OUTLAWS are OPTIONAL

OUTLAWS are OPTIONAL

A Phantasy in XX Acts

DAVID MOSEY

ARPress
45 Dan Road Suite 5
Canton MA 02021

Hotline: 1(888) 821-0229
Fax: 1(508) 545-7580

Ordering Information:
Quantity sales. Special discounts are available on quantity purchases by corporations, associations, and others. For details, contact the publisher at the address above.

Printed in the United States of America.

ISBN-13: Softcover   979-8-89676-024-5
                  eBook   979-8-89676-025-2

Library of Congress Control Number: 2022900546

DEDICATION

To all those actors whose names have been misspelled in
the programme

CONTENTS

Act I
STEMBARK FOREST

Stembark Forest is a huge arboreal smear across the heart of Albion. It is home to the evil forest trolls. It is a place of enchantment. It is a designated environmentally sensitive area of outstanding natural beauty. And a nice place for a picnic on a sunny afternoon.

Stembark Forest is also Don Orlando's Head Office. Don Orlando is the Chief of the notorious outlaws of Stembark Forest.

There have *always* been outlaws in Stembark Forest, just as there have always been forest trolls, but it was Don Orlando who made ***Outlaws of Stembark Forest plc*** into a world-class organisation, one of *Business Greed's* top ten corporations.

It had not always been that way. When Don Orlando arrived in the forest, the band had been a shambles-- a scruffy bunch of herberts who couldn't hit a barn door at twenty paces. They couldn't even tell the rich from the poor. Revenues were derisory, and recruitment had dropped to a trickle. And customers had virtually disappeared. Fewer and fewer travellers even bothered to consider Stembark Forest-- after all, the National Association of Independent Highwaymen offered a service that was more frequent, more reliable and a lot classier.

Don Orlando soon changed that. He simplified the Mission Statement ***Rob from the rich and give to the poor*** to ***Rob from the rich***. Then removed any possible ambiguity by further shortening it to **ROB**. He established a strong corporate identity with a lincoln green uniform. And he established in-house training programmes in marksmanship, deportment and elocution.

The results were dramatic. In Don Orlando's first year as Chief, revenues rose by better than sixty percent. By the end of his second year, travellers from as far away as Nova Castria, almost ninety leagues to the north, were coming to Stembark Forest to experience his new and exciting approach to asset redistribution. And by the end of the third-year travel agents were including a two day trip through Stembark Forest (*Home of the Famous Outlaws*) as a standard part of their high-end package tours. Suddenly it seemed that anybody who was anybody was rushing to Stembark Forest to see the famous outlaws whose yew bows could drive a cloth-yard arrow through a two-inch oak plank at a hundred paces. Thanks to the steady improvement in marksmanship, many of the outlaws could actually *hit* an oak plank at a hundred paces.

The outlaw band had never looked back, Don Orlando reflected proudly as he strolled through the forest glade on a misty spring morning. His outlaws were famous the length and breadth of the land, and beyond. It was a rare day when at least one prosperous party was not riding hopefully along a forest road waiting with eager anticipation for the sight of a group of men in lincoln green, their bows bent and ready for action. And for the summer season parties needed to book months ahead. Stembark Forest was *fashionable* now. It wasn't just the robbing, either. The souvenir shops had more business than they could handle, the tea-room was making money hand over fist and the children's playground was always crowded. And next season, they'd be diversifying into the ransom business.

Don Orlando was far too modest a man to attribute this success to any qualities he might possess. The two miserable years as a clerk in the Shore Enforcement Branch of the Revenue had, he supposed, given him some insight into business organization, asset redistribution and ethical principles, but that was all. In this he did himself an injustice. He was a natural leader who inspired by example rather than governed by precept, and there was not one of his faithful band who would have not cut off somebody's right hand rather than cause him a moment's distress.

"Morning Don!" A cheery shout rang across the glade.

"Morning Walter!" Orlando returned the salute, "bit of archery practice this morning?" He pointed to the big straw target set up against the trees.

"Aye. Qualification shoot." Walter was the band's marksmanship instructor.

"Jolly good!" Orlando made to continue on his way, when something about the positioning of the target and Walter's attitude made him stop in his tracks. "Who's qualifying?" he asked.

"Eric."

The instructor's voice might have been a starting pistol for the effect that it had on Don Orlando. His head down and his shoulders thrust forward, he sprinted for the open door of his office on the far side of the glade. He was less than ten paces from the threshold when his foot caught in a tree root and he measured his length on the ground. As he lay there, winded, there was a vicious hiss above his head followed by the *thunk-pronggg* of an arrow striking home.

"Eric!!" Walter's voice rose in agonized protest, "how many times do I have to tell you: squeeze, don't pull!"

Safely inside his office, Orlando sat down behind his desk and waited to get his breath back. Eric was a mistake. No! He corrected himself, that wasn't fair. If there was any mistake, it had been made by Don Orlando. At the archery trials, where young men from up and down the country competed fiercely to catch the eye of the outlaw leader, Eric's very first shot had flown to the centre of the gold, neatly splitting the last arrow of the previous contender. Don Orlando, his enthusiasm aroused by this display, had not waited to see a second, but recruited the fellow on the spot. He was not to know that Eric had discharged that particular arrow by accident, when a horse had trodden on his foot. But it soon became clear that Eric's marksmanship was of the statistical variety; he had to discharge a statistically significant number of arrows if one of them was to get within shouting distance of its target. Opinion varied on what constituted a statistically significant number. The more charitably disposed suggested it might be around one hundred. The more realistic (or more numerate) were inclined to think this low by two orders of magnitude.

So the new recruit was, much to his chagrin, not assigned to active duties but instead, retained by Don Orlando as an administrative assistant. Orlando never had cause to regret that decision. The eager, gangly youth was not only conscientious, with a meticulous eye for detail, but also had an uncanny insight to the whole business of asset redistribution. A delighted Orlando had given him the post of Special Assistant and soon found himself relying very heavily on the young man. The only problem, Orlando sighed to himself, was that Eric persisted in attempting to qualify for active duty. His shadow fell across the doorway.

"Good morning, Mr Orlando. V-- v-- very sorry about the-- er--"

"Don't worry about it lad."

"I ca-- can't think what the problem is. Perhaps I underestimated the crosswind."

"It really is just a matter of rhythm." Orlando tried to sound encouraging. "Just take the pull, line up on the target breathe in slowly, then all the way out slowly, hold, and squeeze. Didn't Walter tell you that?"

Eric nodded unhappily. "Perhaps there's something the matter with the bow."

"Don't worry about it lad," Orlando repeated, "there's a lot more to the outlawing business than marksmanship."

"But I just don't feel that I'm pulling my weight."

"Listen Eric!" Orlando wagged a finger, "this band has dozens-- well at least half a dozen-- blokes who can split a hazel wand at two hundred paces. If you make it two times out of three, then half the band can do it. But you're the only one who really understands the theoretical side. I mean any twit can prance around the forest in a lincoln green tunic, waving a bow and shouting 'hold!'--"

"Splitting hazel wands at two hundred paces?"

"Yes, that too! But there isn't anyone else in the band who can tell me what we should do about Gentleman Jim." Orlando slapped a sheaf of papers onto the desk.

"Ah yes! Gentleman Jim!" The troubled look faded from the young man's eyes, replaced by a gleam of interest. He sat down opposite Orlando and leafed through the papers. "Gentleman Jim wants our interest in a highwayman franchise in the north... figures look good... untouched territory... fair enough split of the net..." Frowning, Eric read through the papers a second time, then looked up. "I'd recommend we don't."

"We don't? But you just said--

"Not in its present form." Eric spoke firmly and confidently, with no trace of the stammer which sometimes marred his speech. "First thing is he wants to work too close to Nova Castria. And you know what the Nova Castrians are like."

"Right!" Orlando knew very well what the Nova Castrians were like. They were devoted to free trade, eating, drinking and brawling. Their attitude to asset redistribution was liberal in a general sense, but when the assets concerned were specifically theirs it was very illiberal indeed. "Right!" Orlando repeated, "we just wouldn't be able to afford his medical bills."

"And the College of Duellists is located in Nova Castria as well," Eric reminded him.

Orlando shuddered. "Gentleman Jim must be off his nut-- those blokes are deadly! So we tell him 'not on your nelly'?"

"Not entirely, no."

"No? But you just said..."

"The basic idea is sound. There isn't much in our line of business in the north now that Big Bill the Basher and his band are out of business-- just footpads and a few brigands. It's almost virgin territory, and a high-class operation like Gentleman Jim's would clean up a packet. But not near Nova Castria."

"Where then?"

"Other side of the country." Eric smiled. "Just south of Cair Issel. Lots of traffic to and from Nova Castria, and lots more from the south-- especially pilgrims since the Cair Issel Tabernacle of the Redeemer got its Holy Shrine operating licence."

"Brilliant!" Orlando thumped his desk and leaped to his feet. "You see what I mean? Who else could have worked that out. Now I want you to meet Gentlemen Jim as soon as possible. Tell him we're in, but only if he takes the Cair Issel South sector-- I'll leave all the negotiations up to you. Make him an offer he can't refuse."

"You want *me* to handle the ne-- ne-- negotiations?" Eric gulped, "b-- b-- but I c-- c-- could lose--"

"Nonsense lad! You'll do fine-- it'll be good experience for you." At the very worst, Orlando reflected, it would only mean the loss of a lucrative contract-- a bargain price to pay for keeping Eric away from archery practice for a while. "Set up a meeting with Gentleman Jim as soon as possible. I'll leave the whole thing up to you."

Eric was about to begin stammering his gratitude when across the quiet morning air floated the brazen tantivy call of a horn.

"What was *that?*" Orlando stared angrily through the still open door, as if daring the air to transmit the sound once more. It obliged.

"I believe that must be the huntsman, Mr Orlando."

"Huntsman?"

"Yes, the huntsman. I ran across him yesterday morning as a matter of fact."

"A *huntsman?*" Orlando repeated.

"Yes indeed, Mr Orlando. He was quite unmistakable; coat so grey,[1] hounds, and his horn. And everything. In the morning."

"A *huntsman!*" Orlando repeated for the third time, his brow as black as a thundercloud. Don Orlando hated hunting and hunters. The look that crossed his face made Eric almost faint, and reminded him that Mr Orlando had not become the leader of the Outlaws of Stembark Forest just through his commercial acumen.

---

1   The East Castellian nobility favoured grey for their hunting habits despite it not being gay.

"Tell me about this huntsman, Eric." Orlando's voice was deceptively soft.

"I-- I-- just bumped into him yesterday. I didn't get a chance to mention it before--"

"But what's he doing *here*, Eric. Is he just some master of foxhounds of no fixed abode?"

"He said he had come here with his master, Mr Orlando."

"His *master*?"

"Yes. The Duke of Benbrock-Oldstairs, he said."

"What is a duke doing in the forest? Without an appointment?"

"Oh, he didn't come for the robbing, Mr Orlando. He's been exiled."

"An exiled duke!" Orlando scowled. He had little time for the aristocracy. Then his expression changed to one of dismay. "You mean he's being exiled *here*?"

Eric nodded. "The huntsman told me they only arrived a few days ago, and they really like it here. Said something about it being much more free of perils than the envious court."

"He said that did he?" Orlando breathed heavily, "and did he say anything about books in brooks or sermons in stones?"

"Something like that. And good in everything. Mind you," Eric tried to soften the blow, "he did say that the duke always does go on a bit like that, but it doesn't always mean a lot."

"Sermons in stones, eh!" Eric might not have spoken. "We'll see about that!" Orlando crashed both fists onto his desk, jumped to his feet and, flinging his chair to one side, stalked from the office.

"Walter! Form up a squad of six men and follow me!" Eric heard him bellow. His head popped back round the office door. "Where exactly did you say this duke was staying?" he asked.

The exiled duke was closer than they'd realised. With Walter by his side and six outlaws at his back, Orlando had ridden only a few minutes before the smell of wood smoke and frying sausages told him they were close to the interloper's camp. It was a good spot-- a crescent-shaped clearing bounded at its far side by a rampart of sandstone. Ranged about the perimeter were half a dozen caravans-- big ones-- and the dark mouth of a cave gaped in the weathered rock. The set-up was ideal, the outlaw leader had to admit to himself, though he did wonder whether the exiled duke and his followers realized that the cave was the winter residence of a rather large migratory bear.

"I say!" Orlando dismounted and waved commandingly. Nobody took the slightest bit of notice. The clatter of utensils and the chatter of conversation continued unabated. Servants scurried this way and that, bearing platters of food and flagons of ale. Minstrels strummed hopefully on fragile-looking stringed instruments. And at the mouth of the cave, a group of richly dressed men sat around a trestle table toasting each other with brimming tankards.

"Alright then!" Orlando said through his teeth. Walter laid a restraining hand on his arm.

"Perhaps you should try again, sir," he suggested anxiously, "we don't want to provoke an incident."

"Alright!" Orlando made an impatient gesture. He raised his hand once more. "I say!"

"By your leave, sir!" A servant bearing a boar's head on a tray brushed past. Steam began to issue from Orlando's ears. "That does it!" he hissed, and before Walter could intervene, he drew his bow and loosed off a shaft. There was a vicious hiss and a twanging *prongggg*. The servant gazed open-mouthed at the boar's head impaled to the side of the nearest caravan.

"Oi!" he said.

Orlando nocked another arrow. "And there's more where that came from!" he shouted. Silence fell, save for the plaintive notes of a zither drifting hollowly from the cave. "I warned you!" Orlando's bow bent. The zither stopped abruptly. "That's better! Right! Who's in charge here?"

Nobody spoke or moved. The servant made to remove the boar's head from the side of the caravan, but stopped at a threatening gesture from one of the outlaws. Orlando decided to try again. "Are there any dukes here?... any exiled dukes?"

"I am Harold, Duke of Benbrock-Oldstairs." One of the men at the trestle table rose to his feet. His voice resonated with the confidence of one whose every request sets countless lesser beings scurrying.

"Ah, yes! I see." Orlando gazed at the man, wondering what he should say next. The duke certainly had presence. He was slightly above average height, broad shouldered and deep-chested with curly shoulder-length dark hair and a beard framing round-fleshed features. "And who is it I have the honour of addressing?" he asked with the suggestion of an ironic bow, "a band of honest woodcutters perhaps?" There was a burst of sycophantic laughter from the other men at the table, clearly the duke's toadies.

"I am Don Orlando, leader of the Outlaws of Stembark Forest," the outlaw leader snapped.

"You are a don?" The duke's eyebrows arched in surprise and enquiry. "You are not native to these shores, then sir, bearing a foreign title?"

"No, no! I mean my *name* is Don Orlando. Don is short for Donald."

"Dead giveaway, *that* is!" one of the toadies sneered, "positively lower middle-class."

Orlando frowned. The conversation wasn't going the way he'd planned. "What I wanted to know is what you're doing here--"

"Outlaws!" One of the servants darted forward. "These are the notorious outlaws, your grace."

"Oh of course!" the duke smote his brow, "how could I have forgotten the Outlaws of Stembark Forest! Robbing from the rich, and giving to the poor, isn't that right?"

"Half right." Orlando smiled thinly. "But I fear that we had no warning of your coming, your grace, and are ill-prepared--"

"Do not trouble yourself, good sir. We come not to Stembark Forest for the robbing, but to live."

"To live!" Orlando's worst suspicions were confirmed.

"Aye sir, to live. A brother's sudden envy, at one blow deprived me of my dukedom, palace, court, fortune and followers."

"Not all your followers, good sir!" said one toady hastily.

"Nor all your fortune," added a second, with a quick glance at one of the caravans.

"But now we find he does us kindness," ignoring these interruptions, the duke swept on, "for thus sweet are the uses of adversity. This wild wood holds no such perils as the envious court. Here is our roof the vault of heaven, our lanterns the stars. We find sermons in stones, books in running brooks, and good in--"

"Alright, alright!" Orlando interrupted. He might have known it! "How-- er-- long were you thinking of-- er-- staying? You see, our busy season is coming up and..."

"Fear not honest outlaw! We'll not be a burden to you. Berries, the honey from the wild bee, and the forest's sportive game shall be our sustenance-- not at your charge."

"Ah yes... about the hunting. You might find it easier to pick up your meat from Horsefred's-- he's the butcher in Lecter. Only a league or so that way, and his prices are very reasonable."

"And deprive my brave hounds of their sport? You jest sir! But yesterday they killed a stag this high. A noble beast!"

There was a disapproving growl from the outlaws. They all loathed hunting.

"Want me to take him out now, boss?" whispered Walter

"Can't do that!" Orlando hissed back, "exiled dukes are protected, I think." He drew a deep breath, wishing he'd brought Eric along. The lad was *good* at this kind of thing-- he had a talent for negotiation. "Well... er... I suppose we should be getting along now." He lowered his bow.

"For the moment, then, farewell." The duke beamed at him. "You will come and feast with us soon. 'Neath the greenwood tree we shall eat, drink and make merry. There will be dancing, singing and sweet music." The zither started up again. Orlando raised his bow again. The zither stopped. "Perhaps not the music," agreed the duke. "Farewell. The gods prosper thee, honest outlaw."

"What was he going on about, boss?" Walter asked, as they rode back, "did he really mean he'd moved in for keeps?"

"Looks like it Walter."

"Well I think that's a dead liberty!" someone grumbled, "I mean there must be hundreds of them, what with the toadies an' the minstrels an' the huntsmen an' all."

"Their caravans could sort of catch fire, accidental like," someone else suggested.

"'Fraid not lads." Walter shook his head. "You heard what the boss said. Dukes is a protected species."

"*What!*" exclaimed one incredulous outlaw, who followed the sanguinary reports in the "Court Circular" column of his broadsheet with a mixture of horror and fascination. "But the nobs is *always* knocking each other off."

"*Exiled* dukes are different, I'm afraid," Orlando told the man regretfully.

"Well what are you going to do about it then?"

Orlando's tightened his lips and set his jaw. "I'm going into Lecter to see Constable Dixon," he said decisively.

Lecter was a town on the Basingstoke road where Constable Dixon enforced the Law with that intelligence and selectivity that is the hallmark of the really top class copper. Orlando's relationship with the constable was a warm and long-standing one, based on mutual respect, enjoyment of a few pints, and a shared understanding of the iniquitous nature of the Revenue Service. On this day Orlando found Dixon in the parlour of the Three Pigeons where the landlord had, in deference to the policeman's sensibilities, tactfully covered the clock with a dishcloth[2] .

---

2   Licensing hours at the Three Pigeons were honoured more in the breach than the observance

"Don!" Dixon got to his feet with a welcoming smile, "come and sit down. Another two pints of the best, master Rowley!" he called to the landlord.

Orlando sat down with a grateful sigh and took a long swallow of beer. "There's trouble in the forest," he told the constable, "it looks as though I've got an exiled duke on my hands."

"Exiled duke, eh?" Dixon sucked his teeth dubiously. "They say that's the worst kind." He drew his chair closer to the table and opened his notebook. "Perhaps you'd better tell me all about it."

His indignation increasing as he spoke, Orlando recounted the events of the morning while the constable busily scribbled away in his notebook. "And it's not just the noise and general disruption," he concluded, "but the swine *hunts*."

"Hunts?" Dixon looked shocked. "You mean grey coat, hounds, horn and so on?"

"In the morning," Orlando confirmed.

"Doesn't sound very good, if you don't mind me saying so, Don." Dixon shook his head gloomily as he read through his notes. "Sermons in stones... books in running brooks--"

"And good in everything," Orlando reminded the constable.

"Didn't say anything about tongues in trees, I suppose?" Dixon asked, "that'd be the clincher."

"Don't remember that he did."

"He will," the constable prognosticated gloomily. "I'll tell you what Don, you're going to have to do something about this. It's what we in the Force call the 'Arden caper'. If you don't put a stop to it soon, it'll get worse. Courting couples--"

"Courting couples!" Orlando was aghast.

"Courting couples," Dixon confirmed, "and amateur dramatics, nightclub comedians, fairies, magicians-- there'll be no end to it."

"But this is awful!" Orlando gasped, in his agitation reaching for the constable's beer. "We're coming up to the summer season! Isn't there anything you could do..."

"Sorry." Dixon shook his head. "You know I don't do any constabling in the forest, no more than you do any outlawing in Lecter."

Orlando got up and went to the bar to collect fresh drinks. He walked like an old man, and when he returned to his seat he slumped, defeated at the table. "It feels like some kind of insane nightmare... I spend years building up the outlaws into one of the best--"

"*The* best," Dixon tried to comfort him.

"-- and for what? To see it all ruined by an exiled duke with his huntsmen, minstrels, servants and toadies, not to mention courting couples and heaven knows what else. *Magicians*!" He sneered helplessly.

"Just a minute!" Dixon grasped his friend's arm, "you've just given me an idea. What you need is a magician of your own-- or rather a mage."

"A mage?" Orlando looked very dubious, "aren't exiled dukes protected from mages too?"

"Yes."

"Well what's the use of a mage?" Orlando asked crossly, "fifty guineas an hour for some bloody consultant to tell me that he's not permitted to transform an exiled duke into a slug? No thanks!"

"I wasn't thinking so much of that, Don. But supposing the mage managed to persuade the duke to leave of his own accord?"

"How would he do that?"

"Ah well," Dixon gave a quiet laugh, "if we knew that sort of thing, we could charge fifty guineas an hour, couldn't we?"

The outlaw leader gave a brief, humourless laugh. "I didn't think they did this sort of thing-- I thought sitting around making ambiguous prognostications was more their hammer."

"You're thinking of oracles" Dixon told him, "not the same thing at all."

"A mage..." Orlando considered the idea. "You know Dixon, it might be worth a try!" He sat bolt upright in excitement, then slumped once more. "But who'd be interested in a job like that? I mean it doesn't sound much of a challenge-- getting rid of an exiled duke."

Dixon flipped back through the pages of his notebook. "I wouldn't know about that, the maging not being the sort of thing one encounters very much in my line of work, but there is one..." The constable reached the page he'd been looking for and scanned it carefully, following his notes line by line with the tip of his pencil. "Here we are... this may be the man for you. But he's not-- er-- your usual kind of mage..."

"How do you mean? Which guild does he come from?"

"Well..." Dixon hesitated. "The gentleman is a crimson mage--"

"Crimson mage! But the Guild of the Crimson Mages has been out of business for hundreds of years-- even I know that."

"I said he wasn't your usual kind of mage," Dixon continued imperturbably. "He is, in fact, a Wardmaster, and comes--"

"A Wardmaster!" Orlando almost dropped his drink in his agitation, "but that's the highest rank!"

"A Wardmaster, crimson mage," Dixon confirmed. "The gentleman is not native to Albion. He has been brought over on temporary assignment from Earth Three several times, but now I understand he is here permanently, based in Nova Castria."

"Ah..." Orlando nodded. Like everybody else, he was aware that there existed a theoretically infinite number of parallel words, similar roughly similar in topography and climate but laughably dissimilar in every other way. The concept was of academic and scholarly interest, but had little practical commercial application. Earth Three, he understood, was principally remarkable for being an evolutionary dead end, without occult technology. "But there's no magic there!" he protested, "isn't that the place where they still worship sub-atomic particles?"

"Something like that." Dixon gave a short, cynical laugh. "Electrons... that sort of thing. Amazing when you come to think about it."

"Well what's a Wardmaster doing, coming from a place like that?"

Dixon shrugged. "Beats me. Perhaps he's some kind of throw-back. Or a mutation. Anyway, he's here now, and permanently."

"Just a minute!" Orlando's finger jabbed the air in front of Dixon's nose, "wasn't he the one involved in the Basingstoke business almost two years ago?"

"That's right." The constable nodded gravely, "fine job he did there, by all accounts. Even if his methods were a bit... unusual."

"But isn't he with a team? I can't afford a full war party and a Wardmaster."

"Call themselves Mission Implausible," the constable nodded, "and I wouldn't worry about the expense--"

"All very well for you to say!"

"-- because if they find the job interesting they'll probably forget to charge. And if they don't find it interesting, then they won't do it."

"Not very good business sense." Orlando frowned censoriously. "Where would I be if I decided to pick and choose my customers?"

"I believe you will find Mission Implausible' s business sense alarmingly well developed." Dixon's face wrinkled into an expression mid-way between disapproval and reluctant admiration.

"Who are they?" Orlando felt a twinge of concern.

"Let me see..." the constable returned to his notebook, "there's Sir Tiresome. He's a knight of Albion, a fine man!" Dixon's face registered unambiguous approval now, "and then there's Kodswallop-- Nova Castrian fighter."

"A Knight of Albion! And a fighter!" Orlando whistled, "you can't get better than that!"

"Right. Nothing much is going to get in *their* way-- at least not for long. The leader is an elf by the name of Janus. A *very* sharp fellow."

"Leader? Doesn't the mage lead?"

"Only in the maging." Dixon observed the puzzled look on his friend's face and explained, "it's like your band, Don. You're the Chief-- no doubt about it. But in matters of marksmanship, for example, you'd defer to Walter, wouldn't you?"

"I see what you mean," Orlando nodded, "it's a team of specialists."

"That's right. Clumpface the dwarf is their master-artificer, and he's a useful fellow in a punch-up, by all accounts. And Cecil is their marksman. Crossbow specialist from Nova Castria, *and* a master of disguise. A bit of a bolshie, by all accounts."

"Good," Orlando snapped. A bolshie marksman was just the sort of bloke to deal with an exiled duke. "So... a team of six?"

"No. Seven" Dixon paused to take a drink, and an observer might have noticed a slightly uneasy expression on his face.

"Who's the seventh then? A scholar? Some kind of clerical gentleman?"

"Not exactly, no. Actually he's a nicker-- name of Ratbag."

"A nicker!" Orlando jumped to his feet in alarm, "no wonder they don't charge. With a nicker[3] around they don't need to!" The last nicker to come through Stembark forest had not only evaporated with the week's takings, but had also made off with the customer data base and stripped three of the souvenir shops to the bare boards. "A nicker!" Orlando repeated, shaking his head as he resumed his seat, "I think I'd be further ahead to keep the duke."

"I would not go quite as far as that." Dixon put his notebook away and reapplied himself to his beer. "Didn't you say that this duke of yours seemed well provided?"

Orlando thought for a moment, remembering the duke's rich clothes and the rings that had sparkled on his fingers. "Yes, that's true. And he had all those people with him-- servants, huntsmen, toadies and the like. Toadies don't come cheap these days, so he must have brought a fair bit of cash with him."

"Quite traditional that is, with exiled dukes, I understand." The constable wagged his head knowingly.

"So perhaps this nicker would concentrate on the duke?" Orlando asked hopefully.

"Almost certain, I'd say. Your actual nobility always like to travel with a well-filled treasure chest. And nicker are very partial to gold, jewels, rich ornaments and so on, I am led to believe."

---

3   The Nicker are a diminutive tribe (distantly related to elves) who can, and will, steal anything not nailed down, covered with 30 feet of reinforced concrete and guarded around the clock.

"Well in that case..." Orlando sighed with relief.

"That doesn't mean you might find you misplace the odd item here and there," Dixon warned him, "but if you ask nicely you usually get it back. Sooner or later."

"Very well! You've made up my mind for me, Dixon. I'll send a message tonight."

"If you don't find him at this address..." Dixon scribbled a couple of lines in his notebook, tore out the page, "try the Duellists' College."

"The Duellists' College?"

"Yes. The mage is by way of being a Master Swordsman there. A very useful man with the duelling sword he is, by all accounts."

"But a mage!" The outlaw chief was incredulous. It was unheard of for an occult professional to use conventional weapons.

"Oh yes." Dixon began to fill his pipe. "As I told you, this bloke isn't the usual kind of mage."

"Well what's his name?" Orlando took his own notebook from his belt.

"Glad you asked me that." Dixon gave a lugubrious smile and returned to his notebook. "He's used quite a few... let me see..." he flipped the pages over, "...ah yes. Anything addressed to Andrew Cruickshank should find him."

"What was that again?" Orlando scrabbled for a pencil.

"Cruickshank," Dixon repeated, "Andrew Cruickshank."

Act II
NOVA CASTRIA

odswallop stood at the bar in the Nine Lapsed Abstainers and
cast a benevolent yet watchful eye over the crowd. A careful
observer would have noted that though his eyes flickered rapidly, and
seemingly idly, around the smoky, noisy room, they lingered on the
far corner, where the dartboard hung. "Who's that playing with him?"
Kodswallop jerked a thumb.

Motley did not need to ask who "him" was. The tall, slender mage
with the slightly thinning hair and the permanent look of vague surprise
was a familiar figure at the tavern. He was not wearing the crimson
robe of his office, nor did his staff hover menacingly in attendance,
for Andrew Cruickshank was a considerate man and knew that such
things could put people off-- indeed he only appeared formally garbed
and equipped on such special occasions as when a visiting darts team
turned up. The landlord squinted at the mage and his companion.
"Frank Arbuthnot, I think his name is. Up from the south." Motley
shook his head disapprovingly.

"Bit of a shark, is he?" Kodswallop nodded at the dartboard where
Arbuthnot was just pulling three darts from the treble twenty.

"That's what they say. Want me to have a word... sort of warn him
off?" Motley looked at the big fighter nervously. Kodswallop stood
seven foot-six in his socks and was built proportionately, and he took

his self-appointed role as Andrew Cruickshank's particular guardian with great seriousness. And *that* could mean, the landlord reflected unhappily, that any moment now the new furniture in the far corner of the room would be reduced to matchwood. What Frank Arbuthnot might be reduced to, he didn't want to think about. To his great relief, Kodswallop shook his head.

"Nah. Don't say anything... for the moment, that is." His eyes glinted, and he dropped his voice to whisper into Motley's ear. The two men gave a conspiratorial laugh, then leaned back against the bar to watch the darts game.

Frank Arbuthnot was getting excited. He had, with the unerring instinct of his kind, spotted the pigeon as soon as he entered the tavern; the man sitting by himself at a table by the dartboard. Within five minutes he was chatting to the fellow, and minutes after that they were playing darts. Arbuthnot lost the first match with skill and precision and accepted the condolences of his opponent with a rueful laugh.

"Got your eye in good tonight, squire." He nodded with the experience of an expert, "you was putting them just where you wanted them."

"Bit of bad luck, you missing that double sixteen," Andrew Cruickshank offered sympathetically, "I was sure you were going to get it."

"That's the way it goes." Arbuthnot shrugged. Missing double sixteen so convincingly was his speciality. "Fancy another one, then?"

"Why not." Andrew smiled happily. He enjoyed darts but seldom got a partner-- the regulars at the Nine Lapsed Abstainers were by and large a little diffident about playing darts with a mage, and Kodswallop's first and last enthusiastic attempt had left gaping holes in the tavern's wall.

"Best two out of three?" Arbuthnot enquired hopefully, and felt his pulse quicken as Andrew nodded agreement. He would propose a modest wager during the first game, and then lose convincingly. The second game, he would keep run close and, in the excitement, propose an increase in the stakes. He would win the second game by a whisker, allow the pigeon to get a good start in the third, increase the stakes once more, then win. And walk away with a jingling purse, leaving behind a pigeon who didn't even realize he'd been plucked.

"Closest to the centre?" he suggested. The game started.

Andrew was lucky, getting a double with his second dart, and by the time his opponent finally broke in with his starting double, he was down to a hundred and five. Arbuthnot chuckled. "Like I said, squire, you've got your eye in tonight."

"It looks as though you're getting yours in now," Andrew observed with some admiration, as Arbuthnot scored an effortless hundred and seven.

"Got lucky that time." The shark grinned disarmingly, "how about a little wager on it, just make it a bit more exciting, like."

"Good idea!"

Quivers of mercenary expectation tingled along Arbuthnot's veins.

"The loser buys a round!" Andrew concluded in the manner of an impecunious aristocrat placing the last of his inheritance on the table at Monte Carlo.

Arbuthnot deflated slightly. "Er-- OK guv," he agreed weakly, "you're on." In a fit of absent mindedness he threw three treble twenties.

"Bloody good!" Andrew slapped him on the back, "that's only double seven to win!" Arbuthnot gritted his teeth and concentrated on getting himself down to double one in the most plausible fashion.

"Lovely finish, squire!" he was able to exclaim some minutes later, "thought I had a chance there for a minute."

"So did I!" Andrew shook his head in sympathy, "you had rotten luck with the wire."

"That's the game, squire. So it's mugs away." Arbuthnot turned back to the board quickly in an effort to get his opponent's mind off the curious quirks of fortune.

Some minutes later Arbuthnot was pulling his darts from the board, and shaking his head in simulated wonder. "I never thought I'd make that, squire, never in a million years. Your game, by rights, that was."

"Nonsense! Bloody good win!" Andrew slapped him on the back. "One-all, so this is the decider." He prepared to throw.

"Want to up the stakes a bit?" the shark suggested with an insinuating smile.

"Well..." Andrew considered the idea. "Why not!"

Once again Arbuthnot's heart began beating faster and he felt his palm grow moist in anticipation of the gold which would surely cross it ere long.

"Yes! Loser buys two rounds!" Andrew decided.

"Er-- yes." Arbuthnot gritted his teeth. This was a tough customer.

From the bar, Kodswallop and Motley watched the third game begin. "I think I might have a word with him now" the landlord muttered, and strolled to the other end of the bar. He waited until Arbuthnot had completed his turn to bring his score down to one or two points ahead of Andrew's, then beckoned the shark over. "Know who you're playing against?" Motley asked casually.

"No. Young gent out for a night on the town, is he?" Arbuthnot gave a confiding grin, sensing a possible ally in his pigeon-plucking plans.

Motley shook his head sadly. "No. Matter of fact he's a wardmaster mage. Only one in Nova Castria. Quite a regular here, he is."

Arbuthnot's face turned the colour of parchment and his knees buckled. "A mage?" he croaked.

"*Wardmaster* mage," Motley corrected him, "you know, one of the really powerful ones."

Arbuthnot knew all right. Or at least he knew enough about what even an ordinary mage could do when put out. What a wardmaster might be capable of didn't bear thinking about! He tried to pull himself together. "A gent like that wouldn't get narked just by losing the odd game of darts?" He turned pleading eyes on the landlord.

Motley gave him a reassuring smile. "No, of course not. Good sports those mages are... most of the time..."

Arbuthnot did not feel reassured. He shot a quick look at the door, but the way was blocked by Kodswallop; seven foot six of doom propping up the far end of the bar.

"Come on!" his opponent called cheerily, "it's you to chuck 'em!"

"Right squire," he swallowed nervously, "let's get on with it."

Ten minutes later Arbuthnot felt ten years older, and the dartboard was swimming before his eyes in a mist of sweat. His efforts to play worse had been matched by a deterioration in his opponent's game, and now they were both stuck on double one. He dug his fingernails into his palms and *willed* the mage's dart towards that little green segment, nestling treacherously next to double twenty. The dart bounced off the wire.

"Always the same!" The mage smiled a terrible smile in which Arbuthnot read unspeakable torments. "Once I get to double one, I'm done for. Just finish it off, there's a good chap!"

"Arrg." Arbuthnot moistened his throat with a couple of swallows of beer, and took aim. This must be artistic. He couldn't miss by a mile-- that would be too obvious-- instead he would slide the arrows in, just kissing the outside of the wire. One!

"Oh bad luck!" Andrew clucked in sympathy.

Two!

"Again! Stop messing about, and finish off the agony!"

Three! Arbuthnot closed his eyes with relief as the last dart left his hand. He knew that was going to finish up next to its fellows. There was a joyful shout from his opponent. He opened his eyes, and saw to his horror his third dart sitting solidly inside the wire.

"Jolly good win!" Andrew shook his unresisting hand, "now let me get you that drink!"

With a faint whimper Frank Arbuthnot collapsed on the floor in a dead faint.

"I can't understand what came over the poor chap," Andrew shook his head in perplexity, "one moment fine, the next, flat on the floor. I hope he's going to be alright."

"Sure to be!" Kodswallop reassured him, "it was a simple sort of fainting fit-- could have happened to anybody."

The two were walking along Primrose Path on their way back to Andrew's place-- a short enough distance, but Kodswallop would not hear of his mage going about alone after dark. It was true that so far no suicidally inclined asset-redistribution specialist had even attempted to interfere with their progress, but Kodswallop lived in hope. From the narrow, ill-lit alley, their way took them across a broader thoroughfare, along another narrow chasm hacked out between anonymously dark buildings and then into the small square that was known as Cobbler's Court. By day it was a pleasant little spot with benches, a little bit of grass with iron railings about it and a fountain that sometimes actually worked. But after dark it was a mysterious, deep pool of shadow brooded over by the blank stare of shuttered windows. Andrew's house was diagonally across the square, and they were about halfway across when Kodswallop heard the faint scuffling. It could have been the wind chasing dead leaves across the flagstones, but there was no wind, and there were no dead leaves either.

Kodswallop stole softly away in the direction of the noise. To Andrew it was as though he had evaporated, so silently did the big man move. There was another scuffling sound, a muffled exclamation, then Kodswallop reappeared at Andrew's side. Under his arm was a human shape which twisted and struggled violently.

"What on earth have you got there?"

"Found him lurking by the dustbins!" The big fighter spoke with the satisfaction of a dedicated lepidopterist who has netted a particularly rare specimen.

"But what was he doing?"

"Lurking," Kodswallop explained patiently. "Thief, assassin, double glazing salesman-- I can't tell in this light. But he was lurking, alright. That's always a sure sign."

The shape struggled even more violently and made strangled "mmmmggrrnph" noises. Andrew peered at the captive. "I say,

Kodswallop! I wonder if this chap can breathe properly. His face does look a bit on the purple side."

"Probably not," the fighter said equably, "but it doesn't really matter."

The squirming figure redoubled its struggles.

"Let's take a proper look at him," Andrew suggested.

Kodswallop rotated the man until he was vertical and plonked him onto the ground firmly enough to make his knees buckle. "Right then!" He glared aggressively, "who are you?"

"Mmmmggrrnph."

Kodswallop gave a disgusted shrug. "It's not worth wasting time on this one."

"Perhaps if you took your hand off his face...?"

"What?" The big fighter looked puzzled for a moment, then light dawned. "Oh yes." He removed his hand. "Now, who are you? What do you want?" he demanded, accompanying each question with a vigorous shake.

"Don't do that!" Andrew protested as the man flopped back and forth, "his head'll fall off."

"Wouldn't be much loss," Kodswallop grunted, but nonetheless he desisted.

"Aarrk!" the prisoner gasped, fighting for breath.

A window slid up with a bang. "What's going on out there?" a querulous voice demanded, "don't you know what time it is?"

Andrew flinched. "It's just me, Mr Newkes," he called in conciliatory tones, "sorry about the noise. We're going inside right away." There was a gasp of terror, and the window slammed shut very quickly indeed. "That's Charlie Newkes," Andrew whispered, "he's a Sidesman at the local Tabernacle of the Redeemer. Has to get up early for the morning mortification."

In the darkness Kodswallop grinned broadly as he reflected that at this moment Mr Newkes was almost certainly regretting his intervention very heartily indeed. "Let's get this fellow inside," he suggested, "oh no you don't!" he added sharply as the captive showed further signs of life. He replaced his hand firmly over the man's face, tucked him back under his arm and followed Andrew up the steps to his house.

While Andrew bustled about, lighting lamps, feeding the big, tiled stove some more chunks of wood and unearthing a bottle of brandy and three glasses, Kodswallop placed his prisoner in a chair and stood back hands on hips, scrutinizing the fellow intently.

He was of unremarkable build, though his disproportionately long arms gave him a faintly ape-like appearance, and his face was a weathered reddish brown that is the hallmark of one who spends much time in the open air. His eyes were bright and flickered about the room with the furtive appraisal of a successful lawyer or confidence trickster. Kodswallop guessed that in those few quick glances he had valued the furniture and fixtures, assessed the doors and windows for ease of access and estimated the price he'd be likely to get for his loot. The big fighter favoured him with ferocious smile. "Don't even think about it!" he warned.

"I dunno what you're talking about!" The man had recovered enough breath to give a good impression of outraged innocence. "Besides," he added after a pause for reflection, "I don't do houses."

"You don't do this one, anyway," Kodswallop told him calmly. "Now who are you, and what do you want?"

"Two-nine-eight-seven-six-oh, Outlaw First Class, Lenny," the man recited briskly. "I come to see the mage. Got a message for him, haven't I?" he added with an ingratiating smile.

"A message! Who from?" Returning with the brandy, Andrew caught the man's words and pressed forward eagerly. It might be news from the rest of the band, who were still travelling in the Western Marches.

"From Mr Orlando."

"Mr Orlando?" Andrew and Kodswallop eyed each other in mystification.

"Mr Orlando," the man repeated. "*The* Mr Orlando."

"I'm awfully sorry," Andrew began, "but I'm not sure..."

"He's the boss."

"The boss of *what*?" Kodswallop demanded.

"OSF," Lenny replied, "*you* know... Big Green."

"I don't know."

"The Outlaws of Stembark Forest," Lenny spoke as though articulating a self evident truth.

"Oh aye." Kodswallop looked unimpressed.

"And he needs a mage."

Suddenly Kodswallop stopped looking unimpressed. This sounded as though it might be a call to action-- a chance for some excitement. Things had been very quiet for the last six months, and anything to do with the notorious outlaws of Stembark Forest would almost certainly offer unlimited opportunities for action, adventure and exploring new taverns. To Kodswallop's dismay, Andrew did not seem to be grasping the opportunity with both hands.

"A mage? Whatever for?" Andrew shook his head. "Anyway, I'm not really a mage. If I were you I'd tell Mr Orlando to go to one of the Guilds."

"Bu-- bu-- but Mr Orlando said--" Lenny began to stammer.

"What the *Wardmaster* means is that he's not the *usual kind* of mage." Kodswallop said quickly, then paused for a moment to work out what to say next. By rights Andrew should jump at the chance of getting a contract, but one of the mage's little eccentricities was the distaste he affected for good healthy punch-ups. And maybe, Kodswallop thought, he didn't want to look too anxious. Well, he'd soon fix that! "Of course the Wardmaster would be delighted to help if your boss really needs his uniquely specialised skills," Kodswallop said smoothly, priding himself in his phraseology.

"Kodswallop! What are--"

"That's exactly what Mr Orlando wants!" Lenny nodded in enthusiastic agreement, "he don't want the usual kind of mage. You know, the type what costs fifty guineas an hour."

"Kodswallop!" Andrew hissed through clenched teeth.

"Sounds really interesting, Andrew," the fighter encouraged, "and Stembark Forest is really nice at this time of year."

"But--"

"You might at least read the letter." The big fighter pointed to the oblong of parchment Lenny was holding.

"Well, I suppose..."

"Good!" Kodswallop beamed and patted the mage on the back encouragingly. "Here you are!" He took the parchment from Lenny's unresisting fingers and passed it to Andrew, then gently introduced him into a chair, and followed up this immediate tactical advantage by pressing a glass of brandy into his hand.

"*Alright* Kodswallop, I'll read it!" Andrew snapped, by no means taken in by his friend's sudden devotion to his creature comforts. He broke the seal, unfolded the document and began. As Kodswallop anxiously watched Andrew's eyes scanning swiftly through the closely written pages he realised, with a jolt of joyful anticipation, that whatever it was the outlaw chief had written, it had certainly served its purpose in arousing Andrew Cruickshank's intense interest. The mage's eyebrows jumped up and down, he uttered an incredulous squawk of laughter, and looked up from the letter.

"There really is an exiled duke?" he asked Lenny.

"No doubt about it. He had his servants an' huntsmen an' toadies with him," Lenny confirmed. "Mr Orlando says that's always a sign of an exiled duke."

"He's absolutely right!' Andrew jumped to his feet and began pacing the room excitedly. "And he talked about sermons in stones? Books in running brooks? Tongues in trees?"

Lenny, who had been nodding in answer to each question, raised his hand. "He didn't talk about tongues in trees *as such*," he said cautiously, "but he *did* mention good in everything."

"Good heavens! This is incredible! With obvious difficulty, Andrew stopped his pacing, and flung himself back into his chair. Kodswallop was delighted-- he had never seen the mage so animated.

"So we'll go?" he asked.

"Of course!" Andrew jumped to his feet again, "We'll let Janus and the others know at once. We should leave tonight!"

"Tonight! But it's nearly midnight!"

"Oh yes, so it is. Well, tomorrow morning." Andrew began pacing again.

"Er... by the way..." Kodswallop hesitated, "er... what are we supposed to be doing?"

"Doing?" Andrew looked up surprised. "Oh... yes of course... doing." He took up the letter once more. "I see... so Mr Orlando would like us to persuade this exiled duke to leave?"

"Yes please," confirmed Lenny, "before the courting couples an' the nightclub comedians an' everybody else arrive."

"Well, we'll do our best. Now what's this about grottoes?" He looked up, mystified.

"Ah yes." Lenny began to recite: "We understand that a magician, or mage requires something of the nature of a grotto or an enchanted island. A grotto less than half a league from Outlaw Headquarters has been installed in accordance with IOS[4] -286.3 specifications--" Lenny stopped his recitation. "Actually it's dead pretty. There's an underground stream, an' those mights and tights things what drip water and grow down from the ceiling to the floor and up again, an' we got lots of bits of coloured glass an' stuck them in the walls so it looks dead tasteful."

"Sounds awfully damp."

"It *is* a little on the moist side," the outlaw admitted, "I think some of the lads have been growing mushrooms in it. But we'll soon get them cleared out," he added hastily.

"Not on our account!" Andrew told him, equally hastily, "I don't really need a grotto."

"Ah, well..." Lenny thought for a moment, "well, we *can* do an island, though it's not what you'd call enchanted, actually."

"An island?"

"Yeah. You see, we got this lake-- we've been doing it up a bit as a boating lake, an' there's this island in the middle with a maze an' a tea room. But I think you'd be much better off with the grotto."

---

4   International Occult Standard

"I don't want a grotto, or an island," Andrew dismissed these arcane accommodations, "is there anything like an inn or guesthouse where we could stay?"

"Well... we *do* have some guest accommodation," Lenny admitted unwillingly, "finished just last month." He assumed a confidential air. "Keep it to yourselves, but we're diversifying into the ransom business next year."

"That sounds fine," Kodswallop said quickly, anxious to clinch the matter before Andrew could have second thoughts.

"They're not really very magical..." Lenny sounded doubtful.

"Oh don't worry about that," Andrew hastened to reassure the outlaw, "the less magical the better. So long as they're reasonably comfortable."

"Comfortable!" Lenny waved his hands about, "these rooms is five star class! Designed for the quality. Don't want no riff-raff in the ransom business-- we want people who are used to the best!"

"That's right in the forest?"

"Oh yeah. First glade to the left after the Headquarters."

"And what do you do about... er..." Andrew made a vague gesture, which Lenny promptly misinterpreted.

"We got indoor sanitation, of course!" he said indignantly, "like I said, these accommodations is for the quality."

"What Andrew meant," Kodswallop explained patiently, "was whether there was any sort of tavern there."

"Oh I see. Well, there's the Recreational and Social Club, though what they have on tap does depend a bit on who's been travelling through the forest recently. Then there's the Three Pigeons in Lecter-- less than a league away."

"The Three Pigeons!" Andrew smiled with happy reminiscence.

"So we're going?" Kodswallop tried not to make it sound like a question.

"Of course!"

"I better be off, then." Lenny got up, "can I tell Mr Orlando you're on your way?"

"You can tell him we will arrive three days from tomorrow." Kodswallop favoured Lenny with a fierce glare before the outlaw could protest against so leisurely a progress, then ushered him firmly to the door.

While the big fighter closed and secured the front door, Andrew dragged his equipment case out of its cobwebby hidey-hole under the stairs. It didn't look like much-- just an inconveniently large box of dark close-grained wood. In fact it was a shielded storage unit Mark IVb, manufactured by Sproggit and Axel Ltd to IOS 286.9, the top-of-the line model and guaranteed to resist anything up to and including Armageddon. Andrew flung back the lid, and clicked his tongue in exasperation as he surveyed the enigmatic collection of gadgets and instruments whose functions (if they had any) he had never been able to fathom. But the ivory box of Tarot cards and the manual *Using Tarot 5.1* might, *in extremis*, come in handy. In *bloody* extremis, Andrew told himself grimly. And there was the Dalton WM-40 Spellcaster... he'd have to have that along if he was to do anything serious in the way of maging. He put cards, manual and spellcaster to one side, then upended the equipment case to tip out the remaining contents.

"What *are* you doing?" Kodswallop asked disapprovingly.

"Making space." Andrew selected *The Collected Works of William Shakespeare* from the bookcase and dumped the big volume into the equipment case with a scholarly thud. He tossed in the spellcaster, tarot cards and manual, then rather more carefully, added two bottles of brandy. There was still a bit of space-- at least enough for his binoculars and, as an afterthought, the *Arden* edition of *As You Like It*.

"What about all that stuff?" Kodswallop demanded, pointing to the pile of gubbins Andrew had so briskly discarded, "all that technical stuff? You're supposed to be a wardmaster mage-- you can't go waltzing off on field operations without..." the big fighter peered into the cupboard, "without a complete set of fulminator indexing elements!" he said accusingly, "you'll look a right charlie if you're in the middle of an operation and suddenly you need a fulminator indexing element."

"Kodswallop-- have you any idea of what a fulminator indexing element is used *for*?"

"No. But I'm not the mage."

"Neither have I."

"But--"

"I am *not* humping a load of temperamental occult equipment about the place," Andrew said very firmly. "Face it; we know it either won't work or it will work. If it doesn't work, then we've wasted effort lugging it about and if it does work, then we'll probably wish it hadn't."

"It still looks a bit amateurish," Kodswallop grumbled.

"So? I'm a lot of an amateur."

"Ha!" Kodswallop snorted. "I suppose I'd better see about transport. I'll check with the Vita Brevis Stables first thing in the morning. We'll need two mounts and two packhorses."

"Yes," Andrew agreed, without enthusiasm, "just make sure I get a quiet one; I don't want another of those bloody great black things that snorts smoke and flame."

Kodswallop sighed. Another of Andrew's idiosyncrasies was that he didn't understand the importance of keeping up appearances. "I'll speak to Hobson, but you know what he's like. He says it's more than his reputation's worth to have a wardmaster mage riding on anything but the best. And Gehenna's the best he's got."

"Gehenna's not a horse, it's maniacal aggression with a leg at each corner!" Andrew retorted, "hasn't he got a nice, calm, old horse about the place? The sort of thing that wears a nosebag, munches apples and answers to the name of Dobbin?"

"Wouldn't do at all." Kodswallop shook his head firmly.

Almost a hundred and ten leagues away, on the flanks of a little valley cutting into the dark hills of the Western Marches, a camp fire blazed brightly, casting the five figures surrounding it into lurid silhouette. There is nothing like a camp fire, especially on a chilly spring night in the Western Marches, for drawing people together in companionship.

The flickering flames against the velvet night act as a lodestar for good fellowship and contentment.

"Bloody 'taters, it is! Feels like rain, too." The complaint came from a bullet-headed man of medium height whose features seemed to have been carefully assembled for the expression of scepticism and discontent-- the set of the mouth, the crease between the eyebrows and the brooding, hooded eyes told of one who has seen it all before, and knows it's going to get worse.

"It could be worse, Cecil." The gnarled figure of a dwarf tossed another branch on the fire, producing a brief fountain of sparks.

"How?" The sudden sparkle from the fire revealed a glint of sardonic amusement in the first speaker's eye. "You think it's going to snow instead?"

"No. But they could have caught on to Ratbag at the Kraken's Lair instead-- excellent beer they had there." There was a collective sigh.

"Well there you are!" A diminutive figure sprang to its feet, "it's much better to be out here in the fresh air than frousting away in a stuffy old place like the Fakir's Turban-- their beer was sour! I'm sure they can't clean their lines properly." His long, delicate fingers waved hypnotically to emphasise the point.

"Oh, so *that's* why we left, Ratbag!" Cecil's voice dripped sarcasm (or possibly irony; he was working on both). "I *am* sorry. I was labouring under the misapprehension that it was something to do with a sudden loss experienced by the landlord. A sudden loss that he inexplicably attributed to you."

"Be that as it may, we are here and are warm, dry and well fed." A new voice cut in, "let us have no more of these recriminations. It was undoubtedly some simple misunderstanding, and could have happened to anyone." The voice was one accustomed not so much to command, as to lead. But it wasn't bad at commanding either. A silence fell... for a moment.

"We are warm and dry and all that *so far*," Cecil agreed, "but you should know by now, Tiresome, that as soon as somebody says 'it could be worse' it usually is."

In the darkness the knight smiled, took a sip from the flask that Clumpface had passed him, then handed it on to the man at his right. "What now Janus?" he asked, "you want to stay any longer?"

"I think not." Janus sipped and passed the flask on to someone he thought was Cecil but turned out to be Ratbag. "We should start back to Nova Castria soon."

There was a rumble of unanimous approval from the company. "Andrew *is* doing *Blood on the Rooftops* for the Summer Festival?" Cecil asked.

"That's what he was planning," Tiresome nodded.

"Fine play," Clumpface puffed energetically at his pipe. There was another collective sigh, this time of approval and agreement. *Blood on the Rooftops, Blood on the Tiles* was generally regarded as Albion's greatest revenge tragedy.

"We should get back before he does any casting" the marksman reminded them. "He--"

"Hush!" Janus interrupted, "did you hear anything?"

Absolute silence fell, save for the hissing crackle of the fire. Cecil was about to say "not a sausage," when he became aware of a thin, high-pitched whistle. It increased in volume and harshness, cutting through the night air like a glass blade. It was accompanied by a deeper throbbing roar.

"I think--" Cecil got to his feet.

"I know!" Tiresome jumped up, "scatter!" As they all ran for the nearest cover, the noise increased to an unbearable level. *CRASH!* There was a flash of violet light and the ground shook to a tremendous concussion. The light of the fire became blurred as a cloud of dust rolled outwards from the point of impact. The echoes rolled back and forth about the hills. In the far distance a wolf howled.

"What the bleedin' hell was *that?*" Cecil tiptoed back into the circle of firelight like a man crossing a chasm on a single rotting plank of timber.

"Technical stuff. Didn't you see the Heron-Gough discharge?" Clumpface seized a dead branch and thrust it into the heart of the fire, sending a stream of sparks whirling up into the night. The dry wood flamed busily and, when it was well alight, the dwarf held the makeshift torch aloft.

"There it is!" Ratbag pointed. Not fifteen paces from the fire an amorphous mass loomed. The nicker darted forward.

"Watch it!" Clumpface called sharply. Ratbag skidded to a halt as he remembered the Heron-Gough discharge. That manifestation was the invariable accompaniment to any occult phenomenon and Ratbag knew well enough that, even for a nicker, anything associated with occult phenomena could be very hazardous to the health.

"What is it?" asked Cecil, from a prudent distance.

"Looks like a pile of rubble," Clumpface grunted. He waved the nicker back and went to take a closer look. Despite the violent manner of its arrival, the dwarf noted that it had materialized at the one spot that had not been occupied by any of the five-- no-one need have moved. That was suggestive. And then he saw, perched on the top of the pile, a little oblong package. "I believe it's a message," he called, his voice alive with excitement, and I bet it's from Andrew!"

"No takers on that one!" Cecil sniffed. Everyone knew that mages sent hard-copy signals by wrapping the written message about some small heavy object (a half-brick was traditional) and using a simple generic matter transmission routine. And everyone also knew that while Andrew had no difficulty with the routine, he did have difficulty in confining the routine to the half-brick. Invariably his transmissions were accompanied by a sizeable chunk of the local geography. The marksman prodded the pile of rubble with his toe. "It looks like a bit of the rockery from Mr Newkes's back garden," he observed, grinning, "he isn't half going to be pissed off about that!"

Clumpface pushed Cecil aside and, with some caution, took the wrapped half-brick from the top of the pile, untied the string and unwrapped the message. Burning with curiosity though he was, he did not read it himself but at once passed it to Janus; the old dwarf had very firm ideas about the proprieties. Never constrained by any proprieties, Ratbag stooped to retrieve the half-brick and tuck it away in his kitbag-- it would make a nice souvenir.

Janus looked up from the letter, his normally grave features illuminated by an anticipatory smile. "This *is* from Andrew. It appears that we shall not be returning to Nova Castria just yet," he told them, the smile on his face widening. "Andrew has been given a contract by the chief of the Outlaws of Stembark Forest-- his first as an independent mage. We are to meet him in Stembark Forest as soon as possible."

There was an awed silence for a moment. Cecil made a harsh noise that could have been a mocking laugh. "Like I just said," he grated, "things just *did* get worse!"

Act III
UNDER THE GREENWOOD TREE

Two riders moved at a leisurely trot along the forest path. The leader was so hung about with weapons that he looked like total war in search of a declaration, but he was big enough that he didn't look overdressed. The second horseman, slighter and muffled up in a grey cloak, would have been altogether unremarkable, had it not been for the noble black charger he rode. Its hooves struck fire from the ground, its nostrils flared like the air-intakes for high-bypass ratio jet engines, its eyes flashed blood red and its long, predatory teeth glinted in the sun. The four horsemen of the apocalypse would have had second thoughts about the creature. The huge animal stepped haughtily along as though it were grinding hereditary enemies underfoot. The rider joggled uneasily in the saddle as though he had got on during a moment of mental abstraction and was wondering how to get off again.

"Kodswallop! It's doing it again!" Andrew shouted as his horse snorted like a flame-thrower just getting warmed up.

"Doing what?" Kodswallop turned in his saddle to look behind him. The horse returned his gaze with the rigorous detachment of a duchess ignoring an under-gardener.

"It's stopped now. It always does when you turn round."

"What's she stopped?"

"Making this fearful threatening noise. And baring her teeth. When did this horse last eat anyway?"

"She can't be hungry." Kodswallop urged his mount alongside Andrew's, "I think she just wants a little attention."

"She wants a bloody exorcist!"

The big fighter fumbled in the pouch at his belt and took out a lump of sugar. "Here you are," he offered and made a reassuring clucking sound. The horse gave a vicious snarl, revealing long yellowing fangs.

Kodswallop frowned. "Now, now!" he cautioned, and gave the creature a warning tap across the snout with his free hand.

Andrew almost fainted as he waited for the vicious beast to spring into lethal action, but to his considerable surprise it did no such thing, contenting itself with a "well-you-can't-blame-a-gal-for-trying" sort of whinny. It stretched out its head and, very daintily, took the sugar lump with the faintest of scrunching sounds.

"There, there!" Kodswallop gave the horse an affectionate pat. "I told you she only wanted a bit of attention." The horse turned its head (Andrew refused to acknowledge that such an assembly of mindless malevolence possessed any attributes of any sex) and gave a sneer of confirmation.

"It's doing it again!" Andrew cried. The horse blew noisily through its lips making an unpleasing sound, redolent with contempt.

"Hold!" A stentorian voice boomed, making the trees quiver. Open mouthed, Andrew stared at a crowd of men in lincoln green who had materialized not forty paces away.

"Hold!" the voice roared again.

"Hold *what?*" Andrew shouted back, but even as the words left his mouth, Kodswallop caught him round the waist and pulled him from his horse. Andrew had a vague sense of wind whistling past his ears as the big man dashed to the side of the road, then there was confused thud as they crashed into the ditch.

"Kodswallop! Wha-- what the bloody hell are you up to?" Andrew gasped for breath.

"Keep down!" the big fighter whispered urgently, "outlaws!" As if to underline the warning two arrows whistled overhead and smacked into a tree trunk somewhere with a lethal *proinnngggg*!

Andrew tried to raise his head, but Kodswallop forced him back down. "I suppose they *were* expecting us?" he asked, wriggling back a bit. He raised his head cautiously. More arrows clacked and rattled through the branches above them.

"Hold your fire!" snapped a commanding voice. Kodswallop and Andrew exchanged relieved glances-- obviously some kind of silly mistake was about to be rectified. "Those arrows is expensive!" the voice continued, "Pringle! Martin! Target is base of bushy top tree. Five rounds, rapid application, fire!"

With an evil hissing sound another volley of arrows whizzed overhead, slicing low enough to part the longer stems of grass at the lip of the ditch, and thunked into the tree-trunk behind them. Kodswallop and Andrew exchanged thoroughly disconcerted glances. "Sod this for a game of soldiers!" Kodswallop crawled along the ditch a little way, scrabbling with his right hand in the soft earth. With a grunt of satisfaction he disinterred a large stone. He rolled half onto his back and, the muscles in his shoulder and forearm bulging with the effort, lobbed the missile in the general direction of their attackers. It landed with a perfectly satisfactory crash.

"Rocks! They're chucking rocks at us, Bert!" came a scandalized shout.

"That's *Section Leader* Bert to you Pringle!"

"Don't say nuffink about rocks in the Outlaw Regs, Section Leader!" Pringle responded dubiously.

"Don't you worry about ORs, lads! Now spread out-- don't bunch up-- we don't want to give 'em a concentrated target, now do we?" The Section Leader's voice resounded with good-humoured encouragement.

"Don't want to give 'em any target."

"Quiet there! Right! Two volunteers-- that's you and you; Martin and Will! Deploy to the right and take the ditch in enfilade fire. Five rounds each, on the order."

"Enfilade fire, eh? We'll see about that." In the ditch Kodswallop had unearthed two more stones. With unerring accuracy he lobbed them from the ditch to drop within feet of the reluctant enfiladers, and they scuttled back to the shelter of the trees.

"I just looked, Section Leader, and there's definitely nuffink about rocks in ORs."

"Then we use our initiative, lad!" The Section Leader was clearly not a person to be unduly troubled by bureaucratic considerations.

"This is getting ridiculous!" Andrew hissed, "there must be *something* we can do."

"Don't worry!" Kodswallop gave him a cheery grin, "I've just found some more stoness."

"I mean apart from throwing stones."

"We could put a hat on a stick and hold it up and see what happens."

"Why?"

The big fighter shrugged. "*I* don't know. I've just heard about it being done."

"Well do you have a hat?"

"Not exactly, no."

"Neither do I." The two exchanged glances once more. From beyond the ditch they could hear shuffling noises as the outlaws exercised their initiative. Kodswallop hurled another stone. The noises stopped.

"Right!" Section Leader Bert's clarion tones echoed among the trees. "Parsley and Martin! Fall back fifteen paces. On the word of command commence high angle fire!"

"You want us to drop 'em into the ditch, Section Leader?"

"That's right, lad! Soon take care of the opposition that way."

"Er... Section Leader..." It was the voice of the OR scholar. "That might expose the customer to the danger of physical injury, in contravention of our Customer Service Code, Section 7."

"Never you mind about that my lad!"

"But Section Leader--"

"Listen mush: we are dealing with an extraordinary situation. We are dealing with violent adversaries. We are dealing with people who refused to Hold when clearly requested to do so by a duly authorised Outlaw Section Leader and who subsequently chucked bloody great rocks at us. That's aggression, that is. So we've got to be aggressive back!"

"Well... I dunno..."

In the ditch Andrew had come to the conclusion that he did know. At least he knew what he was going to do next, and he reached for his staff. This was a fairly ordinary looking stick about seven feet long, slung from his shoulder by a piece of ordinary looking string. Of dark, close-grained wood, smoothed to a satin finish, the stick carried a hexagonal crystal at its top. In fact the stick was the powerful and temperamental Sproggit and Axel Mk XXVIb Voice Interactive/Enhanced Performance mage staff. But the string was perfectly ordinary string. Andrew gripped the staff near its top, and triggered the destructor beam.

From the tip of the staff an incredibly thin, incredibly bright beam of red light lanced out. Where it touched tree or branch, the wood either exploded in a cloud of splinters with an ear-splitting concussion or the limb crashed to the ground, sliced cleanly away. For fully six seconds Andrew played the deadly, destructive beam of light across the tree tops. The noise was prodigious, almost completely drowning the terror-stricken shouts of the outlaws as they desperately tried to dodge the year's supply of firewood that was falling about their ears.

"That should slow them down a bit!" Andrew muttered rather breathlessly-- he was mightily relieved the staff had actually worked.

"What do we do now?"

"Let's see if they send any more arrows over." Andrew squirmed into a crouching position, "if they don't, I'm going to pop my head up and blast at the road for a second or so. That might encourage them to get lost."

"I don't know." Kodswallop shook his head dubiously. "Perhaps we'd better put a hat on the end of your staff first, and hold it up and see what happens."

"I told you, I don't have a hat."

"Shh..." Kodswallop flapped his hand urgently, "let's try to hear what they're up to."

"That was sorcery, that was!" came an aggrieved cry, "it don't say nothing about sorcery in the ORs."

"Oh yes it does," the OR scholar contradicted him, "it's right there in the index after 'search and seizure'."

"What does it say, then?"

There was an urgent rustling of pages. "Ah, Gottit... oh!"

"Well?"

"It's not very helpful," the voice sounded hesitant, "it just says *Outlaw policy with respect to customers from the supernatural sphere or ethereal plane is currently under review. Pending approval of a formal policy, decisions will be made on a case-by-case basis at the senior executive level. We must avoid a repetition of the unfortunate business with the fairy godmothers last year.* That's all."

"Come on lads!" Section Leader Bert could feel his authority slipping away. "We're not going to be put off by some mountebank with a few cheap technical tricks, are we?"

"It says 'senior executive level', Section Leader," the OR scholar reminded him.

"Besides, that weren't no mountebank," claimed another voice, "mountebanks sell love philtres an' hair restorer an' double glazing."

"It were a mage, I betcha!" chimed in a new voice, "there were something in Daily Orders about a mage."

"Don't talk rubbish, Will!" the Section Leader admonished, "you think I don't read Daily Orders?" There was a rustling of paper. In the ditch Andrew and Kodswallop exchanged very tentative hopeful looks.

"Ahem!" There was the sound of paper being screwed up into a very small ball indeed and stuffed out of sight. "It appears, lads, that there's been a little bit of a mistake..." The Section Leader cleared his throat once more and strode a few paces towards the ditch. "Would either of you gentlemen, by any chance, be a mage?" he inquired.

In the Great Council Room of the Outlaws, Don Orlando surveyed his guests with a welcoming, if slightly apprehensive eye. It was the first time he had seen them all together, and they certainly looked like a capable lot. He coughed loudly. "Gentlemen, first let me formally welcome you to Stembark Forest. I hope your stay with us will be a happy and-- er-- profitable one... from all points of view. And let me take this opportunity to once more apologise for the... er..." he cleared his throat self-consciously, "the unfortunate misunderstanding yesterday. I er... cannot comprehend..."

"Don't worry about it mate!" The scruffy, bullet-headed man with the crossbow slung across his back interrupted cheerfully. "This sort of thing happens all the time. You get to sort of expect it after a while." He leaned forward with a confidential air and jerked a thumb at Andrew. "With him around anything can get buggered up, and usually does."

"Quite! Ah..." Accustomed though he was to the relatively free and easy management style of his own organisation, Orlando found this degree of informality unusual. He took a surreptitious look at his notes and confirmed that this man must be Cecil, the crossbow specialist. His weapon was quite unmistakable-- Orlando had never seen a self-loading crossbow with telescopic sights before. "Ah..." he repeated vaguely, and looked towards the mage.

"Oh please don't give it another thought." Andrew waved a hand dismissively. "Simple accident, could have happened to anybody."

"That's most understanding of you."

"Of course Cecil wasn't there."

"Quite."

"So he doesn't know what he's talking about."

"No." Orlando looked helplessly around the table. From the tone of the mage's response he'd been sure that the next moment would see Cecil as a little scrunched up cinder, or perhaps a newt. But no, the marksman still wore his knowing grin and the mage was still glaring back at him. Suddenly the mage seemed to realise he was being looked at.

"Awfully sorry about the trees," he said, quite misinterpreting the outlaw leader's pensive gaze.

"We have plenty." Orlando shrugged. He decided he'd had enough of the preliminaries. He placed both hands on the table, and leaned towards the mage. "Now, do you think you can help me get rid of this Duke Harold?"

"We can try. But why do you want to get rid of him? This is a huge forest."

"Not big enough for the two of us," Orlando said firmly, folding his arms across his chest.

Andrew stared at the square-built man with the dark brown, crinkly hair, and tried to think what to say next.

"What Mr Orlando means is that the environmental and economic equilibrium of the forest is very delicate," Eric cut in smoothly, "it would take little to cause a fatal disturbance."

"Right!" Orlando nodded in emphatic agreement. "They've set up their camp right on Sycamore Ride, the route most of our customers from the north and east follow--"

"Sucker's Alley" Eric explained.

"Sucker's Alley *North,*" the outlaw chief corrected him. "I mean it just couldn't be worse! Imagine: you've come forty leagues or more for a nice bit of robbing, *plus* the kiddies' playground glade, Ye Olde Forest Shoppe, the archery display and the boating lake, and then you find yourself surrounded by exiled dukes and their toadies, all roistering and hunting and turning over stones to look for the sermons. It'd destroy the whole atmosphere. You'd probably turn right round and go home. *And* ask for your money back!"

"Sounds quite simple to me." Kodswallop leant back in his chair, which creaked dangerously in protest. "All we have to do is go along there, and bop them."

"I don't think we can do that," Andrew told him, "apparently exiled dukes are a protected species or something. He's got to leave of his own accord-- he's got to *want* to leave."

"Well of course he will!" The big fighter dismissed the objection. "Most people want leave after they've been bopped enough times. Being bopped seems to have that effect on them," he concluded with the judicious air of a scientist advancing a well-supported hypothesis.

Janus shook his head regretfully. "I fear we must be more indirect."

"I can bop them indirectly," Kodswallop offered.

"If it was just a matter of bopping, then they wouldn't need us," Andrew reminded him.

"Don't see why we have to treat the southern aristocracy with bloody kid gloves," the big fighter grumbled, "they need a lesson. They need a sharp shock!"

"Are all dukes protected, or only *exiled* dukes?" Andrew asked the outlaw leader.

"Only exiled ones, of course." Orlando was puzzled by the question.

"Ah. And ordinary exiles aren't protected?"

"Good heavens no!" Orlando looked shocked.

"I see... so if this bloke *either* stopped being exiled *or* stopped being a duke, then there'd be no problem."

"Eh?" Orlando struggled with the concept for a while then gave up and looked helplessly round the table. Perhaps the mage's colleagues understood what he was going on about.

The others looked at each other blankly. Perhaps the outlaw chief understood what Andrew was going on about, but they hadn't a clue. "Do you mean," Janus began hesitantly, "that if Duke Harold's exile were revoked, or if it could be shown that he was no duke, then Don Orlando could have him removed from the forest by whatever means proved effective?"

"That's right!"

"Isn't this all a bit academic?" asked Cecil, "I mean it's a bit like saying that if my auntie was a man she'd be my uncle?"

"I hate to agree with Cecil," Clumpface favoured the marksman with a glare, "but I really cannot see how we can alter the fact that this Harold *has* been exiled and is a duke."

"Easy!" Andrew smiled. "For the exile it only needs... who did the exiling?"

"His brother, I believe," Orlando informed him, "traditional sort of thing."

"That is so," Tiresome agreed, "they never did get along well together." The knight was the only one of the band who hailed from the south (though he didn't like to be reminded of the fact) and he knew something of the subculture of the aristocracy.

"Well, the two brothers could become reconciled," Andrew suggested.

"Reconciled! How?"

"Well... er..." Andrew thought quickly, "suppose the usurping brother met some hermit who convinced him to revoke the exile, and live in humble simplicity?"

"Where's this hermit living?" Orlando demanded, instantly suspicious.

"Doesn't sound very likely to me." Cecil broke in before Andrew could answer, "look at it from his point of view. Here you are, a perfectly happy duke--"

"Usurping duke" Andrew reminded him.

"Alright, usurping duke. Nice house, lots of boodle, lots of servants and all that sort of thing. Would *you* knock it off just because some itinerant god-botherer suggested it might be a nice gesture? I mean after all, the career prospects for an ex-usurping duke aren't that promising."

"He could be persuaded," suggested Kodswallop with enough animation to suggest that he would be quite willing to make the attempt.

"They don't have to be reconciled." Andrew decided to offer the alternative. "Suppose it was found out that this Harold character never was the duke in the first place?"

"Eh?" All eyes turned to the mage.

"If this is another one of those conundrums like the one about who shaves the barber..." Cecil muttered rebelliously.

"No, but suppose it were discovered that just after the son of the *previous* duke of Benbrock-Oldstairs was born, the baby had been exchanged for another baby who grew up to become Harold, then clearly Harold wouldn't be the duke."

"How would you find something like that out?"

"His old nurse could confess to the deception on her deathbed."

"I fear that will not do in this case." Tiresome shook his head regretfully. "The former Duchess of Benbrock-Oldstairs was a strong-minded woman with modern ideas of child raising. She resolutely refused to consider a nurse for any of her children."

"Ah, well then..." Andrew thought some more. "A document giving details of Harold's true parentage could be discovered in a casket somewhere."

"What a good idea!" Ratbag squeaked with excitement. "I can start work on it at once." In addition to his other talents, Ratbag was a superb calligraphist.

"It doesn't sound very plausible..." Cecil shook his head doubtfully.

"It doesn't have to be *plausible*!" Andrew thumped the table, "it only has to work!"

"I'm afraid there is a trifling problem..." Tiresome regretted scuppering what had looked like a perfectly good plan, but had no choice. "The title of Benbrock-Oldstairs, like all such in the south, is in the gift of the First Speaker of East Castellian. Titles can descend from father to son, and some have indeed done so. Once or twice. But whether or not Harold was *biologically*, his father's son is quite irrelevant to his possession of the title."

"Oh. But what about his brother. Isn't *he* the duke now?"

"He is the *usurping* duke. Harold remains the *exiled* duke," Tiresome said calmly, "it is a not uncommon situation."

"Alright then!" Andrew sprang to his feet, "we'll go for the reconciliation."

"But--"

"At the point of a sword, if necessary!" Andrew started striding about the room waving his arms excitedly, much to the alarm of the outlaws. "Those two are going to get reconciled if it kills them, *and* they will leave the forest. Horizontally if necessary!"

Orlando growled with approval.

"But how--?" Janus was looking puzzled and a little worried, for he had never seen his mage in such a state of excitement and determination before.

"Now this may take some time." Andrew continued pacing up and down the room, "and I'm afraid, Mr Orlando, you will have to reconcile yourself to the appearance of one or two courting couples and perhaps-- er-- one or two other things. But it won't be anything we can't handle. Might be a bit of bad weather too." He stopped suddenly as a thought struck him, and he swung round to face the outlaw leader. "How are you off for supernatural beings in the forest-- fairies, tree nymphs, that sort of stuff?"

"Well..." Orlando tried to gather his wits. "All we really have here on a permanent basis are the forest trolls. Vulgar little buggers, but they usually leave us alone. There might be the odd fairy godmother passing through, but none in residence, so to speak. As for things like princes transformed into frogs or spirits trapped in trees, well there's nothing like that these days. I don't suppose there's been an amphibious prince around for years-- not in my time, anyway."

"How about enchanted plants? Slips of yew slivered in the moon's eclipse? Love lies bleeding? Mistletoe? Four-leafed clover?"

Orlando shook his head to each.

"Good! Excellent!" Andrew began pacing again. "Now wild animals: how are you off for those? Lions? Tygers-- symmetrical or otherwise? Ravening salt sea sharks?"

"No, not really."

"Oh." Andrew seemed a little put out. "You're sure you might not have the odd lion kicking about the place?" he asked, coming to a halt and fixing the outlaw chief with a persuasive eye.

"Quite sure." Perceiving that the mage seemed disappointed by this deficiency in the lion department, Orlando tried to make amends. "We do have a bear, though."

"A bear!"

"Yes. A rather large, brown bear. It arrived here last autumn and, in fact," Orlando permitted himself a nervous chuckle, "it took up residence in the very cave that Duke Harold is using."

"You mean the duke chucked him out?" Clumpface was looking very threatening.

"No. You see this seems to be a migratory bear and he was not in residence when--"

"A migratory bear!" Andrew exchanged significant looks with his comrades. "Would you describe this creature as a useless ursine layabout who spends his time cadging buns?"

"Well er..." Orlando, who liked to think the best of everyone, hesitated. "In a manner of speaking, yes," he admitted at last.

"It's bloody Horace!" Andrew shouted, "it must be!" Everybody looked accusingly at Clumpface who wriggled slightly.

"He was migrating," the dwarf explained, "went south for the winter. I expect he's heading up to Nova Castria now, for the summer."

"Horace is a Nacandian migratory bear," Janus explained to the mystified outlaw leader, "we met him there about a year and a half ago, and he came back with us. He's quite-- er-- harmless."

"Pity," Orlando frowned, "I was hoping he might come back."

"He probably will." Cecil rolled his eyes, "he never has managed to get his mind round this migration lark properly."

"But what are you going to *do*?" Orlando had traversed incomprehension, mystification, stupefaction and was now entering the terminal phase of extreme irritation.

"It's really quite straightforward." Andrew was speaking rapidly and had resumed his pacing. "We go through the standard stages: initial conflict, misunderstanding, confusion of identities, culminating in resolution, reconciliation and reunification."

"With some bad weather thrown in?"

"If necessary, yes. Pity about the lion... but I think we can work Horace in somewhere." Andrew fell silent, but his mind was racing. For the first time he felt totally in control of a situation, and the realization came to him that the secret to control was not trying to understand and come to terms with a situation, but re-defining it in his own terms, and dealing with it on that basis. Andrew would have been the first to admit that he didn't know much about the maging business, and his efforts in that direction tended to be dangerously unpredictable. But he *did* know about exiled dukes in forests...

"Ah..." Orlando rose to his feet. He hated to interrupt this pregnant silence, but he was due at the Weekly Planning Meeting in five minutes. "I must leave you now. Is there anything I can tell my Section Leaders about your plans?"

"You may tell them that we have the situation in hand," Janus told him, "and will leave no avenue unexplored nor any stone unturned in seeking the solution." The elf looked hopefully at Andrew who was still staring blankly through the window. He sensed that his assurance was slightly lacking in specificity. Tiresome rose to the occasion.

"I recommend as an interim measure that you re-route Sucker's Alley North to bypass Duke Harold's encampment. And perhaps station some of your men along the route to prevent interference, and act as guides if necessary."

"Excellent idea!" This was practical advice to which Orlando could relate. "I'll see to it at once. They could be disguised as honest woodcutters, perhaps."

"Most traditional." The knight gave an approving smile.

"We shall meet tonight for dinner, I trust," Orlando looked around for his cloak, but it seemed to have disappeared. He gave up on it, and swept out. The door thudded shut behind him.

The contemplative silence which followed the outlaw chief's departure was broken by Janus. "What do you have planned, Andrew?" he asked, cheerfully expectant.

Andrew fidgeted absently with his sleeve. "I think the first thing we'd better do is take a look at this duke-- confirm he really does mean to stay. And I want to find out as much about his brother as possible. But really the important thing is to--"

"To case the joint?" Kodswallop and Tiresome said together.

"Right. I want him to start feeling a bit discontented about his living conditions. It's hard to stay enthusiastic about sermons in stones and books in brooks when it's pouring with rain and your tents are leaking or falling down."

"But it's not raining" objected Cecil, "and how do we know his tents leak?"

"Both can be arranged," Clumpface reminded him.

"You mean we're going to do the place over?" Kodswallop gave an anticipatory smile.

"No we are *not* going to do his place over! We are merely going to take a shufti and chat the bloke up a bit."

"Chat him up?"

"Andrew means we are going to carry out a preliminary reconnaissance and conduct an interrogation of the subject," Tiresome translated, adding in a lower voice, "with a view to doing the place over later on if necessary."

"Right," Andrew agreed. He took out his notebook "Now this is what I thought we'd do..."

Act IV
STORMY WEATHER

Very carefully Cecil pushed some brambles aside, wriggled forward and peered over the edge of the cliff. The precautions were probably needless, for nobody in the crescent-shaped clearing sixty feet below seemed to have eyes for anything but their own activities. A rumble of conversation, punctuated by the occasional raucous laugh, floated up on the still afternoon air, together with the fragile sound of stringed instruments being plucked, and an undulating drone which might have been a hautboy. A plaintive tinge was provided by the faint nasal twanging of a zither. Cecil shrugged-- he was no music critic-- and concentrated his attention on the scene below. His lip curled slightly as he took in the ill-positioned caravans and the rapidly growing pile of rubbish about which a small cloud of flies already buzzed eagerly. Cecil was not a fastidious housekeeper, but even he could see that it would not be very long before this exiled duke and his retinue had turned a perfectly serviceable forest glade into a squalid slum that any self-respecting sewer rat would disdain as unfit for rodent habitation. Cecil sneered again, then readied his weapon. From this position he commanded the whole glade. And he was almost directly above a trestle table at which a group of richly dressed men were quaffing hugely and throwing bread rolls at each other-- the exiled duke and his toadies. From this position a flick of a wrist would drop a pebble in the punchbowl that was set before them. A little more muscular effort would send down a sizeable rock with equal accuracy. For a moment Cecil was tempted, but after a short struggle business won out over pleasure, and the marksman returned to his scrutiny of the clearing, his finger resting delicately on the trigger. For some minutes he lay so, motionless, then stiffened. The two spear-carrying guards at the entrance to the clearing had suddenly jumped high into the air and curved gracefully backwards to crash into the bushes. Kodswallop had arrived.

"Sorry about that." Kodswallop casually snapped the spears in two and tossed the pieces to one side. "They moved so quickly I thought I'd better stop them before they did anything we might have to make them regret."

"Never mind," Andrew found himself whispering, "are the others in position?"

The big fighter nodded confidently. Tiresome and Janus were concealed in the bushes nearby to cover them should a fighting retreat become necessary, while Clumpface and Ratbag were slipping through the trees to investigate the perimeter of the encampment. And Cecil should be overlooking the glade. Andrew took another look around the clearing. No-one appeared to have noticed them or, more surprisingly, the unusual behaviour of the two guards. "Alright." He squared his shoulders. "Let's go."

He stalked across the springy turf feeling like a very lonely actor on a very large stage before a very large audience. But it was a very inattentive audience. People were scurrying this way and that bearing huge platters of meat or, more properly Andrew reminded himself, viands. A small group of minstrels made twanging and droning noises, punctuated by the odd thud or tinkle. And a man wearing a grey coat and a funny hat, with a hunting horn hanging at his waist, was throwing sticks and trying to urge a couple of floppy looking hounds to run after them. But there was no doubt where the focal point for all this activity lay, and that was the trestle table drawn up at the mouth of the cave where four richly dressed men sat, or rather lounged. Even at this range it was plain that they were messy eaters and sloppy drinkers. Behind them and to their right, stood a fellow in green livery and a powdered wig.

"Good afternoon!" Andrew called out, cheerily enough. Nothing happened except that a servant bearing an unusually large platter pushed his way in front of them and made to advance to the table.

"By your leave, sir," he said with the studied insolence of the privileged servant or executive secretary.

Kodswallop reached out and grasped the man by the scruff of his neck and held him aloft, his feet vainly peddling at the empty air. "Out of the way, lad," he rumbled, and tossed the man to one side, dropping him neatly at the feet of the minstrels. The music stopped with a discordant twang and a wheezing groan. The chattering and laughter died away until the only sound was a waft of zither music from the cave. Kodswallop glared ferociously, and the music stopped.

"Good afternoon!" Andrew repeated. At the trestle table a broad-shouldered, dark-haired man rose to his feet. The toadies on either side of him looked up curiously and stopped throwing bread rolls.

"Welcome, gentle sirs, to our humble camp!" The mellifluous voice resonated through the glade.

Perched on his cliff-top vantage point, Cecil sneered.

"Welcome, again!" The exiled duke threw his arms wide in an extravagant gesture. "You are pilgrims?" he suggested.

"Not exactly, no."

"No, I see." Duke Harold took another look at the un-pilgrim-like form of Kodswallop. "Perhaps honest woodcutters?"

"Not exactly." Andrew cleared his throat, and began speaking quickly. "My name is Andrew Cruickshank, that is Doctor Andrew Cruickshank, and my research assistant and I are conducting a survey into migratory patterns of the aristocracy. We would be most grateful if you could give us a few moments of your time to answer a few questions. Of course your answers will remain confidential and the information gained in this survey will be of long-term benefit to the aristocracy as a whole." Andrew took out his notebook and stylus, and gave them an inviting flourish.

"A travelling scholar, sir! You are welcome!" Duke Harold eyed the two narrowly. The Doctor lacked the unctuous delivery that the duke associated with academics, and had a hard-bitten look about him. And he could have sworn that beneath the coarse grey cloak, the man carried a sword. And as for the research assistant! He shuddered to think what kind of assistance he might be capable of providing. But then, competition in the universities *was* pretty fierce these days. "I shall be happy to provide you with such poor assistance as I can. Be quiet, Bushy!" he admonished one of the toadies who was attempting to compose a mocking limerick.

"You are very kind, your grace," Andrew hurried on, "first: is this your principal residence?"

"Indeed yes! Here, under the greenwood tree where we see no enemy but winter and rough weather. Not that we have been here for the winter, you understand."

"You arrived recently?"

"Just a couple of weeks ago." The duke struck his hand to his heart. "A sudden stab of envy from my brother at a stroke deprived me of my court, my friends, my fortune."

"Hard luck!" Andrew commiserated, "but you do seem to have brought some friends along."

"Ah! My co-mates and brothers in exile! Together, we find books in the running brooks, sermons in stones, and good in everything!"

"How about tongues in trees?" asked Andrew, wanting to make assurance doubly sure. The duke looked startled.

"I had not thought of that, but 'tis a noble conceit. Palindrome!" He waved commandingly to the man in the green livery. "Make a note to remind me about tongues in trees."

"Would you say," Andrew continued insinuatingly, "that young gentlemen flock to you every day, and fleet the time as carelessly as they did in the golden world?"

"Not yet..." the duke gave a judicious frown, "but I have no doubt that when 'tis known that all the treasury--" he brought himself up with a start. "Ah-- that is to say, when the young gentlemen become aware of how much more free from peril we are here than in the envious court, then..."

"Quite!" Andrew tapped his notebook invitingly, "your brother, would his name by any chance happen to be... er... Frederick?"

"No." The duke shook his head.

"Ah! Andrew thought furiously. He had been *sure* the usurping duke was called Frederick. "Of course! Silly of me. I meant Ferdinand."

"No." The duke shook his head again. "My unnatural brother goes by the name of Roger."

"Roger!" Andrew nearly dropped his stylus but recovered quickly. "Any other family?" he asked.

"One daughter--"

With relief Andrew began to scribble down the name Rosalind, then nearly dropped his stylus a second time as the duke continued.

"My daughter, Julia, remains in Benbrock-Oldstairs with her cousin Anne."

"Er... yes." Andrew recovered again, but not so quickly. "That would be-- er-- Roger's daughter?" The duke nodded agreement. "And are their loves," Andrew pursued determinedly, "dearer than the natural bond of sisters?"

"So true, alas," the duke agreed, "but not in any way unnatural," he added hurriedly, "nothing like... er... that sort of thing."

"Of course not," Andrew agreed. He scribbled a couple more lines, and shut the notebook with a snap. "Well, thank you for your co-operation. You have been most helpful."

The duke made a gracious gesture of dismissal. "I am happy to have been of service. Pray visit us again and feast with us beneath the stars. We shall drink wine, and sing old songs, and listen to sweet music." The brittle notes of a zither drifted out from the cave. Kodswallop gave another ferocious glare. The zither felt silent. "Perhaps not the music," the duke concluded equably, "and so, farewell."

Andrew and Kodswallop turned to go, and all might have gone well had not the toady Bushy decided to play a practical joke on this travelling scholar. Throughout the conversation his eyes had been fixed upon the staff the man carried slung from his shoulder. It didn't look like anything special, but this itinerant academic obviously set great store by it, and it would be a good giggle to take it from him, and have him chasing about the glade after it. Bushy was easily amused. He darted from the table as soon as the scholar turned his back, chased after him and reached out to grasp the staff.

It was a mistake. There was a vicious *crack*, a violet flash of Heron-Gough discharge, and a scream of terror. Bushy flipped through the air to land with an unpleasant squelch on the rubbish pile.

"Sorcery!" There was a collective gasp.

"Er... sorry about that!" Andrew apologised, his face scarlet with embarrassment.

"Sorcery!" The cry was re-echoed from a dozen throats.

"No! It's not that at all! Just a simple little novelty item-- got it in a joke shop in Nova Castria," Andrew gabbled, "but it never seems to work properly. You know, springs and that sort of thing."

There was a rasp of steel as the two other toadies drew their swords and began to advance cautiously. There were more rasps of steel as others, seeing that the quality were prepared to get involved, drew their swords too. There was a menacing whisper as Kodswallop drew his five foot blade and whirled it eagerly about his head. Things were looking up!

Andrew, sick with apprehension but nevertheless feeling the stirrings of anger at the tomfoolery, whipped out his own duelling sword and dropped into a fighting stance. It did occur to him that this might not go too well with his role as a learned doctor, but then Kodswallop didn't look much like a research assistant at the moment. The weapon he was waving about looked like a girder stolen from a rather large railway bridge, beaten flat, then honed by the grindstones of hell to a razor edge. It hissed menacingly as the blade cut the air.

Still gasping, the duke surveyed the scene with pop-eyed amazement. The transformation of two humble scholars into two very stroppy fighting men was just too much. And they looked as though they were about to make mincemeat of his toadies. "Bagot! Greene!" He shouted, "put up your swords. Leave them to my huntsmen!" With obvious relief, the two sheathed their weapons. Disconcerted, Andrew looked round to see a number of grey-coated men bending their bows, obviously with hostile intent.

There was a flat hiss, a *thunk* and a scream. One of the huntsmen dropped his bow and stared wide-eyed at the crossbow bolt that had nailed his sleeve to a tree.

"Any more for any more?" The tone was that of someone who rather hoped there would be.

All eyes save those of Kodswallop and Andrew swivelled up to look at the little black dot of a head on the rim of the cliff overlooking the glade.

"Now everybody stand nice and still and--" There was another hiss and a thud, and another scream. "Naughty, naughty!" Cecil admonished. Everybody froze. Kodswallop scowled ferociously once more.

"You might have waited!" he shouted up.

"Never mind that!" Andrew hissed angrily, "let's go."

"Got all you want, then?" The big fighter turned back to the duke with an attempt at a reassuring smile. "Thank you for your valuable assistance" he said, "and you may rest assured that the information you gave us will be treated confidentially." He turned on his heel and, swinging his sword casually, followed Andrew out of the glade.

More than thirty leagues to the south and the west, at the Guild of the Black Mages, a young man toiled up the stairs of a grim hexagonal tower of gleaming basalt. He reached the solid slab of ebony that was the door to the turret room then paused, his heart in his mouth. He believed the information he had was important enough to warrant disturbing the mage-- but if it was not... He swallowed, and raised his hand to tap upon the door. But before his knuckles could contact the gleaming black surface, the door swung open on silent hinges.

"Yes, Bellingham?" Mage Montmorency raised his eyebrows inquiringly.

Bellingham swallowed again, and tried not to look at the grim, black-cloaked figure, but his eyes were drawn against their will to the thin, almost emaciated features, the short-cropped black hair, and the dark eyes with violet flashes darting in their fathomless depths. "I apologise for the intrusion, Mage Montmorency--"

"Pray do not apologise, Bellingham," the mage waved away the apology, "being disturbed by their graduate students is what supervisors are for. How can I be of assistance"

"I just detected some anomalous occult activity, very similar to yesterday's. A little unusual, Mage. There were certain features..."

"Yes?"

"It *looked* like a late-model Sproggit and Axel staff, but with peculiarities."

"Individual modifications?"

"Ye--es..."

"But you don't think so, eh?"

Wordlessly Bellingham shook his head.

"Good!" Montmorency smiled with approval. "And what else took your attention?"

"It was the signature, Mage Montmorency. I have never seen anything like it. It was off-scale high *and* low. And I remembered that you--" He got no further as Montmorency jumped to his feet and pushed past to the door.

"Come, Bellingham! Let us see this curious phenomenon!"

In the laboratory, Montmorency stared intently into the crystal sphere. "Yes!... That is the trace you just picked up?"

"Yes, Mage. See, here is yesterday's." Bellingham passed his hand over the crystal and a new image flashed into existence, just above the original.

"Remarkable!" breathed Montmorency, "quite remarkable!" He opened a cabinet with a wave of his hand, and a small black tablet floated across the room. He plucked it out of the air and slipped it into a receptacle at the base of the crystal sphere. "And now, Bellingham, take a look at *this*." He waved at the crystal, and a third image appeared. Bellingham caught his breath. Even to his untutored eye the jagged peaks and valleys of the crimson lines of the signatures were identical. "You have done very well, Bellingham!" The voice was so warm, the student almost fainted with shock. Greatly emboldened he decided to risk a question.

"Who would have a signature like *that*?"

"A wardmaster mage, Bellingham. None other than Wardmaster Cruickshank!"

Bellingham gasped and nearly fainted once more. Everyone at the Guild of the Black Mages had heard of this man-- Montmorency's Designated Opposite, and the only mage to have bested the great Montmorency!

Montmorency removed the tablet from the crystal and returned it to the index rack. "And where did this signal come from?" he asked.

"It-- it appeared to originate in Stembark Forest," Bellingham stammered.

"Stembark Forest, eh?" Montmorency stroked his chin, "now what, I wonder..." He stood silent and motionless for some minutes, and Bellingham began to wonder whether he had gone off into some kind of trance. Then abruptly the tall gaunt figure snapped back into life.

"Well, Bellingham" he said with a smile, "I think you are ready for some field work."

"I think we're going to have to do a bit more field work. I want to take a look at the Usurping duke in Benbrock-Oldstairs." Andrew stopped his pacing and returned to staring broodily through the open window. The accommodation more than lived up to Lenny's promises, yet Andrew could take no comfort in the elegance and luxury of the surroundings. "We're going to have to see that usurping duke," he muttered, "just to make sure."

"But why?" Janus asked, "what more do you need to see?" The elf was anxious. The confrontation with the exiled duke that morning had shaken him. It was quite at odds with tradition and good practice for a mage to take such an exposed role, especially a mage like Andrew. "When you've seen one usurping duke, you've seen them all," he explained, in case Andrew was motivated by simple curiosity.

"I never heard of a duke-- usurping or not-- that was worth going twenty paces to see, let alone twenty leagues," Tiresome agreed. "And remember, it'll mean travelling through East Castellian, and none of us are exactly the flavour of the month there," he added.

"It's just that I need to confirm the bit about young men flocking to him every day," Andrew explained, "that is, flocking to the exiled duke-- and I want to see the two girls."

"I shouldn't be at all surprised if all kinds of people were flocking to him every day." Ratbag began to unlace the bulging kitbag he had brought back from the duke's encampment, "you should see what he has in that caravan!"

"Don't you mean 'had'?" asked Clumpface, directing a disapproving glare at the growing pile of loot the nicker was unpacking.

"He seems to be unusually well supplied for an exiled duke," Tiresome observed drily.

"He is very well supplied!" The little figure almost hopped with excitement, "three large chests, all of them just crammed with gold."

"Doubtless they are considerably less crammed now!" Clumpface gave a snort that was not entirely mirthless. Usually he was unremitting in his denunciation of the nicker's propensity for the one-way re-distribution of other people's assets, but when the other people were the aristocracy he was prepared to make an exception.

"It surely is not usual for an exiled duke to be so well provided, Tiresome?" Janus asked, "what is the customary practice in these matters?"

"It is most unusual," the knight agreed, "traditionally, following completion of all the preliminaries, and ratification of the usurpation licence by the First Speaker, an exile may be given a few days to prepare before he must make himself scarce, but that is all. Duke Harold appears to have used those few days very profitably, or else his brother has been pathologically generous."

"In any event it means that you need have no fears about young men flocking to him every day, Andrew." Janus smiled with relief.

"I should think not!" Cecil snorted, "they're probably queuing up."

"I'd still like to check on the girls..." Andrew did not seem convinced.

"But why? What have they got to do with this?"

"Well they should be running away to the forest, because the exiled duke's daughter gets banished by the usurping duke, and the usurping duke's daughter goes with her."

"So?"

"So the usurping duke takes off to the forest as well--"

"After the two girls? But I thought you'd said he'd just banished one of them."

"No, not just after the two girls, but after his brother."

"Why?"

"Well because all the young men have been flocking to him every day, so he get's worried that they may be plotting against him--"

"May!" Tiresome gave a short laugh, "there would be little question about *that!*"

"So he goes chasing off to the forest, then meets an old hermit or somebody like that, and then he decides to give up the dukedom and live in simplicity in the forest."

"I don't think Don Orlando will go for that." Clumpface shook his head. "Bad enough having an exiled duke hanging about the place, but an ex-usurping duke..."

"I still don't believe the usurping duke will go for it either," opined Cecil, "if it were me I'd come to the forest, scrag the duke and take the treasure back. Only makes sense."

"But the exiled duke's protected," Ratbag reminded him.

"Oh, yeah... I'd forgotten." Cecil looked glum.

"Andrew, do you believe you can effect a reconciliation? Without further dealing with Duke Harold?" Janus asked.

"Bugger the reconciliation!" Kodswallop scowled. "We should just go in and give that lot a good thumping-- exiled duke or not. A treacherous bunch, they are! A good thumping would be just the thing to make them want to leave"

"Unfortunately we cannot," Tiresome shook his head regretfully, "however there are other incentives that could be applied."

"Such as?"

"Inclement weather. You might remember that Andrew suggested it at our meeting with Don Orlando."

"That's right!" Elated, Kodswallop jumped to his feet and darted to the window. He peered through, then turned and gave a disappointed shrug. "Just fine outside. Not a cloud in the sky."

"There is no reason why that should continue." Tiresome looked at Andrew as he spoke. Everybody looked at Andrew, as the significance of the knight's remark sank in.

"Now just a minute!" Andrew protested, "you can't mean..." his voice trailed off as he realised that it was very clear that this was exactly what they did mean. "Oh, no! Listen; the whole point about this thing is that there's no magic involved. No magician. No enchanted island. No enchanted plants. No fairies. Nothing unnatural at all."

"You mean you don't call it unnatural for a perfectly successful usurping duke to call the whole thing off and retire to a monastery or something just on the say-so of some scruffy god-botherer?" Cecil challenged.

"Well..."

"You did yourself mention that inclement weather was a distinct possibility," Janus traitorously reminded him, "and I am sure Tarot 5.1 includes weather modification routines."

"But I still think we should go and see this usurping duke."

"Perhaps we may do so, after suitable weather conditions have been arranged for the exiled duke," Janus offered, privately determined to do his utmost to prevent such a foolish and hazardous expedition.

"But..." Andrew looked round the room for support, but saw only the implacable gaze of his comrades. "Well... I suppose I can give it a shot." Reluctantly he opened his equipment case and took out the ivory box of tarot cards, the Dalton spellcaster and Using *Tarot 5.1*. With nervous distaste he opened the manual. *Welcome to the world of Tarot 5.1,* the introduction told him enthusiastically, *with the advent of Release 5.1, the list of Tarot features has become even longer than before, and includes context-sensitive help, improved macros, staff support and, of course, the unique Spell-Check feature. No more memorizing arcane command sequences! Just "point and click" with the Sproggit and Axel Mage staff (system requirements are Mk XX or later with Voice Interactive capability). The staff should be in the Voice-Interactive mode. Remember that inadvertent exclamations can result in spurious input with unpredictable and possibly hazardous results. Sproggit and Axel are not liable for any damages arising from inadmissible oral input. Watch your language!*

Andrew needed no warning of the possibility of unpredictable and possibly hazardous results when the staff was in the voice interactive mode, and he quickly raised a finger to his lips to warn his comrades. Cecil gave a nervous squawk and tried to sidle towards the door, only to be grabbed by Clumpface, and firmly sat down to await events with the rest of them. Andrew switched the staff to voice interactive, and a faint blue glow filled the hexagonal crystal that decorated the top of the instrument. He took up the manual once again, and trying to avoid rustling the pages, turned to the *Meteorology* section. *Weather modification,* it announced briskly, *in the past this required the memorizing of long, complicated incantations, considerable manual dexterity with the staff, and the handling of a number of quite unspeakable substances. But now, with Sproggit and Axel's Tarot, the whole meteorological spectrum is only the turn of a card away. And the new staff support feature makes it even quicker and easier than before!* Andrew turned the page quickly, then several more pages, passing over drought, lightning, controlled cloud cover, fog patches, deep depressions, ridges of high pressure, hurricanes and sunny intervals, until he got to *RAIN*. He studied the page briefly, made a couple of adjustments to his spellcaster, then inserted the required tarot cards into the clip on the back of the instrument. Then he grasped the staff and, feeling a little self-conscious, said; "Precipitation: execute."

The crystal atop the staff filled with a cascade of yellow letters. *Precipitation loading... Please Wait...* they announced, then flickered briefly, changing *to precipitation has been turned ON... parameters loaded... precipitation running... precipitation will terminate in five hours, fifty-nine minutes, thirty seconds.* The message shivered briefly and then dissolved. The blue light faded. His lips tightly shut to preclude any inadvertent exclamation, Andrew put the tarot cards back in their box and slipped the spellcaster into its leather case. He heaved a sigh of relief. "Well at least nothing went horribly wrong."

"Yet," Cecil reminded them, the eternal optimist.

They all crowded over to the windows and peered outside. "You know, I do believe something *is* happening," Andrew remarked with the nervous surprise of an incompetent conjuror who at last, against all probability, has succeeded in producing a rabbit from a hat. The cloudless blue sky darkened to a steel grey, and dank, chill gusts of wind rattled the trees.

"Bit cold, isn't it," Cecil remarked, wrapping his arms about himself.

"Good!" Kodswallop glowered fiercely, "that'll show 'em."

The sky changed from grey to opaque white, and then the snow came down. It came down in thick, enthusiastic, impenetrable swirls, cold and dry, spilling from twigs and leaves like fine sand and, with the faintest rustling, sifting up against the boles of trees and over the paths and generally transforming what had been a bright spring afternoon into the cold silence of a Christmas card winter. All that was missing was a sprig of holly and a log with a robin perched on it.

"That *was* rain you ordered, wasn't it?" Cecil's eyebrows rose interrogatively.

"Er..." Andrew forced himself to look through the window. "I'm not sure..."

"You said 'rain'," the marksman continued inexorably, "*that*," and he pointed, "is snow."

"You know, I believe you're absolutely right!" Andrew wriggled uncomfortably.

"Just the thing!" Kodswallop gave the swirling flakes an approving look, "that duke talked about winter and rough weather-- now he's getting them."

A league and a half from headquarters Don Orlando wrapped his second-best cloak more tightly about him. Snow! Unheard of at this time of year. He frowned-- the outlaw business was very weather-sensitive, although he comforted himself with the thought that the extensive indoor facilities offered in Stembark Forest made them much less vulnerable that sort of thing than, for example, the highwaymen. He shivered and urged his horse forward-- the sooner they were both home the better. The mage *had* said something about the possibility of bad weather, he recollected, and cheered himself with the thought that clearly the man was losing no time in getting down to work. A few unseasonable inches of snow was a small price to pay for getting rid of an exiled duke. Orlando hummed under his breath. This was just the sort of thing to make exiled duke bloody Harold rue the day he left Benbrock-Oldstairs for Stembark Forest.

Act V
OVERCAST... FOG PATCHES... SUNNY PERIODS

Duke Roger of Benbrock Oldstairs (Usurping) stared at his lawyer in outraged disbelief. "What are you trying to say, Pinchbeck?" he snarled, "are you telling me there is *nothing*?" He took half a dozen angry strides across the immaculate grass. "*Nothing*?" he repeated, and kicked viciously at a gaily-coloured plaster toadstool. The toadstool crumbled. Pinchbeck winced, for he had a soft spot for such decorations. The duke snarled once again and lashed out at a plaster gnome fishing from a plaster bridge. The gnome's head splashed into the little stream that trickled its way through the rock-garden. Clutching his briefcase under one arm, Pinchbeck strutted to the duke's side.

"I do not say there is *nothing*," he said, with the calm deliberation of one whose interests are not directly affected, "I am merely informing you that there appears to be very little. Only sufficient, in fact," he coughed discreetly, "to meet our own account."

"But how could he do this to me? His own brother!" Duke Roger's tones switched from enraged to tragic, "I mean, I know we had our little disagreements, but to make off like that, without a word, and with the whole treasury--"

"Most unfortunate, I'm sure," the lawyer agreed.

"How did he expect me to keep this place up!" Roger waved rhetorically at the gracious facade of white marble that swooped along the river. "I'm down to one toady and one trainee. Me-- The Duke of Benbrock-Oldstairs-- with only one full-time toady!"

"Most unfortunate," repeated the lawyer, with a professional shake of the head, "your brother's behaviour seems incomprehensible. So unfraternal!"

"And it's not as if I didn't really put myself out over the usurpation-- nothing but the best--"

"You did all a brother could be expected to, and more," the lawyer patted his arm, "you may at least comfort yourself with that thought." The duke shook off the arm impatiently.

"I tell you this is only just the beginning, Pinchbeck. Before you know it there'll be young men flocking to him every day."

"Most understandable," murmured the lawyer, thinking of the three large treasure chests.

"*And* fleeting the time as carelessly as they did in the golden world, mark my words."

"It would seem to me your grace, that bearing in mind what his former grace took with him, they will be fleeting their time in a *solid* golden world." Pinchbeck permitted himself a dry lawyerly chuckle.

"Very humorous, I'm sure!" His usurping grace was not in the mood to appreciate legal humour-- at least not at the present time. He grasped the lawyer by the elbow. "Now Pinchbeck, I want to take this to the First Speaker. Do you think I have a case?"

"Really your grace!" Pinchbeck shook himself free with a fastidious gesture. "I could not possibly undertake to advise your grace on this matter, or indeed on any matter, given your current circumstances.[5] "

"Listen Pinchbeck," the duke's face darkened with anger and suspicion, and his free hand toyed with the dagger at his belt, "you drew up those articles of usurpation. *Your* name was on the application for the licence. Are you saying you didn't do a proper job?"

"Your grace!" Pinchbeck drew himself up to his full height. "I can assure you that the Articles were drawn up in a thoroughly professional manner. And the licence application was in perfect accordance with all

---

5   "Current circumstances"= totally skint

requirements. Pinchbeck, Frustum, Cade and Pinchbeck are not in the habit of making mistakes in such matters!"

"Well then...?"

The lawyer hesitated. Properly speaking he should not vouchsafe any opinion until he was reasonably assured of receiving payment for it, and he was intimate enough with the usurping duke's current financial position to know that Duke Roger didn't even have the money for the parchment, let alone enough for any legal opinion that might be written upon it. On the other hand his firm had a long history of profitable association with the family, and the present representative of that family was grasping his dagger in an unpleasantly threatening fashion. He decided for old times' sake to offer an informal opinion. "Ahem! As I said, the relevant documentation for your usurpation is of unchallengeable validity. However, as we advised you at the time, it is not altogether clear that your Preparatory Motions absolutely meet the criteria traditionally applied in these matters. It would of course, ultimately be a matter for the Courts to decide, but it is my opinion that a Motion in Challenge to your Preparatory Motions might possibly have a chance of succeeding, should such a motion be filed, of course."

Duke Roger stared uncomprehendingly. "What are you talking about, Pinchbeck? What about the preparatory motions?"

"As our Mr Cade informed you quite clearly some months ago, a formal Application for a Usurpation Licence must be supported by evidence of at least two serious attempts to effect the incumbent's removal."

"You mean the poisoning?"

"Yes. And the assassination attempt. It is my belief that a clever counsel might well be able to demonstrate to the satisfaction of the Court that these do not meet the accepted criteria."

"What would that mean?"

"Your grace!" Pinchbeck spoke with the shock and disgust of any lawyer faced with an impecunious client. "I have already said far too much! I cannot possibly vouchsafe any opinion under the present circumstances. And now I must wish you a very good morning." He turned on his heel and strutted off.

"I'm going to take this to the First Speaker!" Roger shouted after him, "and I'll see he knows all about *your* part in this, Pinchbeck, if it's the last thing I do!"

Pinchbeck paused and turned his head. "With the First Speaker," he said, "it probably will be." The iron gate clanged behind him. His brow as black as thunder, Roger listened to the clatter of hooves and rumble of wheels as the lawyer's carriage drove away and, cursing under his breath, swung his leg at another plaster gnome. There was a soft crunch and Duke Roger screamed in agony. Some of the figures had been cast in cement.

Titus Handcarte, First Speaker of East Castellian, sat at his desk in the Brown Study, the Benbrock Oldstairs file open before him. The First Speaker had a round, pale face set on a less-round body, with light blue eyes inadequately sheltered beneath sparse gingery eyebrows. Those eyebrows were raised slightly as the eyes swivelled back and forth between the closely written papers in the file and a thick ledger whose pages were heavy with annotations and whose cover bore the title *Jane's Guide to the Aristocracy: Southern Albion*. Every now and again he would nod with satisfaction, or click his tongue with irritation, and make some note on a little yellow piece of sticky paper.

The title of First Speaker was both informative and misleading. Informative in that, as the title explicitly stated, he was the man who spoke first in the East Castellian House of Sycophants and, by implication, he was the leading member of that assembly. It was also informative in that it suggested the existence of a Second, Third and Fourth Speaker. Where it was misleading was in the implication that the Second, Third etc Speakers actually might *speak*[6]

---

6   The Second, Third etc Speakers were constitutionally designated successors to the First Speaker should Anything Happen to Him (like dying suddenly of a severe cold following discussions with three hooded figures down a dark alley) with the result that the First Speaker regarded them with the liveliest suspicion. Since he firmly believed that offence was the best form of defence, he ensured that any of his potential successors who exhibited any stirrings of ambition whatsoever (like actually trying to speak) were shortly thereafter involved in full and frank discussions with hooded figures down dark alleys. As a consequence of this amiable policy, the current Second, Third and Fourth Speakers were all men of particularly shy, silent and retiring dispositions.

The First Speaker turned a page, half stifled an irritated grunt, then closed the file with a slap. He was a busy man, and he had little time to devote to the affairs of the current duke of Benbrock-Oldstairs (Usurping). At the same time, Benbrock-Oldstairs was one of East Castellian's most desirable titles-- men would kill for it, and most of the holders of the title had done so. In fact the father of Duke Roger (Usurping) had received the dukedom at the hands of the First Speaker himself in recognition of signal services to the state (unspecified, but involving hooded men, long knives and dark alleys). In a fit of abstraction, Handcarte had allowed the title to descend to the elder son following a tragic accident when the father had fallen down a flight of stairs to land upon a number of daggers that had been carelessly left about the place. And Handcarte had further acquiesced in the usurpation. He shook his head angrily-- what could he have been thinking of! He should have insisted that the younger brother complete adequate Preparatory Motions and then, with Harold disposed of, arrested Roger for fratricide. A sudden thought struck the First Speaker as he scanned the file. Like a hungry cat pouncing on a mouse, he seized one page from the file, and studied it intensely. His tensed shoulders relaxed slightly and a smile spread across his face.

There was a respectful tap on the door, and his secretary slid into the office. "The gentleman to measure for the new carpets is here, First Speaker," he whispered, "do you wish me to show him in?"

"Right away please, Leeper."

The door swung fully open and a stooping figure in immaculate grey overalls sidled in. Under one arm he held a very large portfolio which might have contained wallpaper samples, and a partially unrolled tape measure dangled from his breast pocket. About his neck was knotted a strip of fabric patterned with diagonal stripes of contrasting colours. He closed the door behind him as though it were made of fine china, then advanced slowly to Handcarte's desk.

"Z!" Handcarte greeted his secret service[7] chief with a smile that didn't quite reach his eyes, "do sit down!"

---

[7] Despite its rather shopworn cover as an interior decorating studio the East Castellian secret intelligence service was efficient and effective-- for given values of efficiency and effectiveness.

"With respect, First Speaker," the man eased himself into a chair with a cautious sigh.

"Roger, Duke of Benbrock-Oldstairs, (Usurping)-- you have a file on him?"

"We maintain active files on *all* the East Castellian aristocracy." Z opened the portfolio and withdrew a bulky folder.

"Excellent! I am a little concerned about the duke, Z."

"You believe he may be about to suffer from poor health?" Z asked, a gleam of interest in his eyes.

"Not yet. But I want him watched. Put your best men on him. I believe he may shortly be leaving for Stembark Forest."

"Stembark Forest..." Z made a note, "I'll assign a team to him immediately, First Speaker."

"And if he does not leave for Stembark Forest, Z, you may rest assured that my concern for his health will become acute!" Handcarte dismissed the man with a wave and returned to his perusal of the file on his desk. He was still reading some forty minutes later when Duke Roger (Usurping) of Benbrock-Oldstairs was announced.

"How pleasant to see your grace," Handcarte greeted him, concealing the pleasure with some skill, "but you are injured!" he added as the duke limped across the faded carpet.

"A minor accident, First Speaker," Duke Roger gritted his teeth, "It is very good of you to see me at such short notice."

"Nonsense! The interests of the current holder of East Castellian's most honoured, and most expensive, title must ever be to the fore of a First Speaker's attention."

Roger flinched-- the First Speaker was being more than usually direct in his threats today.

"Now how may I be of assistance to your grace?" Handcarte allowed his eyebrows to rise in interrogation.

Swallowing nervously, Roger began. "The fact is, First Speaker, I fear that my brother is in breach of the Usurpation Licence."

The First Speaker's eyebrows climbed higher. "How so, your grace? Did he not leave your court within five days?"

"Yes."

"And has his banished trunk subsequently been encountered within your dominions?"

"Er-- no."

"Then how has he violated the terms of the Usurpation Licence?"

"He took the whole treasury with him when he left!" Duke Roger's voice was thick with rage and mortification.

"You shock me, your grace! How unfraternal can you get!"

"Well, we never did get on..."

"All great families have such problems," the First Speaker tried to comfort him, "but I am not clear on the nature of the violation. I do not recollect anything in the Standard Form of Usurpation that mentions the treasury specifically."

"But he's not supposed to take anything!" Roger yelped, "he gets five days for provision to shield himself from disasters of the world, and that's it! Nothing about treasure chests or anything."

"A clever counsel might argue that taking the treasury would be a thoroughly effective way of shielding yourself from the disasters of the world," the First Speaker suggested mischievously, "but I believe you are right that the *intent* of the terms of the Standard Form of Usurpation was not to include the treasury." He gave a reassuring smile, and the duke gulped in relief. Then froze as the First Speaker continued.

"Of course that is always supposing that the Usurpation Licence has been issued on the basis of, valid Preparatory Motions. Were that not the case, then I am afraid you would have no recourse."

"I-- I am sure that..."

"It so happens that I was just glancing through the records in question... just to familiarize myself with the matter, you understand."

"Most-- er-- kind of you, First Speaker."

"Not at all. I want to make sure that I have this quite right. Now let me see..." Handcarte riffled through the pages. "Your Preparatory Motions..." He leaned back in his chair, placed his elbows on the desk and steepled his fingers. "As you are aware, application for a Usurpation Licence must be supported by evidence of at least two Preparatory

Motions-- that is serious efforts to remove the incumbent. This is in order to discourage frivolous applications."

Duke Roger nodded in understanding, and tried frantically to remember what it was that Pinchbeck had said about his Preparatory Motions. The First Speaker continued in his didactic manner. "Now I see here that your Preparatory Motions were poisoning and assassination. Either one would seem to be fairly effective. What went wrong?"

"Well, we tried the poisoning first--"

"And you miscalculated the dose?" Handcarte nodded understandingly. "A very common problem."

"Not exactly..."

"No?" Handcarte glanced down at the pharmacologist's report, and his eyes widened in simulated surprise. "Good heavens man! This stuff would drop an elephant in its tracks. And you used a *pint*?"

The duke nodded unhappily.

"Then what on earth went wrong?"

"He woke up when I poured it in his ear."

"*What!*"

Shocked into loquacity by this unprecedented display of emotion in the First Speaker, Roger gabbled on. "I followed the instructions on the bottle. While he was sleeping in the orchard-- it was a habit of his after lunch, you know-- I stole on him. I filled a pint mug with the juice of cursed hebona, then poured the leperous distillment in the porches of his ears, just like it said on the bottle."

"You fool! Don't you understand symbolism?"

"I had a friend at school who played them in the orchestra," Roger offered, then wished he hadn't when he saw the look on Handcarte's face.

"And the assassination...?" Handcarte's voice caressed the word.

"Well there I had a bit of trouble. You see my man Charles--"

"Refused to do it," the First Speaker looked up from the file, "you should have known better than to ask a duellist. So what did you do?"

"We-- er-- arranged an accident with one of the gargoyles. I worked it loose and, while the under-gardener asked him for some instructions regarding the lupins, I pushed it over."

"And missed, I see."

"Well, he wasn't a very good under-gardener."

The First Speaker's eyebrows shot up way past the extreme hazard level. "My dear duke (Usurping)" he began with a formality that froze Roger's blood, "it seems to me that you are in a singularly unfortunate position. I am sorry to have to tell you that these Preparatory Motions would be almost certainly dismissed as invalid by any East Castellian court. And you know what that means?"

"Surely a formality, First Speaker!"

"Far from it, I fear. Any attempt by you to invoke the provisions of the Usurpation Licence would almost certainly result in that licence being declared invalid."

"But I'm ruined!" Roger sprang to his feet, his agitation turning to indignation. "Now look here, First Speaker, you know very well that the title was conferred on my father as a reward for certain-- ah-- services to your government. If you won't support me on this I shall have no alternative but to... to..." His voice trailed off as he caught the First Speaker's eye.

"I would not advise that. The dukedom of Benbrock-Oldstairs is a much coveted title..." Handcarte gave a little shrug. Roger flopped back into his chair as his legs abruptly refused to support him.

"I-- I-- only meant--"

"Quite." Handcarte's lips narrowed in a lupine smile. "But I have a proposition for you by which you may recover your fortunes. Come over here." The First Speaker rose and moved to a large map of Southern Albion which hung on the wall just by the fireplace. "Now what do you see here?" He tapped the map with a long pointer.

"Stembark Forest, First Speaker."

"Quite right!" The First Speaker nodded approvingly like a schoolmaster who has at last elicited a correct answer from a rather dull pupil. "And for what is Stembark Forest noted?"

"It is where my brother has taken shelter. Along with three treasure chests!"

Handcarte sighed-- the pupil had let him down. "Yes, but besides that?"

"Er-- tree nymphs?" the duke suggested without much hope, "enchanted princes? Bears?"

The pointer snapped in half as Handcarte tried to control his irritation. "Come, come! You should know very well that there never has been an authenticated sighting of a tree nymph in Stembark Forest. And the last amphibious prince was reported more than fifty years ago. As far as bears are concerned, they are not native to Albion. And--" he raised a hand before Roger could speak-- "migratory bears are immaterial."

"With respect, First Speaker, not if you happen to get in their way."

There were two sharp cracks as the pointer was snapped into quarters. "I am speaking of the outlaws."

"Oh, the outlaws! Of course!" Roger nodded energetically. "What about them?"

"I want to put them out of business. East Castellian can no longer tolerate the existence of a totally lawless band of-- er-- outlaws virtually on its own doorstep. What is more, they have consistently refused to submit any form of tax return for the last fifteen years."

"Deplorable! But is this not a task for um-- er-- a sheriff, rather than a First Speaker?"

"It is certainly not a task for a First Speaker." Handcarte smiled again, like a python measuring up a rat for breakfast. "But it is a task for you. Let me explain..."

In the depths of Stembark Forest there was a subdued flash of Heron-Gough discharge and two black-cloaked figures materialized. The taller one threw back his hood and looked about him, his eyes gleaming with interest. "That was quite satisfactory." Montmorency reached out an arm to steady his companion, who was swaying drunkenly. "Come now Bellingham! You really must work on that recovery!" Bellingham nodded dumbly, took one or two tottering paces forward and went up to his knees in a snowdrift. Montmorency shook his head and tut-tutted. "The final phase of materialization *must* be accomplished slowly and smoothly, Bellingham. Suppose you had landed on water! Then where would you be?" The black mage floated slowly across the drift, his feet fully an eighth of an inch above the surface, and descended to the path. There was an almost imperceptible shimmer, and his feet sank through the snow onto solid ground. "Like that, Bellingham." He once more offered his arm and, none too gently, tugged the struggling graduate student out of the snow.

"Snow! At this time of year!" Bellingham stooped and picked up a handful, squeezing it into a snowball, as though trying to reassure himself of its reality.

"Yes, Bellingham, that white substance is snow right enough," Montmorency agreed, "and yes, it is quite unseasonable. But in this sun, it will not last very long." Bellingham looked nervously about, acutely conscious of the fact that an extraordinarily powerful, if impossibly unpredictable, wardmaster mage might be in the vicinity.

"Is there-- er-- anything we should-- er-- do?" he asked with the diffidence of a trainee bomb disposal officer faced with an ageing thousand pounder that's just started ticking.

"*I* should be asking *you* that question, Bellingham," Montmorency gave a wintry smile, "after all it is just such a situation as this you will face when you take your practicals. Now think: what is the first thing we do following arrival in the field?"

"Er... STEM! Survey the immediate vicinity for spirits, trolls, elementals and mortals?"

"Correct! STEM. And for STEM you will use...?"

"Er... SALAN?"

"Correct again! Search And Locate And Nullify. I begin to have some hopes for your future, Bellingham. You may proceed."

With obvious nervousness, the graduate student took out a very tatty copy of *Frogson's Modern Spells*. He consulted the book, then held up his staff and muttered a short incantation. There was a crackle of static followed by a shrill beeping.

"Congratulations Bellingham! You appear to have located something." Montmorency watched keenly as the graduate student took out a small crystal sphere and peered hopefully into it. "And what have you found?"

"I-- I'm not quite sure..."

"Let me look." The mage peered into the crystal, then straightened up with a sigh. "That, Bellingham, would appear to be a badger. An omnivorous nocturnal mammal. Might I suggest you re-check the settings."

Mortified, Bellingham tapped the instrument with his index finger, then scrutinised it once more. "Ah! Now I have something!" He held the crystal up proudly. Once more Montmorency examined it, and this time his sigh was one of satisfaction.

"Well done! And what do you make of it?"

"A party of humans, less than a league distant."

"Quite right, although I estimate the distance as being no more than half a league onward. Let us proceed." Montmorency struck off down the path, Bellingham trotting after him.

They had not gone a hundred paces when the mage halted their progress with an upraised hand. "A moment Bellingham! I think--" His voice was drowned out in an unearthly wailing and the clatter and swish of wind sweeping through the trees. The sky darkened to a lowering yellowish grey, and a hot, dry blast of air coughed from some gigantic oven, swept through the forest. The wind dropped as suddenly as it had started, leaving an astonished silence. Bellingham made to speak, but Montmorency stopped him with a quick gesture. "I recommend you activate your local personal protection at once. There is more to come."

Even as Bellingham fiddled with his staff, the rush of the wind resumed, but now it was damp. Huge raindrops began to splatter through the trees, building to a steady drumming as a deluge of tropical magnitude hammered down. Montmorency stood there calmly enough, the sheets of rain cascading off the perimeter of his personal protective shield with a faint hiss and a smell of sulphur. Bellingham, he noted with little surprise, had activated the wrong protective routine, for already he was soaked to the skin, though he was infallibly protected against falling rock. The drumming roar of the rain began to slacken, then died away to a gentle intermittent patter. Montmorency was just about to de-activate his protective routine when he became aware of intermittent crashes and thumps, as of objects falling from a great height, smashing through the trees and slamming into the soft ground. He gave a start of alarm-- perhaps Bellingham had been more perceptive than he'd realized. There was a loud *splat*! and a shower of mud and snow flew up into the air. Montmorency dashed forward, stooped, and with a cry of triumph, straightened up, waving something large and floppy. "A fish!"

"Wha-- wha--?" The graduate student squelched towards him, his eyes wide.

"This is a fish," the mage explained patiently, "now what does that tell us?"

"Ah--" Bellingham's eyes were popping out of his head, but under the cool, quizzical gaze of his supervisor he regained some degree of equanimity. "I do not know," he admitted at last.

"It tells us that this cannot go on much longer. Even someone like Cruickshank cannot keep this sort of thing up indefinitely."

The crashes and splatting noises became more infrequent, then stopped completely. The sky began to lighten once more. Four livid flashes of lightening tore through the air at treetop height, followed by ear-splitting detonations which shook the ground beneath their feet.

"A dramatic display of irritation, but quite understandable under the circumstances." Montmorency's lips twitched in a sympathetic smile. "It's Cruickshank, without a doubt!" Montmorency did not quite rub his hands in anticipation. "Come, Bellingham. Let us investigate more closely." Picking his way fastidiously between the fish that littered the path, Montmorency set off.

The two had covered barely half a league before a sudden turn in the path brought them face to face with two spear-carrying guards leaning up against a tree. At the sight of the black-cloaked stranger and his assistant the two sprang into action, darting behind the tree and into the bushes. This display of military preparedness was followed by the appearance of two spear points from the bushes. Montmorency stopped.

"Was there anything?" he asked the trembling vegetation.

"Er... Halt? Who goes there?" One of the bushes asked apologetically.

"Belt up you twit!" The other bush rustled agitatedly. "We don't want them to *stop*. Tell them to move along there."

"Tell them yourself," the first bush replied, "you're senior."

"Now listen," Montmorency began, "I'm a busy man, and--"

The spear points vanished. There was a squelching thudding sound as of panic-stricken guards setting off in urgent pursuit of Higher Authority. Montmorency raised an eyebrow to his puzzled assistant. "They seem to be unduly agitated. Let us follow them."

They turned off the path, and found themselves in a crescent shaped clearing bounded on the far side by a wall of rock. On either side large caravans were drawn up in rows, and the ground between them was trampled into a grey-brown porridge of snow and mud. A fire sputtered and smoked in the centre of the clearing, where servants and scullions were busy preparing lunch. Two men were resentfully gathering up the fish that littered the ground. Before the mouth of a cave in the rock wall an awning had been set up, beneath which was a large trestle table where four richly dressed men lounged, toasting each other with bumpers and tossing bread rolls about. A group of minstrels twanged, droned and thumped their way through some merry tune. The notes of a zither wafted from the cave. Montmorency frowned. Though he had never encountered the outlaws of Stembark Forest, he was certain they could not be this shower. His cold eyes ranged over the encampment, taking in the servants, toadies, lackeys, guards and huntsmen. His lips tightened slightly, for he despised incompetence, and clearly whoever had set up this camp was gifted with more than his fair share of that quality.

"Who can these people be?" Bellingham's eyes were round with amazement.

"I do not know, but if I were to guess I might suggest an exiled duke and his retinue." Montmorency was coldly disapproving-- he didn't have much time for the aristocracy.

"An exiled duke!"

"The signs are all there. See, the toadies, the minstrels, the servants and the huntsmen-- they're the ones in the grey coats. With the horns. And, of course, the hounds. But let us see..." Montmorency strode across the clearing, Bellingham following nervously.

Duke Harold watched them approaching with growing uneasiness. The last couple of days had not been relaxing ones, what with the appearance of those sorcerers or brigands, or whatever they were. And then the terrible weather! There had been no question of fleeting the time carelessly in that snow. And now these two! As they approached the minstrels fell silent, and even the zither music trembled in anticipation. Harold viciously elbowed his toadies to draw their attention to the visitors, then rose from his chair.

"Good morrow, gentle travellers! Welcome to our humble camp." His voice rolled majestically around the clearing with all the resonance and sincerity of a cabinet minister's statement.

"I thank you." Montmorency threw back his hood and eyed the duke narrowly. "You are not, I take it, here on holiday?" he asked. Harold winced. There was something deeply disturbing about that voice, as cold as polished granite and precise as steel.

"Alas, no." Harold struck his hand to his heart in a well-practised gesture. "A brother's sudden envy at one stroke deprived me of my dukedom, friends and fortune. And yet--"

"Quite." Montmorency raised his hand. "Most regrettable. But doubtless you find this place much more free of perils than the envious court?"

"Indeed yes, sir! You have hit it quite, for here, 'neath the greenwood tree--"

"You may find sermons in stones and books in running brooks?"

Harold frowned at the interruption-- it was not the sort of thing he was used to, being a duke. "I was about to say, sir, that we are taking an active interest in tongues in trees." He gave a self-satisfied nod of his head as though he had just placed a trump over an ace.

"No doubt about it!" Montmorency muttered, "an exiled duke!" He returned his attention to Harold. "Have you been long in exile, your grace?" he asked.

Harold was so taken aback by the directness of the question that he answered immediately and truthfully. "Only a few weeks, as a matter of fact. We're still getting settled in, as you can see." He waved an apologetic arm at the sordid mess of the camp.

"Just so." Montmorency gave a frosty smile. "But doubtless the young men will soon be flocking to you every day and fleeting the time as carelessly as they did in the golden world?"

"I sincerely hope so!" Again taken off-guard, the exiled duke had answered candidly. But he rapidly recovered. "Now tell me sir," his voice returned to the unctuous boom of professional sanctimony, "what make you and your companion in these woods so far from hearth and home?"

"I am but a poor travelling scholar, your grace," Montmorency made a keep-your-mouth-shut gesture to Bellingham, "and this is my faithful research assistant. We seek some secluded space where he may complete the necessary field work for his dissertation. It is one of my duties, as his supervisor, to accompany him," Montmorency added by way of explanation. The effect of his words was dramatic. The duke's face turned grey, and he slumped heavily back into his chair with a gasp. One of the toadies shouted "sorcerers! More of them!" and the air creaked to the sound of bows being bent; the huntsmen were ready this time. Montmorency sighed under his breath. Some people were so predictable! He was aware of Bellingham's squeak of alarm as bowstrings twanged and the arrows started on their way. Then he raised his staff.

Six and thirty arrows exploded in smoke and flame in mid-flight. And six and thirty bow-strings drooped like over-laundered knicker elastic.

"That's better!" The mage lowered his staff. "Now we can discuss matters like civilized beings--" He broke off as one slow learner darted forward, spear in hand. Before the man could actually throw it, Montmorency frowned in his direction. There was a faint flash, and a six-foot high mushroom stood quivering with surprise.

"Sorcery!" The thin cry wailed up from everybody's throat.

"Not quite, but close enough." Montmorency smiled pleasantly. "Merely a couple of simple routines. As I was saying, now we can discuss matters calmly."

"Wha-- wha-- what would you with us, wizard?" the duke croaked.

"Less of the wizard, fellow!" Bellingham was scarlet with rage. "My supervisor is a Senior Level Black Mage! You trifle with him at your peril!"

"I think they may have gathered that already, Bellingham, but thank you all the same," Montmorency said, quite gratified by the young man's loyalty. There was far too little of that sort of thing around these days. "Ahem!" He addressed the terror-stricken duke. "Your grace has penetrated our innocent subterfuge. I am indeed a mage, and thesis supervisor to young Bellingham, here. We wish you no harm--" Montmorency broke off as the plinking notes of the zither, carried by some freak of the wind, echoed tinnily in his ear. He raised an admonitory finger and the music stopped. "That's better."

"People do not seem to be musically inclined in this part of the world." Duke Harold found his voice at last. "Now, sir mage, what would you with us? And what," he added, with an anguished glance at the huge mushroom, "about my servant?"

"The man will return to his usual form within the hour and should suffer no ill-effects save perhaps for a perverse predilection for the dark. And I would have nothing with you. I wish you no ill, I am merely curious about the peculiarly inclement weather that seems to attend you."

"You noticed it too?" Since Montmorency hadn't turned anybody into anything for almost a minute, Duke Harold was beginning to get his courage back. Like all members of the aristocracy, his memory and attention span were numerically similar to his IQ. "I have never known the like. First snow, then desert wind, then teeming rain, and then fish! I ask you! This sort of thing really doesn't encourage the young men to flock, and it's a positive disincentive to fleeting the time."

"Most unfortunate." Montmorency nodded sympathetically.

"In fact," the duke continued with some petulance, "I get the distinct impression that we're not wanted here."

"That is difficult to credit!"

"The outlaw chief was most offhand when we met him. And as for those two sorcerers or brigands, or whatever they were, they were positively hostile!"

"Sorcerers?" Montmorency's voice betrayed no great interest, but Bellingham could tell from his stance that the mage was intent on the answer.

"Aye, sorcerers!" Harold confirmed indignantly. "Not of course of *your* stature, sir, but disquieting none the less. Called themselves travelling scholars too! But I soon saw through that and sent them packing."

"Indeed! And did they identify themselves?"

"One did. A wild-eyed fellow, called himself Cruickshank-- *Doctor* Cruickshank, if you please!"

A sizzling flash of scarlet fire shot from Montmorency's staff and disintegrated the nearest tree, but it only took a fraction of a second before he regained control. "You must excuse me, your grace, a simple accident. But what you tell me is very serious."

"It is?"

"Most certainly. This man is indeed a potent mage. And what is worse, he harbours great resentment against the aristocracy."

"He does?" The greyish tinge began to return to Harold's cheeks. "But surely not against *exiled* dukes?"

"I fear, your grace, that it is against such that he harbours the liveliest of ill-feelings."

"But this is terrible! What am I to do?"

A suggestion, unbidden, rose to Montmorency's lips, but he restrained it. There was bigger game afoot than some paltry exiled duke! "Perhaps *I* could offer such poor assistance as is in my power," he said smoothly. "Young Bellingham must spend some time in hermit-like contemplation-- this is necessary field work for his dissertation-- and I as his supervisor must remain nearby. If there were some place in this vicinity we could lodge, then I should be honoured to remain at your disposal."

"You would!" Colour returned to Harold's cheeks. "You should not be the poorer for it, good mage!"

Bellingham froze with horror at the insult, but Montmorency seemed to ignore it, though a close observer might have seen a cheek muscle twitch. "No need to speak of that, your grace. Some modest shelter is all we seek-- and out of earshot," he added quickly as he remembered the minstrels.

"There is that island we saw yesterday, your grace," suggested one of the toadies, "magicians often live on islands."

"I thank you for the suggestion, Bushy, an' I fear it be not enchanted."

"How about that grotto?" a second offered, "the one we found when we were sheltering from the snow. It might be quite acceptable if we pulled out all those bits of coloured glass somebody stuck into the walls-- awful!" He gave a fastidious shudder.

"As I remember it, Bagot, 'twas passing damp," the duke objected.

"Both will be suitable," interrupted Montmorency, "for Bellingham the grotto will provide the solitude and tranquillity so necessary for really effective contemplation. And I," he said with a firm glance at Bellingham, "shall take the island."

"There *are* some swans," Bushy warned. Montmorency smiled and raised his staff.

"Not now," he said.

Act VI
CURTAIN RAISER

The palace of Benbrock-Oldstairs buzzed with activity. The forecourt was crowded with wagons, and servants were scurrying about loading them with packages, boxes, furniture-- anything that wasn't actually nailed down and might be worth something. And immediately before the palace gates, two companies of Castle Guards were drawn up with military precision, their breastplates and weapons flashing in the sun. The First Speaker wanted Duke Roger of Benbrock-Oldstairs (Usurping) to get to Stembark Forest safely-- and soon.

In the Audience Chamber, Duke Roger irritably waved away the servant who was tugging at the throne. "Not now!" he snapped, "go and do something else. Somewhere else." He took a quick turn up and down the only piece of purple carpet that hadn't yet been taken up. Buckingham, his chief toady, followed two paces behind and slightly to the right. Duke Roger completed his short constitutional and looked around hopefully in case the two young ladies had got bored and gone away. They hadn't. They were standing there still, simmering with discontent: Julia, his niece, was tall, slender and raven-haired, while Anne, his daughter, was shorter and plumper, with red hair and a temper to match. He restrained a sigh. "All packed and ready to go, then?" he asked with the hollow heartiness of a condemned man.

"But father!" Anne protested, "I *still* don't understand. If you have to see Uncle Harold on particular business, why must the whole household go with you?"

"As I have explained, the First Speaker has-- er-- convinced me that it is necessary that we all go. A family excursion."

"Family rubbish!" Julia snorted, "there is surely no business that you have with my father that couldn't be done by a removal company. In fact," she continued helpfully, "there's this new firm, ex-secret service Medical Directorate, and they're offering a special introductory rate-- ten guineas plus expenses *and* a full money-back guarantee."

Duke Roger shuddered. His niece's devastating practicality always shocked him. "It's out of the question! Explain it to her, Buckingham," he ordered the toady.

"The situation is a little complicated, Miss Julia," Buckingham tried an ingratiating smile, "it involves matters of state and high business interests, not to mention some potentially pretty tricky legal problems. All a bit tedious for young ladies like yourself."

Julia's eyes flashed angrily and her hand began to move to the knife at her belt, but her cousin stopped her with a quick gesture. "What Buckingham means is that should your father-- er-- become fatally unwell, then the dukedom of Benbrock-Oldstairs would be vacant."

"How can that be? The Usurpation Licence was granted!"

"You can ask my father to explain *that*!" Anne shot a contemptuous glance at the duke.

"Er..." Duke Roger looked helplessly at Buckingham.

"What his grace was about to explain was that the First Speaker believes your uncle's Preparatory Motions might not meet the traditional criteria, hence the Usurpation Licence could be declared invalid."

"Not meet the criteria!" Julia looked astounded. "The assassination attempt I can understand, but the poisoning?"

"It was the pouring it in his ears," the duke mumbled.

"But that's what it said on the bottle!"

"I know, but the First Speaker said it was percussive."

"Percussive?" Julia looked blank

"I believe that what the First Speaker actually meant was that the instructions on the bottle were symbolic or metaphorical in nature," Buckingham explained, "they were not to be taken literally."

"Well why didn't they say so?" Julia scowled. "So now you're saying you have to traipse all the way to Stembark Forest to get this sorted out?"

"Just so."

"Taking all the household? And us?"

"Yes."

"And what are *we* supposed to do when we get there? Sit in front of the fireplace knitting? Take jars of calves-foot jelly to old ladies? Keep bees?"

"Now here I have a surprise for you. Have you seen this before?" Duke Roger held out a brightly coloured sheet of paper. Julia gave it a quick glance and passed it onto her cousin.

"It's a travel brochure. What about it?"

Before the toady could answer there was a squeak of excitement from Anne. "Julia, it's all about the outlaws! Listen to this: *Romance and Adventure in Stembark Forest. See the legendary Outlaws who, for hundreds of years, have been plying their trade in Albion's largest forest, robbing the rich to give to the poor.*"

"A likely story!" Julia laughed.

"No, it's perfectly true," her cousin contradicted.

"Better check the small print."

"How cynical you are, Julia!" Anne took a second look at the brochure. "Oh! There is something... *some modifications in this policy have taken place in recent years,*" she read aloud.

"The Business Section of the *Basingstoke Bugle* said something about them going into the ransom business," Buckingham said carelessly. "They do have a reputation as a go-ahead organisation."

"Oooh! How thrilling!" Anne's eyes lit up. "Just imagine being held hostage in Stembark Forest!"

"No thanks!" Julia sneered, "shut up in some awful tree house with a lot of hairy oafs shooting off arrows and shouting 'Hold!' all the time."

"Have you no romance in your soul!" her cousin protested, "just listen: *see the mighty bowmen whose clothyard arrows can pierce a two-inch oak plank--*"

"If they can hit it!"

"Julia, of course they can hit it! It says here they can split a hazel wand with an arrow at two hundred paces, or at least--" Anne's eyes narrowed as she struggled to decipher the small print in the footnote, "-- a lot of them can, two times out of three." She looked up from the brochure, her eyes shining. "Oh, father, are we really going to see the outlaws?"

Duke Roger sighed. "I am afraid that we will not be able to afford the robbing. No, what we shall be doing is..." he held out another pamphlet.

His daughter snatched it greedily. *"Fleet the time carelessly in the golden world,"* she read, *"feast and roister in the glades of Stembark Forest! Hunt with the hounds in the morning. And in the evenings, as the shadows lengthen, relax to the music of Clarence Snout and his Arboreal Arcadians--* father, what is this all about?"

"We are going into business," the duke explained with pride, "it's a new concept the First Speaker explained to me the other day-- we are going to offer people a rural roistering experience."

Anne curled her lip. "We're going into *trade?*" she demanded, incredulous.

"Yes-- but in a very exclusive way. This sort of enterprise will soon be all the rage, and we have a chance to get in on the ground floor."

"What your father-- and your uncle-- means," Buckingham hastened to explain, "is that we-- or rather the First Speaker's most trusted economic advisers-- believe that Stembark Forest is ripe for commercial development. Thousands of people pay every year just to go through the forest and get robbed by the outlaws--"

"They have souvenir boutiques as well, you know," Anne had been reading the first brochure carefully.

"*And* a boating lake," added Julia, exhibiting some faint enthusiasm for the first time.

"But what we shall be offering is a *total experience*," Buckingham spoke with the fervour of the recent convert, "what they call a-- a motif garden, I think. Imagine it! Arcadian adventures with the aristocracy in the enchanted forests! Hunting! Feasting beneath the stars in the forest glade. Dancing with fairies and tree-nymphs! Sweet music!"

"Might want to forget about the music," the duke pointed out, "I understand a lot of people aren't awfully keen on that sort of thing."

"Why?" Julia asked bluntly.

"I don't know," the duke looked vague, "it's just something I heard about from someone or other."

"She didn't mean the music!" his daughter stamped her foot. "She meant why do we have to do this? And now? I mean we are awfully glad that you've finally decided to stop being an economic parasite, and for a man of your age a career change might just be the right thing. But for *all* of us--"

Duke Roger finally lost his temper. "Listen, you pair of ninnies!" he shouted, "we don't have a choice. Your precious father--" he jabbed an accusatory finger at Julia, "your father took off with the whole treasury. There's no money! And the First Speaker won't enforce the Usurpation Licence."

Anne gasped. "But-- but-- what are you going to do?"

"We are going to set up in business in Stembark Forest," Duke Roger enunciated clearly, wagging his finger in time to the words, "we will persuade Harold and his toadies and lackeys and huntsmen to join with us."

"Persuade?" Julia was looking puzzled.

"I shall make Harold an offer he can't refuse," her uncle told her with a reassuring smile, "after all, we only really need the money and his followers."

"But he's protected, isn't he?"

"Under the circumstances, and in view of the vital economic interests of the state, the First Speaker might waive the protection provisions."

The two girls stared at each other, round eyed. For the First Speaker to be taking so direct a hand in the matter suggested mighty business indeed. "So we must leave now? This very minute?" Anne asked in a rather small voice. Her father nodded. "Our escort is waiting," he pointed through the window to rows of plumed helmets.

"But we cannot leave until after the duel!"

"Duel?" The duke frowned, "what are you talking about, girl?"

"That young man-- your junior toady-in-training-- he challenged Charles to a duel!"

"I'm not sure I remember..."

"The young man Herbert," Buckingham reminded him, "son of Sir Roger de Coverly. He had applied to you earlier, you might remember. I took the liberty of recommending him myself-- first-class toady potential there!"

"Sir Roger de Coverly," the duke nodded, "one of my father's closest friends, I recall. Whatever happened to him?"

"A severe cold, your grace," Buckingham murmured.

"Ah yes! And his son is very promising, you say."

"Very promising."

"And he wants to fight Charles? The man must be a lunatic! Charles is a master swordsman twice over!"

"Nevertheless, he *has* challenged him."

"Well, he can wait till we get to the forest-- we don't have any time for that now."

"But uncle!" Julia protested; she had been looking forward to seeing Herbert get thoroughly trounced.

"But me no buts and uncle me no uncles!" the duke snapped peevishly, "Captain Spalding of the First Speaker's Personal Guard has orders to see I leave before sunset-- vertically or horizontally."

Julia sighed. There was no reasoning with Uncle Roger when he was in this kind of mood. Then another thought struck her. "Will Pebblestroke be coming with us?"

"Pebblestroke?" Anne made a grimace, "surely not!"

"I fear so." Buckingham looked regretful. "A court jester is a *sine qua non* for a motif garden, I am led to believe."

"I sent him out to entertain Captain Spalding's troops," Duke Roger cast a nervous glance through the window, "perhaps they will appreciate his humour." Through the open window there floated a chorus of jeers and catcalls, a scream of rage and a dull thud. A figure in motley, clutching a bladder on the end of a stick, sailed over the courtyard wall and thumped to the ground.

"Or perhaps they won't," the duke concluded.

Montmorency explored the island with growing approval. At the eastern end was the tea house, screened from the lake by some trees. It was a modest structure, jutting out from a rocky escarpment running across the island, and came complete with a terrace furnished with green wrought-iron tables. And then there was the maze. It was one of the most complex Montmorency had seen, and covered most of the island with its deceptive, symmetrical geometry. Beyond this, at the extreme western end, there was a landing stage, marked by a white-painted flagpole. There were no swans. The whole place was ideal for his purposes.

The mage lost no time in establishing himself comfortable quarters. Of course occult operations cannot be used to *create* matter, but they can shift it around in a number of interesting ways, so it was not very long before Montmorency had arranged a very attractive little villa, complete with a back door leading to a tunnel cut through the escarpment-- even senior level black mages find it reassuring to have an emergency exit.

A few more simple operations sufficed to create a suitably equipped study, and into this Montmorency withdrew and settled down to consider his strategy. It was clear, he told himself, that Cruickshank was involved in some way with this exiled duke, and not as an ally. But what *was* he up to? Montmorency's most frequent exhortation to his graduate students was "understand your opponent," and it was a precept he followed assiduously. With a wave of the hand he opened his equipment case. Another gesture brought forth his wide-band scanning crystal. He placed it on his lap, tapped it gently with his fingertips to establish contact with the Guild network, then stared into its depths. For a few seconds he remained motionless, then he gave the crystal another tap, considerably less gentle than the first-- he was as usual having to wait to gain access to his *own* records. He stifled an angry retort, but not quite soon enough. A very large black bat materialized above his head, and flapped sombrely from the room. Outside a riot of honeysuckle turned brown, and withered.

In the Black Guild's Data Centre a thoroughly alarmed System Operator ducked as a cascade of sparks showered from the wall. He swiftly gabbled the necessary cancellation routines to clear the system. Obviously Mage Montmorency was in a hurry. Wherever he was.

With a sigh of satisfaction, Montmorency settled back in his chair and stared into the crystal. In its glimmering depths all the information he had gathered about Cruickshank through previous encounters scrolled steadily across a luminous background. Every now and again he halted the movement with a wave of his hand and paused to scribble a short note. At last he came to an end and, pushing the crystal to one side, began to study his notes. A faint cheeping noise from the instrument interrupted him, and he glared at it angrily.

At the Data Centre the System Operator jerked his hand away from the control crystal as it glowed an angry red. Clearly Mage Montmorency hadn't quite finished.

Montmorency hadn't quite finished. In fact he hadn't quite started to finish. Eyes half-closed, he ran over what he had established so far. For some reason, Cruickshank was trying to encourage the exiled duke to leave Stembark Forest, though whether he was doing this at the behest of the Outlaws of Stembark Forest or on general principles because he didn't have much time for the southern aristocracy wasn't clear. While Cruickshank's objective was wholly praiseworthy, it did not alter the fact that he must be thwarted. But he must be thwarted in a manner which did not in any way benefit the exiled duke-- the reverse if possible. It was an interesting problem.

Montmorency frowned. This systematic thinking was all very well, but he still had no idea of exactly what Cruickshank's plans were-- if indeed he had any. He glared at the crystal as if daring it to cheep at him again, then returned to his notes. "Understand your opponent" might be an essential rule, but it was a rule very difficult to apply to an opponent like Cruickshank, who defied rational analysis. Montmorency smiled-- he enjoyed a challenge. *Cruickshank* he wrote, in his neat, angular handwriting, *unpredictable... ingenious... outrageous impostures... implausible plots... barefaced effrontery... play-acting...* Play-acting! Something clicked. The mage sat up and tapped the crystal, summoning up a list of the deplorable impostures perpetrated by Cruickshank in the course of his activities. They scrolled through the heart of the instrument-- Guy Fawkes... Errol Flynn... Jack Cade... William Shakespeare... Sir Francis Walsingham... Mr Bunbury... Sherlock Holmes... With deliberate slowness, Montmorency ran a finger over the crystal, stopping the scrolling and highlighting the fourth name. William Shakespeare-- a playwright from Earth-Three, whose name Cruickshank had borrowed for some inscrutable reasons of his own. Montmorency also knew Cruickshank was particularly familiar with the plays of this William Shakespeare.

During his first encounter with Cruickshank, Montmorency had inadvertently transferred himself to Earth-Three. The few days he had spent in that cacophonous and primitive society had not been pleasant, but he had put the time to good use, principally in a local library, and had managed to bring back with him a number of volumes. (Had he known that innocent people had been placed under the severely prejudicial scrutiny of an enraged librarian as a result of his depredations, Montmorency might have suffered a momentary pang of regret. But he would not have returned the books)

The mage replaced the crystal in its case, murmured a short signing-off incantation, then seized his staff. He thought for a moment, then speaking with painful clarity, said "retrieve real-time WS zero zero one." There was a hissing whistle, a violet flash of Heron-Gough discharge, and a pop! of displaced air. A bulky copy of *The Complete Works of William Shakespeare* materialized on the floor, the linen of its cover slightly scorched by its journey. Montmorency waved it onto his knee. Slowly almost casually, he began to turn the pages as though he felt that too great a demonstration of eagerness on his part would make the book hide its secrets from him. He was not totally unfamiliar with the volume, but he had never read it through systematically, instead contenting himself with such lighter pieces such as *Titus Andronicus*. But now he did not examine the plays themselves, but just checked the *dramatis personae* for each play. It was at the ninth that he stopped: there it was! *"Duke Senior, living in banishment"*, he read aloud, *"Duke Frederick, his brother and usurper"*. Montmorency made a noise that was halfway between a shout of laughter and a cry of triumph. It was all there! More or less. The names were different, it was true, and the introduction said there were no outlaws, but these were minor details. With increasing excitement, Montmorency skimmed through the text, his eyes gleaming with triumph. *Now* he knew what Cruickshank was up to, and now he also saw his own course, mapped plainly through the closely printed lines on the pages before him. This would be an excellent contest! His own expertise as a top occult professional, balanced against Cruickshank's obvious familiarity with dramatic works of this Earth Three playwright. Without haste he flipped back through the pages until he came to *A Midsummer Night's Dream*. He checked the *dramatis personae* and nodded with satisfaction. It would make an excellent start! Stylus poised over his notebook, he began to read.

Don Orlando was in a particularly genial mood when he greeted his guests in the Headquarters Glade that morning; by and large things seemed to be going very well indeed. The mage had done a most impressive job with the weather-- the snow had been dramatic, the rain had been first-class, but the fish had been magnificent. For the life of him Orlando couldn't have thought of a better way to persuade an exiled duke of the drawbacks to the pastoral idyll.

"A beautiful morning Wardmaster! Gentlemen!" he beamed, tactfully moving so as to put the maximum distance between himself and Ratbag (he still hadn't found his cloak). "I trust you won't feel it necessary to make any meteorological adjustments today. We are expecting some special clients-- a party hosted by the Nordician Ambassador."

"Oh, certainly not!" Andrew answered with some relief. He had found the exercise with Tarot 5.1 sufficiently nerve-wracking that he would be quite happy not to have to repeat it. The snow hadn't been too bad-- it was the simple sort of mistake that could have happened to anyone. But the fish had really shaken him.

"Perhaps you would like to join me?" Orlando offered, "I was planning to inspect Sucker's Alley North-- make sure all my men are on the top line. I don't want any mistakes when there are distinguished visitors concerned."

"We should be delighted," Janus replied, with a warning glance at Kodswallop who had earlier suggested a brisk walk to the Three Pigeons, "that is if it would not interfere with your duties...?"

"Not at all!" Orlando dismissed the concern with a gesture, "follow me." Still keeping his distance from Ratbag, he led them along a broad path which wound picturesquely between the ancient trees. They passed a small group of outlaws who, clad in leather shorts and jerkins, were receiving woodcutter instruction from a section-leader. "I've got forty men on woodcutter duty already." Orlando gestured to the group, "by the end of the day we should have all the northern and eastern routes into the forest covered. What do you plan next?" he asked abruptly.

"I-- er--" Andrew struggled to think of something.

"I believe we intend to carry out additional reconnaissance," Tiresome suggested helpfully.

"Oh, right!" Andrew grasped at the straw, "I'd like to find out if there are any hermits kicking about the place. And we do need to know something about the usurping duke's activities."

"Don't think there are any hermits around these days," ruminated the outlaw leader, "what with the Sublime Tabernacle of the Redeemer in the south and the Ineffable Tabernacle of the Redeemer in the north-- you know how it is with those big chains. They've got the whole market sewn up; small business just can't compete with them. But I'll ask Eric to look into it, just in case. As far as duke Roger is concerned, I can send a couple of men into East Castellian to see what they can pick up."

"We were thinking of taking a quick trip ourselves--" Andrew began, but was interrupted.

"That would be most kind," Janus said quickly, "we have a lot to do here."

Andrew gave Janus an angry scowl to which the elf returned a bland smile. Orlando did not notice the exchange. "A lot to do!" he exclaimed heartily, "You've done a lot already. I can't tell you how grateful I am for your help. That weather was amazing!"

"Oh-- er-- thank you. Nothing to it really," mumbled Andrew, "sorry about the fish, though."

"Don't apologise! It was inspired! Mind you, the rain was spectacular enough. Do you know that one of my section-leaders told me this morning that the nine men's morris was filled up with mud? Quite choked with it, by all accounts. Unheard of!"

"The what!" Andrew stopped dead. "What did you say?"

"That the nine men's morris was filled up with mud," Orlando replied, "or at least, that's what he said."

"The nine men's morris..." Andrew repeated.

"Right."

"Filled up with mud...?"

"Completely!" Orlando nodded. "The nine men's morris is a kind of traditional rural diversion," he explained, "and unlike most traditional rural diversions, it is suitable for family viewing. More or less. We were thinking of..." his voice died away as it became clear that the question had not been prompted by an interest in local folkways. "I say! Is anything the matter, old man?"

"No..." Andrew waved the question away. That line from *A Midsummer Night's Dream* had given him something of a shock. But, he told himself, it must be just coincidence. Like the bit about biting thumbs from *Romeo and Juliet* that the duellists used in their challenges.

For some minutes they walked on in silence, Andrew preoccupied with worrying thoughts about *A Midsummer Night's Dream*. The last thing he needed was the intrusion of that play. The beauty of *As You Like It* was that there was no magic in it, but the *Dream* was stuffed with it.

"I don't remember this!" Orlando's sudden exclamation aroused Andrew from his reverie. The path had dipped slightly and with a sudden left turn, opened up into a small clearing. No more than a dozen paces wide, it was like a carefully tended arbour in one of these highly elaborate gardens where generations of toil have been devoted to making the place look as natural as possible-- in a highly manicured sort of way. A tiny brook emerged from the trees on the far side, tinkling softly between mossy stones to fall into a little fern-fringed pool then, thickly bordered with wild flowers, meander back into the dark depths of forest. From the margins of the brook the ground rose into a shallow hump or bank, covered with springy turf.

"I say, what an attractive spot!" Even Andrew, usually insensitive to the pastoral aesthetic, was impressed.

"Very pretty" Orlando agreed, "but I just don't remember it. And I should." He gave the brook a quick reproving frown as if it were to blame for this memory lapse. "This is most remarkable!" he exclaimed, his eyes gleaming with the enthusiasm of the dedicated amateur botanist. "In this one spot there seem to be examples of every species of flora you can find in the forest. It is quite unheard of!" He stooped to examine the bank where Andrew rested. "See, even here!" He held aloft a small sprig of vegetation. "Wild thyme!" he announced, "and there's some luscious woodbine! And, I do believe, musk roses! How remarkable. Especially the wild thyme."

"What?" A cold hand gripped Andrew's vitals.

"Wild thyme," Orlando repeated, "I never realised that it grew in this part of the world.

"Wild thyme, eh?" Andrew rose to his feet and subjected the bank to an anxious stare. Methodically, sector by sector, he scanned the innocent-seeming green turf with its bright polka-dots of wild flowers, hoping against hope he would not find what he was looking for. The cold hand let go his innards and gave him a heavy thump in the chest as he saw the small purple flower nestled coyly close to the ground. "What might that be?" he asked, pointing. Orlando bent to examine it, then straightened up with a look that was both puzzled and expectant.

"I am not quite sure. It might almost be the sanguinary libido, perhaps a hybrid version..." he stooped again.

"Don't touch it!" Andrew told him sharply.

"Come, wardmaster!" Orlando laughed, "there's nothing to that old wives' tale about sprinkling the juice from the sanguinary libido on somebody's eyes. It's just symbolic-- like pouring poison in the ears, you understand."

"Orlando!" Andrew grabbed the man's arm, "just leave it alone for the moment. What do you mean by sprinkling the juice from it?"

"Like I said, it's just an old wives' tale."

"Tell me!"

"Well..." Orlando wriggled from Andrew's grip, and rubbed his arm to get the circulation back. "the tale goes that if you crush up the flower and sprinkle the juice from it on somebody's eyes while he's asleep--"

"Then when he wakes up he'll fall in love with the first person he sets eyes on?"

"Good heavens no!" Orlando looked shocked, "nothing like that... well not *exactly* like that. It's supposed to give you more a sort of out-of-body experience. But of course, that's all wrong." He gave a short laugh. "In actual fact it's the *root* you have to crush up. And you don't use the juice on its own. You have to add finely chopped onions, some vanilla essence and a tiny bit of wild honey. With a glass of brandy it tastes surprisingly good."

"But what is it supposed to do?"

"It's a mild hallucinogen, with er... aphrodisiac tendencies. Not that I've ever tried it of course!" he added hastily, "at least not for many years."

"Is there much of it about?"

"Not in this area. That's what makes it so interesting."

"What's the matter?" Janus was puzzled-- Andrew had never shown any interest in botanical matters before. Before Andrew could respond there was a sudden bleep from his staff. Wrenching it off his shoulder he stared at it furiously. It gave another bleep, louder this time.

"There's something going on in the maging line, alright." Cecil gave the staff a distrustful look and began to edge back to the shelter of the trees. "What are you doing with that thing anyway?" he demanded.

"I'm not doing anything with it," Andrew retorted, holding the instrument gingerly between thumb and forefinger.

"It's probably detected something," Clumpface suggested.

"Like what?"

"Like that!" the dwarf suddenly pointed over Andrew's shoulder. Andrew spun round. Violet light flickered briefly and into the clearing floated a small, shimmering bipedal figure, improbably airborne on rudimentary wings from which green, gold and silver light sparkled. One hand brandished a short wand with a flashing silver star at the end. A faint violet glow of Heron-Gough discharge hovered above its head.

The creature dipped its wand in salute. "Over hill, over dale, through bush, through briar, over park, over pale, through flood, through fire, I do wander everywhere," it chanted in a voice like a cheap tin whistle, "but now I'm here to welcome you mortals to these enchanted woods. My name is Peaseblossom, and I am your fairy for tonight. A wish for the little boy?" The wand swept round to point at Ratbag.

Andrew reacted quite instinctively, and very fast, swinging his staff up. But before he could trigger the destructor beam, a ribbon of silver light curved from the fairy's wand and wriggled eagerly towards the tip of the outstretched staff. As it touched there was a crimson flash. The glitter faded, the Heron-Gough discharge disappeared and the fairy fell heavily to the ground.

"Sod it!" said the fairy. With a shout of triumph Kodswallop leaped forward, grabbed him, and waved him aloft. "Gottim!" he shouted, "now let's have a look."

Beneath the yards of muslin, tinted green and glittering with sequins, beneath the wings made of wire-stiffened gauze and hastily fastened to the shoulders with knotted string, and beneath an inch of greasepaint, was the unmistakeable squat shape, and the revoltingly familiar features of a forest troll.

"It's a fair cop," he mumbled.

"Put him down, Kodswallop, but carefully," Andrew instructed, "we want him in one piece."

The big fighter shrugged. "Can't see why." He placed the troll firmly, but not destructively, on the ground and glowered at him. "Now you stay there, wacker," he warned, "or..."

The troll struggled back to his feet and, with an angry snarl divested himself of his theatrical finery, using the gauze from the wings to smear the worst of the greasepaint from his face up into his hairline and down to his neck. It was difficult to say whether or not this was a net improvement, revealing as it did almost ape-like features dominated by a bulbous purple nose and a gaping, narrow-lipped mouth from which a few yellowing teeth protruded. "Morning, gents!" he gave a villainous grin, "what seems to be the problem?"

"I am surprised at you!" Orlando protested, "you know very well that we have always scrupulously honoured our agreement. Have my outlaws ever strayed into your bounds of the forest?" he demanded of the troll. "No!" He answered his own question with a rhetorical gesture.

"Well, why would you want to? It's all swamp, innit." The troll sniffed. "Swamp's not much fun except for trolls-- and we're not that frilled wif it if it comes to that."

Janus drew the indignant outlaw chief to one side. "Perhaps we might ask him a few questions," he said quietly.

"Of course! Please go ahead." Orlando withdrew a pace, "sorry to interrupt," he whispered.

"Now then!" Tiresome said briskly, with the eagerness of the professional military interrogator. The troll recoiled.

"Three nine four seven, Leading Forest Troll, Peregrine," he snapped out, "that's all I have to tell you, under the rules."

Kodswallop gave a menacing growl

"But then, I wouldn't want to be pedantic about it," Peregrine added hastily.

"Look, we don't mean you any harm," Andrew said hastily. He wanted answers, not obliteration. "All we want to know is what you're doing here, and why that fancy-dress?" he asked with an ingratiating smile.

"Ah, well now guv..." a sly look wrinkled across the troll's unpleasing features, "it's like a special project, see?"

"Special project?"

"Yerst. There's this bloke, see, an' he's got me an' free of me mates to act as sorta goodwill ambassadors to visitors to the forest."

"Now you listen, Peregrine Peaseblossom, or whatever your name is," Clumpface moved menacingly close to the troll, "don't give us any of that rubbish. What are you doing dressed up like that and aviating about on high-level magic? And don't you tell me that you got some flying spells from a bloke you met in a tavern who let you have them cheap because they'd fallen off the back of a wagon!"

Peregrine recoiled once again-- he had been preparing just such an explanation. "Nah... it's not like that at all..." He struggled to think of something else-- anything but the truth.

"There's a mage involved-- there has to be!" Clumpface turned away from the creature in disgust. The troll's face turned an unpleasing greyish brown with terror, and his knees buckled under him. Had Kodswallop not been supporting him by the collar, he would have crumpled to the ground. "We won't be getting anything out of *him*," the dwarf spat contemptuously.

"Just one thing!" Andrew tried to speak softly, but his voice had a nasty sounding edge to it. "Let me see if I can guess the names of the others-- your three mates." He paused, as someone pauses just before diving into water that he is sure will be teeth-chatteringly cold. "Are they by any chance called 'Cobweb', 'Mustardseed' and 'Moth'?"

The troll gasped. "'Ow did yer guess that, guv!"

"It's *Midsummer Night's Dream!*" Andrew roared, sending darts of green fire slashing into the undergrowth, "he's bloody well doing a *Midsummer Night's Dream* on me!" He straightened up, almost crackling with anger and frustration. Peregrine quailed, and even Andrew's friends felt nervous-- they had never seen their mage so agitated. His staff was visibly quivering in response to his excitement, and a corona of Heron-Gough discharge flared about his head.

"Take it easy, Andrew!" Kodswallop remonstrated, "I really wouldn't worry about this midnight thing. I mean, look how easy it was to take care of this fellow--" he jerked a contemptuous finger at the ex-Peaseblossom, "the other three should be just as easy. And at night they'll show up even better with all that glitter."

"That's not the point, Kodswallop. It's just that... no, I'll explain later." Andrew himself had formed no very clear idea of exactly what was going on yet, though he had the distinct impression that it *was* directed at him. But one thing was clear. He returned his attention to the troll, but more calmly now. "Alright, now this bloke you're working for..."

"He's some kind of boffin, guv." Peregrine spoke quickly, anxious not to give this terrifying figure the slightest reason for dissatisfaction. "Very intellectual type. You can always tell, you know."

"Tall bloke, is he?" Andrew encouraged.

"Oh yes. Very commanding presence. Mind you, the eyes help."

"The eyes?"

"They flash a lot" the troll explained.

"It *must* be Montmorency... but why?"

"Because it's you" Clumpface shrugged.

"He *said* his name was Oberon, but just for the time being." Peregrine blenched at the expression on Andrew's face.

"*Oberon*! It's Montmorency alright!" Andrew took a couple of furious paces back and forth, then turned on the quivering troll, arm outstretched and finger pointing. "Now you get back to bloody Montmorency, and tell--"

Before Andrew could complete his message the troll vanished with a flash of violet light and a sharp clap! as air rushed to fill a vacuum.

The crash and the scream of terror broke Montmorency's concentration. With a rumble and a solid thud, the troll rolled down the roof, bounced off the gutter and slammed into the ground. Montmorency nodded thoughtfully. Cruickshank had been commendably quick off the mark with that transport routine-- obviously the man was learning fast. He resumed his seat and picked up the *Collected Works* with a smile of anticipation. He had fired the warning shot across his opponent's bows, and it had been tossed straight back. Now to open combat! At Montmorency's gesture the book fell open at *The Tempest*, Act I Scene i. He began to read

Act VII
A CLEARING IN THE FOREST

I still don't understand this midnight dreaming business." Cecil got up to refill his mug, "I mean, what's it matter if Montmorency dresses up a few forest trolls and sends them flitting about the place?"

"There's more to it than that," Kodswallop told him, "it's a matter of context."

"Eh?" Cecil blinked.

"Context," repeated the big fighter, as though stating a self-evident truth, "exiled dukes and fairies don't go together."

"I'm not sure about that," the marksman sneered.

"If Andrew could explain it to us again..." Janus suggested, with more tact than accuracy. Andrew hadn't explained anything so far, at least not coherently, and was now alternately glowering through the window and glowering at his beer. The outlaws' Social and Recreational Club served a good pint, but Andrew didn't seem to be enjoying it. He looked up and attempted a smile.

"It's all a bit complicated, but I thought we'd be able to sort this whole problem out the way Shakespeare sorted it out in *As You Like It*."

"As I like what?" Cecil looked mystified.

"It's the title of a play about an exiled duke and his usurping brother."

"And outlaws?" asked Ratbag.

"No, not in Shakespeare's version."

"Well, I suppose you're bound to forget some of the details when you're writing a play." The nicker gave an understanding smile.

"You could always mention it to him," Tiresome suggested, "in case he decides to do a revised version."

"Well not exactly-- he died more than four hundred years ago. On Earth-Three, that is."

"Just let me get this straight," Cecil waved a grubby forefinger, "you thought you could sort this out on the basis of a play written on Earth-Three by a bloke who died four hundred years ago?"

"Well... yes." Andrew couldn't help feeling that put that way, his rationale sounded a bit thin.

"Is there a good part in it for me?" the marksman asked.

"Never mind that!" Tiresome elbowed Cecil aside, "does it have any good combat scenes?"

"What about comic characters?" Clumpface asked eagerly, "anything like the gravediggers Ratbag and I did?"

"What about the French army?" Kodswallop asked hopefully.

"Hold it!" Andrew jumped to his feet. He had forgotten about his companions' passion for the theatre. "We are not, repeat not talking about putting on a play!" he shouted, "what I meant was *interpreting* what went on in terms of *As you Like It*."

"You mean the play is a paradigm for our situation?" suggested Orlando diffidently.

"Er... yes... I think."

"But surely are we not all playing parts?" Tiresome asked, "I have heard it said that all the world's a stage, and the men and women merely players. They have their exits and their entrances," he added by way of elaboration.

"And one man in his time plays many parts," agreed Janus, "certainly I did in Nova Castria."

There as a tense silence. "What did you just say?" Andrew asked at last.

"Just that I had played many parts in Nova Castria," Janus replied, puzzled.

"No, before that."

"Tiresome said that the world's a stage and everybody merely players."

"Less of the 'merely'," growled Cecil.

"But *that* comes straight out of the play!" Andrew was almost shouting in jubilation.

"No it doesn't," contradicted Cecil, "Tiresome just said it."

"Yes, but perhaps Shakespeare got the idea from him," Ratbag whispered.

"Never mind! You see the important thing about *As You Like It* is that there's no magic in it." The silence that greeted this pronouncement reminded Andrew that it was not his comrades who found occult activities disturbing. Sensing a possible ally he turned to Cecil. "It removes all the possibilities for technical errors," he told the marksman. "Using *As You Like It* as a model, I was sure we could sort things out for Mr Orlando-- it would just have meant a minor adjustment to the ending."

"No hermits in the forest," Orlando wagged a finger.

"Now someone is messing around, introducing stuff from another play called *A Midsummer Night's Dream* and that's absolutely *filled* with magic-- fairies, spells, enchantments and heaven knows what else."

"The French army?" Kodswallop still hadn't given up hope.

"No."

"Would there be a part for me in it?" Ratbag asked, very softly.

Andrew looked at the nicker and thought of Puck. "I'm afraid there would be," he said. "And this is the problem--"

"What other characters are there in *A Midsummer Night's Dream*?" Cecil interrupted.

"Oh loads. Two courting couples, a king and queen, *and* the king and queen of the fairies. And a bunch of amateur actors. They're the funniest part about it, actually. As soon as the words were out of his mouth, Andrew realised he had made an error of some magnitude.

"Strolling players!" Kodswallop's face shone like sunrise on a clear day.

"No! They're not professionals-- they're rank amateurs, and pretty bad ones at that."

"Well, *we* cannot claim professional status," Tiresome observed, "although I must confess with all modesty that I do believe my Prince Hal was not without merit."

"For the life of me, I can't see what you're worrying about, Andrew." Clumpface paused to excavate the bowl of his pipe with a stubby finger. "You know all about this man's plays-- you shouldn't have any trouble adapting any events from this 'Nightmare' thing to your own plan."

"But *A Midsummer Night's Dream* has got all this magic stuff in it... and then omigod there's *The Tempest*!" Andrew walked back and forth distractedly as he tried to remember the other Shakespeare plays in which magic played an important part. He rather thought there were quite a few.

"And a good thing too!" Clumpface made a no-nonsense sort of snorting sound through his pipe, "you could use a bit of practice. You are supposed to be a wardmaster mage, you know. Mind you, the way you got rid of that troll was pretty smooth."

"What do you mean, *I* got rid of him?"

"You transported him." Clumpface blew again through his empty pipe.

"But I didn't do anything!"

"Rubbish!" Janus snorted. "You told him to get back to Montmorency. You pointed your finger. There was a flash of Heron-Gough discharge, and he went.".

"He went where?"

"Ah, well! That's another question." The elf smiled. "Only *you* know that."

Andrew looked helplessly at his comrades. Between their thirst for any new experience, no matter how bizarre, and their sublime confidence in his occult abilities, he was trapped.

"Don't look so worried!" Janus gave him an encouraging smile, "it was a first class transport routine. Montmorency's going to find you've become much more adept-- it's going to be something of a shock for him. And of course you know all about the plays, and can anticipate all his moves. Or if not anticipate them, interpret them and suggest countermeasures."

"I suppose... But it's so ridiculous! Why does Montmorency have to do this?"

Janus gazed blankly at him as though he had questioned the earth's passage about the sun. "But Andrew, he has explained it to you very clearly several times. You and he are Designated Opposites."

"You mean he spends all his time trying to knock me off? Thanks a lot!"

"By no means!" Clumpface spoke sharply, "Montmorency holds absolutely no ill-feelings whatsoever; rather the reverse, in fact. No, this is simply a professional obligation on both your parts. And I must say..." the dwarf paused to light his pipe, "I must say that he has chosen an almost ideal confrontation."

"There is something to that." Orlando perked up, "you know *Clash of the Mages* might go down rather well with the punters. We could fit you in after the robbing and before the festivities in the glade. There's a nice little place--"

"No!" Andrew snapped.

"*It would* be family entertainment?" Orlando pursued hopefully.

"NO!"

"Well, let me know if you change your mind."

"Perhaps you could suggest some precautions in case Montmorency introduces material from this other play-- the... er..." Janus hesitated.

"*A Midsummer Night's Dream*," Andrew told him. "Yes, right, er... the first thing is not to have your men about on their own-- they must stay together at least in pairs."

"Even the woodcutters?"

"Especially the woodcutters."

"Looks a bit odd, two woodcutters together, you know." Orlando shook his head dubiously.

"Not half as odd as having one of them turned into an ass," Andrew told him, "or worse. And another thing: they're not to go to sleep-- at least not in the forest-- without at least two men standing guard."

"No-one to kip unless at least two people on guard," Orlando repeated as he wrote it down. "Why?" he asked.

"Because someone could come along and squeeze the juice from that 'sanguinary libido' onto their eyes-- could be most embarrassing."

"But I told you, that isn't the way it works--"

"If Montmorency tries it, it will be. Take it from me."

"Very well." With ill-concealed scepticism Orlando underlined the instruction.

"And Montmorency might have someone-- or something-- attempt to confuse your men by imitating the voices of their comrades. You know the sort of thing: 'oi! come 'ere Bill, behind this bush and see what I have found!' 'Just coming Sidney. Now, what is it? Oh I say, where did the silly fellow go?' You know the sort of thing."

"I think so. Though in Stembark Forest we do not encourage the use of such expressions as 'oi'." Orlando sniffed disapprovingly. "But I shall tell them to stick together in groups as much as possible. And to use passwords and countersigns."

"Good idea."

"I was wondering, Wardmaster...?"

"Yes?"

"Whether you would explain things to the men yourself?"

"Certainly."

"And you will wear your crimson cloak?"

"I could. Why?"

"It would help to establish your identity. Some of the men have been asking about the scruffy herbert in the tatty leather jerkin. They seem to think you've come about the drains."

On the outskirts of Lecter, Constable Dixon was just completing his afternoon's patrol. It was, he calculated, just about time to head back into the town and visit the Three Pigeons. Ralph Spratt, landlord of the Travellers' Rest had laid an Information concerning after-hours consumption of alcoholic beverages at the Three Pigeons, and Constable Dixon took such an allegation very seriously indeed. He would stop off at the Rest and have a pointed interview with Ralph Spratt: there would be no more such complaints, he told himself firmly, or he'd know the reason why. He was about to turn his horse back along the road to Lecter, when he became aware of a distant rumble and clatter. He halted, and stared curiously down the road as a cloud of dust, punctuated by the bright pinpoints of weapons came into view. The cloud resolved itself into a long procession of horses, carriages and wagons, flanked by an escort of mounted troops-- better than four score by the look of it. They were moving slowly but steadily, the eyes of the leading riders scanning the right side of the road, in search of a break in the blanket of greenery that was the southern margin of Stembark Forest. Dixon urged his horse forward into the middle of the road, and raised his hand to halt the oncoming procession. "Allo, allo, allo," he said, "what's all this then?"

With a confused clatter, and much snorting of horses, the cavalcade halted. Captain Spalding of the Castle Guard cantered forward to see what the hold-up was. "Good afternoon, officer," he beamed genially, "what seems to be the trouble?"

"No trouble, sir, just routine." Dixon took out his notebook. "Come a good distance today, have you?" he asked with a quick glance at the dusty vehicles and the travel-stained riders.

"We've come from Benbrock-Oldstairs, constable. It is my duty to escort this party to Stembark Forest."

"VIPs, eh?" Dixon gave a sympathetic smile. "Be glad to see the back of 'em, I'll warrant. And then you'll be back to East Castellian?"

"Escort duties are trying at the best of times," Spalding agreed with a humourless laugh, "but after we have seen this party safely into the forest we continue to Basingstoke, to await reinforcements."

"Reinforcements, sir?"

"Yes!" Spalding's eyes glittered with excitement, "The Seventh Heavy Dragoons are to rendezvous with us at Basingstoke within the week! A special operation!"

"Indeed, sir? That's very nice."

"Yes! The First Speaker himself--" Spalding checked himself abruptly-- his orders had laid particular and threatening emphasis on the need for security.

If Dixon noticed Spalding's lapse he gave no sign of it, contenting himself with an encouraging smile. "Expect you're glad to be out of the city for a change, sir," he said, with a knowing wink, "I won't delay you any longer, if you could just let me know the identity of the party..."

"Of course, constable." Spalding lowered his voice, "it is none other than Duke Roger of Benbrock-Oldstairs (Usurping) and his retinue!"

"I see, sir." Dixon made a brief entry in his notebook. "That's most satisfactory, sir," he closed the notebook with a snap. "If you proceed some five hundred paces you will come to the Southern Ride-- that'll take your party straight into the forest. There's a big sign on the right-- you can't miss it."

"Thank you very much, constable. You are most obliging."

"Just doing my duty, sir." Dixon put his notebook away, and moved to the side of the road. Spalding turned in his saddle and shouted an order. A trumpet brayed, and the procession lurched into motion.

Dixon waited impassively until the last rider had disappeared, then he took out his notebook and jotted down a few lines. This done, he allowed his horse to amble back along the road to town. The constable was intrigued. Such a large escort was unusual, even for the aristocracy. And the escort was not returning to East Castellian, but instead awaiting reinforcements in Basingstoke... It wouldn't hurt, Dixon decided, to have a quick word with Don Orlando; the outlaw chief would certainly be expecting a party of this size, and might know the reason for the military build-up in Basingstoke. He would send him a message that evening, Dixon decided. With the briskness of one who has determined on a course of action, he whistled his horse to a smart trot. A minute later he got to where the Southern Ride turned into the forest, and he reined in sharply. The signs of recent passage of a large party were unmistakable, including an unsightly scatter of empty crisp packets, choc-ice wrappers and lolly sticks. Dixon clicked his tongue disapprovingly; duke or no duke, this lot would be getting a few summonses for littering. Muttering under his breath, Dixon dismounted, and gathered up the scraps of rubbish. He was about to stuff them into the big litter box at the roadside, when a few words on a brightly coloured scrap of paper caught his eye. Curious, he smoothed it out and began to read. *Fleet the time carelessly in the golden world*, he was encouraged, in rotund green lettering, *feast and roister in the glades of Stembark Forest! Ride with Huntmaster John Peel and his hounds in the morning. And in the evenings, as the shadows lengthen, relax to the music of Clarence Snout and his Arboreal Arcadians.* Dixon shook his head-- something very odd indeed was going on, and the sooner Orlando heard about it the better. He was just about to secure the paper in his notebook when he saw a line of small print at the bottom of the page. *Outlaws are optional,* it said.

It was about an hour before sunset, and the wagons and carriages of the Duke of Benbrock-Oldstairs were drawn well up into the trees on the edge of a small clearing. With much heaving and tugging the ducal throne had been unloaded and was now perched more or less securely on a small eminence constructed of hastily gathered stones. Duke Roger eyed it approvingly, then sat down with a sigh. "So this is the pastoral life!" He stretched his legs, and the throne teetered. "Buckingham!" he turned his yelp of alarm into a commanding shout, "have some of the servants prepare a fire, and then they can cook something on it." He drew a deep appreciative breath. It was a lovely spot, and far too early in the year for insects to be a problem.

"Father!" Duke Roger's pastoral idyll was rudely interrupted by his daughter who stood before him, her foot tapping impatiently.

"Ah, what is it my dear? Cannot you and your cousin find some suitably rustic tasks to occupy yourselves? Milking a cow, perhaps? Fetching water? Gathering pretty nosegays of wild flowers?"

"The duel, father!" Anne fixed the duke with a basilisk glare, "you remember? Young Herbert de Coverly has challenged Charles, and would be satisfied."

"Ah yes, of course. Well, see if you can find them, and they can sort things out now."

"I'll find Herbert, Julia," Anne called to her cousin, "you get Charles. I last saw him over there somewhere." She waved vaguely.

Charles, Master Swordsman and First Member of the Senior Division of the College of Duellists, was sitting quietly on a log behind some bushes, as always, keeping himself to himself. He was a slight man with a thin face and a neat, pointed black beard. His receding hair cascaded back from a high forehead, and his eyes were large and a dark, lustrous brown, giving his face in repose a rather soulful expression. Soulful, that is, unless you looked closer and saw the pattern of fine lines around eyes and mouth, suggesting determination, calculation and, surprisingly enough, a readiness to laugh. But today Charles wasn't smiling and it wasn't due to the unspeakable Pebblestroke. Charles had originally signed his contract with Duke Roger's father. It had been a bit of an impulse really, since the duellist had found himself at a loose end in the south, and not quite ready to take up the faculty position at the College that Sir Arthur Scratch-Itchbag was pressing upon him. A couple of years with the southern aristocracy might be a relaxing and not unprofitable way to complete his active service career. It had been relaxing, alright! Charles could not have imagined the mind-numbing tedium of the experience. He was a fair-minded man, and he was willing to believe that not all southern aristocrats were tasteless, ignorant, inarticulate slobs. It was just that the ones *he'd* landed up with were tasteless, ignorant, inarticulate slobs. Of course when the old duke had died so suddenly, Charles could have terminated his contract, but the duellist was rather old-fashioned in his views of business ethics, so gritted his teeth and stayed on. The fact was that neither the old duke, nor his two sons, had the faintest concept of the abilities of a professional duellist. They knew that the upper classes had such people around, so they got one too. The duellist's lips curled into an involuntary sneer as he recollected how Roger had tried to persuade him to eliminate Harold-- the man obviously thought that he was some kind of assassin!

Charles winced at a distant, raucous laugh-- Pebblestroke was *still* walking about the place. Why no-one had scragged the witless little git yet was a mystery. The thought of witless little gits reminded him of Herbert de Coverly, and he groaned to himself. Herbert was tall, broad-shouldered and well-muscled, especially about the head, but to Charles he was just another witless little git. The young man had light blond hair, one unruly lock of which was guaranteed to flop over his eyes in an engaging fashion-- Charles was convinced (with justification) that it took Herbert several hours in front of a mirror every day to achieve that effect. He was the kind of man who had captained the First XI at school. And probably the First XV as well. Or if not, he'd been to the kind of school that had First XIs and First XVs.

"Charles! Cooee! Charles!" The duellist rose to his feet, but his tense features relaxed as he saw Julia approaching. Not that he had very much time for any of the brood, but anyone who would tell Herbert that the next time he tried to touch her he'd be wearing his goolies round his tonsils couldn't be all bad.

Julia watched the lithe figure of the duellist flow to his feet and, despite herself, felt the tiniest of shivers crawl up her spine. Though he had not appeared to move hurriedly, the man was on his feet in an instant. Though his hand was nowhere near his sword, his stance had a look of menace about it.

"It's only me, Charles. Uncle wanted to know whether you could attend him presently."

"I shall be delighted." The duellist gave Julia the slightest of bows and followed her to the clearing.

"Ah, Charles, so there you are!" Duke Roger acknowledged him with a lordly wave. "All ready for a bit of sport, eh?"

"Oh aye! Such are sports to the gentlefolk that truly should be sports![8] " cackled Pebblestroke, capering madly.

"Pebblestroke." Buckingham beckoned the motley-clad figure aside.

"Yes, my liege?"

"Bugger off for a while. And, Pebblestroke--"

"My liege?"

"Please do not refer to the duke as 'nuncle' any more. He finds it tedious."

"It's traditional!" the jester protested.

"It's dangerous, Pebblestroke," Julia reminded him grimly. With a defiant flourish of his bladder he withdrew.

"As I was saying..." Duke Roger looked around to confirm that Pebblestroke had indeed gone, then continued with an air of palpable relief, "so you're all ready, Charles?"

"With respect, your grace, I must record my reservations. This young... er... Herbert, has to my knowledge no formal training with the duelling sword. Nor any experience in combat.."

"Nonsense!" Duke Roger gave the expansive laugh of someone who, regardless of the outcome of the discussion, knows he will not have to engage in a swordfight with a duellist. "Nonsense, Charles. I expect he did all that stuff at school, eh Herbert?" He wagged his head at the tall, blond youth who was trying to adjust his profile to the best advantage of the young ladies.

"Head of House, your grace," he said proudly, forgetting the profile for the moment. "And I captained the school team once."

"Excellent! So there you are, Charles. The young feller's sure to give you a good run for your money."

Charles grimaced. *None* of these people had the faintest conception of the capabilities of even the most inexperienced duellist. He made one last attempt. "If the young man must go ahead, then I strongly urge that we used bated swords. It is usual for sporting engagements."

---

8   A play on different meanings of the word "sport" that remains almost totally incomprehensible to the modern reader

"That would take all the fun out of it," Herbert protested with a complacent smile, "you're not afraid of a minor flesh wound, are you?"

Charles shrugged helplessly. "In that case, sir, I am at your disposal." He inclined his head slightly, and took up his position. With an eager bray of laughter Herbert faced him, and drew his sword with a flourish. The bits of coloured glass that studded the guard winked merrily in the last light from the setting sun. "May the best man win!" he declared.

"He will," confirmed Charles, with the hint of a smile.

To the uninformed observer the pair looked hopelessly ill-matched. On the one side, the magnificent youth, his silver-trimmed blue cloak thrown carelessly back from his shoulders, his teeth gleaming almost as brightly as his sword. On the other, the slight figure of the duellist; copper-coloured cloak hanging from narrow shoulders, face impassive, and his sword a dull grey pointer.

"Will you--" Charles began, about to ask the duke to signal the opening of the bout, but he was interrupted by a shout of "excelsior!" as Herbert charged forward, waving his sword like a conductor's baton. Charles stepped back and unhurriedly parried the wild blow, disengaged and made his riposte, stopping his point at least an inch short of Herbert's neck. It was done with such economy of movement that there were those among the spectators who were prepared to swear that the duellist had never moved.

Herbert gave an uncomprehending gasp, jumped backwards, tripped, and fell heavily. Charles waited for him to get up, wondering to himself whether the young man realized what had happened. He obviously hadn't for, from a crouched position, he made a prodigious leap forward, sword outstretched before him. Charles politely stood to one side and Herbert crashed, arms flailing, into a bush. Charles moved back a few paces, turning to face his opponent who had paused for a moment to brush some dead leaves from his hair. Perhaps he had learned something, for instead of another full-blooded charge, Herbert advanced more cautiously, a pace at a time, swinging his sword vigorously back and forth in a vain effort to contact his opponent's weapon and produce that thrilling clash of steel upon steel of which he had read so much.

Charles slid his weapon smoothly under Herbert's flailing blade, then tapped the man lightly on the shoulder with the tip. Perhaps this time he would get the hint. But Herbert seemed immune to hints, and waved his sword about even more violently, with a shout of "have at thee!" At this Charles finally lost patience and with a quick, economical movement, thrust at Herbert's sword arm, hitting him cleanly just below the shoulder. Herbert gave a yelp of surprise and pain, dropped his sword, clapped his left hand to his shoulder and stood swaying dramatically.

"That, sir, is what we in the business call a palpable hit." Charles cleaned off the point of his sword with a scrap of linen, and returned the weapon to its sheath. He gave a perfunctory bow to his erstwhile opponent, an even more perfunctory one to the duke, and retired into the shadows to find a spot for his tent.

"Young Herbert, you are well?" Buckingham asked solicitously.

"Aaahh!" Herbert swayed still more and rolled his eyes up till only the whites showed.

"Brandy for the gentleman!" the duke ordered.

At once Herbert began to recover. His eyes returned to normal and he took two or three wavering paces to a convenient log, onto which he sank with a most dolorous sigh, his left hand still tightly clasped about his shoulder.

"Let the girls look to your wounds, young Herbert," the duke suggested.

"That's *wound* father," Anne corrected him, emphasising the singular, "and it doesn't look much to me."

"Nay, good my grace," gasped Herbert, justifiably alarmed at the prospect of receiving first aid from either girl, "the brandy will suffice. As the lady says, 'tis but a scratch."

"Looked more like a puncture wound to me," Julia suggested, with the authority of one experienced in such matters, "take your hand away so we can see."

Unwillingly the young man removed his hand. A red stain, the size of a small coin, showed on his sleeve. Julia rolled her eyes.

"Heh! Heh! Heh!" Pebblestroke capered up, grimacing horribly, "I'll riddle you a riddle, young master." He struck Herbert smartly over the head with his bladder to indicate to which young master he was referring.

"What is your riddle?" Herbert asked unwillingly. He would have liked to tell the vile creature to get lost, but it seemed to him that telling a usurping duke's Court Jester to hop it might be a career-limiting move. Pebblestroke capered a bit more, then crouching down till he was at Herbert's level, thrust his grubby face forward. "Riddle me this! Why is a duellist like a good joke?" he demanded.

Herbert recoiled from the reeking breath. "I cannot tell, Pebblestroke. Why is a duellist like a good joke?"

"Because if you can't take his point, then the joke's on you!" Pebblestroke dissolved into paroxysms of helpless cackling.

Duke Roger covered his face with his hands.

Cecil, Kodswallop and Clumpface were waiting at the outlaw headquarters for the others to get back. Janus and Tiresome had gone with Andrew and the outlaw leader on yet another tour of inspection of the outlying woodcutter guard posts, and Ratbag was off on some inscrutable, and undoubtedly disreputable, errand of his own. While Clumpface was beating Cecil at chess for the third time running, Kodswallop was deep in thought. So far their adventure had provided absolutely no opportunity for violent conflict resolution (save, of course, for those of a routine nature on their journey from Nova Castria) and, though he knew Andrew affected disapproval of such diversions, Kodswallop felt keenly that these affrays were the most important contribution he could make to the success of their mission. It weighed heavily upon him that fortune had been so ill-favoured as to deny him the opportunity of exercising his talents. But the big fighter was too intelligent and practical to waste time in vain regrets; there were other ways in which he could help. An idea, planted in his mind when Andrew was first told them of *As You Like It*, had sprouted into life. He leaned over the table just as Clumpface said "checkmate!" for the third time that evening.

"Checkmate? Never!" Cecil howled, as he tried to slip his queen and two bishops back onto the board.

"Never mind that now!" Kodswallop removed the chess pieces from his grasp and replaced them in their box. "Now listen you two: I've got an idea."

"Nah, it's a bit of a hike to the Three Pigeons," Cecil replied, misunderstanding.

"No, not that! At least, not right now," Kodswallop added prudently, not wishing to foreclose on any options. "Do either of you know anything about hermits?"

"Not much." Clumpface scratched his head, "not a business that's ever attracted me, the god-bothering," he mused.

"But yer actual hermits aren't full-time god-botherers," Cecil objected, "I mean I've heard they do things like astronomy, botany, chemistry, an' all. They're big on herbs an' poisons 'n stuff like that."

"No, what I meant is what do they look like?"

"Look like?" Clumpface shrugged. "Like hermits I suppose."

"They wear hair coats," Cecil suggested, "or habits of some coarse material. Why do you want to know."

"Well, it's like this..." Kodswallop hesitated, torn between the desire not to reveal his plan until he had everything completely worked out and the equally powerful urge to share his idea with his friends, "you remember that Andrew told us that in the play the usurping duke meet a hermit who persuades him to give up his usurping?"

"Yes... but Orlando says there aren't any hermits in the forest."

"There are now." Kodswallop tapped his chest.

"You!" Cecil choked with laughter, "a *hermit!*"

"Why not?"

Cecil stopped laughing. The big fighter was looming over him, a scowl of ferocious enquiry on his face. "Er... no reason at all, Kodswallop. If you want to be a hermit, that is. But... er... why?"

"So I can convince the usurping duke to give up his usurping, just like Andrew wanted. I think I could persuade him."

"You might at that." Clumpface gave Kodswallop a thoughtful look. "Mind you, he's got to be able to walk afterwards."

"So you'll help me?"

"I think it's worth a try. Cecil, what have you got in the way of coarse habits?"

"I'm not touching a line like that with a ten foot pole," Cecil muttered as he threw open the hamper that held their theatrical costumes, and rooted about busily. "How about this?" he offered a few moments later, holding up a rust-coloured blanket-like object with bits of string hanging from it, "it's Sigismund the Mad Monk's costume from *Blood on the Rooftops, Blood on the Tiles.*"

Kodswallop took it gingerly between thumb and forefinger, and gave it a cautious shake. A choking cloud of dust billowed forth, and with a high-pitched squeak a small creature dashed across the floor and vanished into the wainscotting. "Pongs a bit," he commented, "not got anything fresher, have you?"

"Not really-- at least nothing that's suitable. Try it on."

With ill-concealed reluctance, the big fighter draped the costume over his shoulders. He gave a loud sneeze.

"Pull it together at the front," instructed Cecil, "and put the hood up."

Kodswallop complied. "How do I look?" he asked. There was a long silence, broken only by a muffled choking noise from Cecil. At last Clumpface spoke.

"Whatever you look like, you do not look like Kodswallop."

"Well, that's a start. And perhaps with some make-up--"

"No!" Cecil took a deep, shuddering breath. "You don't need any make-up, Kodswallop. In that outfit no-one's going to want to get near enough you to make it worthwhile. Besides, I'm not sure there's anything I could add to... that." His arm trembled as he pointed.

"Looks alright then?"

"You look like one of the four horsemen of the apocalypse-- pestilence, I think-- after a very hard season of being pestilential." Cecil covered his eyes.

"Belt up, Cecil," Clumpface admonished, "it looks fine. All we have to decide is where he's going to hang out."

"Somewhere to the south," Kodswallop suggested, "that's the way this usurping duke'll be coming."

"Come on, then. We must find you a spot before dark." Clumpface got up and led the way out.

After an hour of steady riding, then another half hour of wending their way along a maze of wriggling paths too narrow for the horses, they found a spot. Here the land rose into a gentle ridge and, years ago, a small landslide had left a shallow saucer-like scar in the rising ground, as yet imperfectly camouflaged by the new growth. "Here we are!" Clumpface surveyed the spot with great satisfaction.

"Here?" Kodswallop looked it over. "Looks a bit bleak."

"Well, you're supposed to be a hermit aren't you?" Cecil told him unsympathetically, "hermits *like* bleak environments. It goes along with their coarse habits."

"It's ideal," the dwarf told him firmly. Secluded-- nobody's likely to stumble across you-- and very close to the Southern Ride-- almost in earshot, in fact."

"Aye... I suppose." Kodswallop began to wonder whether he should reconsider the idea. Perhaps Clumpface would be better as a hermit... or Cecil. They both seemed to know a lot about the habits of the species. Then his determination returned when he remembered that for all their knowledge of hermit habits, they would simply be at a loss when it came to the persuading of usurping dukes to stop usurping. With some justification, Kodswallop felt that of the three of them, he was best qualified for that kind of thing.

"Let's see if we can't fettle you up some kind of shelter." Clumpface took his axe from his belt and began trimming the lower branches of the nearest tree.

"Properly speaking, hermits should live in caves. Or cells," Cecil pointed out as, seated comfortably on a rock, he watched the dwarf go to work.

"Cell? I'm not doing any hermitting in some bloody cell, thank you very much!" Kodswallop glowered angrily at Cecil then suspiciously at Clumpface.

"Of course not. Belt up, Cecil, and cut some of that bracken over there if you want to be useful-- or even if you don't."

Quite soon the three of them had completed a simple, sturdy shelter tucked inconspicuously into the trees on the verge of the scar. "That should do you fine," Clumpface observed, taking a well earned swig from the bottle Kodswallop had had the foresight to bring along, "the shelter looks pretty hermit-like, but it'll keep you warm and dry."

"Shouldn't he be growing herbs and making potions?" asked Cecil, "hermits are pretty much in the potion making line."

"No time for that," Clumpface pointed out, "he'd better just concentrate on the meditating. That's always a safe bet for hermits."

"I am going to concentrate on moral persuasion, "Kodswallop told him firmly, "or at least, the persuasion anyway," he added as he saw the expressions on the faces of his two friends.

"Alright then, we'll leave you to it." Clumpface began to repack his tools.

"Do you think he should put a notice up on the Southern Ride?" Cecil asked, "you know the sort of thing: 'Marcus Kneetrembler, Hermit. Full-scope hermitting, no job too small, free estimates and no obligation'?"

"Don't be bloody ridiculous!" Kodswallop gave the marksman a pitying look. "That's the daftest idea I've heard today. I don't look anything like Marcus Kneetrembler."

"I don't believe you need that kind of notice," Clumpface told him hastily. The dwarf was beginning to have second thoughts about the venture.

"But I do need a name," the hermit pointed out. He thought for a moment. "Could I be Knacker?"

"Knacker would be a most unsuitable name for a hermit." Clumpface shook his head.

"Don Pedro d'y Angina?" Kodswallop suggested hopefully.

"Doesn't sound right," Clumpface objected, "it's not a god-botherer's name."

"There's that one Andrew's always talking about," Cecil suggested, "you know..." he snapped his fingers urgently, trying to remember.

"Wakefield...? "Proudie...? Cranmer...?" Clumpface offered, recalling the names he had heard Andrew use in an ecclesiastical context.

"Nah. None of those... no I've got it!" The marksman jumped into the air in excitement, "it was Chasuble! Canon Chasuble!"

"Strange sort of name." Kodswallop shook his head dubiously, "was he from foreign parts?"

"No Kodswallop, he was not," Clumpface told him very firmly, "so he would *not* say 'caramba!'[9] Come on, Cecil." The dwarf fastened the straps on his toolbag, slung it from his shoulder and set off back down the path, shaking his head and muttering "caramba!" under his breath. Cecil gave Kodswallop an unsympathetic grin and followed the dwarf.

A little sadly, the big fighter waved his two friends farewell. Then he cheered up as it occurred to him that the usurping duke would have no way of knowing whether or not Canon Chasuble was a foreigner. He would be able to say 'caramba' as much as he liked.

---

9   Kodswallop was proud of the multilingual abilities he had developed for his
     role of the French army, a couple of years before.

Act VIII
ANOTHER PART OF THE FOREST

—◇—

Montmorency stood at the grotto entrance and sniffed. "Really, Bellingham! Is this the best you could do?"

Bellingham sneezed. "It is a little damp, Mage," he admitted, "but the duckboards help a lot. And it's almost dry where my bed is."

Montmorency illuminated his staff and moved a few paces inside. From a slit-like entrance it widened out into quite a respectable cave, though a very damp one. The stalagmites and stalactites glistened with moisture and the wall on the right was running with it. On the left a narrow shelf had been hacked out from the rock, and above this a lantern was insecurely suspended. Dark water lapped ominously at the duckboards underfoot. The Black Mage shook his head. "I am aware that graduate student accommodation is not generally the most luxurious, but surely even a graduate student might find this a little basic. Running water is very convenient, Bellingham, but not running all over the place. Why did you not take steps?"

"But Mage Montmorency, are we not enjoined from using our powers for self--" the graduate student began, but stopped at an impatient gesture from his supervisor.

"The fact that there exists a long and honourable tradition of not using our powers for trivial personal gratification of a momentary interest does *not* mean we have to take up residence in some subterranean slum and part-time aquarium. Now, take your equipment case outside and wait for me there."

Greatly puzzled, and not a little unsettled, Bellingham stood just far enough from the mouth of the grotto so that he could not see inside-- there were some things, he reminded himself, that it was much better he didn't even think about seeing, especially when Mage Montmorency was involved. He did not have to wait long. After a few minutes of ominous silence, made even more ominous by the occasional violet flash of Heron-Gough discharge, Montmorency summoned him back. "You may come in now, Bellingham, and do mind the step."

Nervously the graduate student sidled into the grotto, and then stopped dead. He gasped with amazement. Gone were the bare rock walls, glistening with moisture. Gone were the highly picturesque, if inconvenient, stalagmites and stalactites. And gone was the ankle-deep water. Where before there had been a gloomy, dripping hole in the ground with bits of coloured glass stuck into one of the walls, now there was a cosy chamber with bright whitewashed walls and a shiny parquet floor punctuated by sheepskin scatter rugs. On one side was a fireplace with a yellow cuckoo clock hanging from the wall above, while opposite was a sofa-bed with a bright red bedspread flanked by bookshelves. There were, alas, no books-- after all there were some things even Montmorency could not do in a hundred and fifty seconds. "Mage Montmorency!" Bellingham caught his breath, "this is-- is--"

"Tut man, it is nothing!" Montmorency shook his head impatiently. "This is the sort of task any undergraduate could accomplish; *you* should be able to do it standing on your head! Remember, Bellingham, the first rule for a mage in the field: get a cosy billet and keep your feet dry. Now at least you might light the fire." He pointed to the logs laid ready in the grate. Bursting with pride, Bellingham stretched out his hand in the direction of the fireplace, and murmured the standard ignition routine. The logs obediently burst into flame and smoke poured into the room. Montmorency sighed. "My dear Bellingham. It is usually considered a prudent move to open the damper before lighting a fire."

Sick with embarrassment, Bellingham summoned up a generic clearance routine. There was a dull clang and a large iron plate crashed down into the fireplace. Sparks flew and the fire began to draw furiously. Montmorency gave a dry chuckle. "The routine you wanted was one to *open* the damper, Bellingham, not remove an obstruction." He chuckled again. "Quite an understandable mistake under the circumstances." He stretched out a hand. The iron plate disappeared up the chimney and the fire stopped imitating an enthusiastic blast furnace and began to crackle in a thoroughly domestic way. Montmorency held his hands out to the blaze, and rubbed them together. "Now if you are settled comfortably Bellingham, I should like to explain the task I have in mind for you. I believe you will find it challenging and rewarding."

Bellingham quailed a little. The rewarding bit was fine, but it was the challenge that worried him. "I-- I-- am anxious to start work as soon as possible, Mage," he lied.

"Good!" The Black Mage beamed approval and walked to the sofa bed, sat, and lounged back comfortably. He made a negligent gesture with his left hand, and his equipment case materialised on the floor, its lid swinging smoothly open. "Before I outline your assignment, I should explain something of the background. You may take notes if you wish."

Bellingham jumped for his notebook. By now he was familiar enough with Montmorency's style to know that last remark meant: "you'd better take this down in great detail and get it right, for woe betide you if you make a mistake." Stylus poised, he looked up expectantly. The Black Mage conjured two glasses of brandy out of thin air and passed one to Bellingham. He took a short sip, and then began.

"You will observe that I have removed myself from the island. You should be aware that this is not a temporary absence. For reasons which will shortly become clear, I can no longer remain there and shall take up residence in this grotto."

Bellingham stifled a sigh-- he might have known it was too good to be true.

Oblivious to the young man's disappointment, the Black Mage continued. "I intend to put in place, centred on the island and encompassing the whole lake and its shoreline, a continuous, full-scope, interactive illusion."

Bellingham could not stifle his reaction this time and his gasp was audible. A full-scope illusion over such a wide area, and continuous *and* interactive, was unheard of! He looked up questioningly from his notes.

"You heard aright, Bellingham," Montmorency confirmed, "a full-scope interactive illusion with a radius of almost two leagues, running continuously." He spoke with some pride. "It is the first time such a thing has been done, I believe."

"Incredible!" Bellingham whispered.

"Of course it is based on the set of illusion routines that the Guild system has used for many years, but it is very considerably expanded. Why, I added an extra seven hundred lines of code to support the peripherals alone!"

Bellingham nearly dropped his stylus. Peripherals referred to individual details of an illusion-- for example the blood dripping from the fangs of a phantom hound would be a peripheral that would require but one line of code-- if that. Bellingham rather thought that the latest version of Sproggit and Axel's Necromancy Utilities could do all that sort of thing using batch spells. But seven-hundred lines of code! "What ki-- kind of illusion is this, Mage?" he stammered.

"It is a storm," Montmorency answered, "or perhaps I should say, a *tempest*." He gave the word particular emphasis, and laughed softly. "That, of course, accounts for the complexity. Waves dashing on rocks, the wind shrieking, the spray flying, and all interactive, it does quite add up. You *did* make a note of that, Bellingham?" he asked, with a keen glance at the graduate student, "the seven hundred lines of code?"

"Indeed yes, Mage! It is an amazing achievement."

"Thank you. And you understand why I must take up residence here?"

"Of course!" Bellingham could quite see why Montmorency had no wish to sit at the centre of such a powerful illusion for any length of time. "But what, if I might ask, is the purpose of the illusion? Or is it just a demonstration or field test?" he added hastily. He knew very well that some mages got quite offended by questions about the practical applications of their work.

"It is a device by which I mean to neutralize Cruickshank for an indefinite period. Or at least seriously inconvenience him."

"But surely as a mage he will not be affected by it?"

"Of course not! But consider this, Bellingham: Cruickshank is formulating his strategy on the basis of a play written by Shakespeare, from Earth Three. The play is called *As You Like It*. You may care to glance through it," Montmorency flicked his wrist and the *Collected Works* floated from his equipment case, "later," he added, as Bellingham reached for the book. The graduate student dropped his hand and began scribbling rapidly once more as Montmorency continued. "My strategy has been to introduce elements from other plays by this man, elements that Cruickshank will recognise and, I trust, find most disturbing. I have already made a start with material from *A Midsummer Night's Dream,* material which Cruickshank recognises and has, he believes, dealt with quite effectively."

"You are lulling him into a false sense of security, Mage?" Bellingham asked.

"Exactly!" Montmorency beamed approval. "So Bellingham, the situation is this: Cruickshank recognises what I am doing, and believes he is countering it. Now suppose that he encounters yet another element from yet another Shakespeare play, a fierce storm which is obviously an illusion routine, what is he going to do?"

"But of course! He will attempt to nullify it-- from the centre, and it is being relayed from here!" Bellingham was astounded at the elegant simplicity of the scheme, and the labyrinthine thinking that had engendered it. An illusion spell could only be completely nullified from its source. Usually the source would be at the centre of the illusion, but not in this case. Of course a powerful enough mage-- and from what he understood, Cruickshank was easily powerful enough-- would have no difficulty in shrinking the illusion. Indeed he could free the whole area of the illusory phenomenon. But-- and this was the crucial point-- he could not disperse the illusion. "It will shrink to him!" he cried, "to within..." Bellingham tapped his forehead as he tried to work it out, "to at least forty paces!" He looked at Montmorency for confirmation.

"You will get a more accurate estimate if you rate Cruickshank at a Mage Index of 12.5." Montmorency smiled broadly. "You should also remember that for such a level the linear approximation is inadequate."

"Oh!" Bellingham reached for his Dalton spellcaster and twirled the circular approximator scales on the back of the instrument. He stared wide-eyed at the result. "But-- I cannot-- it is *impossible*!" he stammered.

"Not impossible," Montmorency told him, "inevitable."

Bellingham looked again at the approximator. Once again he manipulated the rotating scales, and once again came up with the same result. Any attempt by Cruickshank to nullify the illusion spell would result in the illusion shrinking to within a hand's breadth or less of the Wardmaster. It was unheard of!

"It is a classic example of allowing your opponent to use his own strength against himself," Montmorency continued, "while Cruickshank will not be deceived by the illusion, and while he will almost certainly be able to remove its influence from the lake, he may find it rather difficult to communicate, or otherwise interact effectively, with his colleagues after he has done so." Montmorency leaned back and took a long sip of brandy. "While Cruickshank's comrades may be used to his eccentricities, I believe that even they will be hard put to it to work with a seven foot diameter cloudy sphere."

"Especially when it's howling like a banshee!" Bellingham giggled.

"Indeed. And now, Bellingham, we come to your part in this. With Cruickshank out of the way, we can take over, and our first task must be to intercept this exiled duke's brother-- Roger, I believe his name is." The Black Mage waved a hand, and the *Collected Works* floated into his lap. He opened it at *As You Like* It and riffled quickly through the pages. "Shakespeare is a little sketchy about details, but he leaves us in no doubt that the usurping duke falls in with a hermit who convinces him to return the dukedom to his brother."

"With all respect, Mage, that does not sound very plausible."

"It does not have to be plausible, Bellingham," Montmorency told him severely, "it merely has to work."

"I do not believe there are any hermits in Stembark Forest, Mage, indeed I have heard that there are very few left anywhere in Albion."

"You are quite correct, Bellingham, and that is why I want you to be the hermit that the usurping duke shall encounter."

"Me! But Mage-- I-- I do not believe I know enough to maintain such an imposture."

"Nonsense Bellingham! Assume a devout air if you have it not! Piece out your imperfections with your spells! A hooded robe of some coarse material, a pair of open-toed sandals and a few minutes with the reference section of Frogson's Modern Spells, and you will be perfectly prepared."

Bellingham thought to protest more-- then thought again. Questioning the instructions of your thesis supervisor was not a prudent move for a graduate student. He swallowed nervously. "Can you give me any further instructions, Mage?"

"You should proceed to the southern region of the forest." Montmorency conjured a map onto the wall and pointed at it with his staff. "Just about here. Close to the Southern Ride, but not on it. That is the route I should expect duke Roger to come."

"And you wish me to intercept him?"

"It would be better if he sought you out. Or at least one of his retinue."

"How could that be, Mage, when he is unaware of my existence?"

"Really Bellingham! Do you expect me to do all your thinking for you?" Montmorency snapped impatiently, and the map burst into flames. He extinguished it with a careless gesture, then returned his attention to the shrinking graduate student. "Use your initiative, man! Notices on trees advertising your services, of course!"

"Notices on trees?"

"Exactly. Shakespeare does call for notes pinned to trees throughout the forest, so that will be quite appropriate. You know the kind of thing: 'Hermit Services for All Occasions-- Special Rates for Parties-- Twenty-four hour Express Service'."

"And should the duke seek me out?"

"Then seek to delay his progress. Advise caution. Explain that these things take time... that Rome wasn't built in a day. Suggest that this might not be the right moment. Suggest the omens are inauspicious."

"I understand, Mage!" The light of comprehension dawned in Bellingham's eyes, "DPD!"

"Delphic Phrases of Discouragement! Excellent, Bellingham!" Montmorency beamed, "I begin to have hopes of you after all. And another thing: there should be two young ladies with the duke-- his daughter and his niece. Encourage them to separate themselves from the main party and travel ahead alone."

"Would not that be... rather... er... questionable, Mage? Two young ladies travelling by themselves through the forest?"

"One of them may disguise herself as a man," Montmorency suggested carelessly, "or they could take the court jester with them for protection."

"I understand Mage." Bellingham scribbled furiously. He hadn't the foggiest idea what Montmorency was going on about, but he did understand the Mage wanted the two women to be detached from the main party. "One more thing, Mage. What name should I assume? I had rather thought of Marcus Kneetrembler."

"Bellingham, Bellingham!" Montmorency shook his head in sorrow, "sometimes I wonder! Marcus Kneetrembler indeed! You look nothing like the man. Now let me see..." The Black Mage peered into his crystal. After some thoughtful scrutiny he looked up with a smile. "I have the very name, Bellingham. It is one which Cruickshank will recognise instantly. You may call yourself Canon Chasuble."

At the Headquarters Glade Don Orlando frowned anxiously at the note he had just received from constable Dixon. "The usurping duke entering the forest! And we are in no state to receive him!" He ran his fingers through his hair.

"He did not book ahead, Mr Orlando." Eric appeared at the outlaw leader's elbow, "if a party as large as that does not book ahead, they can scarcely expect special treatment. And we don't have to give the group discount either," he reminded his chief.

"There is that." Orlando cheered up slightly, "but even so, I just don't think we have the staff. What with half the men on woodcutter duty and another two sections laying false scents for the exiled duke's hounds, I just don't see how we can fit him in for at least..." he consulted a pocket diary, "...at least two days."

"Actually I think you'll find he hasn't come for the robbing," Andrew pointed out, trying to hide his delight at the turn events had taken, "this may be our chance to organise things so that we can get rid of the exiled duke."

"Er-- yes-- I was going to mention that." Clumpface was feeling a little doubtful now.

"Mention what?" Janus looked interested.

"About the usurping duke. Actually it was all Kodswallop's idea." Clumpface wasn't feeling doubtful any more; he was feeling downright dubious.

"What about the usurping duke?" Janus pursued.

"And what was Kodswallop's idea?" asked Andrew, a nasty feeling beginning to grow in his stomach.

"It was the hermit," Clumpface answered, taking the plunge at last, "he thought that if he could be the hermit he could persuade duke Roger to give up the usurping. He is very good at the persuading, Kodswallop is," the dwarf pointed out, "when he puts his mind to it."

"Kodswallop! A hermit!" shrieked Andrew.

"Just what we said," Cecil agreed with the gloomy satisfaction of one whose direst predictions have come true.

"But he must be--"

"Yes," Cecil agreed once more, "but he was that set on it..." There was a pensive silence.

"Pardon me for asking," Orlando said diffidently, "but is this not perfectly in accordance with the paradigm you had adopted for this situation?"

"No!" Andrew snapped. "I mean yes. But I wasn't thinking of a spurious hermit."

"For the life of me I cannot see what difference it makes!" Tiresome looked mightily satisfied with the way things were working out. "After all, as Don Orlando has told us, there is a complete lack of hermits in the forest. Kodswallop has simply rectified that deficiency. And with commendable initiative."

"Well, I did get him the costume," Cecil pointed out, anxious that credit be fairly shared.

"Tiresome's right, Andrew," Janus tried to calm their mage, "you said that we need a hermit, and now we have one."

"I suppose..." Andrew's mind was still boggling on all cylinders as it tried to come to grips with the idea.

"And," the elf pursued his advantage, "if nothing else, Kodswallop will be invaluable as an advanced look-out post-- he will give us early warning of the usurping duke's approach."

"How?" Andrew demanded.

"I can go back and forth," Clumpface offered hastily-- he still felt more than a little responsible-- "nobody notices a dwarf."

"Then all is settled satisfactorily?" Orlando asked hopefully, "we can proceed with our disruption of the hunt as planned?"

"Of course!" Janus nodded, and everybody looked a little happier. Disrupting duke Harold's hunting was a labour of love for all.

"There is one thing I find disquieting," Orlando tugged at his chin, "Constable Dixon writes of a large force of castle guards-- better than four score-- that escorted the usurping duke to the forest. It seems they are not returning to East Castellian, but are going to Basingstoke to await reinforcements. What, do you suppose, can that mean?"

"Nothing good." Tiresome looked grave. "Four-score castle guards, with more to follow, signifies serious interest on the part of the First Speaker. It could," he concluded judiciously, "be construed as unfavourable comment."

"Has East Castellian ever attempted action against you?" Janus asked.

"There have in the past been one or two incidents," the outlaw chief conceded, "simple misunderstandings really, amounting to the dispatch of a few revenue officers. I had thought we'd cleared all that business up long ago."

"They do keep sending us final notices," Eric pointed out, "but we always took that to be some kind of administrative problem."

"Tiresome?" Janus looked to the knight for advice, for he knew more of the curious habits and behaviour of the East Castellians than anyone else. And now he looked troubled.

"It is possible the First Speaker has decided to attempt direct action against our friends," he said slowly, "but four-score castle guards!" He laughed-- it was an absurdly small force.

"With reinforcements to come," Eric reminded him.

"We must find out." Janus turned to Orlando. "Could you send someone to Basingstoke to make enquiries?"

"Lenny can go. He has some business to attend there in any case."

"But what about East Castellian?" asked Tiresome, "that is where the answer will lie."

"I'm not sure about that." Orlando looked doubtful. "While my men can find friends and informants in every tavern, we do not number the senior officers of the Castle Guard among such, still less members of the First Speaker's inner circle."

"We can handle that." Cecil stood, arms folded and a confident smile on his face. "It'll take a couple of days, but I reckon to get anything we need out of the First Speaker's office. 'Specially if Ratbag can come along."

"Of course!" Andrew exclaimed, "Mrs Plantagenet!" The previous year, in another operation, Cecil had got into Castle Downing disguised as a cleaning lady. The impersonation had never been detected.

"'Sright." Cecil grinned happily, "worked alright before, and like I said, they never notice the cleaning ladies."

"If you believe you can manage the impersonation..." Janus considered the matter.

"Piece of cake," the marksman was still grinning, "and Ratbag can come in with me and do the actual searching." Cecil was the first to recognise that his burglarious talents, formidable as they were, paled into insignificance alongside those of the nicker.

"What do you think, Tiresome?"

"There is no question about it, Janus," the knight told him firmly, "much as it goes against the grain to separate in this manner, we must find out what the First Speaker's got on his mind. And we know Ratbag and Cecil can gain entrance to Castle Downing without arousing suspicion."

"So long as Ratbag isn't allowed near the souvenir shops," Clumpface interjected. Ratbag gave him a reproachful look.

"We could ask Don Orlando if he would be prepared to send two of his men with them to keep an eye on things from the background," Andrew suggested, "just in case things go badly wrong."

"I should be delighted!" The outlaw leader had lost his air of concern now that there was the promise of real action. The Castle Guard, indeed! Things were looking up, especially when he had a Knight of Albion fighting on his side. "You believe there is a possibility of conflict?" he asked hopefully.

"We can only guess," Tiresome shrugged, "but we can be prepared." He had a hopeful look about him too.

"Hadn't Cecil and Ratbag better get going right now?" Andrew asked, anxious to lose no time.

"Oh, not this very minute!" the nicker protested, "I have some particular business to attend to first."

"I'll bet!" Clumpface gave an almost humourless laugh, "you can't be going back to duke Harold's *again*! That'll be the sixth time, to my certain knowledge."

"Eighth," the nicker responded automatically, "he does have such an awful lot of stuff," he added, with a woebegone look, "and so heavy."

"You mean *had*," Cecil corrected him, "I'm surprised the man's got anything left if you've been there seven times already. But I don't mind waiting till you've finished. We'll probably travel safer by night anyway."

"Very good!" Orlando smiled even more broadly, relieved that the nicker's activities seemed to have been concentrated on the exiled duke. "I shall detail Amiens and Jacques, two of my best men, to go with you."

"*Who* did you say?" Andrew's voice twanged like an overstressed harp string.

"Amiens and Jacques," Orlando repeated, "Section-Leaders both of them. Excellent background, good schools, all that sort of thing. Of course Jacques is a bit of a joker..." Orlando's eyes narrowed as he considered the humorous Jacques for a moment. "Anyway," he concluded hastily, "they're both highly reliable chaps, I can assure you."

Andrew did not look totally convinced, though just of *what* he was not totally convinced was difficult to say. For a few moments more he stared at Orlando, mouthing the two names silently, then shook his head helplessly. "It doesn't matter," he sighed.

The next morning the sun shone brightly over Stembark Forest. It struck green-edged golden light into a little clearing where a very large hermit was cooking his breakfast over an open fire. Intermittently screened by a fluttering leafy canopy, it flickered on a very much smaller hermit not four hundred paces away affixing a notice to a tree. It splashed welcoming light about the dark entrance to a secluded grotto in which a Black Mage moved carefully about a mysterious and complex assembly of equipment, making final adjustments. And three leagues away it glinted off the polished horns of duke Harold's huntsmen.

Duke Harold was feeling cheerful that morning. For a start the weather seemed to have settled down-- doubtless thanks to that travelling magician. And for another thing, his chief huntsman had promised there would be good sport that day for had he not located the veritable emperor of the forest in the form of a huge stag whose antlers must spread more than twice the reach of a man's arms from tip to tip? The horns tootled hopefully, the hounds bayed mournfully and duke Harold and his toadies partook of a stirrup jug apiece.

"Hope we get some good sport at last, your grace," Bushy slurped the last of his drink, "those hounds have been demmed hopeless the last few days."

It was true, Harold reflected, that the hounds had seemed to be unbelievably ineffective recently, wandering aimlessly from tree to tree, running round in circles and, once or twice, rolling on their backs making shrill yapping sounds. "Can't think what's been getting into them" the duke agreed, "but Peel is sure we'll have a run today. We're riding further to the north, this time. Fresh ground." Bushy's reply was lost in the urgent yapping of horns and the yowling, hooting call of the hounds. Followed eagerly by the hunters, the hounds streamed off through the trees.

Two leagues away a large brown bear half-opened one of his eyes, gave a moody growl, and rolled over, shielding his face from the glare of daylight with a forepaw. Horace was not in a sunny mood. He was weary from walking many tens of leagues, he was stiff from sleeping outside and, if the truth be known, he was the slightest bit hung-over from the previous night he had spent at the Ferret and Drainpipe on the northern margin of the forest. Horace was sick and tired of this migrating business-- it never seemed to work out the way he planned it-- and he was seriously considering taking up hibernation instead. Over the morning air he heard the brazen note of a hunting horn and the excited baying of hounds. He growled ill-temperedly, rolled over once more, then clambered to his feet. Where there were hunting horns there were people, and where there were people there could be buns. Although, Horace admitted to himself as he wriggled his way through the undergrowth, the kind of people who blew hunting horns were probably pretty low-life and might not be too well equipped in the buns department.

The noises grew closer. Horace could hear the thudding of hooves above the yowling call of the hounds. He rose to his hind legs, and began to forge his way through the chest-high bracken. Quite suddenly he stopped dead and listened intently. Something large and heavy was smashing its way through the bracken towards him. He had hardly begun to react when, with a crash, a huge stag bounded into view. The animal staggered as it landed, then stood, swaying on its feet and its legs trembling. Its sides heaved as it fought for breath, and its eyes were dull with exhaustion and despair. Horace eyed the beast curiously. He didn't have an awful lot of time for deer, intellectually or gastronomically. He found them dull conversationalists and he didn't care for venison. At the same time he couldn't find it in himself to tell the beast to buzz off. He was about to mutter something like "nice day. Well, I must be getting along," when a huge dog burst through the undergrowth and launched itself at the stag. Horace didn't think twice, but swayed forward and clouted the creature hard on the side of its head, knocking it spinning through the air, back the way it had come. It gave a shrill yelp of surprise and outrage as it landed heavily on its back then, wriggling to its feet it scuttled off.

Horace growled angrily and stepped forward a pace, swinging his muzzle from side to side as he scanned the landscape for more trouble. He saw nothing, but the scent of dog and man was heavy on the air. And judging by the racket, there were a fair number of both species in the vicinity. He turned to the stag to seemed to have recovered his breath. "Lie down!" Horace gestured urgently with a paw, "lie down you great lummox" he repeated, "they'll see that hat-rack of your for miles!" He pushed hard at the stag's shoulder and at last the animal got the message, and obediently sank to its knees. Two more hounds burst into view, and Horace served them as he had the first, then a grey-coated human figure appeared and Horace abruptly dropped to the ground. The man carried a bow.

In his dealings with humans, Horace took great pains to assume an air of amiable dimness; since all humans were very insecure, it helped reassure them. And it didn't hurt the bun donation rate either. But that didn't mean he was just a thick ursine layabout. In fact he was a highly intelligent and cunning ursine layabout, and knew very well that there were times when even the largest bear had to lie doggo. He gave a warning growl out of the corner of his mouth at the stag, who was showing signs of restlessness. The animal froze.

"Peel! What on earth is the matter with these hounds of yours?" Flushed with the excitement of the chase, the duke was frantic at the thought of missing the climax of this thrilling adventure: watching the stag get torn to pieces by the hounds.

"I cannot understand it, your grace," the chief huntsman removed his hat and fanned his face with it, "they seem to have lost the scent."

"That one seems to have found something." Bagot pointed to half a couple of hounds which was making its ravening way forward in eager leaps. It disappeared. There was a loud yelp. It reappeared, spinning through the air, and landed with a thud at the little group's feet.

"There's something funny going on here" growled Peel, his face darkening with anger, "I'm going to take a look." He strode forward and began pushing his way through the thick undergrowth. One of the hounds watched curiously, from a prudent distance. Followed closely by the duke and the three toadies, the chief huntsman struggled forward, his knife drawn. There was a fearsome roar and, bursting from the ground like some long-buried monster, a huge brown bear rose up before them. For a fraction of a second the five men stood rooted to the ground in terror. Then, with the duke leading by a handsome two lengths, they fled. Another doom-laden roar pursued them.

Horace gave a snort of satisfaction. That had shown the miserable buggers! But he was too wily a bear to believe they'd gone for good. Soon they'd be back, and then they might remember to use their bows and arrows. He muzzled the stag in the ear, then jerked his paw energetically. With a snicker of understanding, the creature rose to his feet and trotted off. Horace was just about to follow when his sensitive nose registered a familiar smell. Very faint, it was, but unmistakeable. It was a smell that meant buns. And companionship. But mostly buns. Horace raised his nose, and sniffed very carefully. This time the smell was stronger, and the direction was clear. With the delicacy and precision of a cruise missile, Horace began lumbering through the forest in search of the smell.

"Well, I must say that went much better than expected!" Orlando rubbed his hands in satisfaction, "though I was concerned when they headed off north. I had never thought they'd go that way, but you chaps obviously had it all worked out." He made Janus an appreciative bow. The elf looked the slightest bit disconcerted.

"But *we* didn't prepare the northern route. At least, *I* didn't. Tiresome? Clumpface? Andrew?" All three shook their heads.

"How very odd!" Orlando scratched his head. "*Something* happened to their hounds."

"Perhaps they just had an off day," suggested Andrew, speaking with the authority of total ignorance, "or perhaps they're just not forest-rated for this area."

"Whatever the cause, we can be thankful for the result," Clumpface smiled, "now I should pay a visit to our good hermit and give him his instructions."

"You've got the notices?" Andrew asked.

"Yes. Here they are." The dwarf flourished a sheaf of lurid posters. *SPECIAL!!!* screamed the headline, *ONE WEEK ONLY!!!* In scarcely smaller type below, the reader was advised that Canon Chasuble was pleased to offer Hermit Services for all Occasions and that Special Rates were Available for Parties. A small sketch map showing the location of the hermit's cell was appended.

"Jolly good!"

"So I just stick these up anywhere?"

Along the Southern Ride first," Andrew told the dwarf, "and don't forget to tell Kodswallop that if he does run across the chap he's to advise delay."

"Yes, I understand." The dwarf peered at a bit of paper. "These things take time..."

"Right."

"Rome wasn't built in a day..."

"Yes."

"This isn't the right moment..."

"Good."

"And the omens are inauspicious." Clumpface carefully folded the scrap of paper and put it away for future reference.

"Brilliant!" Andrew slapped the dwarf on the back. "And don't forget that he's to try to persuade the two women to separate from the main party. And if they're nervous about travelling on their own he could suggest that one of them dress up as a man. And they could take the court jester along-- if there is one."

"I believe there is," Orlando interjected with a slight smile, "and from what I hear of him they may well decide the perils of the forest are a small price to pay for being free of his company."

"Oh. Well, do your best, Clumpface."

The dwarf mounted his horse and was just about to ride off when he cocked his head to one side. "Did you hear anything?" he asked after a moment's silence.

"Hear what?" Andrew asked.

Clumpface did not answer, but dismounted and raised his hand for silence. By now that was not necessary. Everybody was listening intently to a crashing, thudding noise as though something large and impetuous was making its way through the forest with no very great concern for the local flora. Orlando and Eric exchanged puzzled glances, and Eric reached for his bow. Orlando's glance changed from puzzled to plainly apprehensive, and he snatched at his assistant's weapon. Like a brown, furry main battle tank, Horace burst onto the scene.

"It's him!" Andrew shouted superfluously, "it's bloody Horace again!" and he tried to sidle away among the trees. But he was too late for, with a delighted growl, Horace shambled over, gave Andrew a friendly push on the shoulder with his muzzle, then stood back with an expectant look on his face.

"See! He's so happy to see you again!" Clumpface cried delightedly.

Andrew picked himself up. "And I'm overwhelmed." He scowled at the Horace, who gave a deep, rumbling growl, roughly interpretable as "how about some buns then?"

"So his name is Horace! We never knew!" Orlando walked towards the bear with a welcoming smile. In his outstretched hand he held a bun. Horace took it eagerly and gave a gracious bow, then focused a reproachful look upon Andrew as if to remind him that things had come to a pretty pass indeed when a respectable bear had to accept buns from strangers.

"So *that* explains what was wrong with the hounds!" Janus laughed, "Horace may turn out to be useful."

"He'd better not try," muttered Andrew; he was having enough trouble with *As You Like It* and *A Midsummer Night's Dream* without complicating matters still further with *The Winter's Tale*[10]

"He certainly will!" Orlando showed his teeth in a victorious grin, "that exiled duke is using his cave. He's not going to take kindly to that."

"You can't let him go back there!" Clumpface looked horrified, "those men are poltroons, it is true, but they are many poltroons, and they've got bows and arrows. He'd better stay with us for the time being."

A flicker of disappointment passed over the outlaw leader's face, but only for a moment. "Of course. Clumpface, if you will lead him--" he broke off at the sound of urgently thudding hoofbeats. "Now what?"

---

10   A play with which, aside from the stage direction Exit pursued by bear Andrew
       was completely unfamiliar

A horse burst into view, going like the clappers. The rider saw the group only at the last moment, pulled up his horse violently and half-jumped, half-fell from the saddle. His face was grey, his eyes rolled horridly in their sockets and his hands shook as from the ague.

"I say, is everything alright?" Orlando asked solicitously, "it's... er--"

"Hooper, Mr Orlando, Senior Outlaw," Eric whispered.

"Of course, Hooper! Well, how are you, my man?"

Hooper gulped noisily, then shivered. "Mr Orlando," he began, almost stammering, "I should report that which I say I saw, but know not how to do it."

"If he's going to tell us that he thought he saw the wood begin to move..." Andrew muttered darkly.

"Come along, my good fellow," Orlando encouraged the man, "don't worry about the formalities. What's up?"

The fellow seemed incapable of coherent speech. He waved his arms frantically about, gasping as he did so. Clumpface offered a flask. Hooper stopped gasping, and took a long pull. "It's the boating lake, Mr Orlando," he choked, lowering the bottle, "it's-- it's--" his eyes widened in horror at the recollection, "it's gone *mad!*"

Act IX
A TEMPEST

The wind shrieked and howled like a thousand demons from Hell. Heaping grey-green waves exploded into thunderous clouds of spray on black fanged rocks. A seething mass of foam hissed across a steep shingly beach.

"I don't think anyone will be wanting to take a boat out in weather like this." Eric shook his head sadly.

"This is...? What...?" Orlando's jaw dropped. He turned to Andrew. "Did you have anything to do with this?" he demanded.

They were standing at the end of a neatly raked gravel path that wound through the trees back to Ye Olde Souvenir Market Glade. At regular intervals were litter baskets, park benches and little signposts reading *To The Boating Lake*. At the end of the path there should have been a landing stage and a boathouse, not a raging tempest. "Did you have anything to do with this?" Orlando repeated.

"Of course not!" Andrew snapped, "I've never been here before." He stared at the tempestuous seascape, then took a tentative step forward. As he did so he felt his staff quiver in his hand. A faint halo of violet light flickered around the crystal. He stared at it nervously.

"It's an illusion spell!" Clumpface bustled forward with a look of relief on his craggy features, "just walk forward."

"Walk forward? Into *that*?" Andrew gestured at the raging storm.

"It's an occult-generated simulation," the dwarf explained, "it can't affect you."

"What do you mean, it can't affect me. It is affecting me. I can see it and I don't want to go out in it."

"Just walk forward," Clumpface repeated patiently, "and everybody else follow Andrew closely."

Reluctantly, Andrew took a couple of paces forward. The staff quivered more violently, and the air itself seemed to quiver and twist for a moment. The violet glow around the top of the staff grew brighter. Encouraged by this, Andrew took another few paces and, with an eerie suddenness, a boathouse and long wooden jetty popped into view, with a line of freshly varnished rowing boats each with a white number painted on its prow. Beyond the end of the jetty the storm still raged wildly, the howling of the wind a surreal contrast with the quiet lapping of the water against the moored boats.

"Phew! That's some maging!" Orlando gave Andrew an admiring look.

"Nothing to do with me," Andrew mumbled.

"And it's all an illusion?" Orlando eyed the rampaging waves warily.

"Yes. And a very extensive one," Clumpface confirmed, "and it's interactive too. Never seen anything this big *and* interactive."

"What does 'interactive' mean?" Andrew asked suspiciously. Before Clumpface could answer, Eric gave a loud triumphant laugh.

"All an illusion! Just a mirage, eh?" He stepped smartly forward, into the storm.

"I wouldn't advise that--" Clumpface began, but his warning was too late. Unprepared for the onslaught of the wind, Eric swayed dangerously, stumbled, and as he measured his length on the beach a huge wave crashed down with a hollow *boom!* enveloping him in a cloud of spray.

"*That* is what 'interactive' means." The dwarf pointed to the soaked figure.

"It's a prodigious display, even for Montmorency," mused Janus, "but what's it for?"

"Oh, I know *that*." Andrew was beginning to feel in control of the situation once more. "He's using *The Tempest*."

"I can see it's a tempest" the elf agreed, "but I still don't understand *why*."

"No, I mean from the play *The Tempest*," Andrew explained, "and..." he paused as he gave more thought to the play "...of course!" He grabbed Orlando's arm. "Is there an island out there?" he demanded, waving at the violent seascape.

"There *was*," the outlaw chief confirmed cautiously, "quite a pretty one, actually. With a tea room, and a rather nice maze. And swans."

"Right then! That's where he's got to be!"

"Who?"

"Montmorency, of course. You see, in the play all the action takes place on this enchanted island which is under the control of a magician. In fact everything starts with a storm raised by the magician; Montmorency's got to be there."

"So you're going to have a word with him?" Orlando looked hopeful once more.

"Er..."

"There are lots of boats," Eric pointed out helpfully.

Andrew made a vague gesture in the direction of the storm in the hope that Janus or Clumpface would insist that rowing out into a hurricane (even an illusory one) to confront a Senior Level Black Mage was a most imprudent action.

"We should go at once," Tiresome observed, with treacherous enthusiasm.

"Right now?"

"Certainly."

"If you are going, it'll be without me." Clumpface shouldered his pack and made to leave. Andrew felt a surge of hope. If that wise and experienced dwarf were opposed to the venture, then neither Tiresome nor Janus would support it. But his hopes were dashed as Clumpface continued, "I must take Horace back to the Headquarters Glade, then

I have to get these posters up for Kodswallop. But the rest of you go ahead."

"Er... right."

The dwarf gave them all a casual wave then, whistling cheerfully, stumped back along the gravel path.

"You are going to the island?" Eric asked hesitantly.

"Thinking about it," mumbled Andrew

"Of course we're going to the island." Tiresome clambered into the first boat and started fiddling with the painter.

"Well, they're half a crown an hour, and there's a five shilling deposit," Eric informed them.

"Eric! This is scarcely the time to be so particular!" Orlando looked at once shocked by the untimeliness of his assistant's suggestion and proud of the dedication to duty that lay behind it. "Under the circumstances we should certainly waive the deposit."

Andrew recognised there was no help for it. Already Janus was climbing aboard, and Tiresome had untied the painter and was holding the boat to the jetty in readiness to push off. "Where exactly is this island?" he asked.

"Over there." Orlando waved his arm through about a hundred degrees.

"North west of this point," Eric elaborated, "perhaps half a league."

"We'll take a quick look then," Andrew told them with no very great confidence, and climbed aboard.

"Good luck!" Orlando called out uncertainly, and Tiresome pushed off.

It was an eerie, unsettling feeling. Apart from some slight jerking and rolling caused by the knight's less than expert oarsmanship the little boat moved smoothly across the water, yet around them raged foaming mountains that would have overwhelmed anything smaller than a battleship. They sat in the centre of a calm twenty-foot diameter circle of water, ruffled into little wavelets by some breeze they could not detect. The plash and chatter of the water under the bows formed an unreal counterpoint to the shriek of the wind and the hissing of the giant waves. Andrew sat in the sternsheets, his staff firmly held between his knees, and with one hand on a thwart instinctively bracing himself against a lurch or plunge by the boat that never came. The conflict between what his eyes saw and his eustachian tubes registered was making him feel queasy. He concentrated on staring past Tiresome at Janus in the eyes of the boat. Minutes passed and, to the creak of rowlocks and the burble of water past the planking, the little circle of normality crept forward. Eventually Janus waved his hand. "I think I see it!"

Andrew gritted his teeth, and peered forward. Janus was right. Between the rolling hills of water he caught intermittent glimpses of jagged rocks upon which gigantic waves exploded, sending sheets of spray leaping high into the air, to be shredded by the wild wind. Even though Andrew kept on explaining to himself that it was simply a very clever kind of illusion, it was still very difficult not to shout to Tiresome and tell him to turn the boat about and head back. He concentrated on the small patch of rippling water in front of the boat's prow, and started counting Tiresome's strokes. On the fifteenth the seething mass of foam popped out of existence. A mossy bank appeared, sloping gently down to the still water, and overhung by a willow whose dangling branches brushed inconveniently over the boat. Tiresome backed water clumsily and there was a hollow grating thud as the bows slid into, then over a submerged root. Pivoting on this obstruction, the boat swung round slowly until it was broadside to the shore.

Janus made fast the painter and they stepped ashore. At their backs the storm screamed crazily, but before them was sun-dappled grass and a small white painted bungalow with a verandah upon which were arranged some wickerwork chairs and a small table. Black shutters gaped open, but the blank-faced windows they exposed gave no hint of the interior.

"Nice little place he's got here," Andrew grunted as he led the way forward, "I suppose it is Montmorency's?"

"There is little doubt of that," Janus answered with a smile, and pointed to a highly polished brass plate that twinkled on the door.

"Montmorency and Associates. Occult Consulting Services," Andrew read aloud, "he certainly doesn't seem to be worrying about security, does he?"

"Why should he?" Tiresome asked, "what is there to be secure about? You know he's here, and he knows you're here, and he knows you know he knows you're here."

"Er... yes." Andrew decided not to bother trying to sort that one out. He looked at the door. It stayed closed. He gave it a sharp rap with his knuckles. It still stayed closed. He poked the door knob with his staff and, when this failed to trigger any violent reaction, he reached out and gave the knob a firm twist. The lock clicked back and the door swung open. "You two had better wait outside," he said over his shoulder, as he crossed the threshold, "we don't want both of you turned into newts."

"Montmorency wouldn't do anything like that," Tiresome protested, "he's scrupulous about observing the *Unified Code*."

"Oh, alright." Andrew shrugged and led them into the hall, knocking over a brass umbrella stand with a clatter that made them all jump.

"*Definitely* no-one at home," Tiresome observed, as the echoes died away. "Through there, do you think?" He nodded at a door on the right which was open just wide enough to spill a long sliver of light across the tiled floor. Andrew gave it a careful prod with his staff. It swung open without a sound, and they all froze for a moment, anticipating some kind of inhospitable response from an irate black mage. But the silence that flowed through the open doorway was the silence of an unoccupied room, not the silence of a highly expert practitioner of the Black Arts preparing a discouraging reception for some uninvited guests. Even so, Andrew found himself walking on tiptoe as he entered.

It was large for a study, but not large enough for a library. Two walls were lined with bookcases, upon which rank upon rank of leather-bound volumes, gloomy with ponderous menace, stood silent guard. Two high-backed armchairs were drawn up before a stone fireplace. On the mantelpiece above was a battle-scarred leather tome bearing the title *Proceedings of the Two Hundred and Twenty-Fifth Annual Conference of the Guild of the Black Mages*. And on the wall above these a small yellow cuckoo clock ticked busily. To the right of the fireplace hung a dartboard with a small picture of Mage Ponsonby, Guildmaster of the Black Mages, pasted over the double nineteen.

"Cosy little place." Andrew eyed the dartboard, relieved that it wasn't his picture stuck over the double nineteen. He looked around to see if Montmorency had happened to leave any darts lying about the place. "Where do you suppose he can be?" he asked the room at large.

"Aah!" Tiresome took a couple of paces towards the window and gave a sigh of satisfaction. "Now *here* you may have a challenge worthy of your talents, Andrew."

Andrew winced. Whenever anybody made a statement like that he was seized by the panic an incompetent amateur conjuror feels when, before an audience of hundreds, he is handed a perfectly ordinary, empty top hat and asked to produce a rabbit from it. "Er... yes?" He tried to make out what it was that had the others so worked up. Through the window all he could see was the grass, the trees waving slightly in the breeze, and beyond that, like some vast back-projection of unprecedented realism, the tossing waves of the illusory storm. "I don't... er... quite..." he began again. Then he saw it.

It was on a low table, hard against the wall just below the central window. It was some kind of... Andrew stretched his brain to think of a word, and finally came up with "device". It was something that might have been the offspring of a perverse mating between Babbage's difference engine and one of the more imaginative pieces of equipment from a Dr *Who* episode. Tiny gear wheels spun busily, cranks whirled and connecting rods shot back and forth. And a row of hexagonal crystals twinkled and blinked, sending darts of light along the translucent filaments that linked them. At once Andrew realized that this was no common or garden piece of Sproggit and Axel equipment. For one thing, it appeared to be working-- or at least performing consistently. He stared at it, mesmerised by its busy complexity, then turned to Janus. "Have you any idea what this is?"

"Haven't the foggiest," the elf answered cheerfully.

Andrew looked at Tiresome, who shrugged helplessly. "Haven't a clue, either. But it's a pretty safe bet that it must have something to do with *that* out there." The knight gestured through the window at the raging seas.

Andrew leant forward to examine the thing more closely and as he did so felt his staff begin to tremble slightly. He stepped back quickly and the vibration stopped. "The staff is doing something again," he muttered, edging the instrument forward once more. The staff vibrated like a tuning fork, a faint violet glow of Heron-Gough discharge appeared at its tip and there was a slight brown smell of hot insulation. Andrew jerked the staff back and eyed the machine anxiously. It whirled away, seemingly unperturbed.

"Do you think this might be what you're looking for?" asked Janus, pointing under the table at a small highly polished block of ebony. In the centre of the block was a prominent red button, bearing the unambiguous label: *OFF.*

"Like hell!" Andrew recoiled, "Montmorency can't think I'm as big a twit as all that! Pushing the 'off' button indeed!"

"Couldn't it be a double bluff?" Tiresome suggested unhelpfully, "by which I mean that it really *is* the 'off' switch but that he will count on you not believing it because it is labelled so clearly."

"Perhaps Montmorency is counting on him making that deduction," Janus pointed out, "and has merely put the button there as a trap."

"That is possible," Tiresome allowed, "but then he could well believe that Andrew would arrive at that conclusion and not push the button, thus achieving his objective of deterring Andrew from switching the machine off. It is, I admit, a devious line of reasoning, but all mages are a bit like that I understand."

"Stop it, both of you!" Andrew cried, before Janus could carry the endless series of bluff and counter-bluff yet another step, "I'm not pushing the bloody button."

"What are you going to do?"

"I think I'll give the whole issue a bloody good poke with this." Andrew shook his staff. "Or perhaps I'd better just blast it from a safe distance." He drew back a pace and levelled the staff. "You two had better wait outside in case anything violent happens," he added. While Andrew knew that he was more or less immune to any kind of nastiness Montmorency might have set in place for fiddlers-about with the equipment, his friends were not. Reluctantly they moved to the door as Andrew advanced his staff towards the enigmatic device. The staff tingled violently and a violet corona appeared about its tip. The humming of the little mechanisms rose in pitch and the flashes of light from the crystals took on a reddish tinge. Once again the brown smell of hot insulation wafted across the room. Definitely, Andrew decided, a bolt of destructor beam energy from a healthy distance was indicated. He was about to lower the staff and move back when a cry from Janus halted him.

"Andrew! Don't move!"

"What do you mean, 'don't move'?" Andrew snapped, "this thing looks as though it's going to burst into flames at any moment."

"It's doing something to the storm, see for yourself!" The elf pointed to the window. "Don't move the staff!" he warned as Andrew looked up and the instrument wavered in his hand.

With some effort, Andrew maintained the staff in its original position, the tip not more than a foot from the chattering and flashing mechanisms. Then he slowly and carefully raised his head to take a look.

The raging storm *had* disappeared replaced by a translucent screen of mist. Even as he watched, it seemed to ripple slightly, and for a brief moment he caught a glimpse of a sheet of blue water, patched with darker blue by the wind. Then it was gone.

"I must take a closer look at this!" Tiresome bounded from the room.

"Watch it, Tiresome!" Janus called after him.

Andrew braced a forearm against his thigh in an attempt to keep the stick steady. The machine seemed to have settled down a bit and the smell of overheating components had dissipated, but the crystals still flickered with an angry redness. Whatever it was he was doing, the machine was not happy about it.

With a crash Tiresome erupted back into the room. "You've done it!" he shouted, "the storm's gone!"

"Gone?" Andrew echoed disbelievingly, "well what's all that out there, then?"

"Well, perhaps not quite gone," the knight allowed grudgingly, "but very much changed. It has changed into some kind of curtain, only about a hand's breadth deep."

"You mean the illusion has been concentrated?" Janus asked.

"Yes. And it's still interactive. I put my arm through it-- look." Tiresome held out his right arm to show the sleeve of his jerkin dark and sodden with water.

"Excellent!" Janus chuckled, "are you going to disable the illusion completely?" he asked Andrew.

"You mean by poking at this thing with my staff?"

"That would seem to be the way to handle it."

"I don't know..." Andrew gazed through the window at the rippling translucent curtain of highly compressed illusion, then eased his staff back. The effect was immediate-- the slightly laboured hum of the machinery dropped back to an almost inaudible whisper, and the raging seascape leaped into existence. Andrew moved the staff forward again: the storm disappeared.

"A little further forward should do it," Janus encouraged him.

"No... I don't think I want to do that..." Andrew moved his staff back and forth a couple more times, noting that the transition was not instantaneous, therefore there must be a position of his staff which would ensure that the storm reached only halfway from the island to the shore. He lowered the staff, letting the storm reassert itself, then turned to his colleagues. "We aren't going to switch this thing off," he told them firmly, "we're going to use it."

"Use it!" Tiresome expostulated, "but how? Why?"

"I'll explain later." Andrew almost skipped across the room in his delight. Prospero wasn't a part he'd ever hankered after, but he did know *The Tempest* well enough to get by-- a few minutes with the book would be all he would need to refresh his memory. "We'll get back now-- I'm going to want to get a message to Kodswallop." Moving at a brisk trot, he led the way from Montmorency's house.

"What message?" asked Janus, chasing after him.

"I want him to persuade the usurping duke to take his whole party for a nice boat trip on the lake," Andrew told him with a triumphant smile.

The following morning Kodswallop was up before the sun. He ate a hurried breakfast, then strode off through the trees, with extra copies of the posters Clumpface had delivered the night before tucked under his arm. It wouldn't hurt to stick a few more up. Soon he reached the Southern Ride and headed down it, stopping every hundred paces or so to nail another poster to a tree. He had just stepped back a few paces from the tenth one, and was eying it narrowly to ensure it was straight, when he caught sight of a flash of colour just at the edge of his field of vision. He turned to look, and his face wrinkled into a puzzled frown as he saw it to be another poster. He strolled over to take a look.

FLEET THE TIME CARELESSLY IN THE GOLDEN WORLD! he was encouraged, *Feast and roister in the glades of Stembark Forest! Hunt with the hounds in the morning and in the evenings, as the shadows lengthen, relax to the music of Clarence Snout and his Arboreal Arcadians.*

Kodswallop's puzzled frown deepened. Andrew had told him to expect notices on trees, he didn't think this was what the mage had in mind. He tore the offending poster down and was about to crumple it into a ball, when his eye was caught by a line of small print at the bottom. *Outlaws are Optional*, it said. The big fighter scowled angrily, folded the offending document and put it away. Don Orlando should see this, he decided. Kodswallop started off once more. He would walk perhaps half a league along the Southern Ride in the hope of seeing some signs of the usurping duke and his party, then he'd get back to his camp and see about lunch. Whistling tunelessly to himself he strolled along the broad avenue, looking keenly from side to side for any signs of the mysterious bill-poster. A flicker of movement between the trees caught his eye, and he stopped abruptly.

Kodswallop's first instinct was to draw his sword, but then he realised that the fearsome weapon, presently concealed beneath the enveloping folds of his habit, would not go too well with his role as the well-known hermit, Canon Chasuble. Instead he took a firm grip of the stout cudgel he bore-- a six foot length of gnarled tree trunk-- and drifted noiselessly into the undergrowth. A human flitted into view and Kodswallop relaxed a little for it was obvious that whoever it was, he was not moving with aggressive intent. The fighter waited and watched until the man was a scant twenty paces away, and then nearly dropped his tree trunk in surprise. This was no outlaw, nor any member of the usurping duke's party! The man wore a coarse-woven brown habit-- not unlike that which adorned Kodswallop's own shoulders-- and open-toed sandals which undoubtedly accounted for the fellow's very tentative progress through the brambles. Kodswallop felt a stab of gratification that he had insisted on wearing his own stout boots, rather than such footwear, despite Cecil's protests that such things were *de rigueur* in the hermitting business. It was an extraordinary coincidence, Kodswallop told himself, to run into a *real* hermit. He'd have to watch his step, or his imposture might be detected. Perhaps it would be better to stay hidden, and let the fellow go on his way? No, he decided, this was a chance he couldn't miss. "Oi!" he said, and stepped out of the bushes.

Bellingham nearly fainted. The day had started out badly, and was getting worse by the minute. The shelter of brushwood he'd constructed the night before had suffered an untimely structural failure in the early hours of the morning when some large nocturnal prowling creature had barged into it. He had promptly taken refuge in the upper branches of a holly tree, from which he had emerged at dawn, stiff, scratched and demoralised. His attempts to light a fire by conventional means had been a miserable failure and the generic spell he had tried as an alternative had burned a six foot crater in the ground and badly singed his eyebrows-- Sproggit and Axel were going to get a stiff letter about *that*, he promised himself. And now, as he stumbled footsore and weary through this impenetrable jungle, he was accosted by some huge bandit, undoubtedly with violent intent. He was on the point of gasping out one of his protective spells when he realised with relief that this man's intentions did not seem hostile at all-- rather the reverse; the man was a hermit! It was just like Montmorency to lull him into a sense of false security, he told himself bitterly, and he should have known better than to take at face value the mage's assurances that there were virtually no independent hermits in business these days. But Bellingham was confident he would be able to rise to the challenge-- he'd just have to watch what he said in front of this fellow. "Good day, brother, and God be with you," he stammered. "The gods that is," he amended rapidly to cover all eventualities.

"Oh, aye, yes." Kodswallop was nonplussed for a moment. How was *he* expected to respond? Did hermits have secret passwords and countersigns? Special handshakes? The fighter gave a mental shrug; if he just watched what he said it'd be unlikely the fellow would suspect anything, and he *did* have an unworldly look about him. "Grand morning, isn't it?" he suggested with a proprietorial air.

"Er... yes. Quite so." There was a silence as each tried to think of what to say next. Kodswallop decided first.

"Just passing through are you? On a bit of a pilgrimage, like?"

"Not exactly, brother. As a matter of fact I've-- er-- just set up in business around here, so to speak," Bellingham concluded with a nervous smile.

"You have, have you? Well there's a coincidence!" A sociable fellow, Kodswallop was happy at the prospect of having a neighbour, but at the same time he had the uneasy feeling that when that neighbour was a professional hermit-- and potential competition, he reminded himself-- the possibilities for complication were unpleasantly high.

"Coincidence?" Bellingham chirped.

"Indeed yes!" Kodswallop beamed encouragingly. "I'm setting up in the hermitting business around here as well."

Bellingham choked back a gasp. As if his job were not difficult enough already, without a legitimate hermit in close proximity! Now there was an unpleasantly high probability of being unmasked as a spurious hermit-- to say nothing of the competition for customers. He comforted himself with the thought that a sleep spell could, in extremity, be used more or less continuously to keep this hermit out of the picture. Cheered by this, he stepped forward with some confidence, hand outstretched. "A happy coincidence, brother," he observed, "pray let me introduce myself. Canon Chasuble." He shook Kodswallop warmly by the hand and gave him a business card.

"Chasuble!" Kodswallop rocked on his feet. Canon Chasuble, he had been led to believe, was a character from Earth Three. Either a very remarkable coincidence had occurred, or this hermit was not all that he should be. Although Kodswallop habitually affected an air of amiable buffoonery, in fact he had a quick and incisive mind as well as a talent for low cunning. With the role of Canon Chasuble no longer available, he had to concoct some other *nom d'hermitage*. "Delighted to meet you, Canon Chasuble. And my name is Immaterial," he invented quickly then, struck by a happy inspiration added, "that is Don Pedro d'y Angina Immaterial."

Bellingham felt a flood of relief-- from his name it seemed highly likely this man was a foreigner and as such would be unfamiliar with the hermitting conventions of Albion. "May I take it that you are a stranger to our shores?" he suggested cautiously.

"Caramba yes!" Kodswallop exclaimed, happily conscious of the fact that any anomalies in his behaviour as a hermit could be explained by his foreign origins.

"I fear you will find business opportunities sadly restricted in Albion," Bellingham warned him, "what with the Sublime Tabernacle of the Redeemer in the South and the Ineffable Tabernacle of the Redeemer in the North, it is getting harder and harder for the small businessman-- you just can't compete with the big chains, you know."

"Aye... but if you offer a specialist service..." Kodswallop suggested.

"Exactly!" Bellingham hastened to agree.

"Customized hermitting," Kodswallop continued, warming to his theme, "specialisation. It's the way of the future, you take it from me."

"What is your area, exactly?" Bellingham asked with growing confidence.

"Persuading." Kodswallop answered automatically, "that is I do a special line in dynamic prediction and analysis."

"Much demand for that sort of thing in... er... wherever it is you came from?" Bellingham asked with elaborate casualness.

"Sapristi yes!" Kodswallop told him uninformatively, desperately trying to imagine which country Don Pedro d'y Angina Immaterial might call home. "And you," he continued, changing the subject, "do you have any special line of hermitting?"

"I... ah... provide consulting services for new businesses," Bellingham waved an arm in an all-encompassing gesture, "and... ah..." he hesitated further, blushing as he remembered Montmorency's instructions, "and... ah... advice and career planning for young ladies."

"You sly rogue!" Kodswallop gave a knowing leer and dug his elbow into Bellingham's ribs, "say no more!"

Blushing even more furiously, Bellingham staggered under the impact. "It is nothing of that nature, brother, I assure you!"

"Of course, brother!" Kodswallop assumed a contrite expression, "merely my little joke."

"Ha! Ha!" Bellingham responded dutifully, but his heart wasn't in it.

"Well, I mustn't delay you any longer, brother...er... Chasuble." Kodswallop withdrew a pace, and paused. "My cell isn't far from here-- you must come over for a drink some time."

"That is most kind--" Bellingham began, but Kodswallop interrupted.

"And if you come across anyone who needs anything in the way of dynamic prediction, just mention Don Pedro--"

"Don Pedro d'y Angina Immaterial," Bellingham concluded for him, "I will indeed. Fare you well."

"Fare *you* well, brother Chasuble." Kodswallop made a bow that a more acute observer than Bellingham would have detected as unequivocally ironic, then strode off rapidly. With a sigh of relief, Bellingham began to make his way in the opposite direction.

Kodswallop was in something of a hurry. For a start he had to pull down all *his* Canon Chasuble posters before the other Canon Chasuble found them. There was something very fishy indeed about that fellow, he mused as he paused at every tenth tree to remove Ratbag's elegantly lettered testaments to the readiness of Canon Chasuble to carry out any kind of hermitting activity on an hourly, daily or weekly basis. Kodswallop didn't know much about hermits, but he was prepared to eat his boots if the lad he'd met that morning was the genuine article. Canon Chasuble, indeed! Kodswallop snorted to himself. The man was as convincing as a politician, probably as honest as a lawyer, and was certainly up to no good. He would have to get back to the Headquarters Glade as soon as possible to warn the others of this newly arrived imposter. And give Don Orlando that poster with the curious annotation, *outlaws are optional.*

To his very great surprise, Kodswallop found Clumpface waiting for him at his camp when he returned. "Where have you been?" The dwarf asked anxiously, "I've been here since just after dawn."

"Just doing a bit of hermitting to get into the way of it. You'll never believe this, but there's *another* Canon Chasuble in the forest."

"Never mind that for the moment," Clumpface waved the news aside, "we have some different advice for you to give the usurping-- *what?*"

"Another Canon Chasuble," Kodswallop repeated calmly, "a bit odd that is, if you ask me."

"A bit odd? It should be impossible! But how did you find out?"

"I met him, didn't I? Said he was setting up in business here specialising in consulting services and career advice to young ladies." Kodswallop snorted with disgust.

"You're sure he wasn't a genuine hermit?"

"Nah!"

"How can you be so sure?"

"He gave me this." Kodswallop held out the business card. Clumpface scrutinised it suspiciously.

"How does that prove he's a wrong 'un?" the dwarf asked, "all it says is *Canon Chasuble, Purveyor of Executive Hermit Services. Corporate Rates Available.* What's so special about that?"

"Look at the back of it."

Clumpface turned it over and squinted at the microscopic print. *"PrintMaster 3.1 by Sproggit* and Axel," he read aloud slowly. His features hardened into a grim stare. "And we all know what that means."

Kodswallop nodded soberly. "Only a mage uses Sproggit and Axel stuff." Ever since he'd read the small print and realized he'd been in close contact with an occult professional, he'd been feeling a little pensive. "But it can't have been Montmorency," he pointed out, "probably just some understrapper."

"But a mage all the same. We'll have to get Andrew to deal with this. And now."

"The first thing we have to do," Kodswallop corrected him, "is take down all of *our* Canon Chasuble posters before that imposter sees them."

"Right!" The dwarf jumped to his feet.

"Then," Kodswallop continued, "I'll stay around here and keep an eye out for this duke Roger while you get Andrew."

"Is that a good idea?" Clumpface was plainly dubious.

"I can keep out of the other fellow's way," Kodswallop assured him, "and I might just get the chance to do a quick bit of persuading on the duke."

"Wait!" Clumpface grabbed at Kodswallop's arm, "Andrew says to knock off the persuading."

"Knock it off?"

"Yes. What you should try to do is convince the whole party to go for a boat trip."

"A boat trip?" Kodswallop looked puzzled. "Where? Why?"

"It's part of a new scheme Andrew's just worked out," the dwarf explained with a chuckle, "seemingly Montmorency is about to be hoist by his own petard. Here's a map."

"What's a petard?" Kodswallop asked, taking the map. Clumpface shrugged. "Just something people get hoist by, I suppose. If they've got one, that is."

"Pretty bloody silly to keep one about the place if all you do is get hoist by it," Kodswallop pointed out.

"It must be more technical than that," the dwarf said knowingly. He rose to leave, then stopped, struck by one last thought. "Are you *sure* this Chasuble imposter didn't suspect you?"

"Absolutely. He's convinced I'm a genuine hermit."

"How can you be so sure?"

"Ah! That's where I had this idea..." Kodswallop gave a big broad happy smile.

"What idea?" Clumpface wasn't smiling.

"Well, obviously I couldn't be sure that I'd look the part of a real local hermit-- I just don't know enough about the hermitting business. But a foreign hermit..."

"A foreign hermit?" Clumpface's voice had the quivering calm of one braced to receive terrible news.

"A foreign hermit," Kodswallop confirmed triumphantly, "you see, Clumpface, your actual foreign hermit is different from the home-grown Albion variety and so if he does not in all respects conform to your picture of the typical hermit then you put that down to him being a foreign gentleman and not knowing any better. And if he should use the odd foreign phrase every now and again--"

"Like 'caramba'?" Clumpface asked through his teeth.

"You guessed it!"

"I see." Clumpface's teeth remained clenched, though the corners of his mouth appeared to be twitching. "And the name you used was...?"

"Don Pedro d'y Angina Immaterial!" The big fighter gave another triumphant beaming smile.

Act X
ENTER A HERMIT

Kodswallop's shelter looked more a field headquarters than a hermit's retreat. Outlaws stood guard at the approaches to the little clearing and at a hastily erected trestle table covered with maps sat Orlando and Eric, the latter with a handful of coloured pencils ready for action. Tiresome and Janus looked on, the former with the eager interest of the professional soldier. Andrew, Clumpface and Kodswallop were seated a little apart arguing among themselves about the pseudonymous Canon Chasuble.

"According to the latest reports, Duke Roger's party has reached here." Orlando tapped the map with a swagger stick, then exchanged the stick for a red pencil and marked the spot with a neat cross. "From here," he continued, "he can only travel this way along the Southern Ride, or retrace his steps." He took an orange pencil from Eric and marked in a dotted line.

"You are certain of his position?" Tiresome asked.

"I have better than sixty men on woodcutter duty in this part of the forest," Orlando replied confidently, "this usurping duke has but to change his underwear and I shall hear of it... Well perhaps not the underwear," he admitted, "but just about everything else."

"Have they seen anything of a hermit?" Andrew asked from behind Tiresome's left elbow.

"I regret, no." Orlando took a blue pencil from Eric and printed "hermit?" next to the red cross. "Do you wish the man apprehended should he be discovered?"

"That might not be a good idea." Andrew shook his head. The outlaw chief looked rather disappointed-- he was relishing the role of front-line commander and looking for more decisive actions to take. "We don't think anyone should tangle with him," Andrew explained, "because it seems he might possibly be something of a mage."

"A mage!"

"Don't think he was much cop myself," Kodswallop joined them, "that is to say he didn't seem the aggressive type. Quite harmless really. But you never can tell. That's why we thought Andrew should come along."

"Clash of the Mages!" An anticipatory commercial smile flitted across Orlando's face, "you don't think you could hold it off till tomorrow do you? I have a big party booked--"

"No." Andrew interrupted quickly. "There's going to be no clash of the mages if I can help it. With a bit of luck we won't even see the bloke. Do you have those coupons for the boating lake?" Orlando handed over half a dozen bright coloured scraps of parchment, each one entitling the bearer to three hours' use of a rowing boat plus free admission to the Enchanted Island. Andrew glanced at them, then handed them over to Kodswallop. "You know what you have to do?"

"Tell him I know what his quest is," Kodswallop began to tick the points off on his fingers, "tell him it's fraught with peril, that the omens are inauspicious but that if he perseveres he will achieve his dearest wish. Then I give him the coupons and tell him that what he seeks lies on the Enchanted Island. And then I look mysterious."

"Good." Andrew nodded. "And then?"

"Then I tell him I have important advice for his daughter and niece. And I tell *them* that the Enchanted Island can be a bit dodgy for young beautiful girls and that one of them might consider disguising herself as a man--" Kodswallop broke off, his face reddening. "Sounds a bit... er... dubious, that does," he demurred, "are you sure about it?"

"Don Pedro d'y Angina Immaterial would find nothing dubious about it, I can assure you," Andrew informed him with a trace of malice.

"What if the duke asks *me* what his quest is?"

"Look mysterious and tap the side of your nose-- like this." Andrew demonstrated.

"What if he says they've already had their hermitting for the day?"

"Persuade him he wants some more."

"Aah!" For the first time Kodswallop smiled-- that was more like it!

"Remember Kodswallop-- be careful!"

The big fighter got up to leave. "Don't worry about me," he called over his shoulder, "just make sure you keep an eye out for that imposter Chasuble." He reached the edge of the clearing, turned and waved briefly, then disappeared among the trees.

"We should get going after him now." Andrew began to pace anxiously, in truth seriously worried about the hazard his friend might be facing.

"I don't think that'll be necessary." Tiresome jerked a thumb in the direction of the green-clad figures moving silently after the big fighter, "Kodswallop will be well guarded. "I have never seen men move so silently in country like this," he added in admiring tones. Orlando flushed with pleasure at the compliment.

"Well, we do place a lot of emphasis on fieldcraft in the outlaw business."

Eric gazed longingly after the men as they disappeared from view. "Mr Orlando! Section Leader Bert is short two men-- couldn't I go with him?"

"Sorry Eric, but I need you here." Orlando shook a finger. "Remember, there's a lot more to the outlawing business than scampering through the forest and shooting off arrows." Disconsolate, Eric wandered over to the far side of the clearing and stood staring into the depths of the forest.

"Surely you can spare the lad for a while?" Tiresome said in a low voice. He was touched by Eric's obvious disappointment, and admired his keenness.

"Yes, but the problem is he can't shoot for toffee," Orlando explained softly, "great disappointment to him of course, but I can't allow him on operations-- wouldn't be fair to the other men. Besides as an assistant he's indispensable; the whole organisation would go to pieces if I didn't have him around."

"Pity." Tiresome thought for a moment. "Would you mind if I borrowed him for a few hours?"

"Borrowed? What for?"

"We shall be patrolling the other side of the Southern Ride in search of the mage Kodswallop met. It would be a great help if we could have someone with us who knows the forest well, and can move silently through it."

"Eric can certainly do that-- and I know he would be delighted to accompany you. Just make sure, for your own safety, that he does not bring his bow and arrows with him."

If anything, Orlando had underestimated Eric's enthusiasm, for the young man's face shone like the sunrise at Tiresome's invitation. "I shall be with you directly!" he cried, bounding across the clearing.

"You won't need weapons." Tiresome halted him in mid-flight, and his face fell slightly. "This is a reconnaissance mission," the knight explained, "and if there is any conflict it'll be technical stuff-- a job for our mage."

Eric looked dubiously at Andrew who was shrugging on his crimson cloak-- tradition demanded formal dress in the event of a mage-to-mage confrontation. Andrew caught the look and glared back. He had quite enough doubts of his own about his ability to confront a Mage without having to put up with anybody else's. "Let's get going," he said brusquely.

Orlando watched their departure wistfully. He really would have enjoyed a bit of action instead of being stuck behind a desk-- or rather a trestle table-- all the time. With a sigh he laid his coloured pencils out in a neat row, then unrolled the scheduling chart he'd been working on. What, he wondered to himself, was this usurping duke up to?

"I was wondering what exactly your grace's immediate plans might be." Buckingham ducked to avoid an overhanging branch that would otherwise have swept him from the saddle, and urged his mount closer to the duke's.

"What was that, Buckingham?" Duke Roger cupped his hand to his ear and leaned slightly towards the toady, "can't hear you above that awful racket."

The two men rode at the head of a long procession of mounted men, wagons and pedestrians wending its way along the serpentine course of the Southern Ride. In addition to the muffled thud of hooves on the forest floor, the chink and jangle of harness and accoutrements and the creaking rumble of wheels, there was the chatter of some four score family members, men-at-arms, retainers, cooks, scullions and other hangers-on, the woodwind whining and flaccid percussion of the minstrels and the cackling of Pebblestroke.

"I said, your grace," Buckingham raised his voice, "that I wonder what your immediate plans might be?"

"Stop for tea? Certainly not! It's less than an hour since breakfast, Buckingham-- do you think of nothing but your stomach?"

"That was not my question, your grace--" Buckingham abandoned the subject for the moment and turned in his saddle. "Herbert!" he bawled to the apprentice toady riding just behind, "please be good enough to instruct the minstrels shut up. For the next forty-eight hours. And try to do something about Pebblestroke!" Herbert raised his hand in acknowledgement, wheeled his horse about and cantered back along the column. Shortly thereafter the droning and thudding of the minstrels died away, and with a thump Pebblestroke was cut off in mid-cackle. For a second or two the notes of a zither lingered faintly on the air, then they faded.

"That's better!" Duke Roger heaved a sigh of relief. "Now what was it you were asking, Buckingham?"

"About your immediate plans, your grace. What they are, that is."

"First of all, to find brother Harold and... ah... explain the situation to him. Then I shall invite him to reconsider his position."

"I see, your grace. And then?"

"I trust he will propose that the treasury be returned to Benbrock-Oldstairs for safe-keeping while we set up Fleet the Time Carelessly in The Golden World plc. Once the enterprise is properly established on a firm basis I shall return to Benbrock-Oldstairs to co-ordinate the administrative details leaving my brother here as Managing Director--that is if he agrees, of course. The two girls will remain as Executive Assistants. It is high time they had some working experience in the real world."

"You do not anticipate any difficulties with the outlaws?"

"A fig for the outlaws!" Duke Roger dismissed them with a wave of the hand. "I have the First Speaker's assurance that any hint of trouble from them and they will be driven from the forest. In fact," he added carelessly, "my impression was that the First Speaker might well pre-empt any hint of trouble. Those outlaws have been a thorn in his side for long enough!"

"Have we nothing to fear from them?"

"We offer little enough in the way of plunder" the duke reminded him, "and in any event we are a large party and have not booked ahead. They require at least a week's notice for large parties."

"I believe that is a matter of qualifying for the group rate, your grace," Buckingham reminded him.

"Pah! We have nothing to fear from them, I tell you Buckingham! Have you yet seen any sign of an outlaw?"

"Indeed not, your grace. The only humans aside from our party have been woodcutters."

"Woodcutters?"

"Yes your grace. Those rather raggedly dressed fellows with big leather boots and axes. They cut wood."

"I am quite well aware of what woodcutters look like and what they do, thank you Buckingham. My response was rhetorical, to indicate surprise, and the fact that I was about to make an important statement."

"I beg your pardon, your grace. You were about to say...?"

"I was about to say that I, too, have noticed the woodcutters. A very large number in fact. Is there, you suppose, some kind of convention going on?"

"I cannot say, your grace."

"Look!" Duke Roger exclaimed, pointing, "another pair of them!"

The two woodcutters, observing the approaching procession, immediately began to attack a fallen tree with their axes.

"Enthusiastic! Hard working!" The duke nodded approvingly as they rode past.

"With respect, your grace..." Charles, the duellist urged his horse to the head of the column."

"Yes, Charles, what is it?" Roger turned impatiently.

"The woodcutters, your grace. There is something funny about them."

"What do you mean, 'funny'? I found them in no respect risible. Worthy, yes. Honest, doubtless. But funny? No."

"I meant suspicious," Charles explained patiently, "they weren't really doing much woodcutting-- just smashing at a log with their axes."

"Well really, Charles! I cannot see how you can possibly make such a judgement-- those men are professionals, after all. Do you have any formal woodcutting qualifications or experience?" The duellist shook his head. "I thought not. Someone unfamiliar with the finer points of woodcutting technique might well fall into the error of supposing them to be unscientifically bashing away at a log when in fact they were executing a complicated technical operation with commendable dispatch." The duke gave a dismissive snort.

"But we have passed those two men before," Charles pursued, with quiet obstinacy.

"What nonsense Charles!"

"One of them had 'Section Leader Pringle' stencilled on the back of his jerkin," Charles continued, as though the duke had not spoken.

"Coincidence! Pringle is not an uncommon name."

"And the tree trunk was the same. It had the same initials carved in it. *H luvs J.*"

"Are you going completely round the twist, Charles?" Duke Roger tried to control his irritation. "What earthly reason could there be for two rational men to stand over a tree trunk belabouring it with axes while we ride past, and *then* pick up the tree trunk and scamper through the woods to get ahead of us, only to repeat the performance? The idea is preposterous!"

"I have noticed that many of the trees hereabouts seem disfigured by carved inscriptions." Buckingham interposed in an effort to inject some reason. "Doubtless that is the explanation."

Charles shrugged, and slowed his horse to a gentle walk to allow the irascible duke and his toady to pull ahead. He had done his best to alert them to the fact that the procession was under continuous observation-- if they refused to listen there was nothing else he could do. Struck by an idea, he wheeled his horse about and trotted back to where the two woodcutters were energetically hacking away with their axes. Charles said nothing, merely observing their labours, the hint of an ironical smile on his face. Eventually one of the men sensed his presence and straightened up, digging his colleague in the ribs as he did so. The two gazed at Charles suspiciously.

"Warm work on a lovely day like this, gentlemen?" Charles suggested.

"Aye," agreed the taller of the two, "but like the good book says, the honest man mun' live by the sweat of his brow." He swung his axe to and fro carelessly.

Charles held out both hands, open, to indicate his pacific intentions. "I am not here in my professional capacity," he said quickly. The two men relaxed. "In fact I have already done my best to discharge my professional responsibilities to my client," he continued, "I only want to offer a word of friendly advice."

"Eh?"

"When you take up your next position, Section Leader Pringle, you should remove your jerkin. The Duke of Benbrock-Oldstairs (Usurping) may be intellectually challenged, but he can read... after a fashion."

"I *told* you Perky!" the shorter man claimed reproachfully, "I *said* that it wasn't good security."

"Well I wasn't to know we'd be dealing with a bunch of intellectuals, was I?" Pringle grumbled, as he removed the tell-tale garment from his shoulders and folded it carefully. "Much obliged, squire," he gave the duellist a rueful smile, "not got much time for this cloak and dagger sort of stuff, I'm afraid."

"Neither have I, Section Leader," Charles replied with a laugh. "Am I right in taking you gentlemen to be members of the Stembark Forest Outlaws?"

"Section Leader Pringle and Leading Outlaw Makepeace!" Pringle snapped, springing to attention, "Number Two Woodcutter Detachment (Temporary)."

"Pringle, Makepeace," Charles acknowledged each name with a bow. "I am Charles, Duellists' College... Senior Division," he added almost apologetically. There was an awed silence that could have been cut with a knife. "Please remember me to Mr Orlando," Charles concluded, offering his card. Pringle took it as though it were made of the finest china, ran his eyes over the inscription, and wide-eyed, showed it to Makepeace. "Don't forget to give my regards to Mr Orlando!" Charles called over his shoulder as he rode off.

Charles had no reservations about making contact with what might technically be called the 'enemy'. As a duellist under contract to the usurping duke his duties were clear, and he had discharged them. Should the duke himself be physically threatened, then Charles was in honour bound to defend him-- a duty he would discharge no matter how distasteful-- but from what Charles knew of the outlaws of Stembark Forest, the usurping duke was in no physical danger. That being the case, it was important that the outlaws understood that a duellist rode with the duke's retinue, or unfortunate misunderstandings might result. So preoccupied was Charles with these musings, that it was a moment or two before he realised there seemed to be a hold-up, and the procession had halted. Charles whispered to his horse, and cantered forward.

At the head of the column the cause of the delay was immediately apparent; a huge tree trunk, backed up by a hastily woven screen of brushwood, lay clear across the Southern Ride. And strung from the trees a huge banner proclaimed: ***CUSTOMER APPRECIATION DAY!! DON PEDRO D'Y ANGINA IMMATERIAL HERMITTING PLC.***

"What's all this about, Buckingham?" Duke Roger eyed the banner curiously.

"I do not understand, your grace. I rather thought that the two big chains had taken over all this work."

"Could be a subsidiary of the Sublime Tabernacle of the Redeemer, I suppose?" the duke hazarded, "perhaps that will tell us more." He pointed to a brightly coloured poster nailed to a tree on the right.

"That is possible, your grace." Buckingham squinted at the poster in an effort to make out the words.

"How dull you are, Buckingham!" the duke snapped, "bring me that paper!" Flushing, the toady complied. The duke snatched it from him and read it carefully, his lips moving slightly as he did so. "Remarkable!" he observed after a lengthy pause, "there appears to be *another* hermit in practice in the vicinity. And, what is more, one who offers a corporate rate."

Before Buckingham could express satisfaction at this example of traditional market forces at work, the air shook to a mighty shout of "CARAMBA!" and the screen of brushwood trembled, bulged ominously and disintegrated into a cloud of flying fragments as Kodswallop burst through.

He had listened to the duke and his toady with increasing impatience, waiting and hoping for a good entry line, and he could have kicked himself when he realised that he'd missed one of the competition's posters. He had to act quickly before his prospective customers got too intrigued by Canon Chasuble's misleading advertising.

"Morning gents!" He saluted the duke and his toady, "grand day, isn't it?"

Startled by this sudden apparition, the horses reared and plunged in a most spectacular fashion, enabling the duke and Buckingham to withdraw a prudent distance as they struggled with their mounts. Still beaming good naturedly, Kodswallop stooped and, with a grunt of effort, upended the tree-trunk barrier and sent it crashing to one side. He moved forward, shaking off twigs and branches from his head and shoulders.

"What would you with us, fellow?" Duke Roger called as he tried to place Buckingham between him and the gigantic hermit.

"I am Don Pedro d'y Angina Immaterial," Kodswallop boomed, "purveyor of hermitting services to the quality. And you," he continued, his forefinger stabbing towards the riders, "are the fortunate winners of this week's grand prize of a free consultation with Don Pedro d'y Angina Immaterial plc. To claim this valuable prize, all you have to do is answer a single skill-testing question: which one's the usurping duke?"

Instinctively Buckingham and Roger pointed at each other, then Roger dropped his hand, and grabbed at Buckingham's forearm. "It's only a hermit!" he whispered, "non-violent type. Just get rid of him for me, Buckingham."

"He is very large to be non-violent," Buckingham demurred, with a doubtful glance at the titanic figure.

"The bigger they are, the harder they fall. Besides he's unarmed. Now get him out of the way. Tell him we've already got some."

Buckingham hesitated no longer. The man might be big, but he was on his feet and clearly unarmed, whereas Buckingham was on a horse and had a sword. That seemed to even things up nicely. He clapped his heels to his horse and drew his sword. "We don't want any today, thank you!" he shouted, as he charged the defenceless hermit.

Kodswallop's smile broadened. He had been looking forward to this job, but he'd not expected it to turn out to be so much fun. As the horseman bore down on him flourishing his sword, the big fighter casually stepped to one side and stretched out his arm. Buckingham screamed with terror as Kodswallop plucked him from his horse and flicked him aside. The toady described a graceful arc through the air into a tangle of briars.

"As I was saying," Kodswallop dusted off his hands, "which one's the usurping duke?"

"I stand for the duke, foul traitor!" Herbert shouted, spurring his horse forward.

"Good toadying," the duke murmured approvingly as Herbert thundered past, "but perhaps a little impetuous," he added as Kodswallop gently lifted the young man from his horse and tossed him in the general direction of Buckingham.

"Look, I don't have all day, you know," Kodswallop said conversationally, "so perhaps we can get down to business now."

"Guards! Guards!" Duke Roger called, but in vain. His men-at-arms had used their professional military judgement and executed a tactical withdrawal to previously prepared defensive positions-- after all their contract said nothing about oversized homicidal maniacs.

"As I was saying--" Kodswallop advanced on the duke, hoping that by now he had got the man's attention.

"Charles!" the duke screamed, remembering at the last moment that he did have a duellist under contract. Charles rode forward reluctantly; he had found the whole thing quite entertaining so far and had been hoping for more. Some twenty paces from the looming figure of Kodswallop, the duellist brought his mount to a halt, jumped lightly from the saddle, and walked forward slowly, his open hands held slightly away from his body.

Kodswallop's smile did not alter-- at least his lips didn't change. But his eyes at once became hard and watchful. Duellists were not to be taken lightly.

Charles came to a standstill slightly more than two swords' lengths from the big fighter. "Good day, sir hermit," he bowed slightly, "my name is Charles, Duellists' College, Senior Division, currently contracted to Roger, Duke of Benbrock-Oldstairs (Usurping). The gentleman behind me." He jerked a thumb in his client's direction.

"As I said just now," Kodswallop gave the usurping duke a pointed stare, "I am Don Pedro d'y Angina Immaterial, and I have a special message for the duke (usurping). I intend no harm to the gentleman... at the moment." These last words he added in a voice low enough that only Charles caught it.

"I am glad to hear it." The duellist gave the hint of a smile. "From your name, reverend sir, I take it that you are from foreign parts?"

"Sapristi, yes!" Kodswallop exclaimed, delighted at the chance to exercise his cosmopolitan vocabulary.

"Just so. Yet your voice suggests to me you have spent much time in Nova Castria?"

"Er... well I do get about a bit," Kodswallop admitted cautiously.

"Indeed." There was much more than a hint of a smile on the duellist's face now. "We must talk together some time-- perhaps we have acquaintances in common. But for the moment I leave you to Duke Roger." He turned and walked back to the duke. "This man promises you no harm, your grace. He merely wishes to give you some message. I'd suggest you find out what it is, or we're going to be stuck here all day."

"Lot of use you are," grumbled the duke as he dismounted, "can't see the use of a duellist if he won't deal with bandits on the road." Charles did not bother to respond, and simply moved back far enough to be out of the way, if not out of earshot.

Reluctantly, Duke Roger approached. "Well?" he demanded.

"Stay while I unclasp to you a secret book and read you matters deep and dangerous." Kodswallop delivered the line with a flourish.

"I do not see it." The duke gave Kodswallop a puzzled glance.

"See what?"

"The secret book you just said you were going to unclasp."

"I was speaking figuratively," Kodswallop said impatiently "and now," the big fighter continued in tones of deep solemnity, "I have to tell you, Roger, Duke d'of Benbrock-Oldstairs (Usurping), that I am aware of the nature of your quest."

"The devil you are!" Roger scowled suspiciously. "If there's been a leak--"

"Calm yourself," Kodswallop admonished him, "Don Pedro d'y Angina Immaterial sees much that is hidden from the eyes of ordinary mortals. Your quest is fraught with peril--"

"What!" Duke Roger took an apprehensive step backwards, and fumbled for his sword.

"And the omens are inauspicious," Kodswallop continued inexorably.

"He didn't say anything about omens!" The usurping duke felt a sense of betrayal.

"Who didn't?"

"The First Speaker," Roger answered automatically.

"The First Speaker has much upon his mind," Kodswallop answered smoothly enough, "which is, of course, why I have stayed your journey to give you this counsel."

"Ah!" The duke sighed with relief and satisfaction. "You are sent by the First Speaker?"

"Don Pedro d'y Angina Immaterial is not sent," Kodswallop glared, "although we do undertake consulting work for a number of East Castellian Departments. Confidential, of course." He tapped the side of his nose, just as Andrew had showed him.

"Of course."

"Right then! Though your quest is fraught with peril, if you persevere you shall attain your dearest wish. What you seek lies on the Enchanted Island. These coupons entitle you to use of up to six boats on the Lake of the Enchanted Island for a period not exceeding three hours. Take them, Duke Roger of Benbrock-Oldstairs (Usurping) and proceed at once to the Enchanted Island."

"You want us *all* to go to the Enchanted Island?" The duke waved at his massive retinue.

"Of course not all of you!" snapped Kodswallop, "just you and your immediate family, toadies and so forth."

"Does that include Pebblestroke-- the court jester?" Roger looked at the hermit with pleading eyes.

"Especially Pebblestroke," Kodswallop told him mercilessly. "Now hop it. No, just a minute!" He stretched out an arm to arrest the duke. "I want to talk to your niece and your daughter."

"But of course, Don Pedro." The duke backed away, "I'll have them sent for directly. They'll take a moment or two to--"

"Now!" roared Kodswallop, impatient to get the whole thing over with.

"So! You would be private with the ladies? Hee! hee!" Pebblestroke, back on his feet, was capering and leering and swinging his bladder. "Be warned, lusty hermit, that a man who would be private with such as these must guard his privates well!"

Kodswallop's brow darkened, and his fist twitched.

"Allow me, Don Pedro!" Charles swooped on the cackling figure, seized him by the scruff of his neck and tossed him into the bush from which Buckingham and Herbert were still trying to extricate themselves.

"Poor Pebblestroke!" Anne broke away from her cousin and ran towards the struggling tangle of bodies. "And poor Buckingham and poor Herbert, too!" She almost successfully smothered a giggle. Then she looked up and the laughter dried in her throat as she saw the looming, scowling figure of Kodswallop. "Don't show fear," she hissed out of the corner of her mouth to Julia, who was looking distinctly pallid, "any sign of fear, and it'll charge."

"Put a sock in it!" Kodswallop growled. The big fighter knew from past experience that he was a sucker for a pretty face-- and the two young ladies had much more than just pretty faces. As a result, in his determination to counter his susceptibility to feminine wiles, his face was contorted into a ferocious scowl, calculated to freeze the blood. It seemed to be working. The two girls did not have their arms round another protectively in the traditional manner, but they looked as though they might be giving that kind of sentimental exhibition serious thought. "Right then!" Kodswallop felt like a lion tamer who has successfully halted the first impetuous charge of the wild beasts and now is faced with the relatively simple problem of getting them to sit on silly little seats and wave their forepaws about. "Now I want you to listen very carefully."

"Y-- yes," Julia whispered. Duke Roger felt a stab of envy-- how was it that he had never managed to elicit such respectful attention from the two girls?

"You will be going to the Enchanted Island--"

"Oh goody!" Anne gave a girlish laugh of excitement. Kodswallop's face went blank-- he wasn't big on girlish laughter.

"It's not that good," he warned, "in fact it can be a pretty dodgy place; there all kinds of unsavoury characters kicking about on the Enchanted Island, you know. *And* there's a really powerful magician."

"Oh *that's* alright," Anne said calmly, "all the really powerful mages take absolutely no interest in innocent bystanders. And they're pledged to celibacy as well, I think," she added with a sigh of disappointment.

"Not this one!" Kodswallop countered.

"You mean he's *not* pledged to celibacy?" Julia's eyes sparkled with anticipation and excitement.

"I didn't mean that! I was talking about the other bit-- not taking interest in innocent bystanders. This one is a different sort of mage. A right nutter, he is. Turn you into a newt as soon as look at you! Doesn't know his own strength, half the time," Kodswallop continued, inadvertently lapsing into truth, "you'll want to stay well clear of him, mark my words!"

"Oh!" The two girls slumped slightly in disappointment. "Couldn't we watch him from a safe distance?" Julia suggested

"With this one there's no such thing as a safe distance," Kodswallop told them with perfect sincerity. "But it's not just the mage. There's all these unsavoury characters-- dacoits, thugs and other... er... " Kodswallop blushed, "insatiably libidinous creatures."

"We can look after ourselves," Julia said firmly, "if any insatiably libidinous creature tries anything on *me* he'll be wearing his goolies round his tonsils."

"Howay lass!" for a moment Kodswallop beamed with approval. "Well my advice-- that is the First Speaker's advice--" he invented hastily, "is that one of you should disguise yourself as a man, to protect the other." Kodswallop's confidence began to ebb as he watched the changing expressions on the two girls' faces. "That is to say," he stumbled on doggedly, "these insatiably libidinous creatures tend to be much less insatiably libidinous when they encounter a man and a woman rather than two women on their own..."

"Ignoring the sexist implications of that last observation," Anne's voice could gave been used to engrave glass, "are you suggesting that one of us should take part in some bizarre cross-dressing game?"

"Not as such, no--"

"And you can tell the First Speaker that he can take his patronizing patriarchal attitudes and stuff them--"

"Alright!" Scarlet-faced, Kodswallop interrupted the tirade. "Forget the dressing up bit!" He was furious-- hadn't he told Andrew that it was very dubious? "But make sure," and he wagged a huge forefinger threateningly, "that you stick together on the island."

The two girls nodded their agreement.

"Good. I'll be off then." Kodswallop waved, "thank you for choosing Don Pedro d'y Angina Immaterial plc for your hermitting services," he boomed, then filtered off into the trees.

In another part of the forest, Andrew, Clumpface and Janus were poking about in a small clearing, while Tiresome and Eric stood guard. "There's no doubt somebody's been here," Andrew pointed to the wreckage of a shelter.

"And he probably intends to come back," Janus agreed, indicating the cooking pots and eating utensils scattered carelessly on the ground.

"And I think you'll find he's a mage," called Clumpface from the far side of the clearing, "come and look at this!" The dwarf was standing beside a shallow, blackened depression, about six feet in diameter, and he looked extremely satisfied with himself. "No doubt about it," he nodded vigorously, "this is occult stuff alright."

"You don't think it could have been a rather large bonfire?" Andrew asked hopefully.

"Not a chance; see for yourself." The dwarf grinned and held out a small scrap of charred paper. Squinting at the smudged lettering, Andrew could just make out the words *"Sproggit an... Campfire Ser... Light Blue Touch Paper and Retire Imm..."*

"At least it's not Montmorency," Janus pointed out, "he would never leave a camp site in this condition."

"That's true!" Andrew began to feel a little more optimistic.

"Of course, he *could* have deliberately left it in this state, just to put us off the scent," Clumpface pointed out.

"What do you mean, 'put us off the scent'?"

"He might want to make us think that there's another mage in the forest as well as himself."

"But why?"

"I dunno. The dwarf shrugged, "just to confuse us?" he suggested.

"Clumpface! We do not need Montmorency to confuse us. I am quite confused enough without his assistance! Now let's shift that stuff and see what's underneath." He tugged at the debris of the shelter. It was not strenuous work; it was simply a framework of light branches with bracken woven between them, a flimsy enough structure which a good hard look would have been sufficient to topple. Soon most of it was cleared to one side to reveal a rickety camp bed, a toothbrush and a brass-bound chest made of dark, close-grained wood. It was identical in size to Andrew's own equipment chest, but instead of the complex pattern of interlocking rings that decorated the lid of Andrew's there was a single, large red letter 'L'.

"Back everybody!" Janus warned, "that's a mage's chest."

Andrew glared at it. It seemed to glare back with the faintest suggestion of a flickering violet haze of Heron-Gough discharge. Tentatively-- very tentatively-- Andrew pushed his staff forward to give the thing an exploratory poke. The staff leaped in his hand, there was a livid flash of Heron-Gough discharge, and the chest dematerialized.

"Ooops!" Andrew blinked, "I didn't mean to do that!"

"It might be a wise precaution to prepare something to deal with an irate mage," Clumpface suggested with a broad grin. He was by no means disconcerted, and had an absolute faith in Andrew's ability to handle any occult opposition, no matter how potent.

"Why don't we just leave," Andrew countered, "before the owner gets back."

Janus shook his head doubtfully. "The owner of that chest will certainly have detected its... er... departure and will doubtless be anxious to inquire further into the matter."

"Well, if you're sure..." with nervous fingers, Andrew began to leaf through *Frogson's Modern Spells*.

Janus was wrong. The owner of the chest had other things on his mind at that moment. Bellingham was crouched uncomfortably halfway up a tree overhanging the Southern Ride, and preparing to jump down. The Duke of Benbrock-Oldstairs (Usurping) was on his way-- would be coming round the corner in a moment-- and Bellingham was determined to make his first appearance as a hermit a memorable one. Montmorency *had* cautioned him against using any technical routines, but Bellingham was sure a couple of minor illusion spells wouldn't count.

It was time! The clamour of the approaching procession suddenly increased in volume as it rounded the bend and the leading riders came clearly into view. With a quiet cry of triumph Bellingham jumped from his perch, and triggered his first illusion spell.

Back in the clearing Andrew was thumbing furiously through *An Introduction to Tarot 5.1*. *Frogson's Modern Spells* lay on the ground beside him, wedged open at page 97 *(Removal: Generic)* with the Dalton Spellcaster beside it. He looked up at last. "I can use the Generic Removal with the spellcaster and the staff," he mumbled, "or I could use Tarot 5.1 with the spellcaster and rely on their default values."

"Better use Tarot 5.1." Clumpface puffed a relaxed smoke ring.

"Yes, but there's a warning here," Andrew stabbed at the page with a finger, "it says: *High Mage Index users should create a batch spell to limit output before implementing a hot card in a built-up area. Sproggit and Axel will not be responsible for loss or damage caused by inappropriate application of this product.* What do you suppose that means?"

"It means you use Tarot 5.1," Clumpface said very firmly, "this isn't a built-up area."

"Better get a move on," Janus warned, "the owner of that case may be back soon."

Once again, Janus was mistaken. The owner of the equipment case was floating gently to the ground before the entranced gaze of Duke Roger and his party. Flashes of golden light played about his form, and a shimmering golden halo hovered over his head, the effect only slightly spoiled by the thin column of smoke that rose from it. Letters of fire danced across the sky spelling out *Canon Chasuble Executive Hermit plc. Corporate Rates Available.* Deep chords of organ music reverberated through the forest.

"Not another one!" exclaimed the duke, "Buckingham-- tell him we've had all our hermitting taken care of for today."

Before Buckingham could speak, the apparition raised its hands.

"I think I've got it," Andrew said at last. "The Wheel Of Fortune on the Spellcaster with the azimuth set to 100. That seems to be it."

"You have the card ready?" Janus asked anxiously.

"Right here." Andrew tapped it casually with an index finger.

Bellingham had just completed the invocation when, without any warning, he quite suddenly dematerialized.

Act XI
EXIT PURSUED BY BEAR

W ell, Bellingham?" Montmorency sighed, "I trust you have an explanation for this untimely appearance?" The graduate student swayed, failed to regain his balance and fell heavily to the floor. As he struggled to his feet, Montmorency took another sip of brandy. "Really, Bellingham, I must confess myself somewhat nonplussed by this exhibition. I assign you a perfectly simple, nay elementary task, and you fly back here like a ferret to a trouser leg." The voice was calm, but the cuckoo clock on the wall above the fireplace was ticking more urgently.

Bellingham tried to pull himself together. "I-- I--" he stammered.

"This was not an emergency, Bellingham," Montmorency continued inexorably, "for had it been an emergency, you would have not have sent your equipment chest before you."

"But I--" Bellingham stared at the box with its bright red 'L' plate, and his eyes popped. "I do not understand this, Mage!" He reached out to touch the chest as though to reassure himself that it was really there. It was an unwise move. There was a vicious crackle and a violet flash. Bellingham gave a yelp, and jumped back, sucking his fingers.

"That *would* appear to be your chest, Bellingham. And you appear to have neglected to disarm it." Montmorency's stern expression relaxed a tiny bit-- forgetting to disarm one's equipment chest was one of the oldest boobs in the business, and under other circumstances the oversight would have cost Bellingham a round of drinks in the Graduate Students' Lounge.

"I cannot explain this!" Bellingham darted a betrayed look at the chest. "I certainly did not send it here."

"And yourself?" Montmorency asked ironically, "that was involuntary too?"

"Indeed it was, Mage!" Bellingham retorted, "that is to say, with the greatest respect--"

"I do not want respect from you, Bellingham, but information." Montmorency snapped, "and I want *accurate* information; objective reporting, not the kind of jargon-ridden impressionistic claptrap they let you get away with in your social science courses. Do I make myself clear?"

"I did not return the chest, Mage." The graduate student spoke with absolute certainty.

"Then what is it doing here? And what are *you* doing here?"

"I... er..." Bellingham looked helplessly around the cosy little grotto. "I don't know."

"You do not know?" Montmorency repeated incredulously. "Perhaps it was because you had completed your assignment, and wished to report back at the earliest opportunity?"

"Not-- er-- quite, Mage."

"You did *not* complete the assignment?"

"I have not quite completed all phases of the work, no, Mage."

"What on earth are you talking about, Bellingham? *Phases?*" Montmorency snapped his fingers irritably and a bolt of lighting smashed into the ground outside.

"What I mean to say, Mage, is that I did intercept the usurping duke, as instructed--"

"Excellent!" Montmorency beamed and a dove cooed sweetly at the grotto entrance. "And you told him his course was fraught with peril, the omens were inauspicious, and so forth?"

"Not exactly--"

"Well, what *did* you tell him?" Montmorency's brow darkened and the cuckoo clock speeded up again.

"I was not able to tell him anything, Mage. I had just-- er-- prepared the usurping duke to receive my message, and was about to deliver it when I found myself here. I can only think that a dematerialization routine went premature."

"A spontaneous premature!" Montmorency frowned, "that is unheard of-- even for Sproggit and Axel products." Then a thought struck him. "You were not, Bellingham, attempting any technical activity at the time?" he asked in a voice as smooth as the silk thread of a black widow.

"A minor illusion, Mage," Bellingham almost whispered, "in order to attract the attention of the customers."

"Fool!" Montmorency almost spat the word. "How many times did I tell you that you were to use NO technical routines in your dealings with Duke Roger?"

"Er-- once or twice. But it was only--"

"SILENCE!" Montmorency was extremely angry. The scatter rugs on the highly polished parquet flooring of the grotto began to curl at the edges. "I was speaking rhetorically, Bellingham. I was attempting to make the point that I had repeatedly insisted to you that under no circumstances were you to use any technical means in your meeting with Duke Roger. That instruction was given for very cogent reasons. I was not speaking just to exercise my vocal chords."

"No Mage." Bellingham drooped miserably.

"Well, well," Montmorency took pity on the young man, "it's no use crying over spilled brandy. Let us go through your log and see if we cannot determine exactly what happened."

Cheered by this, Bellingham took from his pouch an ebony tablet in the centre of which was inset a hemi-ellipsoid crystal. Montmorency glanced at the crystal, then tapped the side of the tablet impatiently. The crystal glowed, and a short procession of esoteric symbols marched through its interior. "Hmm... all perfectly standard... I think... Just a minute!" Montmorency looked up, his eyes gleaming. "There was another mage in the vicinity when this happened!"

"There can't have been! I'm sure there wasn't." Bellingham protested.

"You mean you *detected* no other mage in the vicinity," Montmorency corrected him.

"But by definition, a mage outside detection range cannot trigger--"

"If that Mage is a Wardmaster, running Tarot 5.1, then he most certainly can."

"You mean...?" Bellingham paled.

"Exactly!" Montmorency handed back Bellingham's log, snapped his fingers, and materialized a bottle of brandy and two glasses. "Clearly Cruickshank detected your presence and removed you before you could give any advice to Duke Roger." He poured a modest amount of brandy into Bellingham's glass and a slightly less modest amount into his own, then took a sip. "This is quite satisfactory," he observed with a vulpine smile.

"It is indeed, Mage!" Bellingham emptied his glass and smacked his lips.

"I did not mean the brandy, Bellingham!" The smile expanded to show teeth. "What I mean is that we have the initiative-- Cruickshank is merely reacting to our moves. His concentration on you doubtless accounts for the fact that he has so far failed to take any action on the storm illusion. That, I must confess, had puzzled me until now, but obviously his attention is still focused on the forest, not the lake." Montmorency smiled again, and dispensed more brandy. "But I should like to know how it was he detected your existence, and inferred your plans."

"I cannot imagine, mage. I encountered nobody, save another-- that is a real-- hermit."

"A hermit! That is most strange. I had thought that the two big chains had a virtually monopoly of the business."

"Not for the speciality services, it appears, Mage," Bellingham told him, anxious to display his newly acquired knowledge, "and of course Don Pedro, being a foreign gentleman, offers the continental touch-- if you get my drift!" Bellingham winked and made to nudge Montmorency with his elbow.

"Don Pedro, you say! Would that by any chance be Don Pedro d'y Angina?"

"Don Pedro d'y Angina Immaterial, actually," Bellingham corrected him, "a very distinguished foreign scholar. Has a little trouble with the language, but I understood him alright."

"Tell me Bellingham," Montmorency's eyes glittered like cold distant stars, "was this Don Pedro d'y Angina Immaterial a large person?"

"No Mage. A *very l*arge person."

"I see. A very large person. And did this very large person use expressions such as 'caramba', 'sapristi' and 'nom de nom'?"

"I did not hear him say 'nom de nom', Mage," Bellingham answered uncertainly.

"Kodswallop!"

"He did not use that expression either, Mage."

"No, Bellingham! I mean that you encountered Kodswallop. One of Cruickshank's mob. Ha!" With that enigmatic exclamation, Montmorency lapsed into silence for some minutes, sipping at his brandy.

Eventually Bellingham plucked up the courage to address him. "Was there anything more, Mage?"

"Eh?"

"Because it's getting on for teatime, and I was wondering--"

"Well done Bellingham! You were wondering if there was anything else you could be getting on with. Good! I like your keenness!" Montmorency smiled approvingly. "As it happens there *are* some tasks you could be getting on with."

"Some tea, Mage..." the graduate student began hopefully.

"For a start I want you to review what we have available in the love spell line. Nothing too elaborate, mind you, just simple and reliable. You might as well check the list of organic components too-- sometimes these old chemical devices are the most reliable."

"The Three Pigeons, Mage. They do a very nice sausage and chips there, I've heard."

"Pigeons? Sausage and chips? What *are* you talking about Bellingham? Since when has sausage and chips been accounted an aphrodisiac?" Montmorency waved an impatient hand. "And the next thing you can do is summon those forest trolls. I want them airborne by sunset. They are to carry out standing patrols over the usurping duke's travel route. No contact at this stage, just monitoring. I shall provide them with more specific instructions later."

"Standing patrols after sunset," Bellingham repeated hungrily as he wrote the orders down, "further instructions to be issued in due course."

"Correct. You may handle the flying spells yourself Bellingham."

The graduate student's hunger almost disappeared, and he flushed with pride at the implied compliment.

"And when you have done that," Montmorency continued, "you may construct a simple invisibility routine to be used in conjunction with rapid movement and aural illusion. Do you understand?"

"You wish to be unseen, to move very fast and to speak in other people's voices?"

"Almost correct, Bellingham. In fact I wish *you* to be unseen, moving rapidly and speaking in other people's voices."

"Mage?"

"I want you to be able to put a girdle round the earth in forty minutes," the Black Mage elaborated.

"A girdle round the earth..." Bellingham scribbled away industriously, "in forty minutes." He looked up from his notes. "What kind of girdle, Mage."

"A metaphorical one. But before you start all that, let us don some inoffensive disguise, and make our way to Lecter."

"To Lecter, Mage!" Bellingham's hopes shot up.

"Yes, to Lecter. I want you to find out if there is an amateur dramatic society in the town. We shall meet at the Three Pigeons; I understand they do a very good sausage and chips."

"It can't have been Montmorency!" Clumpface banged his fist emphatically, "he would have recognised Kodswallop immediately."

"Perhaps he did, and didn't let on," Andrew suggested, "don't forget, he must have detected us waiting for him." Andrew was feeling less than content with the way things had turned out-- he'd got all prepared to do a serious bit of maging with the Tarot 5.1, and then nothing had happened. "Don't forget, Montmorency is a pretty devious sort of bloke."

"I don't *think* it was Montmorency." Kodswallop scowled ferociously, "you see, Andrew, he didn't have the confidence."

"That was just an act."

"No. If it'd been Montmorency, then he couldn't have ignored a line like 'caramba'. I mean," Kodswallop turned to the others for support, "whatever else you say about him, you've got to admit Montmorency knows how to pick up on a good line."

"Then who was it?" Andrew paced back and forth impatiently.

"Perhaps Montmorency brought an assistant along." Clumpface shrugged, "happens all the time. Any graduate student would jump at the chance to work with a Senior Level Mage."

"With Montmorency?" Andrew was incredulous, "I know it's a hard life, but there are limits!"

"Could be a desperate graduate student," the dwarf pointed out, "or a very good one."

"There was that 'L' plate on the equipment chest," Janus reminded them.

"So that leaves us with *two* mages to deal with!"

"Nowhere near!" Clumpface shook his head emphatically, "not more than one and a quarter."

Andrew scowled, then turned to Kodswallop. "Do you think he suspected you?"

"Nah! He was too busy worrying about his own performance."

"Good. At least that means Montmorency doesn't know we've played the hermit card. And you think you got to the usurping duke before that imposter?"

"I think so. I mean they didn't say anything like 'what a coincidence! You're the second hermit we've had today'. And most people would remark on that, you know."

"We'll go ahead and get them to the island as quickly as possible," Andrew decided, "but we'll have to watch them all the time-- Montmorency will be sure to try something. More bloody fairies aviating about the place, I shouldn't wonder, so I'll have to hang around to take care of them."

"He should go back to the island first," growled Clumpface in an aside to Janus.

"Eh?" Andrew looked up.

"Yes," the elf nodded, "you should secure the island against Montmorency-- and the house itself should be screened from your prospective visitors."

"How am I supposed to do that?"

"Tarot 5.1," the dwarf said casually, "that always seems to do something for you."

"Alright, I suppose I'd better get out there and try something." Reluctantly Andrew opened his copy of Using Tarot 5.1, then dropped it, and jumped to his feet. "I've been a twit!" he shouted. Nobody contradicted him-- they all felt it would be impolite. Andrew allowed the silence to go on for a second or so, then continued, "why should we let Montmorency keep the initiative? He knows I'm trying to sort this out using *As You Like It*, right?"

"Yes, if you say so, Andrew." Clumpface was delighted that Andrew had decided to seize the initiative, but for the life of him couldn't understand this as you like it stuff.

"And he's trying to sabotage things by introducing stuff from other plays, right?"

"Like the forest trolls done up as fairies?" Kodswallop ventured.

"Yes. That's from *Midsummer Night's Dream.* And then he introduced the tempest from *The Tempest.*"

"But are you not going to use that yourself?" Janus was looking puzzled.

"Oh yes. But the thing is I don't want Montmorency to think he's got things going all his own way. I want him to realize that we can hit back! I want to knock him for six! I want Horace!"

"Horace?" Clumpface looked mystified.

"Yes. There's one Shakespeare play where a bear appears. It's called *The Winter's Tale,* and there's a scene where this bloke gets chased offstage by a bear. I want Horace to go to the exiled duke's camp tonight, and chase somebody."

"You want Montmorency to think that you might be switching to this winter's tale thing?"

"Right!"

"I don't know how Horace will go for it. It's not a speaking part, is it?" the dwarf looked doubtful.

"Well, he gets to growl a lot. And wave his paws about ferociously."

"But no lines?"

"Of course he doesn't have any lines, Clumpface. He's a bear!"

"And what has that to do with his artistic potential?" Clumpface asked with dignity.

"It's an important part!" Andrew insisted, "it's vital."

"But with no lines..."

"He can't have any lines! Look Clumpface: just get Horace there, have him chase somebody, then bring him back and give him some buns."

"What are you going to do?" asked the dwarf, as he gathered his equipment together.

"Janus and Tiresome and I are going to keep watch on the usurping duke. If Montmorency has any fairies airborne tonight, I may be able to ground them."

"First you must go to the island, and secure matters there," Janus reminded him.

"You think that's really necessary?"

"Absolutely essential."

Andrew got to his feet reluctantly. "Well I suppose I'd better get on with it," he agreed. With the enthusiasm of someone on his way to the dentist, Andrew followed Janus to the boating lake.

Night had fallen over Stembark Forest. Along the margin of the Southern Ride campfires twinkled where Duke Roger and his retinue had stopped for the night. Most had turned in early and were sleeping uncomfortably curled up in odd corners of the wagons they had travelled in, while a few guards prowled nervously about peering into the deep shadows. Duke Roger (Usurping), with Buckingham hovering at his side, sat staring moodily into the embers of the fire, swirling the dregs of wine around the bottom of his glass. In their tent a few paces away Anne and Julia, unable to sleep, chattered in excited whispers about the forthcoming voyage to the Enchanted Island.

"What was that!" Duke Roger jerked upright.

"What, your grace?"

"Didn't you hear that cry from over there?" The duke made an all-encompassing gesture.

"No, your grace. I--" Buckingham broke off as from the darkness a voice shouted "Halt! Who goes there?"

"Jorkins, the sergeant of the guard!" Buckingham reached for his sword and began to buckle it on.

"Who keeps the gate there, ho!" the voice continued, "advance and be recognised!"

With a clatter of equipment three armed figures ran into the circle of firelight. "That was the sarge, alright!" shouted one, staring this way and that, his pike levelled. "You'd better go and see what he wants then," said a second, "I'll stay here and stand guard."

"Wojjer mean giving orders like that!" the first responded angrily, "I'm senior. You two go and see what Sergeant Jorkins wants then report back to me. On the DOUBLE!" The two men seemed reluctant. "The sergeant's a busy man," temporized one, "he might not want to be disturbed."

"You men!" For the first time the trio noticed Buckingham and the duke. They sprang to attention. "You and you," Buckingham pointed, "take this lantern and proceed in that direction." He pointed again. "You," he indicated the third member, "will come with me."

"Sah!" The senior member of the squad stamped militarily, about-turned and marched off, followed at a discreet distance by his colleague. Buckingham picked up a second lantern and turned his attention to the third guard, still rigidly at attention. "Well, my man, we've got a chance for some action at last, eh!"

"Sah!" the guard agreed unenthusiastically.

"Good! Keen spirit! I like that!" Buckingham approved. "Now just follow me. Are you coming, your grace?" he asked the duke.

"Ah... I think not, Buckingham." Duke Roger had no intention of blundering about a dark forest filled with possibly hostile entities.

"Very good, your grace. We shall report back directly." Buckingham and the guard disappeared into the night. Left to himself, Duke Roger began to wonder whether he had not been hasty in declining his toady's invitation. Though he would have been blundering about in the dark, at least he would have been blundering about in the company of two well-armed men, rather than sitting nervously in the semi-darkness on his own. A second later he almost fainted from shock as a huge shadowy figure burst into view.

"What's going on here?" the figure demanded, "sir?" it added, seeing the duke. With a surge of relief Duke Roger recognised Jorkins, the sergeant of the guard.

"We should be asking you that, Sergeant. We heard your call, and Buckingham went to investigate with a squad of your men. I presume you have encountered them?"

"I gave no call. I was... er..." Jorkins had in fact been chatting up an Assistant Cook called Monica. "I was carryin' out an inspection of the cookhouse facilities," he decided.

"Nonsense, man! We heard you call. I heard you call." Before Sergeant Jorkins could respond there came a shout from the depths of the forest.

"There, you see!" Roger jerked a thumb, "Buckingham is out there searching for you now. And moving briskly, too."

"Sah!" Sergeant Jorkins knew that any attempt to make sense of the mental processes of the aristocracy or senior officers was foredoomed to failure. "I'll see to it at once, sah!" he agreed, and pounded off into the darkness. Duke Roger pensively opened another bottle of wine as a chorus of shouts echoed through the trees. It was impressive the speed with which Buckingham seemed to be moving about-- in fact it was difficult to keep track of him.

If Duke Roger was finding it difficult, Buckingham was finding it almost impossible. He had become separated from the guard he had set out with, and though he could hear the man's voice clearly enough, he just couldn't seem to track him down. And to make things even more confusing, Sergeant Jorkins was bellowing something close at hand. Perhaps it was some peculiar acoustic effect caused by the trees, but to Buckingham it seemed that at one instant the man was straight in front of him, and the next, he was at his back. At to make matters worse he had dropped his lantern.

The two other soldiers were faring no better. Buckingham's enraged tone boomed at them from the darkness, yet no sooner had they moved in that direction, then his shouts rang out from behind them. Seasoned soldiers that they were, it took them little time to identify the situation as a traditional cock-up, and fall back on the traditional response of sitting tight and brewing up. Buckingham and Sergeant Jorkins would sort it out in their own good time.

Crouched under a carefully supported canopy of brambles, Bellingham almost hugged himself with excitement. He had to admit that Montmorency had been right to insist that custom-coded routines be used; everything was working together with a smoothness and precision that no generic spell, particularly a Sproggit and Axel model, could hope to achieve. A flick of his finger added two more voices coming simultaneously from six different directions. He giggled as the sounds of confusion in the forest about him redoubled in intensity. Then he caught himself-- this was no time for gloating, with the job only half-done. He took the small, short range crystal from his pouch and touched it lightly. The miniaturised features of Montmorency appeared within the translucent globe.

"Receiving you, Bellingham. You may report."

"All is going precisely as planned, Mage. Already there are at least half a dozen men blundering about in the darkness."

"Excellent work!" Even with the metallic overtones of the transmission spell, there was unwonted warmth in the mage's voice. "Shall we send the fairies in?"

Bellingham gulped. He was having to work hard enough organising the voices-- the prospect of acting as ground controller to a flight of fairies at the same time was a daunting one indeed.

"I shall maintain control," Montmorency reassured him, "and when they have reached your sector I will hand them over to you one at a time for vectoring to specific targets."

Bellingham breathed a sigh of relief-- handling one airborne forest troll at a time would not be unduly onerous. "That will be perfectly satisfactory," he confirmed.

"Very well. I will instruct each fairy to switch to your channel individually. Your call-sign is Bravo Control."

"Bravo Control, Mage," Bellingham repeated, scribbling furiously.

"The call-signs for the fairies are: Mustardseed, Cobweb, Peaseblossom and Moth, and the prefix is 'foxtrot'. Please confirm."

Slowly and clearly Bellingham repeated the words.

"Excellent! Wait five, Bravo Control." There was a click, and the little crystal globe became opaque. Bellingham was almost beside himself with excitement-- here he was not only doing a delicate piece of simultaneous spell-casting in the field, but also acting as ground controller for a Senior Level Black Mage. Out of sheer bravado he conjured up another voice to add to the growing bedlam around him. The raucous crow of a cock split the night air like a blunt saw. Bellingham jumped, then shrugged unrepentently-- you couldn't be a hundred percent all the time.

In the grotto, Montmorency's eyes were fixed on four bright spots of light that hovered deep in the heart of the scanning crystal. The four trolls were there. Montmorency tapped a smaller crystal smartly, and began speaking. "Attention foxtrot, this is Mike Control. Report please." There was a brief hiss as the carrier spell cut in, then the sulky response.

"This is Peregrine. How much longer we going to be hangin' about 'ere?"

"Observe communications protocol, foxtrot Peaseblossom!" Montmorency snapped. There was a faint yelp, then Peregrine's voice returned, sullen but clear.

"Mike Control, this is foxtrot Peaseblossom. In readiness position." One by one the other three trolls confirmed their position. Montmorency's lips bent in a thin smile.

"Proceed to reference golf five november eight at three hundred feet, vector two three zero, twenty five knots, and report." There was a brief silence, broken by Peregrine's petulant voice. "'E means 'op over to the Southern Ride, just where the camp fires are, then call him up."

"I won't remind you about protocol again, foxtrot Peaseblossom," Montmorency said quietly. Save for the hiss of the carrier spell there was silence again for almost half a minute. Montmorency's lips thinned, and he reached for his staff, then halted the movement as Peregrine's voice once more crackled forth.

"Mike Control, foxtrot Peaseblossom. Foxtrot on two three zero at twenty five knots, cherubs three."

"Very good foxtrot. Prepare for course change in two minutes." Montmorency tapped the smaller crystal. "Bravo Control, this is Mike Control. Foxtrot is on its way."

"Frederick, Mike Control."

"That's 'Roger', Bellingham. Now listen carefully. I shall be giving foxtrot a course change in..." Montmorency glanced at the tiny red digits flickering at the base of the crystal, "ninety seconds. Their ETA at your position will be five minutes later. At that time you will provide them their final vectors. Clear?"

"Er... Roger Mike Control." After the initial hesitation Bellingham sounded confident. Montmorency moved to change back to the command channel and just as he did so there was a thunderous knocking on the door. Montmorency hastily issued the course change orders, went off-net, then opened the door with a wave of his hand. Outside stood Bushy, one of the exiled duke's principal toadies.

"Was there something?" Montmorency's right eyebrow flicked up.

"I-- I did not expect to see you here, Sir Mage," gasped Bushy, "I had looked for the young scholar, your assistant, that he might to you from me, this being more seemly than for me to presume to approach you directly. Believe me sir," he swept his hat off and bowed deeply, "I intended no offence." He bowed once more and flourished his hat. "Were you at leisure, sir, I should impart a thing to you from his grace--"

"Yes, yes," Montmorency snapped impatiently, acutely conscious of the seconds ticking past, "I will receive it, sir, with all diligence of spirit. Put your bonnet to his right use. 'Tis for the head."

Bushy bowed and flourished the hat once more. "I thank you, Sir Mage, it is very hot."

Montmorency lost his temper. "I am not interested in meterorological observations," he snapped, "kindly bugger off; I am engaged on particular business"

Bushy paled and dropped his hat. "I crave pardon, Sir Mage, but my business is urgent--"

"Well?"

"There is a kind of witchcraft at our camp, and the Duke my master bids me crave your--"

"Witchcraft? What do you mean?"

"A monster from the depths of hell itself rages unchecked about our peaceful glade--" He stopped at Montmorency's upraised hand, and waited hopefully. The Black Mage considered the matter. On the one hand he was in the middle of a highly delicate operation. On the other... His curiosity was piqued. And Bellingham should surely be able to handle things from now on. "Wait," he commanded Bushy, "I shall be with you directly." Leaving the toady standing in the doorway, he returned to his crystals and brusquely informed Bellingham of the sudden expansion of his responsibilities. The carrier spell vibrated to the graduate student's nervous gasp, but he recovered fast and in an almost steady voice repeated his instructions. Satisfied, Montmorency summoned his staff and made for the door.

Horace had been in a perfectly good humour up till now. At Clumpface's urging he had quite happily trotted along the forest path in the gathering dusk. And he had been happy to lie concealed in the undergrowth, noshing on the odd bun, while things quietened down in the exiled duke's camp. It was only when he got back to his cave that Horace lost his temper. As soon as he approached the cave he scented human occupants. But that didn't upset him unduly. It was, after all, a highly desirable cave and since he wasn't using it right now, anybody, even exiled dukes, would be welcome to stay there. It was only when he got close enough to catch a glimpse of what had been done to his winter home that he blew his cork. It wasn't the carpets that set him off so much as the wall hangings. And the noise! The nasal twanging made his fur stand on end. In a fraction of a second he changed from a large, amiable shadow moving discreetly across the almost deserted clearing, to a charging behemoth. For a second or so Clumpface chased after him, then fell back, defeated, to hover in the shadows.

From the mouth of the cave Duke Harold emerged at high speed. A shaven second behind him ran the three principal toadies. They were followed, some seconds later, by a dense shower of kitchen utensils, empty bottles, boxes, broken bedsteads and macrame hangings. An awful silence fell. Then from the darkened mouth of the cave came grim rumbling noises, as though heavy items of furniture were being shifted about the place.

Steaming with rage, Horace prowled about the cave. He pushed the two cases of full bottles carefully into a dark cleft, from whence his friend Clumpface could retrieve them later, then sidled down to the mouth of the cave and peered out. The initial shock of his arrival had worn off and now the cave entrance was ringed, at a prudent distance, by men with flaring torches and grey-coated huntsmen with their bows ready bent. Horace sniffed contemptuously. That lot out there couldn't catch a cold! Didn't they know that every proper cave had at least one concealed entrance? He pondered his timing-- twenty-five minutes or so for them to get even more nervous, and much more cold and tired, then on Clumpface's signal he'd come out through the number two tunnel (just behind the bramble bush), chase a couple of them away from the clearing, then back to the Executive Glade for some buns. Clumpface had suggested he chase only one man, but Horace was feeling in a generous mood-- he'd chase a couple, at least. Silently he padded back into the depths of the cave where, far from silently, he began demolishing the remaining items of the duke's furniture that were too heavy to throw.

Clumpface was so absorbed by the sounds of destruction from the cave that he almost missed Montmorency's arrival. The mage swept into the glade, cast one contemptuous glance at the cordon of huntsmen and torch-bearers, and addressed himself to Duke Harold. "Are you responsible for this exhibition?" he gestured at the crowd, "you may dismiss your men. The formation is totally impractical and by no means decorative. No migratory bear ever inhabited a cave without at least one concealed entrance."

"Migratory bear? But learned mage, this is some creature from the mouth of Hell itself!"

"Rubbish!" Montmorency illuminated his staff. "Creatures from the mouth of Hell do not leave footprints like that!" He pointed to the ground. "Nor do they let fall items such as this!" He held up a half-eaten bun.

There was a rustling and rattling of movement and bows were lowered and arrows replaced in quivers. From his vantage point in the shadows, Clumpface sighed with relief and satisfaction-- everything seemed to be working out according to plan. The dwarf took the piece of paper Andrew had given him, read the untidily printed words on it for perhaps the fifth time, and shrugged in puzzlement; it was quite incomprehensible. He wrapped the paper round a small pebble, and tossed it into the clearing. Then the dwarf gave a low whistle to remind Horace that his time was up.

Fifty paces to the left of the cave entrance a clump of brambles quivered, then were thrust aside as Horace, eight feet of very stroppy looking migratory bear, burst into view. He gave a great roar as he singled out his first target, the toady Bagot, and started forward. Bagot started forward too, with considerable energy. Horace gave another roar. Bagot gave a shriek of terror and accelerated.

Half a dozen bows twanged and arrows lanced through the air, but in response to an inconspicuous gesture from Montmorency they flew wide. Hotly pursued by the bear, Bagot disappeared into the trees.

"Hold your fire!" Greene shouted, "it's gone now!" So too, he hoped, was Bagot. For good.

"Sir Mage," Duke Harold had partially recovered his composure, "can you tell us aught of what this visitation portends?"

"It is not a portent, I believe--" Montmorency broke off as Horace erupted back into the clearing, roared once again, then fixed his eye on Bushy. The toady tried to avoid his gaze, and moved to place the duke between him and the irate creature, but he did not move fast enough. With a roar that sounded suspiciously like a satisfied laugh, Horace launched himself forward, waving his forepaws energetically. Bushy took to his heels.

"I was about to say, your grace," Montmorency's words dropped into the awed silence like ball bearings into a still pool, "that this was not a portent, so much as a message. And the message is: do not set up your billet in a migratory bear's winter quarters." He turned on his heel and strode away. Just before he reached the trees he halted and half-turned, as though he had forgotten something. He stretched out his left hand, and a small white object-- a piece of paper wrapped around a pebble-- jumped up from the ground and flew to him. He unwrapped the paper, glanced at it for a moment, then folded it carefully and tucked it beneath his cloak. Then he silently vanished into the night.

When Montmorency rematerialized at the grotto he hesitated for a moment. Anxious as he was about Bellingham's progress, he was equally anxious to discover the meaning of the message Cruickshank had left so casually in his path. Certainly Bellingham's task was a challenging one, but not impossible for an experienced, gifted graduate student. And, Montmorency told himself, the lad would do much better if he didn't think that his supervisor was continually looking over his shoulder. And Cruickshank's note was intriguing. He looked at the short phrase: *now is the winter of my discontent made glorious summer...* What could it mean? Of one thing Montmorency was certain: the answer must lie somewhere in the plays. He stood in silent contemplation for a minute, then came to a decision. Bellingham could handle the rest of the evening's operation, while he tracked down the significance of Cruickshank's message. Bellingham would enjoy the chance of doing an independent piece of work.

Bellingham was beginning to enjoy himself. So far everything had gone smoothly. The trolls had been particularly cooperative, not deviating one iota from the flight plan and punctiliously observing the communications protocol. They understood very well that their flying routines were now under the control of an apprentice and one mistake on his part could result in their uncontrolled descent from three hundred feet to ground level. They didn't want him to make any mistakes. Not that they were worried by falling three hundred feet, of course-- no self-respecting forest troll would be-- it was hitting the ground that they wished to avoid.

"Foxtrot, this is Bravo Control. Throttle back to loiter," Bellingham ordered calmly, "commence orbit. Confirm."

"Bravo Control, this is foxtrot Peaseblossom. Orbiting at cherubs three."

Bellingham let out a long breath. All four trolls were circling overhead, awaiting their final orders. With a hand that trembled slightly he activated his smaller crystal. "Foxtrot Peaseblossom. Switch to channel one four."

"Bravo Control. Foxtrot Peaseblossom on channel one four." The voice had the slightly tinny note characteristic of the short range channel.

"Foxtrot Peaseblossom. Vector zero zero zero to beacon then turn red three zero. Descend and activate." The troll repeated the instructions. Staring up, Bellingham saw quite clearly the little flickering glow begin to move slowly off to the north. Quickly but calmly, Bellingham gave the other three their instructions, then went off-net. Fascinated, he watched the four bright flickering spots of light moving northward in line astern. They seemed to be growing brighter-- doubtless due to their steady loss of altitude. Bellingham wanted to beat his chest and shout with triumph. His first solo, major operation! Taken over at short notice, too! He'd get a paper out of this, he told himself. *Some Observations on Multiplexed Flying Routines in a Multi-Channel Illusional Environment...* Maybe too short and simple-- but he had plenty of time to formulate something more impenetrable. Then the taste of triumph turned to ashes as, one by one, the four flickering specks of light gave out a brief violet flash, then vanished.

Less than a mile away Andrew lowered his staff.

"Excellent!" Janus whispered, "Tiresome and Eric had better go and pick them up before they get away."

Act XII
EAST CASTELLIAN

Standing astride the River Hamers, East Castellian is Southern Albion's largest city, the commercial and administrative centre and the seat of government. The city is a cesspit of lawyers, accountants, revenue officials, and other such exploiters of human degradation, but it is not totally devoid of human decency-- if you know where to look.

Ratbag and Cecil did know where to look. The Revenue's Lament was a sprawling riverside tavern under the benevolently despotic proprietorship of "Five Fingers" Schofield, and was about fifty paces from the end of Creek Slime Alley, from which insalubrious thoroughfare Cecil now peered cautiously. The coast was clear. He turned and beckoned to Ratbag who, like a small sheepdog herding a pair of rather dim sheep, chivvied the two outlaws along before him. In an exaggerated gesture, Cecil placed a finger to his lips; Amiens and Jacques had a nasty habit of breaking into yaps of admiration or honks of disdain at the most inconvenient moments. Luckily for them they took the hint, and remained silent.

"It's all clear," Cecil murmured, "just follow me." Walking with quick nervous strides he led the way.

The journey from Stembark Forest had been a bit of a strain for everybody. Jacques and Amiens were both well-born young gentlemen who had both attended good schools and had emerged imbued with the spirit of good sportsmanship, clean living and the desire to serve (ie lead). In spite of these disadvantages, Orlando had admitted them to the outlaw band[11]   and they had both advanced to the rank of senior section leader. They could both split a hazel wand with an arrow at two hundred paces (two times out of three on a calm day). And both, as professional outlaws, had a deep and abiding respect for the sanctity of private property. They were thus ill-prepared for any cooperative venture with Ratbag and Cecil, and the two-day journey to East Castellian had given their whole sense of the natural order of things a thoroughly nasty jolt.

For their part, Ratbag and Cecil were suffering under the impact of Jacques's sense of humour. Don Orlando had suggested that Jacques was a bit of a joker, but he had not warned them that the outlaw's comic effusions made seaside postcards look intellectual. The whoopee cushion on the pilgrim's chair at the first inn they'd stayed at had been bad enough. The imitation dog turds on the dinner table the previous night had been worse. And, Cecil told himself, if he heard the story about the one-legged mercenary, the farmer's daughter and the coconuts one more time, he would throttle the fellow. With an effort, he put these vengeful thoughts from him; at least they'd arrived safely.

"A picturesque looking inn," Jacques drawled as they made their way across the courtyard. Neither Ratbag nor Cecil answered-- they were too busy scanning the environment for any signs of Revenue officers, Castle Guards or the ubiquitous, grey-overalled members of the First Speaker's Secret Service.

"One hopes the landlord keeps a good cellar," Amiens filled in the conversational gap. The two outlaws followed Ratbag and Cecil to the head of a narrow staircase descending to the landing stage where the door to the Revenue's Lament opened. Just as they started down Cecil turned. "What was that?" he asked Amiens abruptly.

Startled, Amiens took a moment or two to register what exactly it was the scruffy fellow was asking. "Ah-- I was hoping our landlord keeps a good cellar," he repeated.

11   He was an equal opportunity employer

"Not really. Not as such, anyway." Cecil shook his head. "He's right by the river, see." He pointed to the sullen grey-brown water lapping at the piles of the landing stage. "A cellar would flood. That is fill with water," the marksman spoke laboriously as though imparting information to a backward child, "and Five Fingers Schofield wouldn't care for that. Doesn't like the damp."

"I see." Amiens gave the river an uncertain look.

"I believe what Amiens meant to ask was whether the fellow keeps good wine," Jacques elaborated. He had once employed a servant and was experienced in communicating with the lower orders.

"Not for long," Cecil muttered as he pushed the inn door open.

At that hour of the day, things were fairly quiet at the Revenue's Lament-- a couple of seamen were discussing the division of their bill with cutlasses while half a dozen more, under the landlord's approving gaze, were attempting to arrive at an equitable division of four bottles of rum. But as soon as the door swung open Schofield quickly broke away from the group and cudgelled his way through the crowds of onlookers to greet his visitors as they crossed the threshold.

"Cecil! Ratbag! Welcome back to East Castellian!" He pumped their arms so enthusiastically that the nicker was almost lifted from the floor. "What fair wind brings you to the city? What about the others-- may I expect them soon?"

"Just us, this time." Cecil waved a hand to indicate the two outlaws. "We got a special job on at Castle Downing."

"Aha!" The landlord gave a delighted laugh, "well you will find your wardrobe safe upstairs, in your old room. Come!" He began to lead the way to the bar. "You'll have a quick one or two while your men look after the luggage? The rooms through that door, up the stairs and first on the right," he told Jacques and Amiens, "and once you've finished unpacking, pop straight down to the kitchen and see if cook can't find you something to eat."

The two outlaws looked at first confused, then furious. Amiens was about to make some indignant remark that would have almost certainly cost him some expensive dental work (Schofield was quite touchy on the matter of insubordination) when Ratbag filtered back from wherever he had been. "Oh no, Five Fingers, these are our colleagues. They are outlaws from Stembark Forest," he added proudly.

"Oh, my pardon, gentlemen!" Schofield greeted them amiably enough, if with some forcing of his disposition. With the keen eye of the professional landlord he had quickly identified them as white wine or dry sherry drinkers and such guests lowered the tone of the establishment.

"So, what roguery do you have planned here then?" he demanded as, drinks in hand, they settled down at a small table tucked discreetly in the corner.

"We need to get into Castle Downing," Cecil said casually, "couple of things Andrew wanted us to check up on."

"Castle Downing!" Amiens choked on his sherry. Nobody had actually mentioned getting inside Castle Downing! Not that it was a difficult matter to get inside, he understood, but it was the getting out again that could often be the problem. He dabbed ineffectually at the spilled sherry with his handkerchief.

"Yes, that's right!" Ratbag confirmed eagerly, "we've been there before."

"Castle Downing!" Amiens was still trying to get his breath back.

"That's just upriver from here," Schofield put in helpfully, "huge place with towers and battlements and things. You can't miss it." The innkeeper gave the outlaw a concerned glance, "look, are you sure you want to drink that stuff? Wouldn't you rather have a small brandy?"

Amiens shook his head. "Thank you, no. A large brandy, perhaps..." Beaming, Schofield jumped up to fetch a bottle, delighted to discover that there was some good in the lad after all.

With a sample of Schofield's latest consignment trickling warmly into his stomach, Amiens felt capable of exploring matters a little further. "How are we going to get into Castle Downing?" he asked, trying to sound casual.

"How are we going to get out?" asked Jacques, less casually.

"We could disguise ourselves as inspectors from the Water Board," Ratbag suggested, "coming to see about the pipes?"

"The *water board?*" Cecil asked incredulously, "why?"

"Well they go into all kinds of places to see about pipes and stopcocks and... er... things like that," the nicker explained, "and we could use these. I found them this morning." From his bulging knapsack he withdrew a large turncock and a metal badge, formerly the property of F Crowther 2978, Inspector, East Castellian Water Board.

Cecil's eyes gleamed-- being a Water Board inspector might be even more fun than being a cleaning lady. But Jacques shook his head. "I'm afraid we could not possible sustain the impersonation-- we know nothing of such technical matters."

"Don't be such a wet blanket Jacques!" admonished Amiens, who was working on his second brandy, "you *must* know something about it-- I've been to your pater's place and that's got running water with pipes and taps and all that sort of thing."

"Yes, but we have a man to work the taps for us," his colleague protested, "it's hardly the sort of thing one would do for one's self, after all."

"Well you could be an *assistant* inspector" suggested Amiens, "learning the ropes, so to speak. I know about taps. *And* stopcocks."

"I have never seen a stopcock," Jacques sneered, "obviously our social circles have been very different."

"I believe, gentlemen, that the question is academic," Schofield shook his head sadly, "since Mission Implausible's last visit to Castle Downing, security measures have become very stringent. An unscheduled inspection team from the Water Board would never be admitted." There was a depressed silence. Schofield leant forward to Jacques who was giving his half-empty glass of white wine a supercilious sneer. "Look, are you sure you really want to drink that stuff? Why not try a sip of this?" He slid the brandy bottle insinuatingly across to the outlaw.

"I suppose I might." Jacques poured himself a meagre measure, tasted it, drained it, then poured a second considerably more liberal one. His expression relaxed. "Thanks-- it's a fine brandy!"

"You need not drink it as though you were going to drink it all!" Amiens reached for the bottle.

"Plenty for everybody, gentlemen!" Schofield said severely, and placed a second bottle on the table. "Now, to business. Ratbag?"

The nicker hesitated. *He* knew that he would have no problem getting into the castle, whatever the security provisions. But he also knew that a thorough job could not be accomplished without Cecil's help. "I think we should go and take a look--"

"You mean case the joint?" Amiens suggested. Jacques and Cecil looked at him reproachfully. The expression had been on the tips of their tongues.

"You'll have to be careful," Schofield warned them. "It's not only the Castle Guards, you know. The place is crawling with the Secret Service-- their Headquarters is right opposite."

"Are you sure?" Cecil frowned.

"'Course I'm sure." The landlord pushed a fresh bottle across to Amiens, "Grey overalls, tape measure dangling out of the top pocket and the book of fabric samples. You can tell them a mile off."

"Well..." Cecil scratched his chin. It was not just a matter of taking a quick shufti, he reminded himself, they needed to get a good idea of the whole operation-- patterns of guard changing, procedures, all that sort of thing. Gathering that kind of information would take time, and must be done inconspicuously. An idea struck him. "How about setting up a souvenir barrow opposite the main entrance?" he suggested, "it'd be ideal cover. There must be dozens of them round there."

"Fabulous!" Ratbag chirped excitedly, and bounded up from his seat, "Amiens and Jacques can run it, and keep an eye on the guards, and you and I can mingle with the crowds."

"I er--" began Jacques.

"Excellent idea!" Schofield thumped the table with approval, "I have an old barrow in the stables you can use."

"But what are we going to sell?" Amiens asked.

"And how?" Jacques sniffed loudly. "I've never been in trade," he added, staring down his nose at the others.

"Of course you have!" Amiens tried to encourage his friend, "you ran the white elephant stall at the last Staff Association jumble sale."

"It lost money," Jacques said with a melancholy sigh.

"But commercial success is not the objective of this operation." Amiens reminded him.

"What are we going to do for stock?"

"I think we can rely on Ratbag for that," Cecil told them, and looked round for confirmation. But the nicker had already disappeared.

From the Brown Study, Titus Handcarte looked down to the bustling crowds thronging Memorandum of Understanding Square. It was a bright sunny day and the First Speaker was in a more than usually cheerful mood since he had just been informed that the Second Speaker had fallen seriously ill and was unlikely to recover. He made a mental note to congratulate the Secret Service chief on the matter; those involved had certainly earned promotions. He waved to his private secretary. "Ah, Leeper, ask the interior decorating representative to see me as soon as possible, please. I should like his views on some new curtains."

"Of course, First Speaker. I will ask him to attend you directly."

"Thank you Leeper. And another thing: what has happened to my secretary today?"

"I fear Mrs Gerund is unwell, First Speaker. A severe cold, I understand."

"A severe cold!" Handcarte half rose from his seat. "I gave no instructions--"

"That is a *medical* severe cold, First Speaker," Leeper said hastily, "there's a lot of it about apparently. I expect her back at the beginning of next week."

"Ah, very well," Handcarte relaxed, "please arrange a temporary with Mrs Newkes. And you may hand these papers to the Attorney General." He indicated an orange file.

"Immediately, First Speaker." Leeper took the file and prepared to go. "And the despatches for Captain Spalding?"

"I don't know about that." Handcarte smothered a yawn, rose from his chair, and stretched luxuriously. "You know, Leeper, it occurs to me that I might just deliver these to Captain Spalding myself. And then ride with the troops on the operation. That should make a pretty good impression, don't you think? The First Speaker leading his troops into action!"

"Quite in the heroic tradition, First Speaker," agreed Leeper.

"Yes... we could even invite some of the broadsheet writers along to record the affair-- indeed in a matter of such national importance we would be remiss not to." Handcarte began to pace back and forth as he warmed to the idea. "The government needs something to raise its profile after that er-- unfortunate business last summer. Something to boost public confidence."

"Quite, First Speaker. I shall make the necessary arrangements at once."

"Excellent, Leeper." As Handcarte paused at the window and looked down once more at the thronging crowd about the souvenir stalls below, something caught his eye. "Leeper! What do you suppose is going on down there?" He pointed to a stall where the crowd was at its densest-- indeed it was almost a solid mass. And some of them appeared to be waving.

"Perhaps that particular stall is having a special sale, First Speaker?" Leeper hazarded.

"That must be it. He certainly must be doing a roaring trade. Those people almost seem to be fighting to get to him."

"I believe I *can* hear them roaring, First Speaker," agreed the secretary.

"That's what I like to see!" Handcarte nodded approvingly. "Enterprise and initiative in the free market economy. That's the mighty engine that drives our society, Leeper."

Ratbag arranged the final items on the barrow, hung yet another string of bunting from the counter, then turned his attention to the two outlaws. "Now there really is nothing to worry about." He passed Amiens a cloth cap. "Just remember that the mugs with the First Speaker's picture are half a crown, with sixpence off for two, the tea towels with the picture of Castle Downing are five bob plus threepence for gift wrapping, and the gift sets with the tray, the mug and the flag are seven and six each."

"Um..." Jacques clumsily tied his apron, then wriggled his shoulders. The rough serge jacket was at least half a size too small, and itchy. "What about the guide-books?" he asked.

"They're free to anybody who buys a gift set. Otherwise half a crown."

"I don't know that I can remember all that," objected Amiens, adjusting his cap to a more rakish angle.

"I wrote it down for you." Ratbag handed the outlaw a scrap of paper. "Can you see the entrance clearly?"

"No problem." Amiens was happy to be on more familiar ground. The entrance to the Administration Wing of Castle Downing was clearly in view, as were the gates in the castle wall from which guards emerged at regular intervals.

"Good. But watch out for the Shore Enforcers-- the ones in the brown uniforms. Cecil said that they sometimes have random patrols."

"Right. By the way, where is Cecil?"

"There." Ratbag smothered a giggle, "the one with the bucket."

Amiens looked, then wished he hadn't. He saw a shapeless form wearing a red gorblimey turban with curlers poking out aggressively from the perimeter. It was carrying a large galvanized iron bucket from which the handle of a mop protruded at a jaunty angle. "By the cringe!" he choked, "what is it?"

"Just Cecil," Ratbag told him blithely, "he's going to take a closer look at reception and registration. I'll be back in a few minutes." The diminutive figure evaporated into the crowd.

"Did you just see that?" Jacques gasped as he caught a glimpse of Cecil.

"No!" Amiens told him firmly.

"Well I did." Jacques reached beneath the barrow for the bottle and took a substantial swig.

"Steady on, old boy!" Amiens cautioned him, "sun's not over the yardarm yet."

"Bugger the sun," his colleague responded, "and the yardarm." He took another swig.

Conversation languished for a while. Both men, when not busily ministering to the needs of their customers, were noting down the movements of the various detachments of Castle Guards and Shore Enforcers. Every now and then Ratbag reappeared and, from a bulging knapsack, replenished their stock.

"I must say that little feller is very well organised," Jacques observed after Ratbag's third visit.

"Absolutely!" Amiens agreed, "but wouldn't it have been more efficient and effective to have brought all the stock here in one go, rather than having him chase back to... to wherever the stores are?"

"There's something to that." Jacques gave the matter some thought. "We should mention it to him."

"Of course he could be using some paradigm based on real-time input from customer demand," Amiens suggested.

Jacques frowned. "That's pretty sophisticated," he objected with a shake of the head, "probably a bit too technical for our little friend."

"Well a lot of these-- er-- chaps that aren't like us," Amiens wrestled with political correctness for a moment, "have this sort of instinctive--"

"Oi!" Both outlaws turned instinctively. Facing them was a flat hat surmounting a pair of accusing eyes and a collection of aggressively bulging muscles that should not have been allowed out without a licence.

"Good morning, sir. How may we help you?" Amiens asked brightly.

"How may you help me?" The eyebrows above the accusing eyes vibrated agitatedly, "I'll tell you how you can help me, squire. You can hand back that stuff there wot you just nicked from me barrer!" A finger the size of a well-developed sausage jerked menacingly in the general direction of the china mugs bearing the likeness of the First Speaker.

"What are you talking about, my good man?"

"I'm talking about the stuff you thieved from me barrer, that's wot I'm talking about!"

"Don't be ridiculous!" Jacques shouldered Amiens aside, and stared at the man as though he were something nasty that had been left on the carpet by an incontinent pet. "Be off with you, fellow!"

Unamused by this response, the burly stallkeeper gave a yell of rage, grabbed one of the china mugs and flourished it aloft. "This is my stock!" he declared to the world at large, "you all seen it on me barrer. You know it's mine on account of the sort of smudge over his nibs' left eye!" There were growls of agreement from a few partisans among the gathering crowd.

"Now you listen here, my man!" Jacques spoke severely, "that is not a smudge. That is known as a 'bloom', and is a characteristic marking on quality ceramics of this kind. It comes from the unique glazing and firing processes used by the master craftsmen who have so painstakingly laboured to create this priceless example of the potter's art."

"Bollocks!" shouted the stallkeeper. Goaded beyond all reason by this slick display of salesmanship, he hurled the mug at Jacques. Amiens, with the lightning reactions of a Stembark Forest outlaw, stretched out his hand and caught the missile, then hurled it back. Unfortunately his marksmanship was not up to his reaction speed, and the mug shattered against the head of a hitherto uncommitted member of the audience. A great shout of joy arose, and the crowd surged forward. Amiens and Jacques made to retreat, but tripped and fell backwards. Luckily Amiens had the presence of mind to wriggle forward and, dragging

Jacques, take temporary shelter under their barrow. The vehicle tilted and creaked agonizingly under the load of enthusiastic shoppers.

"I say, Jacques," Amiens flinched as a shower of china mugs cascaded past his ear to splinter festively on the cobblestones, "where did you learn all that about fine ceramics?"

"It's the sort of thing you pick up when you work on the white elephant stall," the other outlaw explained with a self-deprecating shrug.

"Ah." Amiens gave the matter some thought, then started as though something completely different had crossed his mind. "Do you think we ought to be going?"

"Do you think we should leave the barrow unattended with all that stock?" Jacques countered. There was another splintering cascade.

"It might be prudent. And there is a lot less than we started with."

"I don't know, Amiens. I have the definite feeling that there are one or two dishonest people out there," Jacques assumed a concerned expression. "They might well take something without leaving the money. I had better go and--"

"Come on!" With a fierce whisper, Ratbag materialized beside them. "Follow me!" he urged. The two outlaws blinked in astonishment.

"But the barrow--" Jacques protested.

"Leave the barrow! The castle guards are coming!"

"Just as well." Jacques prepared to stand, "I want to make a complaint."

"Come on!" Ratbag plucked frantically at the outlaw's sleeve.

"But Ratbag! There are thieves about!"

"No!" The nicker looked shocked.

"Yes indeed. And I intend to make a complaint."

"Leave it Jacques!" Amiens grabbed his friend's arm, "we have a mission, remember? And," he added over his shoulder as he wriggled through the crowd after Ratbag, "you can always write to them about it."

"We gotta move fast." Cecil drained his tankard and looked around for a refill.

Amiens finished adjusting his bandage and gingerly sipped at his own drink. "Where?" he asked.

"Castle Downing. We've already been away two days, and Andrew will be doing his nut if we don't get back soon." Cecil spoke sharply, even for him. He was unused to the responsibility of directing any mission and it weighed heavily on his shoulders. Added to which he had the burden of these two upper class twits.

"You have a plan?" Jacques tried to raise his eyebrows inquiringly, but the crust of dried blood impeded him.

"No. I'm just making it up as I go along." Cecil rolled his eyes at Ratbag, who returned him an uncomfortable look. Ratbag was the kindest hearted fellow imaginable, and hated thinking anything but the best of anyone, but Amiens and Jacques did seem a bit useless.

"I don't suppose you managed to make anything of the guard pattern?" Cecil asked, without much hope.

"This was the best we could do." Jacques slid a folded piece of paper across the table. "Awfully sorry about the handwriting."

Cecil unfolded the paper casually and began to read. Then his jaw dropped. Wordlessly he handed the document to Ratbag who, eyes narrowed, scanned it line by line. "But this is wonderful!" The nicker almost bounced from his chair in excitement, "you got everything! How did you manage it?"

"Oh... well... er..." Amiens floundered, "we do make a bit of a thing about plotting guard schedules in the outlaw business. It can be quite important."

"It's vital!" Cecil found his voice at last, "a bloody marvellous job! Running the stall, getting that schedule *and* organising a first-rate punch up." He shook his head in amazement.

"We didn't really organise the punch-- ah!" Jacques clutched at his shin and looked reproachfully at Amiens. "What did you do that for?" he whispered.

"Keep quiet and don't spoil it!"

"Bloody marvellous!" Cecil repeated, relieved and delighted. Not only did they now have a precise and detailed picture of the guard mounting pattern at Castle Downing, but also they the assistance of two extremely capable blokes. "I think this may be a doddle after all," he leaned back in his chair and gave what was, for him, a friendly grin. "Now this is the picture: I can't get in as a cleaning lady-- they check identities against a list with pictures now, *and* there's a secret service agent assigned full-time to each cleaning lady. Distrustful sods!"

"So we do go as Water Board inspectors after all?" Amiens suggested hopefully.

"No." Cecil grinned more widely. "Tell them about the secretaries, Ratbag."

The nicker opened a manilla folder and touched a few sheets of flimsy paper delicately with his little finger. "This is signed requisition form and countersigned admission slip for a temporary secretary, who is to report to Castle Downing this afternoon. The First Speaker's usual secretary is off sick."

"Where did they come from?" Jacques stared at the flimsies.

"I just found them." The nicker shrugged.

"So this afternoon the thoroughly experienced secretary Miss Prism will report to Castle Downing." Cecil leered horribly. "It's only for the one afternoon, and that should give me all the time I need to case the joint."

"But can you do that sort of thing-- the secretarial business, I mean?" asked Jacques, "isn't it all a bit technical?"

"Nah. Nothing to it. Look coldly efficient with just a touch of the fluttering eyelashes to let the bloke know that beneath this cool, self-possessed exterior, throbs the heart of a passionate woman. You know the sort of thing."

"Er-- yes. That is-- no." Jacques flushed slightly. "So you will use the opportunity to spy out the lie of the land?"

"Yerst. And *then*, this evening, lo and behold, who should appear at Castle Downing but the rather flustered Miss Prism? She presents her signed authorization from the First Speaker (remember to update that,

Ratbag) and proceeds under escort to the First Speaker's office where her escort unlocks the door, lets her in the office and locks the door behind her, leaving her to complete those important and confidential tasks for the First Speaker." Cecil leaned back and favoured the company with a triumphant smile.

"And then?" asked Amiens.

"And then Ratbag comes in, and we go through every nook and cranny in the First Speaker's office until we find what we're looking for."

"And what about us?"

"Do you two think you might be able to take over the guard if necessary?"

"Oh yes-- quite straightforward." Amiens felt a little disappointed at being relegated to such a dull, though doubtless important, part of the operation. "Wouldn't we be more help to you as Secret Service officers?" he suggested, "we could even escort you in."

"That would be wonderful!" Ratbag's eyes danced with excitement at the thought, "but how could you manage it-- about the uniforms, I mean?

"Easy. We saw a crowd of those fellows this morning, so all we have to do is discreetly tap a couple on their heads, tie them up, borrow their clothes, and Arthur's your aged relative."

"If you're sure..." Cecil looked dubious.

"Absolutely! We can move fairly quietly, you know."

"Well... if you're sure..." the marksman scowled at the floor for a moment, knowing that he was going to have to be friendly and grateful to somebody, and hating the thought of it. "Well if you're sure," he said slowly, "then I can't think of anyone else I'd rather have along."

"Well *that's* arranged!" Ratbag said happily. "I'll pop out now and get you that attache case, Cecil. You wanted a big one?"

"Yes. About this big." Cecil indicated with his hands, "and don't worry about the initials."

The great bell in the Revenue Tower was just booming two o'clock when a smartly dressed lady walked confidently into the Administration Lobby of Castle Downing. The severe cut of the full length blue skirt suggested a professional woman, and the large shiny black attache case that hung from her shoulder confirmed it. She advanced to the reception desk and handed a flimsy piece of paper to the guard lounging in a swivel chair. The guard stared at the paper, frowning. Then reversed it and tried again. Cecil tapped his foot impatiently.

"What can I do you for, dear?" the man leered, "lost your way, have you?"

"As you see from that requisition, I have come from the Agency." Cecil's voice was low, in both volume and temperature.

"Ar, yeah, I can see that. But what I asked you was what do you want?"

"To begin work!" Cecil snapped.

"Eh?" The guard contemplated this novel and disagreeable concept for a moment.

"May I be of some assistance?" The Secret Service agent who wafted up to the desk was clearly one of the senior ones. His grey overalls were immaculately tailored and a brightly coloured strip of fabric with a complex pattern of diagonal lines hung from his neck. Cecil decided that cool politeness was indicated.

"That would be most kind of you, sir. As I informed this fellow, I am here from the Agency. There is my authorization."

The agent snatched the document from the bewildered guard, glanced at it quickly, then strode to the other side of the office where he and a colleague consulted a ledger. For a second Cecil felt a twinge of concern, but the men appeared satisfied, for the ledger was closed with a heavy thud and the first agent marched back, a welcoming smile on his face. "Do follow me, Miss Prism. I apologise for all the formalities, but State security requires it."

"Of course." Cecil gave the agent a cool look as he fell into step beside him. "I am not absolutely unfamiliar with the procedure."

"Quite, quite! But you have not, I believe, worked with the First Speaker before?"

"No, indeed." Cecil tried to look deferentially expectant.

"Well, you have nothing to worry about." The agent gave Cecil an unpleasantly familiar pat on the shoulder, marking himself out for really severe trouble at some future date. "You will find that the First Speaker is a perfect gentleman."

Cecil did not trust himself to reply to that, so merely nodded briskly. They walked on in silence along an echoing corridor and up a broad flight of stairs at its end. At the head of the stairs, flanked by marble columns, was a massive oak-panelled door. "The First Speaker's office!" the agent said in a hoarse whisper, and knocked softly.

The door swung open to reveal the rodent-like features of Leeper. "At last!" he snapped, before the grey overalled man could say anything, "please come straight in, Miss; the First Speaker is waiting."

Cecil followed the man in and the door thudded closed behind him. He tensed for a moment and patted his dress unobtrusively to confirm that his cosh was ready to hand.

"Miss-- er-- Prism. How good of you to come at short notice." The First Speaker advanced a pace to indicate his recognition of the new arrival, then sat down behind his desk. "You may go, Leeper." The private secretary disappeared noiselessly. "Please be seated, Miss Prism, and we can begin." He waved to an upright chair set before a small table adjoining the corner of his desk. Cecil took his seat, then looked across to the First Speaker, awaiting instructions.

"First of all, Miss Prism, the following memorandum to the Attorney General..."

Four or five memoranda later Cecil began to wonder if he had bitten off more than he could chew. It was the sheer mind-numbing banality of it! By the time he had filled nineteen pages of his notebook he was seriously considering cutting his losses, coshing the First Speaker and buggering off. As Handcarte's voice clicked into silence, Cecil rested his writing hand and allowed his eyes to stray around the room.

"That takes care of our routine administrative tasks, Miss Prism. Tedious, but necessary." Titus Handcarte essayed a thin, confidential smile calculated to make an underling feel party to the burdens that weighed upon the shoulders of the mighty. "And now," he continued, rising from his desk, "the next assignment I must ask you to regard as highly confidential."

"All my assignments are highly confidential, First Speaker," Cecil informed him primly.

"Quite so. And very commendable too, if I may say so. But I must remind you, Miss Prism, for the good of your health, that these are high matters of state to which you will become privy." The First Speaker's lips became a thin line and, for a moment, Cecil felt a chill wind at his back. The First Speaker moved to the wall by his desk and touched a section of panelling. Noiselessly it swung open to reveal a deep closet in which lay half a dozen red or so leather dispatch boxes. Cecil made a mental note of the position. Handcarte removed one of the boxes and, back at his desk, took a file from the box and scrutinised it briefly.

"Now, Miss Prism, please take this down most carefully: *Memorandum to all Staff in First Speaker's Office: In accordance with the recommendations of the East Castellian Task Force on Economic Development, the Government, in partnership with Fleet the Time in the Golden World plc, will establish a world-class motif garden in Stembark Forest. Preliminary survey work and preparation of the required environmental impact report will begin at once. So that this work may proceed expeditiously, relocation of the Stembark Forest outlaws will be necessary. This will be accomplished by a task force comprising detachments of Shore Enforcers, Castle Guards and the Seventh Heavy Dragoons. The First Speaker will personally lead the operation. Mr Leeper will be responsible for organising the spontaneous demonstrations of public support for this operation. The composition of the Task Force and its Order of Battle appear as Annex 1. Documents relating to the composition of the Executive Board of Fleet the Time In the Golden World plc are retained in Dispatch Box 3 under my personal seal--* Miss Prism! Are you unwell?"

Cecil had been unable to restrain a gasp of surprise, and now Handcarte was gazing at him with concern and just a hint of suspicion. Cecil made another noise that came somewhere between a gasp and a sob. "I-- I am perfectly well, First Speaker. It was just the shock at discovering that you--" he allowed his voice to tremble and fluttered his eyelashes in modest confusion.

"That I was to lead a military operation?" All suspicion had disappeared from the First Speakers voice, leaving only glutinous self-satisfaction. "My dear Miss Prism, that is part of the duty of the First Speaker. To be at the head of his troops in times of danger!" Handcarte looked at his temporary secretary with fresh eyes-- she really was a most elegant creature! Despite the air of icy professionalism it was clear that beneath the cool, self-possessed exterior, throbbed the heart of a passionate woman. That plain, almost severe dress might conceal undreamed of delights. He licked his lips mentally. "Pray, do not distress yourself, my dear Miss Prism. He leaned forward and patted her arm. From her dark eyes he caught a momentary flash-- could it be passion, he wondered?

Cecil controlled himself. "I beg your pardon, First Speaker. It was just the thought of you, the man our country can the least afford to lose, placing himself in such peril--" Cecil broke off to dab at his eyes. Was he laying it on too thick, he wondered? A glance at the First Speaker from beneath lowered eyelids convinced him he was not.

"Come, my dear!" Handcarte essayed a gallant laugh, "it is a trifle. A symbolic gesture. After all, we have only to deal with a rabble of outlaws-- not that they cannot be pretty nasty if they put their minds to it," he added hastily, realising that minimising the hazard might not be in his best interests.

"That may be true, First Speaker. But the responsibilities! The planning!" Cecil breathed a wealth of erotic suggestion into the word.

"Well that is why I am First Speaker, I suppose," Handcarte said with a gruffly modest laugh.[12] He smiled understandingly. "My dear,

---

12   There were three reasons he had become First Speaker and

they all had carried long sharp knives when they engaged his

predecessor in full and frank discussions

you still look unwell. You should go home and rest-- I fear I have upset you with my silly chatter."

"I could not leave, First Speaker; there is so much to do."

"Nothing much really-- that is-- well of course there is a fair bit to get sorted out." Handcarte assumed the grave expression of one all but overwhelmed by the cares of office, yet nobly refusing to be laid low.

"Then I must stay. Let us continue." Cecil snapped the pages of his notebook. "We had just got to: *are to be retained in Dispatch Box 3 under my personal seal...*"

"Ahem! Miss Prism!"

"I am afraid I cannot spell a cough, First Speaker."

"I was not dictating. Miss Prism, your devotion to duty is admirable, but I cannot permit you to remain here this afternoon. A woman's delicate constitution requires time to recover from such a shock as you have received today."

"Really First Speaker!"

"No! I insist, Miss Prism. But if you felt sufficiently recovered to return this evening, I should be deeply indebted to you. As you say, there is much to be done."

"I should be honoured, First Speaker!" Cecil felt a surge of triumph.

"And perhaps you would care to join me in a light supper before we begin...?"

"Supper, First Speaker?"

"Oh yes. The position of First Speaker does hold some trivial advantages, and one of them is a rather more pleasantly furnished chamber than this. It is designed for the discreet entertainment of guests whose presence at Castle Downing must, for reasons of state, remain secret." Handcarte almost leered.

"I-- er--" Cecil wondered if he should try to blush, decided he couldn't manage it, and settled for a simper instead.

"Seven o'clock?"

"That will be wonderful, First Speaker." Cecil gathered up notebook and attache case and stepped out of range before Handcarte went into the hand-kissing mode.

"I shall look for you then, dear lady." Balked, he tugged viciously at the bell pull. "Leeper. Please escort Miss Prism out. And register her with Security for re-entry at seven o'clock."

"Surely you've got as much information as you need." Five Fingers Schofield stood at their table, a small wooden box in one hand and a doubtful expression on his face. Cecil wiped away the last trace of eye-liner and tossed his towel aside.

"I haven't got as much information as I want," he said stubbornly.

"But going for a snogging session with the First Speaker..."

"I am not going for a snogging session. I am going for supper."

"Aahhh!" Schofield made a mocking noise.

"And at that supper," Cecil continued, "the First Speaker is going to get very sleepy. Sleepy enough that snogging will be completely out of the question. And *that* is why I want one of your knock-out drops."

"Well, if you're sure..." rather unwillingly Schofield opened the box and took out a little capsule. "In his wine-- it should dissolve pretty fast."

"Will it knock him out pretty fast?"

"In seconds."

"And he'll stay out for...?"

"Three hours at least. *And* when he wakes up he'll have a rotten hangover."

"Good." Cecil smiled happily.

"What exactly is it you are looking for?" Amiens asked, "it does seem to me that, as our friend Schofield said, you have all the essentials."

"I want more information." Cecil set his jaw stubbornly. "The First Speaker talked about documents under his seal and I know Andrew will want those-- he's got a thing about documents. And there's the order of battle for this attack on Stembark Forest. Your boss will probably want to see *that*."

"He might be interested," Amiens agreed.

"Certainly he will!" Jacques said enthusiastically. "Of course you must get that material! We were just concerned that you were going to keep things going just on account of us."

"Eh? Well, if it comes to that we won't really be needing you. Now that I've got the First Speaker's invitation."

"Won't be needing us?" Amiens looked horrified, "of course you'll be needing us. And since you're going in with a genuine authorization, we should have no trouble bluffing our way in as your escort."

"Well... that would be useful," Cecil admitted. And, he told himself, it *would* be reassuring to know that those two would be close at hand.

"And it will be so handy to have someone else around to help carry things," Ratbag pointed out happily.

"Carry things?" Amiens looked puzzled, "what sort of things."

"Oh, you know..." the nicker shrugged, "just things."

"You'll find out," Cecil told them.

Act XIII
ALARUMS WITHOUT

At six o'clock Memorandum of Understanding Square was all but deserted. The tourists had returned to their guesthouses for dinner or, with the blind optimism of the uninformed, had gone in search of East Castellian's night-life. The stallholders had either left or were busy dismantling their booths and wheeling their barrows away.

Amiens and Ratbag strolled along the far side of the square from the looming wall of Castle Downing until they came abreast of an undistinguished grey stone edifice, where they paused to look at the notice that hung over the entrance. *Living By Design Ltd*, it proclaimed, adding in smaller print that "experienced professionals" were available for "consultations" and that "easy" terms could be "arranged".

"That's it?" Amiens indicated the building with the slightest jerk of his head. The nicker nodded.

"Looks pretty deserted. Are you *sure* it's the Secret Service headquarters?"

"There are at least five agents inside at the moment," Ratbag confirmed, "and more on the prowl."

"We'll wait for a moment and see if any customers come along. Where's Cecil?"

"Back there; just behind Jacques." Ratbag pointed, and Amiens tried to stifle a gasp.

"Are you *sure*?"

"That's him alright" Jacques confirmed as he came up to them, "he was just field-stripping his crossbow."

"It's incredible!" Amiens shook his head in amazement. "Perhaps we'd better get started-- before some randy guard starts chatting him up."

"Good idea. Do you want me to do the door or will you?"

"I might as well." Amiens began strolling towards a small door labelled *Deliveries*.

"Just a minute!" Jacques restrained him, "look!" Two grey-clad figures had just emerged from the Administration Wing and were walking across the square. Just beyond the Secret Service building was a narrow alley, and it was into the deep shadow of this that the two outlaws quietly retired. Ratbag scampered back to Cecil and joined him in the doorway of a pie shop, from where they watched with interest. At first sight the two secret service agents looked just like a couple of salesmen making their weary way back to the office after a discouraging day of failing to interest customers in their wares. But a more acute observer would have marked the way in which their eyes flashed continually about them, the almost military precision of the length of tape measure dangling from their top pockets, and the way in which they carried their sample books as if they were weapons.

The two agents were a couple of paces from the mouth of the alley when they halted suddenly, as though something had attracted their attention. Sample books at the ready, they looked about suspiciously. Ratbag and Cecil held their breaths. The agents moved cautiously towards the alley and disappeared from view. There was a clatter as of a dustbin being knocked over, then silence. Nothing happened for a minute or so, then the two agents reappeared and began walking back the way they had come. Rooted to the ground, Cecil and Ratbag exchanged concerned glances. Had something gone wrong? Was it possible that the agents had overcome Amiens and Jacques? It was only when the two men came closer that Ratbag's sharp eyes picked out the outlaws' familiar features.

"How do we look?" Jacques asked, "I fear that we must have waylaid quite low echelon agents-- these uniforms have not been tailored so much as blacksmithed." He tugged fastidiously at the unyielding material.

"You don't look too bad," Cecil told him, "and they can't have been that low echelon if they were wearing those." He pointed to the strip of material with its pattern of diagonal stripes that hung from the outlaw's neck.

"Oh that! That's only my old school tie-- Amiens has one too. I thought they might come in useful when you told me the fellows inside seemed to wear that sort of thing."

"They do." Cecil agreed

"I hope I don't run into anybody I know." Amiens looked suddenly worried.

Jacques smiled a little maliciously. "Not very likely, I should have thought. I believe you have to pass an intelligence test to get into the Secret Service."

"Ah." Amiens looked relieved, for a moment, then his face fell. "But it can't be a very hard one, judging by those two back there." He jerked his thumb in the direction of the alley.

"Yes. But you have to be able to write your name. That should let most of your lot out."

"Well, there was Thorseby Minor. He got fifty percent for that"

"What!"

"But I think it was for neatness."

"Well..." Jacques thought hard for a moment, "if we *do* run into him, you could always turn your face to the wall. Or cover it with a handkerchief or something."

"Are you two ready?" Cecil's foot was beginning to tap with impatience.

"Of course!" Amiens glared briefly at his colleague. "Really, Jacques! If you could restrain yourself from any more ill-timed badinage, we might be able to proceed." He gave Cecil an apologetic look. "Ready when you are, Cecil. What's the form?"

"We go in and I identify myself to the security guard at the desk-
- usually some lout from the Castle Guards. I show him this." Cecil
held up the flimsy piece of paper countersigned by the First Speaker,
or rather, by the First Squiggle. "Now most of the time he can't read it
of course--"

"Better watch out, Amiens," grinned Jacques, "he might be an old
boy."

"Belt up," Cecil said automatically. Jacques belted up. "Now what
usually happens after that is that one of the Secret Service agents on
duty comes over, takes the authorization and compares it with an entry
in the register. If you think you can carry it off, that's what you two will
do. Just wave the First Speaker's authorization about and confirm the
entry in the register. Then you escort me to the First Speaker's office."
Cecil was abruptly seized by last minute doubts. "Perhaps you'd better
just wait for me here and keep an eye on things outside."

"By no means!" Amiens sounded affronted. "Do you know the way
to the First Speaker's office?"

"Of course."

"Then you do the navigation, and leave the escorting to us. We do
learn one or two things in the outlawing business, you know... I say,"
Amiens was suddenly struck by a thought, "what do you suppose we
should call ourselves?"

Jacques scratched his chin. "Shouldn't we have numbers, being in
the Secret Service?" he suggested.

"Wouldn't do at all, Jacques! Your school didn't do counting."

"We certainly did!" Jacques snapped, outraged at this slur on his
alma mater.

"Not as far as double figures, anyway," Amiens replied complacently,
"no, we need names." He folded his arms across his chest with an air
of finality.

"How about Rosencranz and Guildernstern?" Jacques suggested.

"A little too theatrical." Amiens shook his head. "Scylla and
Charybdis?" he suggested.

"No... too classical. Let me think..."

"Assault and Battery!" Cecil snapped. "You," he pointed at Amiens, "are Assault. And you," he jabbed his attache case at Jacques, "are Battery."

"Assault..." Amiens tried it on for size, "I don't know.."

"Assault by name," Cecil said grimly, "or by me. Come on."

At that hour the reception area was virtually deserted-- a guard lounged behind the security desk, yawning, while at the door labelled *Authorized Personnel Only*, a Secret Service agent flipped idly through a book of wallpaper samples. Cecil clicked briskly over the polished parquet to the security desk, Amiens and Jacques a few watchful paces behind. Cecil presented his authorization to the security guard who, predictably enough, examined it with the total incomprehension of the professional illiterate.

"The matter is of some urgency, my man!" Miss Prism's knife-like tones sliced through the somnolent air, "I am here on the authority of the First Speaker, and he expects me directly."

The Secret Service agent quietly laid down his book of samples, and started towards the desk. Amiens nodded slightly to Jacques, and the two advanced, reaching Cecil at the same time as the agent.

"Can I be of assistance, miss?" Not waiting for an answer the agent held out his hand for Cecil's authorization. "My name's ah-- Max, and I am Duty Officer this evening."

"We can take care of this, ah-- Max." Smoothly Amiens reached out and took the flimsy slip of paper. He affected to glance at it briefly. "We shall have to check this with the register of course. As you are Duty Officer, ah-- Max, you might care to confirm?"

"Of course, but--"

"Good." Amiens turned on his heel and with a quick gesture to Jacques, marched to the wall cabinet. "Would you be kind enough, ah-- Max?" He pointed to the cabinet. The agent unlocked it, then hesitated.

"I must check your identities, gentlemen," he said, "as Duty Officer, you understand."

"Field agents," Amiens responded crisply, with just enough emphasis on the "field" to suggest that he had little time for headquarters types. "I'm Assault, and he's Battery."

"I was not informed--" ah-- Max began.

"Not surprised. You will probably see it on the Daily Circular the day after tomorrow, if HQ is up to its usual state of efficiency," Jacques almost sneered.

"But from which--" ah-- Max was still fighting back gamely.

"Operation Golden Age," Amiens rapped out, "temporarily detached to escort this lady at the express instructions of the First Speaker. Please confirm her arrival. Now."

As if they were acting independently of the rest of his body, ah-- Max's hands opened the ledger and began to turn the pages. "Let me see..." he ran his finger down a line of entries and stopped about halfway down the page, "here we are! Miss Prism, authorization signed by Mr Leeper and countersigned by the First Speaker, to arrive at nineteen hundred." As he spoke the words seven strokes boomed out from the great bell in the Revenue Tower. The agent looked up from the page. "I see no departure time entered?"

"The First Speaker has much to get through tonight," Cecil fluttered his eyelashes, "he was unable to estimate when we might be... er... finished."

"I see," ah-- Max leered.

"If all is in order, then we may proceed?" Jacques asked.

"You may proceed," ah-- Max confirmed, closing the ledger. The trio moved off. "Operation 'Golden Age'..." he called after them, "I don't know--"

"Few people do," Amiens said shortly, "we like it that way."

Their footsteps echoed down the deserted corridor, merging with the rustling whispers of plots being laid, rumours started, betrayals negotiated and assignations planned. Though it was after official working hours the First Speaker's administrative staff were a dedicated lot.

"Which way?" Amiens asked quietly. Cecil nodded towards the great staircase.

"Up there. First door on the right. Just knock and wait outside for me."

"What about Ratbag?"

"What about him?"

"Where is he?"

Cecil looked about him quickly. "Probably down at the souvenir stall in the Great Hall. Don't worry, he'll catch us up."

"But isn't it closed?" Jacques asked, puzzled.

"Precisely."

They arrived at the oak panelled door and Amiens rapped authoritatively. It swung about halfway open, and Cecil peered anxiously into the gloom.

"Do come in, Miss Prism," the First Speaker's voice was cold, dry and husky like a November wind blowing through dead leaves, "the escort may dismiss." With a warning grimace to the outlaws, Cecil stepped across the threshold and the door closed behind him.

"Welcome, Miss Prism!" The voice was now warmer, like a May breeze. But it still blew through dead leaves, "please step this way." One small lamp burned in the outer office, but on the far side a yellow glow of candlelight spilled through an open doorway. The First Speaker ushered Cecil through into a richly furnished chamber. Windowless, the walls were hung with deep red velvet, save above the fireplace where there hung a portrait of the First Speaker in the uniform of a full Colonel of the Seventh Heavy Dragoons. Close to the fireplace a table had been set with two places and the flickering light from the ten-branched candelabra flashed and glittered off silverware and glasses. Outside the circle of candlelight, Cecil could just make out the shadow of a huge canopied bed. The place reminded him of nothing so much as the brothel scene *from Blood on the Rooftops, Blood on the Tiles* (where the evil Don Anselmo attempts the seduction of the virtuous Cynthia but is thwarted by the arrival of the avenging Don Pedro d'y Angina).

Cecil began a growl, then hastily converted it into a sigh. "It is all so beautiful, First Speaker."

"It is one of the compensations of the office, my dear." Handcarte smiled complacently, "some wine?" He held out a crystal glass that must have contained nearly half a pint.

Cecil took it gratefully. "Oh, First Speaker! I hope you're not trying to make me tiddley." He noticed with some concern that the First Speaker did not have a glass in his hand. "A girl doesn't like to drink alone, you know!" He smiled roguishly.

"Perhaps I'll take a sip from yours, my dear." Handcarte leaned forward.

Instinctively, Cecil drained the glass. "Down the hatch!" he said cheerfully, and held out the empty vessel for a refill.

A little taken aback, the First Speaker took it and turned to reach for the bottle. While he was thus occupied, Cecil's hand flew to the front of his dress. In a quick movement he withdrew Schofield's knock-out capsule and held it concealed between his thumb and first two fingers-- unlike Cynthia he was not virtuous, and he could not count on the timely intervention of an avenging Don Pedro d'y Angina.

"Here you are, my dear." Handcarte proffered the brimming glass. Cecil affected to sip at it and slipped the capsule into the wine. It fizzed briefly, and dissolved without trace.

"Now my dear First Speaker," Cecil held the glass out with both hands in an offertory gesture, "you simply must have some of this, otherwise I'll think you're trying to get me drunk and helpless." He giggled archly.

"I assure you, my dear, I intend no such thing." Handcarte reached for the glass, "and to prove it I take this chalice from your fair hands." The First Speaker raised it to his lips and took a long draught. He smiled and shook his head. "This wine is not as intoxicating as your eyes!" he uttered, as though it were original. His face changed. "As a matter of fact it tastes distinctly off. I must ask--" He got no further. The glass dropped from his fingers and, with a noise midway between a sigh and a snore, he collapsed.

Cecil watched him, unmoving, for fully two minutes. When he was sure Handcarte was well and truly off into dreamland he tucked his cosh away with a sigh of relief and satisfaction. One of Schofield's knock-out drops was worth any number of avenging Don Pedro d'y Anginas! Unless the role of Don Pedro was being taken by Kodswallop, he reminded himself, and even then the knock-out drop was quieter. He was just about to steal forth to the office when he remembered something. Stooping over the prone form of Titus Handcarte he arranged the unfortunate man's limbs in a particularly contorted position that would ensure he suffered the maximum discomfort when he awoke. He took a slip of paper and scribbled a short note. *Respected First Speaker, please feel no regrets,* he wrote, *undoubtedly the inhuman burdens that you must daily bear accounted for your tired and emotional state this evening. It has been a great honour to meet you.* He signed it with a florid P, and left it propped against the empty wine bottle.

Returning to the outer office, Cecil eased open the door. "Coast's clear!" he whispered. There was a brief rustle as Ratbag wafted in, his eyes flashing acquisitively about the gloomy room.

"Better not," Cecil warned him, "I don't want to leave any traces." The nicker made a face. "Where are Amiens and Jacques?" Cecil asked, as he began lighting more candles.

"Just coming now. They're helping with some of my things."

"What things--" Cecil started, then broke off as he saw Amiens stagger through the door, scarcely recognisable beneath an unstable pile of parcels, packages, bags, and crudely wrapped bundles. Just visible behind him was Jacques, similarly encumbered.

"Just put them down here," Ratbag instructed in the manner of a railway passenger instructing a couple of porters on the disposal of his luggage, "but do be careful. Some of those things are quite fragile."

"Ratbag!" Cecil glowered at the diminutive figure. Oblivious, Ratbag prowled round the office, casting a predatory eye over every cupboard door and every desk drawer. At least, Cecil noted with relief, he was being careful to touch nothing.

"Was there anywhere in particular?" he asked, as he hovered by the First Speaker's desk like a hawk meditating its stoop.

"There," Cecil pointed at the wall, "a concealed door in the panelling."

"Not very well concealed," Ratbag sniffed fastidiously as he went to the spot. He touched the wood, and the panel swung open. "I don't think their locksmith can be out of kindergarten yet, either."

"He could have been at school with Jacques," Amiens suggested, "probably captained the incompetence First XV."

Neither Cecil nor Jacques made any reply-- they were watching, fascinated, as Ratbag ran his sensitive fingers around the inside of the closet and the boxes it contained, checking for any hidden unpleasantness. Apparently he found nothing, and began to remove the red leather dispatch boxes and place them on the desk, neatly lined up in two rows. There were fourteen of them, all with substantial locks and three with the additional security of big green seals.

"One at a time, Ratbag," Cecil instructed, "and don't forget when you open them, be careful."

The warning was superfluous. Ratbag had opened more trickily trapped locks than Cecil had eaten hot dinners, and was very alive to the unpleasant surprises that can lie in wait for the careless. Working with a couple of delicate probes, scarcely thicker than a human hair, he soon had the first box open. It proved to contain nothing more than a thick bundle of cuttings from broadsheets, all on the subject of the First Speaker. With the second box they also drew a blank-- they had no interest in the text of a speech on economic policy. But when the lid of the third was lifted Cecil let out a crow of delight as he saw a familiar manilla folder with *Stembark Forest* stamped on the cover in red ink. He stretched his hand out quickly to stop Ratbag stuffing it in his knapsack. "No! We can't take it. Do you think you could copy it all out?" Ratbag opened the folder and riffled through the papers inside.

"It might take time," he shook his head doubtfully, "this headed stationary is quite fancy."

"We don't need a replica," Cecil explained, "just the information."

"Oh, in that case..." Ratbag sat himself down at the First Speaker's desk and began scribbling furiously, stopping only when he heard Amiens uncork a bottle that, with remarkable prescience, he had secreted beneath his overalls. For half an hour the only sounds that could be heard were the scratch of Ratbag's quill as it raced across the paper, the occasional trickle and plash of brandy being added to someone's glass-- and every now and again a discontented snore from the First Speaker's private chamber. At last Ratbag's pen stopped. He got up stiffly, flapped the last sheet of paper in the air to dry the ink, then carefully replaced the original documents in the dispatch box. "All done. And won't Andrew be interested!"

"Not to mention Don Orlando," Cecil observed grimly. He had been reading over the nicker's shoulder. "What with the Seventh Heavy Cavalry *and* the shore enforcers, he's going to have a lot to think about."

Amiens and Jacques looked shocked. "We must leave immediately!" Amiens started to move for the door, "they must be warned at once!"

"We leave when we have those other papers, not before." Cecil's voice grated with tension, "check the sealed boxes, Ratbag. Look for number three."

"Got it!" Ratbag held up one of the boxes. "The seal looks easy enough-- it will only take a minute or so." The nicker's estimate was over-conservative. With the aid of a knife blade and a candle flame, the seal was removed, intact, from the lock in a matter of seconds. And the lock itself succumbed to Ratbag's ministrations just as quickly. But that was as far as the good news went. The nicker weighed the thick bundle of documents in his hand. "I just don't think I can manage to copy these in anything less than a few hours. And we don't have the time." As if to underline this, a more than usually penetrating snore reverberated through the room.

"We'll just have to take them," Cecil decided. After all, the First Speaker had given no indication of any intention to get at the papers in the immediate future-- he had just said they would remain under seal. "Close the box up, Ratbag, and do something to the lock if you can."

"Something?"

"Something that'll make it much more difficult to get open."

"Oh." Ratbag closed the lock, inserted a couple of tiny pellets of Clumpface's extra special glue, pushed them home into the mechanism and replaced the seal. With Amiens and Jacques to help, the dispatch boxes were soon returned to the closet, Ratbag carefully arranging them so that even the most eagle-eyed observer would not detect they had ever been moved. He closed the panel, then began to move almost casually to the desk. Cecil saw the glint in his eyes.

"No, Ratbag! We don't have the time!"

"It won't take a moment." A desk drawer slid open. "I just need to borrow a couple of things."

"What things?"

Ratbag straightened up holding aloft a metal stamp and a big lump of sealing wax. "I just need to do something about all my stuff," he pointed to the heap of packages and parcels in the middle of the floor, "we can't just leave them here. It would look very suspicious."

"We can't just walk out with them either," Jacques pointed out sourly, "I couldn't move two paces without dropping something."

"Besides it could well give rise to unfavourable comment," Amiens added.

"Not when I'm finished," Ratbag smiled. From the heap on the floor he tugged out two floppy packages which unfolded to become two big sausage-shaped canvas sacks with *Internal Mail: ADMIN* stencilled in large black letters on their sides. Into these the nicker stuffed his loot and laced the bags closed. "See!" He pointed triumphantly.

"We can't just walk out with a couple of huge mail-bags," Cecil protested.

"Don't worry, Cecil. You won't have to carry one."

"That's not the point!" Cecil concealed his relief. "At the very least those people on the desk are going to want to know what's in them."

"Not when they're sealed with the First Speaker's personal seal," Ratbag busied himself with candle, red tape and sealing wax.

"I am not sure that I can act as a postman," Jacques objected, "not really being up with the technical side of it, you understand."

"You don't have to act as a postman," Cecil told him, "just act as a secret service agent carrying a mailbag." He straightened his clothes and picked up his attache case. "It's time we were going." The two outlaws shouldered their heavy sacks and, staggering slightly under the load, started off. Ratbag flittered away down the stairs and was lost to view in the shadows. Cecil took one last careful look around the office, blew out the candles, then left, closing the door softly behind him.

It was almost two hours later when the First Speaker awoke. His head throbbed like a war drum and his arms and legs felt as though they'd been tied up in knots, then pulled tight by a team of enthusiastic elephants. It was characteristic of the man that he made no audible complaint but rose to his feet (albeit shakily) and scanned the room intently for any evidence of recent dissipation. He saw none, but he did see a scrap of paper propped against the empty wine bottle. He picked it up and wrinkled his nose appreciatively at the lavender scent that arose from the note. Another quick glance around the room, lingering on the bed, served to confirm that the note was the only palpable evidence of a visitor to his private quarters. Thus reassured, he bent his eyes to the curiously angular (but distinctively feminine) handwriting. It is one of the disadvantages of holding high public office that one's critical faculties (such as they might be to start with) become severely blunted. Titus Handcarte was no exception to this rule, therefore nothing struck him as being particularly unlikely about the note Cecil had left him. Ladies were, Handcarte knew, highly impressionable creatures, and it seemed to him entirely reasonable to suppose that such a delicate flower would indeed make a precipitate departure when the object of her devotion needed the odd forty winks. He folded the note away carefully for future examination by the Secret Service[13] and walked into his office. Despite the fact that he had no fear that the security of his planned operations had in any way been compromised,

---

13   Just because women were delicate, impressionable creatures didn't mean that one should abandon the habits of a lifetime

Titus Handcarte was a prudent man. He had not gained the office of First Speaker by trusting anybody, or taking anything for granted; the schedule, therefore, would be advanced. He tugged at the bell pull to summon his staff.

"So gentlemen," he concluded some twenty minutes later, "dispatch riders will leave for Basingstoke by midnight and I, Captain Bargemaster and four companies of mounted Castle Guards, *and* the Seventh Heavy Dragoons under Captain Porsena, will start out at oh-nine hundred hours tomorrow. The back-up force of Shore Enforcers will leave no later than midday. The commander understands his orders?" He looked inquiringly at the Chief of Staff of the Shore Enforcement Branch.

The Chief of Staff nodded confidently.

"Good. I anticipate no problems, but it does no harm to be prepared. And it will doubtless be a useful exercise for the men and their officers." It would also, the First Speaker reflected, be a prudent move. A First Speaker away from East Castellian might give rise to unfavourable comment among the Members of House of Sycophants. However a First Speaker away from East Castellian and at the head of about two thousand crack troops was quite a different matter, and any comment it did give rise to would be muted indeed. "I understand that word of this operation has somehow leaked out," Handcarte chuckled understandingly. "An operation like this does attract a great deal of public interest, so liaison with the broadsheets is important. As you will note, your written orders include the assignment of an Information Officer to each Company. He will be the *only* person authorized to speak to broadsheet writers. I want to make quite sure that all your officers and men are very clear on that point. Quite innocent comments can so easily be twisted out of context and give rise to misleading impressions when they appear in print. We must avoid misleading impressions, gentlemen. They can be most injurious to your health." The First Speaker's eyes glittered, and even the tough and experienced Chief of Staff shivered at the threat.

"You need have no fear of that, First Speaker," he said gruffly.

"I am glad to hear it." Handcarte gave a wintry smile. "That will be all, gentlemen. We well meet again at Staff HQ just outside Lecter two days hence."

Cecil had a difficult choice to make. On the one hand, it was a matter of urgency that Don Orlando be alerted as quickly as possible to the First Speaker's plans. On the other, all four of them were exhausted and in no condition to travel that night. Amiens and Jacques agreed, and even Ratbag, whose wiry little frame seemed impervious to fatigue, did not object too much.

But it was a decision the marksman bitterly regretted the following morning when Schofield burst into his room. "They are all on the march!" he shouted excitedly, flinging open the shutters, "see for yourself!"

Cecil had no need to look, for he could hear well enough the urgent bugle calls, the thump and rattle of drums, the clatter and clash of horses and accoutrements, the echoing crunch of hundreds of pairs of boots meeting cobblestones at precisely the same instant and, over all, the operatic roar of NCOs chanting their ritualistic invocations. Cecil jumped out of bed with a curse. "The buggers have started!" He stared disbelievingly through the window. "The First Speaker deceived Miss Prism! The unutterable swine!"

"Terrible!" Schofield shook his head. "The girl's father should take a horsewhip to him-- poor innocent young thing. Used and cast aside like an old glove! 'Tis true, master Cecil, 'tis very true. It's the same the whole world over you know, it's the poor what gets the blame. It's the rich what gets the pleasure--"

"Belt up!" Cecil began to throw his clothes on. Schofield shrugged and departed to see about breakfast. Plainly Cecil was not in the mood for philosophical discussion.

Cecil had just begun to pack his gear when the door burst open once more to reveal the agitated features of Amiens. "I say!" He gestured to the window, "did you notice the place is absolutely *crawling* with troops?"

"I had noticed, yes." Cecil tightened the straps around his travelling bag.

"Well, do you plan to take any steps?"

"Yes. Bloody great big ones. After breakfast. Now, Amiens, do me a favour and sod off." Amiens left to seek out breakfast; plainly Cecil was suffering under the stress and isolation of command. Left to himself once again, Cecil reassembled his crossbow, checked the action, then carefully began to fill the magazine with bolts. There was a knock on the door. Cecil made no answer. The door opened a little and the head of Jacques appeared in the gap.

"I say, Cecil--"

"If you've come to tell me that the place is crawling with troops, you're late."

"No, it wasn't that as a matter of fact--"

"And if you want to know what steps I intend to take, they're bloody great big ones!" Cecil worked the action of the crossbow once more.

"No, it wasn't that, either."

Cecil put his weapon down gently. *"Then bloody what is it?"* he shouted.

"Breakfast's ready," the outlaw said apologetically, and withdrew his head.

"Streets are going to blocked for hours," Schofield joined them at the breakfast table, his face troubled. "And there isn't any way through the back doubles either. They've got barricades up all over the place, an' spontaneous crowds out for the cheering an' everything." Cecil sagged in his seat. The sleep didn't seem to have done him any good-- he still felt exhausted. And what made it worse was that Amiens and Jacques were looking bright and energetic. They had, Cecil reflected sourly, probably already had cold baths and been on three-league runs.

"If we split up into pairs?" he began, but Schofield shook his head.

"Not on. When they've got spontaneous demonstrations of popular support going on no-one moves about unless they've got papers signed by someone at Senior Secretary level at the least. At best you'd get as far as the first Spontaneous Demonstration of Support. And then--" he shuddered, "a whole morning of shouting in chorus 'two, four six, eight, who do we appreciate.' No, there's no way out through the streets."

"Ugh!" Amiens snorted fastidiously, "sounds just like Sports Day."

"You always told me you enjoyed Sports Days." Jacques waved a half eaten slice of toast for emphasis.

"Never did." Amiens did not meet his colleague's gaze.

"But I thought you won prizes? Head of House, and all that sort of thing. Egg and spoon, I believe, was what your school was famous for."

"Couldn't stand that hearty stuff," Amiens growled, not altogether convincingly, "I was interested in the intellectual side of things. No flannelled fools or muddied oafs for me, let me tell you!"

"I wouldn't have thought you'd get very muddy in the egg and spoon." Jacques affected to consider the matter, "unless of course there was some kind of obstacle race combined."

"Belt up you two!" Cecil glowered at them, and made a threatening movement with his fork. He turned to Schofield. "So what do you reckon then?"

"The river," the landlord told them promptly, "Old Fred from Wharf Rats next door could take you upstream a bit-- say one and a half, two leagues. It's in the right direction. Then you go cross-country. With a bit of luck you should get ahead of them that way."

"What are the river patrols like?" Cecil was not thrilled; messing about in boats was no pleasure to him.

"No worry-- not to Fred."

"Then we've got to try it. We can help with the rowing."

"That might be a bit technical for us," Jacques looked a little worried.

"For me perhaps," Amiens nodded, "but I thought you did rowing at your school."

"Of course we did!" Jacques looked offended at the imputation. "But we had a man to work the oars for us. It is hardly the sort of thing one could be expected to do for one's self."

"Don't worry, gents." Cecil leaned back and favoured them with a not entirely unmalicious smile, "you'll soon pick it up-- there's nothing to it, really."

"There wasn't anything to it really," Andrew told the others as they approached the bungalow, "it was just a matter of using Montmorency's significator card on the spellcaster."

"Well done!" Clumpface wagged his head encouragingly. "You see, Andrew, I always told you that you'd pick up this maging business in no time at all."

Together with Orlando and Eric the whole party had taken one of the larger boats and crossed through the illusory storm to the island. The usurping duke was close and was expected to arrive at the lake that afternoon, so at Andrew's insistence everyone had come out to the island to make the necessary preparations. Then Kodswallop and Clumpface would return to the mainland so that Kodswallop, in his capacity as Don Pedro d'y Angina Immaterial, could encourage the duke and his immediate retinue (including the two girls, again at Andrew's insistence) to cross to the island the following morning.

"So you can actually control that?" Orlando asked, jerking his thumb back at the frenzied illusory storm.

"Sort of. I can remove it from the lake for a while anyway-- I just sort of poke my staff at it."

"Amazing! And when you take your staff away, it returns?"

"Yes. The idea is that I keep it in check when the usurping duke arrives at the boathouse, and he starts rowing across, then I let it return just about when he gets to the island."

"So he's trapped here."

"Right-- or at least, he'll believe he's trapped here."

"I certainly would in his position." Orlando gave the raging seascape a nervous glance. Eric, who had been listening intently to this exchange broke in, his eyes alight with interest.

"I wonder, Mr Orlando, if we couldn't keep this as a permanent feature. Make it a 'sea adventure experience'. It could be very popular with the younger customers."

"I fear not." The outlaw chief gave Andrew a calculating glance, "unless of course the wardmaster were prepared to stay with us...?"

"I-- er--"

"We could offer you very attractive terms," Orlando hastened on, "and it would only be for the summer season."

"You don't need Andrew," Janus said quickly, "you could get a site licence from the Guild of the Black Mages. You should talk to Montmorency about it when all this-- er-- business is concluded."

"Good idea! Make a note Eric." With a renewed spring to his stride, Orlando followed them to the bungalow.

"A very nice place indeed!" The outlaw chief eyed the neat little building appreciatively. "Much nicer than the old tea-room-- I hope he leaves it this way when he goes. If we extended the veranda a few feet..." He reached for the door knob, but Clumpface stopped him in time.

"Wiser to let Andrew do it," the dwarf warned, "he used a locking routine to prevent Montmorency getting in. It shouldn't affect anybody else, but..."

"But with Andrew you never know!" Kodswallop concluded cheerfully.

Andrew grasped the door knob and twisted. It did not move. Frowning, he twisted it harder, then tugged. Nothing moved. The whole shooting match felt as solid as the Rock of Gibraltar. "Seems to be stuck," he muttered as he stepped back and scrutinized the door suspiciously as though some message lay hidden in the brightly painted woodwork.

"Would you like me to try?" Kodswallop pushed forward eagerly.

"Thanks. It probably just needs a bit of a nudge. The wood could have swollen in the rain."

Smiling confidently, the big fighter swung his foot at the door. There was a solid *THUNK*, the whole structure shivered and Kodswallop staggered back with a puzzled frown, massaging his leg briskly. "That's pretty solid!" He gave the door a look of betrayal. "Just like kicking a mountain."

Everybody looked at each other in some consternation. Any structure that could withstand a swift boot from Kodswallop was an extremely unusual structure indeed.

"Are you *sure* about that locking spell, Andrew?" Janus asked after a lengthy pause.

"As sure as I can be. All I had to do was put the significator card on the spellcaster and state the command line."

"There must be a bug in the spell." Clumpface shrugged, "typical Sproggit and Axel!"

"Well I'm not going to mess around any more!" Andrew's lips were compressed into a thin line as he raised his staff, "stand back everyone." He switched the selector ring the destructor beam position and levelled the staff at the doorknob. "I don't want to seem unreasonable about this..." he hissed at the door, and twisted the trigger ring. A needle-thin, incredibly bright crimson line of light shot from the tip of the staff to the doorknob with an evil sizzling sound. Everybody involuntarily retreated a step or so, anticipating the violent disintegration of the doorknob and a goodly portion of the door as well.

Nothing happened. Andrew released the trigger ring and, scowling with suspicion, lowered his staff and leaned forward to examine the doorknob. It was completely unmarked. Very cautiously he held his hand close to the polished metal, then allowed his palm to touch it. It was icy cold. "What the hell is going on!" he grated. This was the first time the destructor beam had ever let him down. He shook the staff irritably, subjecting it to such a ferocious glare that the sensitive instrument quivered in sympathy and the grass in the immediate vicinity withered and turned brown.

"I don't think it's the staff." Clumpface had a worried look. "There must be a spell active on the door. And one of yours, Andrew. Look at the way it absorbed all that energy!" Eric and Orlando moved a few steps further back, and even Tiresome and Kodswallop looked faintly pensive.

"Alright. Then we'll have to try something else. There must be *something* in here on opening doors." Andrew began thumbing furiously through the manual. "Ah, here we are: *Locks: release of. Based on Sproggit and Axel's original industry standard Necromancer's Utilities, the Tarot 5.1 Lock Release provides recovery from a misapplied safeguarding routine. With the Hot Card feature and staff support (if implemented) it's just a matter of 'point and click'.*" He looked up from the book. "Does that sound like the sort of thing I want, Clumpface?" The dwarf nodded slightly, but said nothing. Andrew returned to the book. "Right. I see..." He switched his staff to the voice interactive mode. As he did so, Clumpface raised a finger to his lips and made a warning gesture. A voice interactive staff was supposed to respond only to the voice of its owner, but you couldn't be too careful. Andrew pointed the staff at the door and said "unlock: execute," in a clear voice. The crystal at the top of the staff glowed violet for a second, then turned a translucent blue. Yellow numbers and letters flickered in its depths like tiny agitated goldfish. They formed themselves into a line, scrolling through the crystal: *unlock is ON... executing... searching for lock data.... ***please wait*** verifying data...* Then the smoothly scrolling text seemed to hiccough. *can't find lockdata.fil!* it accused. The letters froze, and then rearranged themselves with an irritated flicker to read *irrecoverable error!... illegal function call!... aborting...*

"Bloody *hell*!" Andrew exploded.

"Andrew!" Clumpface tried to shout a warning, but too late.

The voice interactive feature on their enhanced performance model Mage staves was one of which the surviving designers at Sproggit and Axel were particularly proud. Each staff was provided with a basic vocabulary of some 50,000 words and used fuzzy logic in conjunction with some very sophisticated parsing algorithms to respond to oral input from its owner. In this instance, the staff responded promptly to Andrew's oral input then, as a precaution, switched itself into the safe/ standby mode.

A deep rumble of thunder shook the air. The ground quivered to the sonorous notes of a giant organ. To gasps of horror from Eric and Orlando a monstrous black shape materialized before them. Ten feet high, it resembled nothing so much as a knight from some titanic chessboard. Red eyes flamed in a vaguely horse-like head, smoke rose from the nostrils, and long teeth like ivory daggers sprouted from the mouth. From where its shoulders should have been, waved two long tentacles terminating in vicious serrated claws. To Andrew and his friends it was a revoltingly familiar sight. To Eric and Orlando it was simply revolting.

The stunned silence was broken by a three-note chime, then the creature spoke. "Thank you for calling Hades-Four, Torment and Temptation Division. We are proud to offer the discerning customer all the very best in diabolic services at affordable prices. We are committed to prompt service, total quality and customer satisfaction. Excellence is our watchword. Excellence and efficiency--"

"That's two watchwords," pointed out Kodswallop, who had been keeping count.

"Oh very well!" The voice took on a peevish note. "Among our watchwords we include excellence and efficiency. And effectiveness. I am Special Customer Satisfaction Representative Alecto, and it is my mission to be *your* supplier of choice for *all* your diabolic services." The tentacles waved insinuatingly. "How can Torment and Temptation help you today?"

"Ah! Well..." Andrew found his voice at last, and tried to assume a casual, yet conciliatory tone. "I'm awfully afraid there's been a bit of a mistake--"

"Mistake!" Alecto yapped, "what kind of talk is that? We are not in the habit of making mistakes on Hades-Four, let me assure you. If any mistake has been made I can guarantee that the mistake maker will be placed in a non-mistake-making category for quite a few millennia. Oh yes!" A narrow, black strip of tongue emerged from the lipless mouth for an instant.

"That's not quite what I meant." Having recovered from the initial shock of the monster's appearance, Andrew was beginning to feel a little more confident. "You see," he continued, "I think that--"

"It's YOU! *AGAIN*!" Alecto gave an outraged howl and flickered slightly at the edges.

"Ah... Sorry about that."

"Sorry? *SORRY*!" The tentacles quivered with theatrical agitation. "Don't you know how busy we are on Hades Four?"

"Sorry," Andrew repeated. Kodswallop dug him violently in the small of the back. "Don't be so apologetic," he hissed, "you're supposed to be the wardmaster; tell him to avaunt, or something like that."

Andrew stiffened his back and tried an imperious frown. "I hate to pull rank," he began, "but..."

"Say no more, Wardmaster!" Alecto fluttered his tentacles, "your voice is my command. It's just that we are so understaffed-- it's a positive *nightmare*!" Again the tentacles fluttered expressively. "Now how can I be of service?" he concluded, squaring what could have been his shoulders, "the usual package-- world domination, unlimited wealth and beautiful women?"

"Not exactly, no."

"Let's not be hasty about this!" Orlando tugged at Andrew's arm. "There are some elements in his proposal that might be the basis for negotiation."

Andrew waved the outlaw leader to one side. "What I was really after was a bit of information--"

"Ah yes!" Alecto's eyes blazed with the enthusiasm of a salesman about to close a deal. "The winner of the three-thirty at Kempton Park will be--"

"No, not that sort of information." Andrew waved the offer aside. "I want to get that door open, and I've been having a bit of a problem. I was just trying--"

"Sproggit and Axel, eh?" the creature interrupted, "the same old trouble."

"What?"

"See it all the time, we do."

"Oh yes?"

"Notorious for it, Sproggit and Axel," the monstrous head wagged up and down in agreement, "notorious for it."

"Notorious for *what?*" Andrew's temper started fraying at the edges, and an ugly violet corona appeared around the tip of his staff.

"Now just be patient and let me take a look." Alecto did his best to sound conciliatory now; he knew very well how dangerously unpleasant a narked wardmaster could be, and this one was looking very close to narked. "Just a quick check..." One tentacle snaked out until the claw brushed the door knob, then he relaxed and smiled-- or at least exhibited some more teeth. "I see... it's the locking routine, but you really don't have to worry."

"No? Why not?"

"Because of the problems they've had with that series of spells, Sproggit and Axel put in a safety override."

"How do you mean?"

"It's simple: the lock just defaults to a time lock, so after a given interval it automatically deactivates."

"As simple as that?" Andrew felt weak with relief.

"As simple as that," Alecto agreed, his eyes growing even brighter.

"And how long are we going to have to wait?"

"Oh, eight thousand years." The creature shrugged. "Give or take the odd century." With a triumphant laugh and a puff of smoke, Alecto dematerialized.

Act XIV
UNSETTLED CONDITIONS

ZIP-HISS!! The needle beam of crimson light shot forth again. *CRASH-BOOM*! The air shook to the concussion, and fragments of brick and splinters of wood whined through the air like shrapnel. A rumble and crash followed as a section of brickwork subsided reluctantly into a heap of rubble. Since the door of the bungalow appeared impervious to hints (and was likely to remain so for a few thousand years), Andrew had adopted the only alternative and was dealing with the wall instead. It was a tribute to Montmorency's talents that while normally one blast from Andrew's staff was amply persuasive for even the most substantial of structures, it had taken twenty shots to break a modestly sized hole through the wall. But it had been done. To the right of the completely unscarred door a ragged hole now gaped, from which brick dust curled out lazily. "That's about it!" Andrew called, rather shakily, and the rest of the group rose from the prone positions they had adopted earlier and approached cautiously.

"Are you alright?" Clumpface rushed up anxiously.

"Fine. Just need to sit down for a moment." Andrew swayed a little, then flopped to the ground. Almost immediately he jumped to his feet again. "No! Haven't got time for that. Let's take a shufti at that thing inside."

It was remarkable how localized the damage was. While from the outside, the pile of crumbled masonry and the burn marks deeply incised into the brickwork suggested the building had been subjected to a sustained barrage from a battery of anti-tank guns, inside there was only the narrow ragged gash in the wall. There was not even any brick dust on the floor.

Clumpface whistled. "You've got to hand it to Montmorency; he certainly knows his structural spells." He glanced curiously down the hallway. "Where did you find the doings, then?"

"Through here." Andrew led the way down the narrow hall and through the right hand door. "There it is." He pointed to the enigmatic mechanism, still whirring and flashing away on the low table in front of the window.

"It is *that* which causes the storm?" Orlando looked at it with disbelief.

"Yes. And this is how you control it." Andrew held out his staff and carefully moved it closer to the device. The whirring noise rose in pitch and the darts of light from the crystals assumed a reddish hue.

Orlando looked through the window, and gasped. "Amazing! I can hardly believe the evidence of my own eyes."

Andrew lowered the staff, and the storm reappeared. "So that's all I have to do. I'll hold the thing in check as soon as we know the usurping duke is approaching the lake. While Kodswallop gives him his final instructions, Clumpface signals us on the island. Clumpface will wait for Kodswallop, then both of them row over. Janus and Tiresome will be on the alert from the moment they see Clumpface's signal and they'll let me know when the duke's party sets off. When they're ashore on the island, I'll turn the storm back on. Then Bob's your uncle. Alright so far?"

"You may be a long time holding that illusion spell in check." Clumpface looked worried.

"I can't see what else we can do."

"You could disable that device here and now!"

"No. I *need* the storm," Andrew insisted, "it's part of the whole pattern."

Clumpface snorted and muttered something under his breath that sounded remarkably like "sod the pattern."

"What happens when they have landed?" Orlando asked.

"I'd like the party to separate into small groups-- preferably with the girls on their own," Andrew explained, "you don't think one of them will try changing into man's attire?" he asked Kodswallop hopefully.

The big fighter shook his head. "No." He wanted to discuss the matter no further.

Don Orlando felt a tinge of uneasiness. He did not desire the reputation of his outlaw band to be besmirched by any funny business, and what with wanting the girls on their own, and then wanting one of them dressed up as a man, Orlando did wonder if the eccentric wardmaster might not have funny business in mind. The last thing the outlaw leader wanted was to have his island used for some dubious transvestite ritual. Clumpface noted the cloud on the man's face and drew him to one side. "It's alright," he explained in a low voice, "Andrew intends the young ladies no harm-- he is just trying to duplicate the conditions as much as possible."

"What conditions?"

The dwarf shrugged helplessly. "Damned if I know. But he wants to duplicate them, whatever they are."

"The grotto *used* to be right at the back of the tea rooms," Orlando said uncertainly as he edged gingerly past a rose bush, "but all this looks a bit different..."

"How about this?" Clumpface called, "come and take a look!"

They found the dwarf on the other side of a tall, meticulously clipped privet hedge. He was peering into the arched entrance to what looked like a sizeable cave cutting into the angle between the back wall of the house and the steeply rising ground.

"Looks bigger than I remember," Orlando said doubtfully, peering inside.

"Montmorency may have made some minor topological adjustments," Janus suggested, "he is something of a perfectionist in these matters."

"Might as well take a look." Before he could have second thoughts about the matter, Andrew stepped through the portal. The others exchanged uneasy glances; you never knew what Montmorency might decide to do with a grotto, and he did have a reputation for mischievous humour. "Come inside and take a look at this!" Andrew's voice boomed hollowly, but it held a note of grim triumph.

No lamps were lit inside the chamber, but enough light filtered down through a shaft cut in the roof to reveal a stone-walled chamber with, at the rear, a perfectly ordinary-looking panelled door. The floor was smooth flagstones with three or four sheepskin rugs strategically placed and, to the left, a table and two upright chairs. On the table was a chessboard, a couple of old copies of *Private Eye* and a bowl of peanuts, half empty.

"What can this be?" Orlando looked thunderstruck.

"I'll tell you what it is!" Andrew was almost hopping with excitement, "it's Prospero's cell, that's what it is."

"Who's this Prospero character? Do we have a Prospero on staff, Eric?"

"Don't think so--"

"No, no! You don't understand. This is what Montmorency was setting up. He was trying to duplicate the pattern from *The Tempest*, you see, while I--"

"Perhaps you could explain the details later," Janus interrupted gently, "they are somewhat complicated."

"Right. Yes, of course. Lets just take a quick shufti..." Andrew helped himself to a couple of peanuts, then tried the door at the back of the chamber. It opened silently on well-oiled hinges, and Andrew stepped through the doorway-- to find himself in the hall of the bungalow once more. "Brilliant!" He beckoned the others inside. "This is ideal!"

"For what?" Orlando asked, his suspicions of transvestite orgies reawakened.

"I'll explain later," Andrew said hastily, "but the thing is this house makes an ideal base for us. It's virtually invisible from anywhere else on the island, and it's got this highly convenient back door. Now let's take a look at the rest of the island."

They emerged from the cavern-like chamber and Orlando led them across a little semi-circular clearing, up a bank and then pushed his way through a dense clump of bushes. "Here," he said proudly, "we have the Foxglove Bower."

Although they could see no foxgloves, they had to admit that it was a particularly charming spot. Shaded by trees and almost totally completely enclosed by bushes, all it needed was a concealed string quartet to make it the perfect setting for romance. A rustic bench was supplied for comfort, and a litter basket for convenience. Andrew made a careful note of it-- a plan of campaign was already forming in his mind. "Do you have anything else like this about the place?"

"Well we do have the waterfall bower-- that's quite pretty, and then there are two smaller ones in the maze-- we'll get a better view from the top of the ridge."

They followed Orlando up a narrow path that zig-zagged in a series of narrow, rocky steps up the steeply rising ground to the crest of the ridge, fringed with a line of young elm trees. From here the ground dropped away in three rocky terraces, tufted with bright clumps of wild flowers. At the foot of the third terrace was an immaculate stretch of lawn punctuated by flower beds and threaded by a network of paths. Beyond this the deceptively regular green geometry of the maze reached almost as far as the western tip of the island. A flagpole was just visible in the distance.

"But this is amazing!" Janus looked about with wide eyes, "I have seen nothing to compare with it, not even the Duke of Ambridge's ornamental gardens."

"We *are* rather pleased with it," Orlando said with quiet pride. He pointed to the right. "Down there we have the waterfall bower-- most suitable for parties of up to ten. It includes a paddling pool for the kiddies. And in the maze, though we can't see them from here, are two smaller bowers. These are very secluded and more suitable for-- ah-- small groups of adults. Very small groups of adults," he elaborated.

"You could lose better than a hundred men in that maze," Tiresome remarked, running his professional soldier's eye over the scene.

"Very easily," agreed Orlando. "People are always getting lost. We do provide maps, but even so some visitors still get hopelessly confused. It can be quite frustrating-- if they would only follow the signposts there wouldn't be a problem."

"Signposts?" Andrew asked sharply.

"Yes, the maze is quite comprehensively signposted-- it is a requirement of our insurance."

"They'll have to come down. Right now."

"But--"

"I want duke Roger and his mob as confused as possible, and the maze might be just the ticket. But *we'll* need maps. All we've got to do is think of a way to tempt the duke and his party into the maze."

"There will be no difficulty in that regard." Orlando smiled confidently. "The western entrance is incorporated into a small formal garden, so people wander in quite naturally, and before they realize it, they are in the maze. We had to put up warning signs."

"They'll have to come down as well." Andrew snapped his notebook shut, then began to lead the way down, scrambling awkwardly over the rocky ledges.

Three hours later, tired and dishevelled, they stood by the western landing stage, a pile of uprooted signposts as mute witness to their labours. "Phew!" Andrew dusted his hands off. "We got them all?"

Orlando nodded dolefully. "Every one. If the insurance company decides to spring a snap inspection, I really don't know what we should do."

"Tell them the signs are down for routine maintenance."

"Ah! Good idea." The outlaw chief brightened. "Now what do you want us to do?"

Andrew automatically looked at Janus. Everybody else looked at Andrew, and it was with something of a shock that the he remembered that he was supposed to be directing this show. "First thing is to get those signs out of sight. There should be room in the boat for them."

"I'll go and bring it round now!" Kodswallop jumped to his feet and set off.

"No! We've only got the one boat over here." Andrew grabbed the big man's arm just in time. Kodswallop in control of any vehicle was a mobile disaster area of cosmic magnitude. "That is, Kodswallop, I think Clumpface had better fetch the boat-- he's a little more familiar with it."

"But I need the practice."

"And we need the boat," Clumpface retorted unkindly, and stumped off.

"You're staying here?" Orlando asked, eyebrows raised.

"Yes, with Tiresome and Janus. Kodswallop has to intercept the duke, and make sure he's at the lake at the right time. Once the duke is on his way, Kodswallop and Clumpface take a boat and come out to the island. You," he told the outlaw leader, "should make sure that all the rest of the usurping duke's party is rounded up and secured."

"That will be a pleasure." Orlando gave a wolfish smile, "some of the lads are getting pretty fed up with woodcutter duty-- they'll enjoy the change of pace."

"But aren't we coming out to the island?" Eric's voice held an aggrieved note.

"Eric! I really think we should leave things up to the wardmaster," Orlando admonished his assistant.

"I suppose so," Eric agreed, "after all he is the boss." He sounded unconvinced.

"That's right. I *am* the boss." For a second or two Andrew revelled in the exercise of power. Then he saw the thinly veiled looks of disappointment on the faces of the two men. And he also realized that Eric was a young man, and eminently personable. Probably about the same age as the two girls, Andrew reminded himself. "Er... perhaps it might not be a bad idea for you to be out here after all," he said slowly, as he weighed the possibilities.

"We could come out with Clumpface and Kodswallop. We could help row, couldn't we, Mr Orlando?" Eric urged, his face shining with enthusiasm. The outlaw leader nodded.

"It is true we might be best employed in helping our friends get out to the island," he agreed. Rounding up the duke's retinue might be satisfying, but it did sound as though the island was where the action was going to be.

"Right then!" Andrew agreed-- it would be a relief to know that Clumpface could count on some nautically competent assistance. "But you must make sure that the duke's party is taken care of," he reminded them, "we don't want them wandering all over the place."

"Don't worry about that." Orlando permitted himself a relieved smile, "the competition among my men for that job will be fierce."

There was a slight thump and a creak of woodwork as Clumpface brought the boat up to the landing stage. He looked tired and his jerkin was dark with spray. "Just as well that illusion stops just before the shoreline," he said a little breathlessly, "otherwise I don't think I could have made it. There's about three inches of water in the bottom as it is-- those interactive illusions are fierce!"

"I'll get back to the bungalow and turn it off for you. Now you all know what you've got to do?" Everybody nodded. "Good. Let's get going." He started towards the maze, but stopped and turned as he remembered something. "Eric!" he called.

"What?" The assistant looked up from the signs he was stowing in the bottom of the boat.

"When you come over tomorrow, do you think you could dress up a bit?"

Eric looked puzzled. "I could wear my dress uniform, I suppose. But why?"

"You never know who you might run into," Andrew told him, with an enigmatic smile.

Duke Roger (Usurping) awoke to something that sounded like a civil war in an ironmonger's. He stretched, mumbled two or three profanities, rubbed his eyes, reluctantly unfolded himself from his blankets and emerged from his tent. The unspeakable racket came to an abrupt halt. "Buckingham!" He glared venomously at his toady who was trying to conceal the ladle with which he had been belabouring a cooking pot. "Buckingham, what is the meaning of this?"

"First light, your grace!" the toady responded with the insufferable briskness of one who has been up and dressed for at least half an hour before anyone else, "and you know the honest hermit charged us to be on our way 'ere cock crow."

"Hee hee!" Pebblestroke capered unpleasingly about, "he who is up before cock crow has some cock to crow!" He waved his bladder suggestively.

Enraged, Roger seized the cooking pot Buckingham had been bashing and hurled it at the jiggling figure. It missed by several feet, crashing into the tent occupied by Julia and Anne, which sagged under the impact, then gently collapsed in a billow of canvas. The air was rent by shrill oaths and girlish screams of rage.

"I say! Is everything all right!" Still in his nightshirt, but with his bejewelled sword drawn and flashing bravely in the cool dawn light, Herbert rushed forward.

"Another one up before cock-crow!" Pebblestroke cackled, moving slightly further from the confused group-- he might not be so lucky next time.

"Pebblestroke!" Do you go and arouse master Charles, and bid him attend us. Buckingham sent the capering figure on its way with a swift kick, happily killing two birds with one stone; getting rid of the jester and infuriating Charles.

Duke Roger, his good humour restored, extracted the girls from the remains of their tent, then set about arranging breakfast in the only way he knew. "Breakfast ho!" he shouted.

"Father! What are you doing up at this hour of night?" Anne looked around the clearing nervously.

"The Enchanted Island awaits, my dear!"

"Well if it awaits, why can't it wait until a decent hour?"

"Us mortals must be subject to the guidance of the spirit world in such matters," the duke murmured sententiously, "remember, the good hermit bade us be up betimes."

"He's a foreigner, uncle," Julia protested, "to them 'betimes' is anything not too long before noon."

"Really?" The duke looked momentarily disconcerted, then darted an angry look at his chief toady. "I thought you said--"

"I believe in matters of this kind, local time is invariably used." Charles, fully dressed and quietly immaculate, lowered a bulky kitbag from his shoulder and sat down on it. "I have no doubt that Don Pedro will be here directly, as he promised."

"I really don't see why we have to wait, father." Anne glared mutinously. "After all, we know the way." She pointed at the signpost reading To *the Boating Lake: ½ league.*

"Ah, yes... well the good Don Pedro explained all that to us last night, did he not? These things take time... Rome wasn't built in a day... in the fullness of time... one must not rush ahead..."

"If one must not rush ahead, then why have we rushed ahead of the rest of the party and what are we doing up at sparrow fart, father?" she asked, reasonably enough.

"A matter of security, no doubt," Roger snapped. He was beginning to feel the irritation of a man who has not yet had breakfast. "Herbert!" he ordered, "when you have got dressed you may assist Buckingham in preparing breakfast."

In an elegantly renovated grotto a few leagues away Montmorency sat hunched over his volume of the Collected Works, his chair surrounded by heaps of paper covered with his precise, angular handwriting. The lamps showed a sickly yellow in the early morning light. Montmorency straightened, gave a sigh of irritation and frustration, and closed the book with a thudding slap.

Bellingham, who had been dozing beneath a blanket, sprang agitatedly to his feet. "What was that, Mage?" he asked anxiously.

Montmorency waved a hand. "It was nothing Bellingham, go back to sleep."

"But it is after dawn! You have been up all night! I shall make some breakfast."

"No, no, Bellingham, do not trouble. I could not eat a thing." Those who did not know Montmorency might have thought that his voice held a note of defeat. But his graduate student did know he had been up for almost forty-eight hours, and had eaten only once in that time. Besides, Bellingham had been working long and hard on this particular routine, and was determined to invoke it. He muttered the incantation, and twitched his staff. There was a muted violet flash, and a loaded table materialized. From the covered chafing dishes, appetizing smells of bacon and kippers wafted. Pots of coffee and hot chocolate steamed enticingly.

"Your breakfast, Mage."

For a moment Montmorency remained silent, and Bellingham feared he had either been guilty of some arcane solecism, or else had mishandled the routine somehow. "Is-- is everything er-- in order, Mage?" he ventured.

"Most kind of you Bellingham. Most thoughtful." The mage put down his book and looked at his graduate student with red-rimmed eyes. "And very competently executed, as well. You should be commended, and may rest assured I shall record that fact on your evaluation."

"Th-- thank you, Mage!" Bellingham stuttered. A commendation like that from Montmorency was equivalent to a medal!

"Now sit down and join me, Bellingham. No I insist!" He materialized a second chair and waved the graduate student into it.

For some minutes they ate contentedly, and Bellingham was relieved to see some traces of animation returning to his supervisor's features. At last Montmorency looked up from his plate.

"Very tasty indeed, Bellingham. I do not believe I have ever had kippers tandoori before."

"Kippers tandoori?" Bellingham echoed weakly.

"Yes-- an uncompromising dish with which to start the day." He drank some coffee, then rose, rather stiffly, from his chair and began to pace slowly back and forth.

"I must confess that for the first time I find myself at a loss."

"You mean the wardmaster's message, Mage?"

"Yes! I have, line by line, made my way through *The Winter's Tale*-- not I might interpolate, in my opinion one of Shakespeare's finest pieces of work-- and I can find nothing relevant to the current situation, save the reference to the bear. I have also made a similarly detailed progress through the play *Richard III*-- an excellent study of a much misunderstood man, by the way-- which Cruickshank quoted in his message. Again, nothing!" Montmorency slammed his fist on the table and thunder boomed hollowly through the grotto.

"Could it be, Mage, that there is nothing else to it?"

"Nothing else?" Montmorency's eyebrows contracted, "what do you mean?"

"Could it not just be a 'gotcha'?" suggested Bellingham, greatly daring.

"A *what*? What on earth do you mean by a 'gotcha', Bellingham?" The mage's voice was that of a High Court judge asking what the Beatles might be.

"I was speaking of an analogy, Mage. Undergraduates in their first year often play silly jokes on one another-- you know the sort of thing, illusions of holes in the ground, untied shoelaces--"

"Yes, yes. I am aware that such childish japes go on."

"Well Mage, once the joke has been played, the perpetrator of the joke will often say to the victim: 'gotcha!' I am uncertain of the derivation of the term."

"You mean that Cruickshank means nothing by his message?"

"Only, 'gotcha', Mage."

For a second or so Montmorency's face remained impassive as he wrestled with the concept. Then quite suddenly he exploded in one of his very rare, spontaneous laughs. "Bellingham, you are a genius!" Again he laughed. "Of course, you are absolutely right! The one mistake

I have made this time in dealing with Cruickshank is to have fallen into the trap of thinking that there was a rational basis behind his actions. I should know better by now than to be taken in! Well done, Bellingham!"

Bellingham glowed with pride and pleasure. "One thing that I do not understand, Mage..."

"Yes?"

"If it is true that Wardmaster Cruickshank lacks expertise--"

"Expertise!" the Black Mage gave a bark of laughter, "the veriest wet-behind-the-ears undergraduate would be better at spell coding."

"Then why... er..." Bellingham's voice trailed off as he realised there was no really tactful way to frame the question that had risen to his lips.

"Then why has he got the better of me?"

Bellingham nodded dumbly.

"Let me give *you* an analogy, Bellingham. You play chess, do you not?" The graduate student nodded. "And you account yourself an above average player?" Another confident nod. "So I have heard. Then you would suppose that, if you sat down to play chess with a man whose knowledge of the game was limited to the fact that each side starts with sixteen pieces, you would be likely to win?" A third nod. "WRONG Bellingham! And do you know why?" A perplexed shake of the head. "It is because, Bellingham, this hopelessly ignorant player's first move is to take out a large axe and chop the chessboard up into small pieces."

"You mean he's not playing the game, Mage?"

"He is not playing your game Bellingham. Cruickshank does not play my game, and I do not play his. In order to engage we must learn something of each other's methods. In the case of Cruickshank this is not easy since I have yet to determine whether he actually *has* any methods."

"You mean he is... er..." Bellingham pointed his index finger to his forehead and rotated it. Montmorency gave another bark of laughter (he was certainly running rapidly through his annual ration, Bellingham reflected).

"No, Bellingham. If that be madness, then yet there is method in it." The Mage shook his head slowly. "But we *are* learning something of each other, and I must admit that Cruickshank has been most artful. Took me in completely. Well, well! We must see what we can do to recover the situation." He rubbed his hands with anticipation. "Now the first thing we must do is review the logs for the last three days..."

Duke Harold (Exiled) staggered from the sagging tent. He was cold, damp and stiff and it was still some time before sunrise. But even the unwelcoming dawn was preferable to another minute in that tent. Duke Harold had not been sleeping well since he had moved out of the cave, but insomnia was worth it. He shivered at the memory of that ravening creature! It was certainly enough to put you off caves for life. He looked discontentedly about the glade, which now looked more like a municipal rubbish dump than ever. It was manifestly unjust that all his subjects should be lying in hoggish slumber when the Duke himself was up and about. He looked around for means to rectify the situation, and his eyes fell upon the large iron pot that still hung from a tripod over the ashes of last night's fire. He seized a ladle and began belabouring the pot. "Wakey, wakey!" he shouted, "breakfast ho!"

From the other tents, and from caravans, servants, cooks and scullions scampered forth. Peel, the huntmaster, gave a quick flourish on his horn to arouse any laggards. And the three toadies, Bushy, Bagot and Greene, emerged from their tent, rubbing the sleep from their eyes. A fire began to crackle busily and the smell of burning porridge wafted over the glade. Duke Harold relaxed-- this was more like it! But it seemed to him there was still something missing. "Bushy!" He waved his arm, "the minstrels! Let their instruments discourse sweet music!"

"Your grace," Bushy bowed, "the minstrels are not here."

"I can see they are not here, Bushy. Summon them." Harold smiled indulgently, "doubtless the lads are tired after some mild debauch. Ah! Youth, youth!"

"In point of fact, your grace," Bushy spoke slowly and carefully, "the minstrels are waiting to be paid."

"To be paid!" Harold blinked. "With money?" he pursued, seeking clarification.

"Yes, your grace. And while we're on the subject, I wonder if I might mention that Bagot, Greene and I are somewhat in arrears...

"Bushy, say no more! I shall see to it at once. Never let it be said that the Duke of Benbrock-Oldstairs was sparing of his bounty to his beloved friends." The duke turned on his heel and strode towards a caravan of uncompromisingly utilitarian appearance, a slab-sided, heavily built vehicle whose small windows were covered with heavy iron bars. Humming confidently, the duke inserted an enormous key in the door, turned it and, with a grunt of effort, pulled the door open. Still humming confidently he went to the first of three large iron chests, inserted a smaller key in the lock, and opened it. He stopped humming. He stared, horror-struck at the emptiness thus revealed. True it was not quite empty, but the few coins scattered across the floor of the chest would scarce have supported an unaccompanied chorus of hey nonny no's. Frantically he dashed to the next chest and unlocked that: save for his second-best coronet, it too was empty. A gurgling noise came from his throat. Staggering like a drunkard, he opened the final one, only to find it as financially challenged as the others.

For a few minutes Duke Harold stayed unmoving, stooped over the empty chests. He resisted his first instinct to run screaming and shouting from the caravan since he did not want to disturb his many friends outside, nor did he want to disappoint them. He must keep the news of this disaster to himself for a while. But where could he seek help? There was only one possibility-- that sinister black-cloaked figure, the Black Mage Montmorency. He would go to Montmorency at once. And there would be no nonsense about checking the grotto first: they would go straight to the island. With an effort, the duke straightened up, and forced himself to walk calmly to the caravan door. "Bushy! Bagot! Greene!" he shouted, "and Peel! To horse at once! We ride to the Boating Lake!"

"Stand not upon the order of you going, but go at once!" Kodswallop boomed, relishing the line.

Duke Roger (Usurping) flinched before the volume. "All of us?" he asked.

"All of you," Kodswallop confirmed.

"Including Pebblestroke?"

"Including Pebblestroke. And you'd better get a move on."

"Of course, Don Pedro." Roger made a conciliatory gesture. "We will leave directly. Shall we see you on the island?"

"All your questions will be answered on the island," Kodswallop told him generously.

"But Don Pedro!" Roger shouted vainly as the gigantic figure disappeared among the trees.

Kodswallop ran into Clumpface a hundred paces or so short of the water's edge. "They're on their way!" he told the dwarf, "has Andrew turned the storm off?"

"Almost an hour ago. I had better signal."

"Are Eric and Don Orlando here yet?"

"They're with the boat. Don and I will be rowing, and Eric will do the steering," he added hastily before the big fighter could lay claim to any specific nautical responsibilities. Kodswallop looked disappointed, and was on the point of suggesting a different arrangement-- at least taking turns with the steering-- but the dwarf was pushing through the undergrowth to the water's edge, his signal flags tucked firmly under his arm.

"Duke Roger is on his way." Janus turned away from the window and looked anxiously at Andrew who sat, unmoving, his staff across his knee.

"Good. That'll be about half an hour before they get to the lake?"

"About that. The boats are ready." Janus peered through the window once more. "Ah! Tiresome has just signalled that Clumpface and Kodswallop are getting into their boat."

Andrew kept his eyes fixed on the whirring device, the tip of his staff a scant eighteen inches from the flickering machinery. The machine was definitely labouring-- the flashes of light from the crystals were a uniform angry red, and the brown smell of hot insulation filled the room.

"They're here!" Janus cried.

"This must be the place!" Duke Roger pointed to the mist-shrouded island, took a few proprietorial steps onto the landing stage and tripped over a mooring ring.

"If your grace will permit me..." with the expertise borne of long practice, Buckingham seized his master and steadied him. "This might be the most suitable vessel." He indicated a portly craft bobbing at the end of its painter, "Herbert and I will take the oars."

"Ah--" Herbert assumed a thoughtful look.

"You do row, Herbert?" Julia's eyebrows rose slightly.

"Of course! I was Head of House in rowing at school."

"Good! Anne-- you go with your father. Buckingham and Herbert can row. I shall take this boat with Charles and Pebblestroke." Julia climbed aboard a trim, lean skiff, unshipped the rudder and tossed it onto the landing stage. She knew enough about boat handling to be very sure that with someone like Pebblestroke on board, a rudder was an invitation to shipwreck. Before she could issue any further orders, Charles unceremoniously dumped Pebblestroke in the sternsheets, stowed his kitbag carefully beneath an after thwart, then took his place amidships. Julia caught her breath in surprise. For her, the world was divided into two classes of people: those who understood boats, and those who didn't. She had never suspected that her uncle's duellist might be a member of the former class. "*You* can row, Charles?" she asked, as she readied her own oars.

"Everybody in Nova Castria grows up messing about in boats." The duellist fitted his oars into the rowlocks. "If you'll cast off, I'll push us out."

To a squeak of apprehension from Pebblestroke, the skiff slid forward over the glass-like water. Two, three, four strokes, and they were well away from the shore, sliding smoothly along with a gentle chuckling burble of water under the bows. "Rest a moment," Charles instructed, "we should let your uncle catch up."

"That may take a while." Julia sniffed contemptuously, "he belongs in a boat the way a fish belongs on horseback."

That was a little unfair. The usurping duke couldn't lay claim to much seafaring competence but he was not at that moment directly responsible for the erratic progress of the craft on which he was the unwilling passenger. "I thought you said you rowed at school," he glared accusingly at Herbert who, for the fourth time, was reintroducing his oar to its rowlock.

"I did, your grace," the apprentice toady replied with some indignation, "but that was in properly equipped craft."

"And what equipment do we lack?" Roger asked, dodging a capful of water from Herbert's latest stroke.

"A man to work the oars, your grace," Herbert explained aggrievedly, "it is scarcely a matter one should be expected to attend to oneself."

"Perhaps it would help matters if you concentrated on just one oar," Buckingham suggested, drawing upon reserves of patience he did not know he possessed, "and I shall concentrate on the other."

Accompanied by enthusiastic splashing, the boat zig-zagged forward. Julia watched, clicking her tongue in exasperation. "Let's go on, Charles," she suggested, "we can at least land Pebblestroke, then go back and tow them in."

"They seem to be making better progress now," Charles squinted across the sunlit water, "I think your cousin has taken a pair of oars."

"About time! Anne can handle a boat after a fashion," Julia conceded grudgingly, "now let's get going." They both bent to their oars again, and the skiff slid across the water like a varnished dagger. After some dozen strokes, Julia glanced over her shoulder to check progress. "I'm not sure I like the look of that mist."

Charles gave her an approving look-- he did not have much time for the pampered children of the southern aristocracy, but he had to admit that Julia seemed to know her way about with boats. "I don't like the look of it either. But it seems to follow the shoreline very closely. Let's wait for the others to come up with us," he decided, "and we can go ashore together. It might not be wise to become separated."

Montmorency placed his large crystal on the table and laid his log carefully beside it. "Well that was most illuminating, Bellingham! So Cruickshank is actually on the island, yet has done nothing about the illusion..."

"Could it be he lacks the power, Mage?" Bellingham suggested.

"Pshaw! He could handle it with a flick of his finger!"

"But would that not merely collapse and concentrate the illusion about his form as you explained?"

"Certainly. And to disarm it he would need to use a properly coded routine. And the probability that he would successfully complete such a task is negligible."

"Then--"

"Knowing Cruickshank as I do he would most likely flounder around helplessly until he got impatient enough to override his better judgement and try to use Tarot 5.1. Quite what would happen after that is a matter for speculation, but it is certain that Cruickshank would emerge unscathed. However the environment within a ten league radius would become a very confusing and possibly hazardous place. No, I think the time has come for us to pay the wardmaster a visit." Bellingham watched intently as Montmorency made an adjustment to his staff, then murmured an incantation. For a moment the outline of the tall, menacing figure seemed to fade, then flicker at the edges. There was a slight smell of burning. Montmorency lowered his staff and clicked his tongue in annoyance. "There seems to be a minor technical problem, Bellingham..." For a minute or so he scrutinised his high-definition crystal, then gave a short humourless laugh. "Well, well, this is most interesting. Cruickshank appears to have placed a lock on the island."

"A lock!" Bellingham's jaw dropped. Ordinary locks were tricky enough things to handle, but those which could, even temporarily, block a senior level black mage were challenging pieces of work indeed. "Will you disable it, Mage?"

"It appears to be a time lock with a default value of eight thousand years or so."

"How can that be!" the graduate student's jaw dropped, "I understood that the wardmaster's ability in that area was--"

"Negligible. It is. However there are times when in his blunderings he hits upon a routine that reason and sanity would not so prosperously be delivered of."

"Mage?"

"He gets lucky." Montmorency folded himself back into his chair, lips compressed and brows furrowed. "He is on the island, yet he has not attempted to disable the illusion spell... he has placed an irrevocable time lock... what *can* he be up to?"

"Can you not monitor--" Bellingham began, but was interrupted by a shout of triumph from his supervisor.

"Brilliant, Bellingham! You are quite right. And not only can I monitor his movements, but I can transmit." Montmorency chuckled. "I may not be there in person, but I can certainly be there in voice." The mage picked up his loose-leaf binder and flicked through the pages until he found the reference he sought. He was about to make a move with his staff when he was struck by another thought. "I might as well discontinue the illusion now. I don't need it any more, and its disappearance may disconcert Cruickshank. Besides the network charges will be mounting." With a casual flick of the finger he terminated the spell.

"Oh look!" The skiff rocked alarmingly as Julia half rose from her seat, before her training reasserted itself. "Look Charles, the mist. It has gone!"

Charles glanced over his shoulder, and even he was hard put to restrain a gasp of astonishment. The veil that had enveloped the island had vanished without trace, and every manicured detail stood out sharp and green in the glittering sunlight.

Act XV
ILL-MET BY SUNLIGHT

Andrew stared uncomprehendingly at the device as the flashing lights died and the spinning wheels and oscillating levers slowed to a halt. He waggled his staff at the machine in a vain effort to stimulate it back into operation, then lowered the instrument and uttered one short expletive. Twice. The staff, sensitive as always to its owner's mental state, shivered in sympathy and three ragged streaks of lightning cut livid slashes across the clear sky. Andrew looked through the window, and repeated the profanity once again, but this time his heart wasn't in it. The drifting white veil of the concentrated storm illusion had gone, and on the twinkling surface of the lake the dark shapes of two rowing boats showed up clearly. Without much hope he stabbed at the button labelled "OFF" and was quite unsurprised when nothing happened.

"What's happened, Andrew?" Janus rushed in, his face taut with concern.

"I don't know. This thing just stopped working." Andrew pointed to the lifeless device. "I didn't do anything!" he added defensively. "Did Kodswallop and Clumpface make it?"

"Yes."

"Let's go." With Janus running after him, slightly bewildered, Andrew dashed from the room.

At the water's edge the others, screened by the drooping branches of a clump of willows, were watching the progress of the two other boats.

"They'll be out of sight soon," Orlando pointed out, "if they are going to the landing stage. And what happened to that storm, by the way?"

Andrew ignored the question, and trained his binoculars on the boats. He couldn't make out faces, nor would he have recognised any, but he could at least count heads. "Three in the first boat and four in the second." He lowered the glasses. "That's the duke, the two girls, the court jester... and who else, Kodswallop?"

"Must be toadies," Kodswallop scratched his chin, I know I saw two."

"Well, at least we've got the principal characters here." Now that the shock of losing the storm illusion had worn off, Andrew began to feel back in control. After all the storm had merely been a device to make sure they stayed on the island and there was, he realized, another way to ensure that. "As soon as they've landed, we've got to get their boats."

"Get their boats?" Eric looked puzzled, "you mean... *take* them?"

"Yes."

"But they're entitled to three hours!" the assistant protested, "it says so quite plainly on their coupons."

"You can give them a refund afterwards," Andrew snapped, impatient with this display of commercial probity. He was about to continue, when something about the young man's appearance caught his attention. He looked again. Eric had obviously taken Andrew's earlier instructions to heart, for his lincoln green tunic was immaculate, his boots shone with a mirror-like lustre, and a green feather rose at a jaunty angle from his bonnet.

"You did say to dress up a bit," Eric mumbled, conscious of the wardmaster's gaze.

"Absolutely! First rate, Eric," Andrew told him earnestly. The effect was everything that could be desired; Eric was in any case a very personable young man, and in his best uniform he looked the epitome of the young romantic hero. If the usurping duke's party was short on young romantic heroes, then Eric would be just the ticket.

"You were saying about the boats?" Clumpface asked.

"Yes. We need to get them. Is there any wind out on the lake?"

"A light breeze, nor'nor'west," Eric answered promptly.

"Excellent." Andrew grinned. "Can we get to the landing stage without going through the maze?"

Orlando considered the matter. "There is a path along the north shore, though it is badly overgrown-- maintenance is such a problem."

"Right. Then this is what we're going to do: Janus and Eric will keep watch from that lookout point overlooking the maze. You can't actually see the landing stage from there, but you should be able to see anybody moving through the maze. Try to keep track of them-- we must keep them under continuous observation."

"But what are you going to do?" Janus was not anxious to be handed a watching brief while his friends went into the thick of action.

"We'll go along the north shore until we're as close to the landing stage as we can get. Then Kodswallop sets off a couple of smoke candles."

"Then we rush in and bop them?" Kodswallop asked, his eyes shining.

"Not exactly, no. Once the smoke gets going it'll roll along with the wind and hide the landing stage. The usurping duke's mob will be sitting about in the ornamental garden having their sandwiches--"

"What if they didn't bring any?" Kodswallop asked.

"We can offer packed lunches," Orlando suggested, "only half a crown a head."

"Forget the sandwiches!" Andrew snapped. "As soon as Kodswallop's set off the smoke candles, Clumpface, Don Orlando and I will sneak down to the landing stage and take the boats. Kodswallop and Tiresome will make very loud aggressive noises and rush about the place (but stay out of sight) to encourage everybody to stay put."

"What if they don't stay put?" Kodswallop asked hopefully, "or if they have a guard on the boats?"

"Then you can take care of them," Andrew assured him. "Once we've got the boats, we'll row to the far side of that little headland and wait. As soon as the smoke begins to thin out, you two can take off and join us, and then we row back here."

Kodswallop took the two smoke candles and weighed them in his hand. "So I set these off, then we run around and shout a bit while you take the boats..."

"Straightforward enough!" Tiresome encouraged him.

"Yes. But there's that toady I-- er-- ran into. Big lad he is, too. And enthusiastic with it. He might need--"

"Rest assured, Kodswallop, if *anybody* starts getting stroppy, you are to take whatever steps you think necessary to make him un-stroppy," Andrew assured him.

"Ah!" The big fighter gave a relieved smile, "well that's all right then."

"Do you mean *nobody* brought sandwiches?" Duke Roger (Usurping) turned an incredulous and baleful look upon his toady. "Here we are, at a perfect picnic spot with nothing to eat. It really is too bad Buckingham!"

"Your pardon, your grace, but I understood your niece and daughter were preparing--"

"*We* brought *our* lunch." Anne smiled sweetly at her father. "And Julia even brought a bottle of wine. What did *you* bring?" she asked innocently.

Roger was about to say something about the nature of the division of responsibilities on expeditions such as this, but stopped himself in time-- a stern lecture on the nurturing role of the female was unlikely to get him any lunch. He needed the soft answer that encourages sharing of sandwiches. "I-- er-- don't suppose--"

"Sorry father." Anne turned away and strolled across the soft green turf to join Julia, who was setting out the contents of a picnic basket.

Hungry, Roger looked about for any possible source of sustenance. Charles had disappeared and Buckingham, he knew, had brought nothing. He saw Pebblestroke, alternately snuffling and chuckling into a crumpled brown paper bag and waving his bladder about aimlessly, and shuddered. There were limits. Then his eye fell upon Herbert who was returning from the landing stage. "Herbert! Come here, lad!" He waved the apprentice toady over. "Did you happen to bring any sandwiches with you?"

"Of course, your grace!" Pleased at the chance to demonstrate his forethought, Herbert indicated his knapsack.

"Well done!" Roger held out his hand. Herbert looked at it blankly until the meaning of the gesture sank in.

"But, your grace..."

"Don't thank me lad!" Roger reached into the knapsack, retrieved a packet of sandwiches which, with elaborate care, he divided into two unequal portions. "That's good toadying, Herbert," he said, replacing the smaller portion in the knapsack, "always well prepared. I like that in a toady. You'll go far, mark my words!"

Herbert watched disconsolately as the usurping duke swaggered off. He was hungry, and Roger had left him with little enough. This toadying business was not all it was made out to be. At least he had *some* sandwiches left and, he remembered happily, a couple of apples. Cheered by this recollection, he made for one of the benches and was just about to sit when the figure of Buckingham loomed up.

"Ah, Herbert!" He gave a hungry smile, "I couldn't help noticing just now..."

Thirty seconds later Herbert, now sandwichless and bereft of both apples, had come to the conclusion that toadying was a very much overrated occupation. Wherever he looked he could see people eating with every appearance of enjoyment. Except Charles, he noted-- where could the fellow be? Herbert's eye was caught by several rows of tall hedges that marked the landward boundary of the ornamental garden, and defined a number of shady avenues leading inland. The duellist must have gone down one of those, he decided. Perhaps he'd go and look; after all, Charles might even have some lunch.

Charles did have some lunch, but food was not what was upon his mind at that moment. As soon as he had come ashore, the duellist had shouldered his kitbag and set off to investigate the maze. He had recognized the geometric arrangement of hedges at once, and as soon as he entered it he realized that, while less complex than the Nova Castrian training maze at the Duellists College, this was considerably greater in extent. For a duellist, maze training was a required course, and Charles had achieved top marks in it though, he reminded himself grimly, that was more years ago than he cared think about. And it did take him some time to identify the pattern, but then he began making his way between the eight-foot hedges as though he held a plan of them in his hand. As soon as he came to the first bower, he halted. This would do. It was a small enclosure, with a simple bench, a litter basket, and a pair of young almond trees. It was, Charles calculated, less than two hundred paces in a direct line from the ornamental garden, but for someone without a plan of the maze it might just as well have been on the moon. It would make a very pleasant refuge from Duke Roger, Buckingham, the two young women and, above all, from the unspeakable Pebblestroke. He could have his lunch in peace.

Cheered by the thought, Charles had just taken out his sandwiches when he heard the first of Kodswallop's smoke candles explode with a dull thud. Without appearing to move fast, the duellist was on his feet, out of the bower, and slipping between the high green walls of the maze before the echoes of the detonation had died away. Hard on their heels came a second thud, and Charles quickened his pace. He was almost within sight of the ornamental garden when he collided violently with a running figure. He was only temporarily thrown off-balance, and as his left shoulder hit the hedge he was already recovering. A violent push from his left foot brought him back into the centre of the path between the green walls, and by that time his sword was out and he was ready to strike. The other man was still struggling to his feet. Charles recognised him, and lowered his sword.

"I say, Charles!" Herbert scrambled up, "awfully sorry about that. What do you suppose is going on?"

"Let's go and find out."

"But this is some kind of beastly labyrinth. I was completely lost."

"I believe I can find the way. Come!" Charles started off again and, though to Herbert it looked as though the man was strolling in a leisurely fashion, it was still a struggle keeping up with him.

When they reached the entrance to the maze, Charles halted Herbert's headlong rush with an outstretched arm. "It doesn't hurt to see what we have to deal with first," he said quietly.

"But the duke may be in danger!"

"Not immediate danger, I think." Charles pointed to where Roger sat gazing with polite, if slightly apprehensive interest, at the rolling cloud of smoke. From the depths of the cloud fearful sounds emerged, as of large bodies of men in close and fierce combat. The air shook to the thunder of booted feet, the crash of bodies through vegetation, shouts of defiance, and the blood-thrilling clash of steel upon steel. Herbert started forward, hand on sword hilt, but was again restrained by the duellist. "Unless you can see better through that murk than I can, you will do no good."

"But there must be a whole army out there!"

"In that case we are well advised to stay here," Charles observed calmly.

"But Buckingham is attacking-- see!" Herbert pointed to the figure of the toady who, sword drawn, was advancing boldly into the smoke.

"He may well decide to reconsider his position." The duellist watched, arms folded, as Buckingham disappeared from view. A couple of seconds later there was a cry of fear which was cut off sharply by a solid thud, and the toady flew gracefully out of the smoke cloud and hit the grass with a crunch. His sword followed closely after and landed point-first in the ground. "I thought so." Charles nodded slightly as his prediction was confirmed. "You know, Herbert," he took the young man by the elbow and drew him just inside the entrance to the maze, "there is something that strikes me as familiar about all this."

"Familiar?"

"Yes. The way Buckingham flew through the air in that professional manner." Charles cocked his ear to the shouts and curses emerging from the billowing grey cloud. "And I am sure I have heard one of those voices before."

"But what should we do?"

"Well, master Herbert," Charles began ticking the points off on his fingers, "that cloud of smoke lies between us and the landing stage, where the boats are moored. That same smoke cloud is populated by an undetermined number of people. These people do not seem to be encouraging members of our party to enter the smoke cloud. What does that suggest to you?"

Herbert thought hard-- an unfamiliar activity. "They... they do not wish us to get to the landing stage?" he suggested at last.

"Correct! And from that it follows...?" he paused and gave the young man an encouraging look.

"That they do not wish us to leave the island?" Herbert ventured.

"That would be my assessment," Charles agreed, "I suspect that when that smoke finally clears, we will find the boats have disappeared."

"But you still haven't told me what we should do!" complained Herbert.

The duellist took another look around the garden. Buckingham had risen to his hands and knees and was shaking his head groggily. The usurping duke was throwing an apple core at Pebblestroke. The two girls, their eyes fixed on the drifting smoke, were finishing off their wine. "There is nothing constructive we can do here at the moment, so I would recommend we have some lunch."

"Lunch!" Herbert's stomach felt hollow once more. "I have nothing," he mumbled.

"Well in that case you must join me."

"But-- I should stay with--" Herbert stammered, torn between his duty as a toady and his increasing hunger.

"I do not think Duke Roger (Usurping) needs your presence at the moment. Buckingham is at his side, in body at least."

"You're probably right," Herbert agreed bitterly, recalling his disappearing lunch, "he certainly doesn't need me any more. At least not until the next mealtime."

Charles eyed the young man sympathetically. Despite Herbert's offensive good looks and despite his background, Charles felt sure that he was fundamentally an honest, even honourable, fellow. He might be as thick as two short planks, but his heart was in the right place. He was, Charles felt, deserving of a better career than toadying. "Come, Herbert! There are better jobs in this world than apprentice toady to a usurping duke."

"Not for me, there aren't." Herbert scuffed his foot in the dust. "It's what I've been brought up for. Family tradition, and all that."

"Rubbish!" Charles didn't shout (no one had ever heard him raise his voice) but the word rocked Herbert like a box on the ear. "Listen Herbert, your father, Sir Roger de Coverly, was never anybody's toady!"

"Well what was he? I never knew him after all-- he died before I was a year old."

"Your father was... ah..." Charles hesitated. "He was... er... an independent businessman. Import-export. And," he was struck by a happy thought, "one of Albion's greatest experts in asset reallocation."

"Really!" Herbert glowed with pride, "he was well-known?"

"He was much sought after," the duellist answered with perfect truth. "Come along, I'll tell you more about him over lunch."

Breathless and exhilarated, as though they had just pulled off a successful smash and grab raid against overwhelming odds, Tiresome and Kodswallop scrambled up the narrow rocky path to the lookout point, Andrew and Orlando hot on their heels. Janus met them just before they burst through into the open, and halted them with an upraised hand. "We must be careful," he warned, "there is little cover beyond the trees, and any movement against this background will stand out."

"Quite right!" Tiresome growled, furious with himself at forgetting such an elementary precaution.

"There is a need for secrecy?" Orlando asked with some puzzlement, "that performance at the landing stage should leave them in little doubt that there are others on the island."

"They probably think it's a squadron of heavy cavalry," Clumpface observed acidly.

"It's the principle of the thing," Andrew told them, "they may know they've got company on the island, but they don't have to know where we are."

"Quite! Always minimize your opponent's information, even negative information." Tiresome nodded vigorously. He was still hideously embarrassed about forgetting the need for concealment.

"You were successful, we saw," Janus observed with a smile, "but who was it who was so foolhardy as to try to interfere?"

"Interfere?" Andrew swung round sharply. This was the first he'd heard of it.

"Yes. The one man I saw come flying out of the smoke," continued Janus. "You may rest assured that you caused the fellow no permanent physical injury."

"Just a minute!" Andrew glared at Kodswallop-- there was no need to ask who it was who might have made someone fly backwards through the air. "You didn't say anything about any punch-up."

"Well..." the big fighter shrugged, "it was a simple accident-- could have happened to anybody. It was..." he paused, then inspiration came. "It was self-defence!" he declaimed righteously.

"Self-defence?"

"Yes, self-defence. He came at me with his sword-- Tiresome saw. He charged right at me! You tell him, Tiresome!"

"Of course..." The knight met Andrew's sceptical stare with a bland smile. "I saw the man running, with his sword drawn. I also saw Kodswallop running. At the crucial moment my attention was distracted so I did not witness the exact moment of... er.... engagement."

"But you *did* see this bloke running after Kodswallop?" Andrew was beginning to feel anxious; if there *was* someone down there who was prepared to chase after Kodswallop, then they could be facing a dangerous nutter.

"It is quite possible that he changed direction by one hundred and eighty degrees when I took my eyes off him," the knight mused, "so I cannot dismiss that possibility."

"It was *proactive* self-defence, Andrew, honestly!" Kodswallop gave his traitorous colleague a reproachful look.

"Alright!" Andrew tried to glare at the two men. "It had better not have been the usurping duke. I want him in full working order."

"Oh, he'll be alright when he comes to," Kodswallop assured him, "and it wasn't the duke anyway-- just the toady."

"Janus!" Eric's voice, low but vibrating with urgency, made everybody jump. The elf wheeled about and, stooping cautiously, made his way through the screen of overhanging boughs to the lookout point. The others gathered close behind, but remained still and quiet, and careful not to disarrange the drooping greenery that hid them from view.

"Look! There's another boat," Eric pointed.

"Another boat!" Heedless of the camouflage, Andrew pushed his way through to join Janus and Eric. A dark shape was cutting an erratic path across the rippling water, reflected sunlight flashing from the oar blades.

"Five men aboard." The elf narrowed his eyes, "and something else... I cannot quite make it out."

"Let's take a butchers." Andrew raised his binoculars. "You're right, Janus. Five men... the one steering is wearing some kind of grey coat... and..." his voice rose to an incredulous squeak, "...there are two bloody great dogs!" He almost dropped the binoculars. Crouching down, he steadied his hands on a rock and stared long and hard through the glasses. He was rewarded by a glint of reflected light from some polished metal article the man in the grey coat carried at his waist. "It's the huntsman!" he shouted, rising to his feet, "coat so grey, *and* the hunting horn, *and* the hounds!"

"But it's afternoon," Eric objected.

"Doesn't matter!" Andrew was almost hopping with excitement. "We've done it! We've got the exiled duke too!"

Duke Harold (Exiled) glanced uneasily at Bagot and Greene. "Are you two sure you know what you're doing?" he asked.

"Rest assured, your grace." Bagot paused to sweep his oar over the surface of the water, transferring a healthy slice of it to Bushy in the bows. There was a snarled profanity. "Rest assured," Bagot repeated, "we are quite familiar with this kind of activity-- did rather well in it at school, as a matter of fact."

Not particularly reassured by this, Harold shifted uneasily on his seat; at least the water was calm. One of the hounds gave a mournful yodel and Peel made an ineffectual gesture, rocking the boat alarmingly. "Keep still, Peel!" the duke snapped, "I really cannot see why you had to bring those creatures along."

"Traditional, your grace," the huntsman replied, "and you never know what kind of game there might be on that island. Ponto! Sit!" he shouted at the second of the creatures who appeared to be labouring under the misapprehension that a bone lay buried somewhere beneath the bottom boards. "I think they're settling down nicely now, your grace." The first hound gave another yodelling cry, staggered forward on trembling legs and vomited over the duke's feet.

"Do you really think the two brothers will become reconciled right away?" Janus looked sceptical.

"They might need a bit of persuading..." Kodswallop looked hopeful.

Andrew ignored them. "First we need to get the usurping duke's party into the maze-- I want them out of the way of the other lot for the time being."

"I see." Janus frowned. "Kodswallop and Tiresome: go and persuade the usurping duke's party to enter the maze, and quickly!" he ordered. Without a word the two dashed off.

"Wait! Andrew called after them, "don't forget the plan!" But he was too late.

"They won't be going in," Janus reminded him, "all they have to do is chase the others in."

"Yes, but what if they chase after them?"

A look of concern clouded the elf's brow for an instant. "No, they would not be so impetuous."

"One of them's Kodswallop," Clumpface reminded everybody.

"Yes." Andrew gloomily reviewed the additional complications that an unguided Kodswallop would impose upon an already adequately complicated situation.

"I'll be able to find them quickly enough," Eric told them, "I know that maze like the back of my hand."

"You do!" Andrew gazed at the youth with relief.

"Oh yes, Eric could find his way through that thing blindfolded," Orlando told them proudly.

"Brilliant! Okay, Eric, it's going to be up to you. Now which would you say is the most romantically appealing of the bowers?"

"The Waterfall Bower," Eric replied promptly.

"Then I want the two girls taken there. That's your first job, Eric. Get them there, and see they don't leave until I arrive."

"But-- but what should I say?" Eric was crimson with embarrassment.

"Just ask them to follow you. Say you are escorting them to a place of safety. Tell them all things will be explained shortly. Chat them up a bit. If they start asking questions, just be mysterious."

"Couldn't I be mystified? It sounds a bit easier"

Andrew ignored the question. "Next, any young men from either party-- usurping duke or exiled duke-- I want them in the Foxglove Bower. Will you look after that, Clumpface, with Mr Orlando?"

"Right." The dwarf nodded. "And you want them held there until further notice?"

"Yes. Janus and I will deal with the two dukes. We'll keep them apart-- one in each bower in the maze." Andrew folded his plan of the maze and tucked it into his belt. "We'd better get on with it... I only wish Ratbag and Cecil were here-- we're awfully thin on the ground."

Ratbag and Cecil would have been very glad to be there. In fact they would have been very glad to be anywhere but where they were, which was in Frettleigh Gaol, together with Amiens and Jacques. It was the simple kind of accident that can happen to anyone who happens to steal four horses, four uniforms and related accoutrements from a squadron of the Seventh Heavy Dragoons and then happens to be found in possession of such items. Ratbag had obtained the gear without causing the slightest ripple. The uniforms were at least an acceptable fit. And the disguise had stood them in good stead, for no-one had questioned them for the better part of the day. And had not Jacques accosted a trooper, mistakenly identifying him as an old school chum, they might not have found themselves arrested on charges that started with high treason, ran on through espionage, sabotage, mutiny and taking and riding away a horse without the owner's permission, down to failing to salute a superior officer. The East Castellian military establishment prided itself on its justice system and the four accused had been promised a fair trial and a fair execution. Even now they could hear all too clearly the thud of mallets and the ring of hammers as a squad of pioneers put the finishing touches to a perfectly splendid quadruple gallows.

Cecil looked broodily around the cramped cell. He needed something to cheer him up. "Ratbag. Do you remember how many charges they had on the list?"

"Fifteen or sixteen, I think."

"Oh." The marksman drooped. "I was hoping it might be up to twenty. That would be a record."

"You could always ask them to take a few more offences into consideration," the nicker tried to comfort his friend, "I don't think they had loitering with intent, arson or parking in a prohibited area."

"You've got a point there!" Cheered, the marksman peered through the tiny barred window and surveyed the labouring pioneers. "Think they'll be finished soon?"

Ratbag scampered to his side, jumped up and, hanging onto the bars, peered through the window. "Oh yes, I expect so. Probably before lunch."

"Good." Cecil nodded with satisfaction. "I hate hanging around."

"Look, there must be *something* we can do!" Jacques, who had been slumped in a corner, sat up abruptly, "I mean couldn't we entice a warder in here, then take his clothes and walk out in disguise?"

"How about digging a tunnel?" Amiens suggested, scratching with his fingernails at the narrow joint between two flagstones, "we could conceal the entrance with a vaulting horse and--"

"Where would we get a vaulting horse?" Jacques challenged.

"We could make one."

"With what?"

"Ah..." Amiens looked around the unfurnished cell for inspiration, but found none. "Well, perhaps Ratbag could do the digging, and we could all crowd around him in a group pretending to have a sing-song so the warders wouldn't see him."

"Nah." Cecil dismissed the idea.

"Well what are we going to do! We can't just sit here and wait till they take us out and--" Amiens gulped, "and-- hang us."

"'Course we're not. We'll leave about... one o'clock, I reckon, Ratbag?"

"Why-- that is how? I mean why one o'clock?" Amiens spluttered.

"And how?" Jacques added.

Cecil sighed and sank to the floor, where he arranged himself cross-legged. "They'll finish working on the gallows by noon. Then they'll go away. There'll be only a couple of soldiers on guard till... when do they hold executions, Ratbag?"

"Midnight," the nicker told him, "it's traditional."

"Midnight," Cecil repeated with satisfaction, "so that gives us almost twelve hours start."

"But won't they be coming to take us to the trial?" Amiens asked.

"Trial?" Cecil looked blank for a moment. "Oh, the trial! Well they couldn't have that before noon tomorrow at the earliest."

"You mean we don't get a trial!" Jacques was indignant.

"Of course you get a trial!" Cecil retorted, not unkindly, "but not till tomorrow, see?"

"But that's *after* the execution!"

Cecil shrugged. "Tradition," he explained. "Anyway we're going to have to miss it. 'Cause we'll be off."

"How?" Jacques asked again.

"As soon as the coast is clear, Ratbag opens the door. Then we go out."

"The coast is *clear?*"

"Well, sort of clear. There'll be a couple of guards. Maybe three or four. We clobber them, get our stuff from the front office, then bugger off."

"Ah, yes!" Both outlaws had completely forgotten the fact that to a nicker a locked door is scarcely more substantial than mist-- and not so damp. They cheered up considerably.

"Now we're going to have to keep off the roads for a while," Cecil warned them, "until we've got a league or so from here. Then we'll cut back to the main road and the first chance we get Ratbag will find us some more horses. We could be in Lecter by this evening. Just one thing!" He turned on the two outlaws so suddenly that they both jumped. "I don't want either of you, especially you--" his finger stabbed at Jacques, "engaging in casual conversation with anybody. Especially if it's a bloke you happen to think you have been at school with."

"Of course not!" Jacques shook his head vigorously. "Is there anything we can do to help?" he offered.

"As a matter of fact, there is." Cecil's finger wagged emphatically, "you can both of you keep... your... mouths... shut."

Duke Roger (Usurping) and Buckingham were gazing hopefully at the approaching boat when Tiresome and Kodswallop had burst upon the scene. The sight of the two huge fighting men advancing like doom in armour but faster, galvanized Roger into instant action. He dashed from the water's edge, across the immaculate grass, hurdled the stone bench in fine style and disappeared into the maze. Buckingham was scarcely slower, pausing only to shout a warning over his shoulder to the two girls. Julia and Anne were determined to stay put, but this determination faded rapidly as Pebblestroke scampered towards them fearing, with good reason, that the two oncoming figures might not share his sense of humour.

"Come on!" Anne jumped to her feet.

"Do we have any wine left?" Julia hesitated for a moment, her hand straying to the picnic basket.

Anne shook her head. "Come on!" she repeated, and led the way into the maze.

Pebblestroke flung a panic-stricken look over his shoulder, and a definitely worried look at the entrance to the maze. Panic won out over definite worry by five lengths, and he darted after the girls.

Kodswallop and Tiresome sat down on the stone bench. Kodswallop mopped his brow and looked expectantly at his colleague. Tiresome nodded and pulled a bottle from his knapsack. They each took a swig, then another, as they waited and watched the approach of the exiled duke's craft.

"Not very good at it, are they," Kodswallop said contemptuously, as he observed the erratic, splashing passage of the little vessel, "still, I'm not surprised. These southerners always are a bit thick when it comes to technical stuff."

Tiresome was struck temporarily speechless by this example of such a large rock being chucked in such a fragile greenhouse, and by the time he had recovered the prow of the oncoming boat was a scant fifty paces from the landing stage. "They are at least arriving here, Kodswallop," he observed pointedly, "with the boat on one piece and afloat. Now, will you be able to identify the duke for me?"

"I'd recognise him anywhere. He'll be the one talking about books in running brooks and sermons in stones and all that sort of thing."

"Very well. Let us concentrate upon getting him to one of the bowers."

"What about the others?"

"Let me go ahead with the duke-- give me a few minutes, then you may persuade the others to enter the maze."

"Ah..."

The boat hit the landing stage with a hollow thud, and all the occupants tumbled forward. An unearthly howl arose.

"That one's the duke!" Kodswallop pointed to the figure crawling out of the boat, "he's-- what is he doing?"

On the grass, the duke was executing some complex evolution that involved rubbing his feet along the ground one at a time, while turned at some unnatural angle. "Curious!" Tiresome shrugged, "perhaps some obscure propitiation ritual?"

"Looks more like someone trying to scrape shit off his boots," Kodswallop observed, "anyway, he's your lad."

As Tiresome strode forward, the other four men began to clamber out of the boat. Bushy and Bagot were already ashore by the time they caught sight of Kodswallop bearing down on them, and immediately tried to get back in the boat. They were hampered in this by the passive behaviour of the hounds, who were simply being stupid and getting under everybody's feet, and the active behaviour of Peel and Greene, who were trying to untie the boat and push off.

"Just a minute, lads!" Kodswallop cast a glance over his shoulder to confirm Tiresome and the exiled duke were on their way to the maze. "Just a moment-- now now!" Bushy and Bagot, putting an enforced valour on, drew their swords and turned to face this awesome figure. Kodswallop wagged a finger at them. "There'll be no need for that," he said pleasantly enough, "put up your bright swords or the dew will rust them."

Bushy and Bagot did not put up their bright swords. Instead, impelled by one part desperation and two parts realization that Greene and Peele were now ashore with their weapons drawn, they charged the big fighter. Kodswallop smiled happily. In a single movement he drew his own weapon and swept it gracefully across the two blades that were cutting at him. There was a sharp snapping sound as Bushy's sword blade was sheared in two, and an ugly *sproinnggg!* as Bagot's bent like a bow, then leaped from his hand to splash into the lake behind him. There was a clatter as Peel and Greene dropped their own weapons on the landing stage. Kodswallop slipped his sword back into its sheath, then grasped Bushy and Bagot each by a shoulder. "Will you walk this way, gentlemen?" he suggested.

They began to walk. Greene and Peel followed.

Kodswallop ushered them into the maze, walked beside them for a few paces, then allowed them to disappear around the next corner. It was only then that he remembered that he had not brought a plan of the maze with him. And shortly after that he remembered that neither had Tiresome.

Act XVI
VOICES OFF

Everything had gone according to plan-- sort of. Eric, using navigational principles known only to himself, had swiftly located the two girls and escorted them to the Waterfall Bower where he had remained, an acutely uncomfortable guard, until Orlando and Clumpface had appeared. They had failed to find anybody and had lost themselves twice. Eric, thankful to hand over his guard duties to his chief, had set off with Clumpface in search of any young man from either party. They had located Herbert who, separated from Charles and hopelessly lost, had been wandering round in circles. The young man was so grateful to be found that he was happy to follow them to the Foxglove Bower. There he waited, mystified, under the avuncular eye of Clumpface.

By now a little breathless, Eric had finally located Andrew and Janus whose plans had worked to the extent that they had located the two dukes, but failed in that they had been unable to keep them apart. Now the two brothers stood in the eastern bower, glaring at each other in mute hostility while Janus, who had prudently disarmed them both, kept guard. Andrew, whose plans, such as they were, had depended upon the two brothers being kept apart for a while, was trying to work out what to do next.

"At last! I've found you!" Eric burst into the bower, then stopped dead as he saw the two dukes. He beckoned fiercely to Andrew, and drew him some paces away. "We've got the two girls," he whispered, "Mr Orlando's looking after them. And I found one young man called Herbert, from the usurping duke's party.

"Good show! At least something's going right," Andrew grimaced, "have you seen any sign of the others?"

"Not exactly *seen*, but I've heard people running around and shouting. And one of them did sound like Kodswallop. But you can't tell where they are by the sound."

"I know! You can't see anything through those hedges, and anything you hear could be coming from anywhere."

"Yes, we designed it like that," Eric said proudly, "Do you want to talk to the girls?"

"Yes... I suppose I'd better. Janus, will you be alright for a while?"

The elf nodded gravely.

"Right then. I'll be back soon."

"Do not feel you have to rush," Janus gave an ironical smile, "I am sure these two gentlemen have much they wish to discuss."

In the Waterfall Bower, Orlando was chatting amicably enough with Julia and Anne. He was delighted to find that the two young women, far from being pampered ornaments of the aristocracy, were in fact intelligent, practical, good conversationalists and, in the case of Anne, had a remarkable knowledge of the management challenges of the modern asset redistribution business. Indeed he was almost disappointed when Eric appeared with Andrew in tow.

Nor were the two girls best pleased to have their agreeable conversation terminated. This quietly spoken, unassuming, yet authoritative man, was a far cry from the witless little pillocks at Court or the pompous asses from Castle Downing.

Andrew wasn't enjoying the prospect either. The fact was that while his original plan had been a simple one it had also, he now realised, been more simple than plan. Pursuing his original concept of *As You Like* It as the model for the situation he had completely lost sight of the fact there would come a point when he would actually have to start manipulating the characters directly. He was in the position of the director of a play who, at a critical juncture, must come onstage to play a pivotal role using lines he's had to write himself. Worse, it was a role that demanded tact, diplomacy and finely-honed negotiating skills. Andrew's tact, diplomacy and negotiating skills were sufficient to ensure that a simple misunderstanding between two well-intentioned parties would escalate to total war in less than a minute. With very little idea of what he was about to say next, he sidled into the bower.

"Wardmaster!" Orlando bustled forward, "Let me make the introductions." He turned to the two girls. "This is Wardmaster Cruickshank, who I mentioned before. He has just one or two things he'd like to discuss with you."

"Anne Benbrock-Oldstairs," said Anne, sticking out her hand like a weapon.   Andrew shook hands, wincing as his knuckles were lightly ground together. "Jolly good!" he said through clenched teeth.

"And I am Julia."

This time Andrew ignored the extended hand, and gave a sort of vague wave. "Er-- hallo."

"I'll leave you to get on with things," Orlando headed for the exit, "perhaps we could all get together for tea later on?"

"That would be lovely, Mr Orlando," Anne responded with real enthusiasm, "I don't suppose this will take very long," she added, giving Andrew a pointed stare.

"Good! Then I'll make the arrangements and be back in... er... half an hour?"

"That'll be fine," Andrew mumbled. The outlaw chief disappeared, and Andrew turned to Anne and Julia, who were regarding him with looks of cool suspicion.

"Er... I wonder if you'd mind answering a few questions?" he began, taking out his notebook, "just routine, you understand..."

In the grotto, Montmorency slid the short-range high-definition crystal into position on the map board and straightened up with a sigh of satisfaction. "We are about ready, Bellingham." He glanced around to make sure everything else was in place. His staff floated quietly in mid-air at one corner of the map board, the crystal at its top flashing regularly with a green light. Bellingham was seated at the small table, his own crystal before him, and his loose-leaf binder open on his lap. His staff hovered at his side, its crystal emitting the same regular green flash as Montmorency's.

"I am ready, Mage" he said quietly. He was excited and not a little nervous, but was determined to acquit himself well.

"Very well. Once I begin transmitting I will be relying upon you for the tracking. Remember what you are dealing with; if anything, and I mean *anything*, seems anomalous, you are to break contact immediately." The mage fixed his graduate student with a steady glare. "You are *not* dealing with another chess player, but with a nutcase with a very large axe."

"Yes Mage."

"Good. Don't make any mistakes, Bellingham. The paperwork generated by the evaporation of a graduate student while on a field assignment is very tedious indeed, and having to complete it would discommode me. It would colour my attitude in assessing your dissertation, for example. Do you understand?"

"Yes Mage." Bellingham swallowed, and concentrated on his notes.

Montmorency made a couple of complicated hand movements and murmured an incantation. Spots of light flared into life on the map board and the flashing green light from the staff changed to a steady red. "You may begin."

Bellingham tapped his own crystal once. The light atop his staff changed to a steady red. Reading carefully from his notes, he began the opening sequence of his incantation, but had not even got halfway before there was a crimson flash from the map board. The spots of light flickered, then went out, save for one steady crimson spark. Bellingham gasped. "I have him already Mage!"

"Without any transmission?"

"I received his trace before I completed the initial sequence."

"Interesting! Cruickshank must be in a very agitated state of mind." Montmorency stared intently into the high-definition crystal. "Yes, indeed... we must be very careful. With Cruickshank in this state, anything he does is likely to be extreme and uncontrolled. That is *more* extreme and *more* uncontrolled than usual." Montmorency scrutinised the map board once more then, apparently satisfied with what he saw, he resumed his seat and took up the *Collected Works*. "I think we may now proceed to increase Wardmaster Cruickshank's agitation." He opened the book and turned to *A Midsummer Night's Dream*.

"Are you serious?" Anne stared incredulously at Andrew. "What business is it of yours, anyway?"

"I-- er--" Andrew floundered deeper.

"I am sure the gentleman was not trying to be offensive," Julia came to Andrew's rescue, "and I am sure he must have a very good reason for asking the question."

"Yes, exactly. You see--"

"But Julia, honestly, do you really think I'd have anything to do with that drip?"

"Herbert is quite a personable young man," Julia countered, "I always thought you and he got on rather well, as a matter of fact." She gave a faintly cat-like smile.

"Julia!" Anne fairly sizzled with indignation. "Herbert may not be ill-favoured, if you like that kind of clean-cut head-boy style, but he's an utter twit! He doesn't just talk in short grunts; he *thinks* in short grunts. If he thinks at all, that is."

Andrew's fingers gripped his staff convulsively. This was not turning out well. "I take it then, that you are not-- um-- have no interest in-- er--"

"I'm not saying that I wouldn't get off with him at a party-- if I'd had enough to drink and he was the only spare man there," Anne admitted, "but for any long-term relationship..."

"Ah... yes... quite. Then..." Andrew swallowed. After some fifteen minutes all he had managed to do was elicit the information that neither Anne nor Julia had the remotest interest in Herbert. Nor, it was possible to infer, did they have any romantic interest in anybody. "How about Eric?" he asked hopefully.

"Eric?" Julia looked blankly at him.

"That's the very pleasant young man who brought us here, Julia," her cousin reminded her.

"Oh yes! The one with the long feather in his bonnet. Well what about him?"

"Would you say he's more... do you think that..." Andrew stammered helplessly.

"Would I say he's what?" Julia asked sharply.

"I think the Wardmaster is asking if you fancy him." Anne giggled.

"Do I fancy him!" Julia echoed, with a look of mixed indignation and incredulity. "Just what exactly is it you're doing here?" she demanded, "running an introduction agency?"

"Ah... not exactly, no. You see--" Before Andrew could flounder through some weak-kneed explanation, the skies shook to the deep chime of a bell.

"What--" everybody said at once.

"*Through the forest I have gone, but Athenian found I none--*" the voice came from above them, a cool, slightly ironic delivery, which Andrew recognised.

"Montmorency!" he shouted.

"*On whose eyes I might approve this flower's force in stirring love. Night and silence! Who is here? Could it be you, Cruickshank?*"

"*MONTMORENCY!*" Andrew roared, unleashing all his pent up frustration, "Knock it bloody off!" His staff quivered violently and a stream of sparks shot from the tip. A jagged black cloud materialized overhead, turned crimson at the edges, then disintegrated into incandescent slivers which flashed across the sky with a shrill scream. Lacking any coherent input, the staff was doing its best. Montmorency's voice cut off with an audible click.

"Awfully sorry about that," Andrew mumbled.

Pale and wide-eyed, the two girls shrank back from this suddenly terrifying figure. Julia recovered first.

"You were saying?" she asked, in a voice that didn't quite tremble.

"*Blast* Montmorency!" Andrew snapped. As Julia recoiled he added hastily, "sorry about that. Simple accident, could have happened to anyone. I must be off-- I have to-- there are a couple of things--"

"You mean you have other calls of a similar nature to make in the neighbourhood?" Julia asked, coming back to the offensive.

Not trusting himself to reply, Andrew turned on his heel and almost ran from the bower, tripping over Orlando on the way. "Everything all fixed up?" he asked cheerfully. Andrew made a snarling noise, from which the outlaw chief inferred that there might be one or two details that still needed a bit of sorting out.

"I'm going to see if I can get any sense out of the two brothers," Andrew told him, "just keep an eye on things here for a bit."

Orlando watched the crimson cloak disappear from view-- clearly this plan of the Wardmaster's was taking more time than he had envisaged-- then returned the bower. "Now as we were saying," he said to Anne, "the real challenge in this business is the long-term planning..."

Andrew was getting more familiar with the maze and he only made three wrong turns before he came to the small bower where Janus was still standing watch over the usurping duke and the exiled duke. The two brothers were now sitting side by side on the single bench which stood at the base of an ancient cedar tree, and were deep in conversation.

"Ah, good sir wizard!" Roger rose to his feet as Andrew entered, "the time has come when you will make all things clear to us?"

"Er-- yes! Of Course. Absolutely." Andrew took a deep breath. "We want you out of Stembark Forest. Both of you. Now."

"Impossible!" Roger's face flushed with anger, "I am here under the Warrant of the First Speaker."

"The First Speaker, brother! You did not mention that."

"I did not think the time or place propitious, brother," Roger responded, a crafty look on his face. "The First Speaker expressed himself concerned that the House of Benbrock-Oldstairs had been rent by discord, and er-- convinced me that we should make our quarrel up and join our fortunes in a common venture."

"Our fortunes?"

"Yes, you know, Harold. That trifling sum of four hundred thousand in gold you took with you when you er-- left."

"Ah yes, *that* fortune." Harold winced.

"That is very good news," Andrew struggled to regain the initiative, "we were hoping you'd become reconciled. But a couple of urban sophisticates like you two can't possibly want to spend any longer rusticating in this place."

"On the contrary!" Harold sprang to his feet and flung his arms wide, "this place is much more free from perils than the envious court-- at least it was until recently. We can find books in running brooks, sermons in stones and--"

"Tongues in trees, brother?"

"I was coming to that!" Harold snapped irritably. "More importantly, we now have the opportunity and the challenge of setting up Albion's first motif garden."

"You what!" Andrew started forward with such violence that the two brothers dodged back behind their bench. "What did you say?"

Before anyone could answer, the air shook again to a deep chime, and a familiar voice began to declaim: *Love! His affections do not that way tend; nor what he spake, though it lacked form a little, was not like madness. There's something in his soul--*"

"*MONTMORENCY!!!*" Andrew screamed, "Montmorency-- that's bloody *Hamlet!*" Crimson streaks of light flashed from his staff and zig-zagged across the sky. There was a strong smell of ozone-- the staff was doing its best.

"*There's something in his soul o'er which his melancholy sits on brood,*" Montmorency continued, "and yes, Cruickshank, I am perfectly well aware that it is *Hamlet.*" The voice clicked off.

"If there isn't anything else, perhaps we should be on our way," Harold ventured, "I can see you're a busy man and--"

"Just what were you talking about? A 'motif garden'?"

"As part of the First Speaker's new economic development programme, we have been charged with the responsibility of establishing

Fleet the Time In the Golden World plc," Roger explained, "it will provide a unique rural roistering experience for all the family-- hunting through the greenwood, feasting around the camp fire, joining in sing-songs--"

"Clarence Snout and his Arboreal Arcadians," Harold added proudly.

"A partnership made, if not in heaven, at least in East Castellian, which provides a much sounder basis for such arrangements," Roger concluded.

"And we are perfectly reconciled." Harold darted a quick eye at the pile of weapons at Janus's feet.

"Perfectly," agreed Roger, following his glance.

"What--" Andrew began, but was again interrupted.

"And I do doubt," Montmorency observed in measured tones, *"the hatch and disclose will be some danger; which for to prevent I have in quick determination thus set down--"*

What exactly it was that Montmorency had in quick determination set down remained a mystery for, overcome by frustration, Andrew raised his staff and twisted the trigger ring. Instead of the crimson streak of the destructor beam from the tip of the instrument, there was a single bright violet flash accompanied by an earsplitting detonation and a strong smell of scorching insulation.

"Well timed, Bellingham!" Montmorency beamed encouragingly at the graduate student through the billowing clouds of smoke, "the Wardmaster is *very* agitated."

"The relay, Mage!" the graduate student pointed a trembling finger at the little black heap of slag that still bubbled and smoked.

"You cannot make an omelette without breaking eggs, And we still have several others available." The mage smiled happily-- he could feel he had Cruickshank on the run.

Andrew plonked himself down on the grass just outside the maze. He had to admit that Montmorency had got him on the run. He was exhausted, frustrated, and pretty close to hysterical. Throughout the day, any attempt at discourse with the two girls, the two dukes, or the young man Herbert, had been interrupted by Montmorency. He had gone from *A Midsummer Night's Dream, by way of Hamlet, The Tempest, Romeo and Juliet to Two Gentlemen of Verona,* and seemed to be quite prepared to keep it up all afternoon and all night too. If Andrew had been a little less close to distraction, he might have earlier heeded Clumpface's advice to go back to Using Tarot 5.1 and see what methods might be available for blocking this interference, but he had not done so. So far his exertions had gleaned him the information that the two dukes had been reconciled to the extent that they were cooperating in some kind of commercial venture with the encouragement (or more likely at the behest of) the First Speaker. That neither Julia nor Anne were romantically interested in anyone at the moment. That Herbert (who looked type-cast for the young romantic hero) was definitely *not* interested in Julia and that anyway a chap in his position with no prospects could not consider paying court to any young lady, indeed a chap was so hard up that he couldn't begin to think of paying anything.

It was not a cornucopia of intelligence. For some minutes Andrew sat staring into space, soothed a little by the sound of the lapping water. It was no good sitting here brooding-- he'd have to get back to the bungalow and then sit down with the others and try to hammer out some plan of campaign. Wearily he got to his feet and began to trace his way back through the maze. He was so preoccupied with the complexities of the situation that he did not see the duellist until he cannoned into him.

Charles had become increasingly disturbed as the day progressed. Despite his experience, the maze was of such a fiendishly complex design that it had all but defeated him as he had penetrated deeper. He had not actually got lost, but it had required all his concentration not to become so. When, therefore, the man stumbled across his path he reacted automatically, and very quickly indeed. He slipped his cloak from his shoulders, drew his sword, and was advancing upon the stranger before the cloak actually hit the ground.

Andrew was hardly slower. Even as he recoiled from the collision his eye registered the copper-coloured cloak-- the uniform of a duellist--

and he flung his staff backwards, dropped his cloak and whipped out his sword. The two blades shone grey, slender and deadly in the late afternoon sunlight.

For a moment neither man moved. Charles waited for his opponent to make the first move-- he always preferred to get the measure of the opposition that way. Andrew too, waited, for it was his technique to invite an early attack, and draw the attacker on.

One, two, three seconds passed, with the tips of the two blades making small circling motions. Then Charles decided to move; obviously his opponent was a wily fighter who would not be drawn. He dropped his blade slightly, and in a beautifully fluid motion, lunged for Andrew's sword arm. He was quite taken aback by the ferocity with which his sword was beaten aside, and the speed of the other man's riposte. It was so fast and direct that he was forced to give ground as he parried. He launched his own response and was gratified to see that it regained him the ground he had lost. The whole exchange had taken scarcely more than a second, and the two swords had darted back and forth faster than they eye could follow. Now there was another fractional pause while the two swordsmen reassessed the situation.

Charles was impressed with his opponent's speed and energy but he was not unconfident of the end result. He had almost thirty years fighting experience and though the other man might be fast, Charles was hardly slower and, he suspected, that this fellow could not keep up that speed for very long.

Andrew had come to the same conclusion. At the Duellists' College in Nova Castria he was accounted one of the better fighters-- his rank of Master Swordsman had been honestly earned. But the man who now faced him was the best he'd ever crossed blades with. If he was to stand any chance at all he must attack fast. He fluttered the tip of his blade slightly and saw his opponent's begin to move in anticipation of an attack to the left. Good! He did it again, then had to whip his sword across as the other duellist ignored the move and launched his own attack. The blades clattered and scraped together, then disengaged, the tips inches apart. Andrew prepared to make his feint again. His muscles tightened in anticipation of the move, and--

"Oh, he is the courageous captain of compliments. He fights as you sing prick-song, keeps time, distance and proportion; rests me his minim rest, one, two, and a third in your bosom; the very butcher of a silk button, a duellist, a duellist; a gentleman of the very first house, of the first and second cause. Ah, the immortal passado! The punto reverso!"

"Grrr!" Andrew snarled, his frustration boiling over. His left arm straightened convulsively, the index finger pointing at the staff which hovered quietly a few feet behind. It responded to the signal immediately-- at last here were some coherent instructions!

As Charles watched, amazed (though his sword remained steady) a ribbon of violet light flared from Andrew's fingertip to the staff. The staff rotated smoothly until its tip was pointing upwards then, with a hissing snap like the crack of a giant whip, a needle-thin grey line shot skywards. Montmorency's resonant tones cut off. The staff quietly returned to its normal vertical orientation and hovered smugly.

For the first time Charles noticed not only the staff, but also the crimson cloak his opponent had flung to the ground. Could there have been some kind of misunderstanding? He moved his sword so that it was merely in a guard position, its point no longer threatening. He coughed. "Sir, before we continue might we not exchange introductions?"

"Eh?" Andrew's sword jerked fractionally. "Introductions?" he echoed.

"Yes, that is the usual courtesy, after all." Charles shrugged slightly. "I fear that the current circumstances prompted us both to precipitate action. I regret that."

"Oh, absolutely! So do I."

"I am Charles, Master Swordsman of the Senior Division, and I entered this engagement in the sporting, or the professional spirit, as the case may be, and without apprehension of personal malice."

"Oh, me too!" Andrew agreed, then remembered the correct formal response. "That is to say I am Andrew Cruickshank er-- Master

Swordsman in residence at the Duellists' College. And I am aware of no difference between myself and my challenger."

"Andrew Cruickshank!" The duellist's face broke into a smile of recognition, "the Wardmaster Mage?"

Andrew nodded.

"My dear sir, I am delighted to meet you!" Charles sheathed his sword and stepped forward, hand held out, then hesitated. "My apologies Wardmaster, I was forgetting. You would doubtless like to finish our little er..."

"No! Not at all!" Andrew hurriedly sheathed his own weapon and shook the proffered hand. "I've heard of you from Sir Arthur Scratch-Itchbag, of course. But I thought you were retiring from active service and coming up to Nova Castria."

"I am. I did have a short-term contract with the old Duke of Benbrock-Oldstairs and felt in honour bound to stay with the family for a while after his death. But the current situation certainly voids any contractual obligation I might have."

"Good!" Andrew was greatly relieved. He knew enough of the reputation of this veteran duellist to recognise that had their engagement continued it could have had but one outcome.

"Again, I must apologise for my impetuosity," Charles picked up his cloak, "even if I failed to recognise the uniform of a Crimson Mage, the staff should have been a dead giveaway."

"No harm done."

"True. And we must try a sporting engagement together some time."

"Um..." Andrew fastened his own cloak and summoned his staff with a flick of his hand.

"Perhaps you could tell me what it is that brings Nova Castria's Wardmaster Mage to these parts, and what interest he has in the unhappy feuds of the Benbrock-Oldstairs family?"

"Well... it's a little complicated." Andrew waved a hand vaguely. "Look, would you like to come back with me and meet the others--

we're all at the other end of the island-- and then we can explain things to you."

"That would be splendid. Am I right in understanding that among your company you number a very large clerical gentleman?"

"Er... not exactly, no. Very large, yes. But clerical, no."

"Very large... I see." Charles smiled slightly, "I am sure it must be the same person." He smiled again, this time more broadly. "Come, Wardmaster Cruickshank, I am anxious to meet your friends."

His ears still ringing with the fearful concussion, Bellingham scrambled to his feet and flapped his hands ineffectually at the swirling smoke. "Mage Montmorency!" he choked, "are you injured?"

"I am perfectly well," the voice sounded faint and tinny in Bellingham's ears, "just a little shaken. You are unhurt?"

"I think so, Mage." By now the smoke was thinning, and Bellingham could make out Montmorency's gaunt form, still seated and seemingly relaxed in the chair by the map board. Greatly daring, Bellingham essayed a simple air movement routine to clear the rest of the smoke from the grotto. To his surprise and relief it functioned perfectly, and soon the last black wisps were disappearing through the splintered remains of the door.

"Good thinking Bellingham." Montmorency rose from his seat and glanced quickly round the chamber. "We must determine exactly what has happened here, but check your relays first and if you find any that are still functioning, disable them at once."

"At once, Mage?"

"At once. Unless you wish to risk a repeat performance of that." The mage gestured to the map board, or rather where the map board had been. All that remained were a few charred scraps, some still with little curls of smoke rising from them. The graduate student shuddered, and immediately set about the task. It did not take long for, so far as Bellingham could tell some massive broad-spectrum spell had simply erased every trace of the network he had so laboriously assembled. Nevertheless he conscientiously activated the several routines with a couple of incantations, then returned his attention to Montmorency who was gazing pensively at the large charred patch on the floor.

"What happened, Mage?"

"Perfectly simple, Bellingham. Cruickshank got it right for once. A rare event, but not unknown."

"But a response like that is most disproportionate!" Bellingham protested indignantly, "we should register a formal protest!"

"As I keep telling you, the normal rules cannot be applied to Cruickshank. The man simply has no idea of his own strength."

"But even so, Mage, it is unheard of to use such power. And in a broad-spectrum spell, too! It must have been in the Mega-Gough[14] range."

"Something over seven MG, in fact," Montmorency responded calmly, "And it is true that even for Cruickshank that seems a trifle extreme. Whatever his deficiencies in the technical area, Cruickshank is not vindictive. Let us review the logs." Montmorency took out the black ebony tablet and activated the crystal at its centre. "Let me see... here we are..." he tapped the crystal lightly. "Ah! *Now* I see."

"What, Mage?"

Montmorency's face went very still for a moment, then his features hardened slightly. "I can see I have been guilty of a grave error. At the time of that last contact, Cruickshank was engaged in combat."

"But he cannot--"

"Tush, Bellingham! The man is a duellist, and a good one too. That means that from time to time he will find himself engaged in combat. Why or with whom he was fighting on this occasion, I cannot possibly say, but fighting he was."

"And that accounts for--"

"A purely instinctive reaction-- he would have no time to consider the situation. No, if anyone has been guilty of unprofessional behaviour it is myself. I should have checked more carefully."

"What are you going to do?"

---

14   One Mega-Gough is sufficient occult energy to transform 100,000 Standard Human Persons (STP) into 1 million newts.

"Well, I shall of course write Cruickshank a note of apology for the misunderstanding, and send a copy to Guild Files for the record." Montmorency looked around the grotto once more. "Perhaps we should make no more attempts to contact Cruickshank today," he decided, "let us give ourselves the evening off and pay a visit to the Three Pigeons in Lecter." He stretched and yawned, "I don't know about you, Bellingham, but right now I could murder a plate of sausage and chips."

It was dusk and the road was still a mass of troops. Just where the Southern Ride into Stembark Forest joined the road they were at their thickest and a small tent city had sprung up, in the centre of which the First Speaker's personal standard hung limply from an improvised flagpole. Patrols stamped with military regularity about the perimeter and beyond, in the deepening dusk, the fires of outlying guard posts twinkled alertly.

From a the concealment of ditch four pairs of eyes stared at this prodigious display of armed might.

"*How* many troops did he say he was sending?" Amiens asked weakly.

"The total came to something like sixteen hundred," Cecil muttered, "but they weren't all due to get here by today.

"There are quite enough to be getting on with." Jacques wriggled lower in the ditch. "We're never going to be able to get through that lot."

They were tired, dispirited and travel-stained. Even Ratbag's natural resilience seemed dampened. "*I* could get through on my own," he pointed out, "if we wait till after dark."

"That's what you may have to do," agreed Cecil, "we have to get that information to Orlando. What are you two doing?" He stared at Amiens and Jacques who were carefully stringing their bows.

"Preparing for our doomed but glorious attempts to cross the enemy lines, of course." Jacques laid his bow down and began sorting through his arrows.

"It is a pity there is no artist on hand to record the event," Amiens sighed.

"Are you out of your tiny minds?" Cecil hissed at them, "you wouldn't get forty paces before they cut you down."

"Jacques can't count," Amiens replied complacently, "not big on mathematics at his school."

"You don't have to be able to count, you ninny!"

"Just as well. But the numbers don't matter; we must make the attempt, no matter what the odds, to get this information to our chief."

"Of course it will mean we get our names up on the Honours Board," Jacques pointed out, "possibly with some quite poignant annotation about devotion to duty. Makes a chap feel quite humble, really."

"Sorry mates. No Honours Board for you this time. You're not going prancing across there causing a lot of disturbance. No." Cecil shook his head firmly then, to add emphasis, casually worked the cocking lever of his crossbow. A bolt slid into place behind the tensioned bowstring with a menacing *snick-click*.

"Well, if you insist on putting it like that..." Jacques gave a helpless shrug.

"Do you have any other plan," Amiens asked, his voice tinged with a shade of contempt.

"Yes. We're going along to the Three Pigeons to get a drink and something to eat."

"But this is scarcely the time for--"

"I'm judge of that. We're tired and hungry and thirsty. Particularly thirsty. People who are tired and hungry and thirsty, particularly thirsty, tend to make mistakes. And I want to have a word with Constable Dixon-- he's usually at the Three Pigeons at this time of the day--"

"He's usually at the Three pigeons most times of the day," Amiens sniffed.

"Good." Cecil ignored the outlaw's implied criticism. "So we'll go there and see if he's got any ideas about how to get through this lot.

And if all else fails, Ratbag'll go ahead on his own after dark. Any questions?"

"Er--" Amiens began, but a slight movement from Cecil's crossbow suggested that the question had been rhetorical.

It was not until a good hour later that they were able to clamber over the garden wall of the tavern and creep up to the back door. A quick word with the landlord, Rowley, established that there were no troops on the premises and it was with the extravagant relief of a desert traveller who has at last arrived at an oasis that Cecil swung wide the door to the saloon bar. As he stood in the doorway, he suddenly realized he had failed to ask Rowley one important question; at a table in the corner, with a full glass in front of him and an empty plate at his elbow, sat the Black Mage Montmorency.

Cecil started to back through the door, but Jacques and Amiens were crowded behind him. Ratbag, swift and deadly as ever, flitted across the room to a position from where he could bring the mage under attack from an entirely different angle.

Montmorency, startled for a moment by the unexpected appearance of the marksman, recovered himself first. "Cecil! What an unexpected pleasure!"

"Ah... er..." Cecil tried to smile. He knew he had nothing to fear in the way of physical damage from the mage (at least, nothing *permanent*, he reminded himself) but the question was; would Montmorency regard himself as being on- or off-duty at the moment? The mage resolved the question with his next words.

"Bellingham and I have given ourselves an evening off-- will you join us for a drink?"[15]

"Don't mind if I do." At Cecil's signal, Ratbag materialized at Montmorency's elbow while Cecil himself sat down opposite the dark looming figure. Amiens and Jacques joined them a few seconds later, slightly bemused by the turn of events.

---

15   The universal term for being off-duty

"So what brings you two here?" Montmorency inquired pleasantly enough, "is it by any chance related to that prodigious display of military might out there?"

"Yes... and er... no," Cecil replied cautiously. He was inexperienced in dealing with mages and not well aware of the conventions that governed their actions so was dubious about telling Montmorency anything. Ratbag, on the other hand was quite confident in his own mind about the mage's position.

"Mage Montmorency, those soldiers out there *are* part of our business, but of yours as well." His delicate, mobile fingers fluttered expressively. "The First Speaker has launched a campaign to drive the Outlaws from Stembark Forest."

"Indeed? And how do you make that *my* business, master Ratbag?" The dark eyebrows rose quizzically.

"Of course it's your business!" Ratbag was not impressed by raised mage eyebrows-- he had seen too many of them. "He's interfering in your engagement with Andrew, isn't he? And besides," Ratbag hastened on, his diminutive figure almost vibrating with intensity, "the First Speaker is attempting a major disturbance to the *status quo*. You are *required* to take a hand!"

Cecil flinched. He'd always heard that instructing a Senior Level Black Mage in his duty, and at close range, could be distinctly hazardous to your health.

"Theoretically there is something in what you say," Montmorency agreed, after a significant pause, "but in practice all I see is a rather large number of soldiers running about the place with the military precision one has come to expect of the East Castellian forces. It could simply be some kind of tattoo the First Speaker has in mind."

"Read this!" Ratbag pulled a handful of notes from his pouch and slapped them onto the table. Everybody watched in tense silence as Montmorency ran his eyes over the papers.

"Most interesting." He looked up with a smile, "and where, may I ask, did you obtain this remarkably comprehensive summary?"

"The First Speaker's office of course!"

"So!" The dark eyes glinted with amusement, "am I to assume that Cecil has been once again employed on the cleaning staff of Castle Downing?"

"Secretary, as a matter of fact," Cecil told him gruffly.

"Another preposterous impersonation to add to your already impressive record!" Montmorency chuckled, "your comrades will be proud of you."

"Nothing much to it," mumbled Cecil, absurdly gratified by the compliment, "'cept for the bit with the candle-light dinner."

"Ah!" For a moment Montmorency's habitual imperturbability threatened to desert him. He coughed. "You are quite right. If the matters in this paper be certain, then we have mighty business in hand. Cruickshank and I will reluctantly have to set aside our diverting little contest. The most immediate problem, I take it, is getting into the forest?"

"Yeah," Cecil agreed. "Ratbag can do it, no problem, but the rest of us..." he shrugged.

"That will be simple enough to arrange. Bellingham!" The research assistant jumped eagerly to his feet, "we shall go out to the back garden. Will you begin a four-person short-range transport sequence-- the usual precautions."

Cecil flinched and Ratbag tugged him by the sleeve. "Don't worry," he whispered, "remember, it's not Andrew. The precautions are probably just a formality."

They trooped out into the garden. At this hour it was deserted save for a small knot of dedicated drinkers who gazed incuriously after the six figures as they disappeared into the shadows. Montmorency halted them at the back fence, next to the chicken coop. "I must first make contact with Cruickshank." He raised his staff and murmured a short incantation. The crystal atop the staff gave a brief flash. A low *breep-breep* sounded half a dozen times, until it was interrupted by a loud crackle and an angry crimson flash from the crystal as contact was established. Montmorency shook his head slightly-- Cruickshank was clearly still in a very agitated state of mind. The others strained to listen, but could only hear Montmorency's side of the conversation.

"Cruickshank-- before you do or say anything, listen very carefully... No, I am not going to unfold a tale whose lightest word would harrow up thy soul. Ratbag and Cecil are with me--" Montmorency ducked as a violent flash of crimson light shot from the staff. "Please, Cruickshank! They are safe and well and have brought me important news." He spoke very rapidly, anxious to preclude yet another display of concern from Andrew. "That is correct..." He relaxed slightly. "Yes, since you ask, there are some chickens here. The state of their health is not relevant... I do not dispute, Cruickshank, that it may be relevant to the chickens; it is just not relevant to me!" The Black Mage masked a sigh of exasperation and tried again. "Cruickshank, we must temporarily postpone our little diversion-- we have more serious work afoot that concerns the First Speaker... that is quite correct, Cruickshank, I should have said the First Speaker and a very large number of well-equipped troops. I shall conduct your friends to the Headquarters Glade... yes the outlaw chief should certainly come too, after all it is his band that is the target of this operation... very good, Cruickshank, we shall meet you at the Headquarters Glade within the hour." Montmorency was just about to break the connection when he paused, and a slightly malicious smile tugged at the corners of his mouth. "Stand not upon the order of your going, Cruickshank," he concluded, "but go at once."

Act XVII
DRUMS AND COLOURS

The Council Room of the Outlaws of Stembark Forest was ablaze with light. Tiresome, the First Speaker's Order of Battle and Operational Orders in his hand, was tracing the route of the enemy advance on the map table, exchanging occasional muttered comments with Janus and Kodswallop, while the others listened intently. Orlando himself sat at the head of the table, a heap of coloured pencils at his elbow and a saucer full of little flags on pins in front of him, while Eric hovered at his side taking notes.

"It is a pedestrian plan," Tiresome mused, running his eye once again over the Order of Battle, "but they do have a lot of pedestrians. Not to mention mounted troops."

"What about those 'roving patrols'?" Andrew asked, pointing to one paragraph of Ratbag's closely written notes.

"The idea is sound enough," Tiresome admitted, "but the men have no training or experience in the forest environment. Their only idea of camouflage is sticking twigs and leaves in their hats, and they think guerilla warfare is what happens between rival tribes of monkeys. No, I don't believe that they pose any threat. The principal thrust is along the Southern Ride. We may expect their first move at dawn tomorrow-- or rather today."

Orlando took a red pencil and wrote *dawn advance* at the top of a sheet of paper and underlined it twice.

"The intention of the enemy is to proceed along the Southern Ride in half-league stages. At each stage they will establish a guard post.

"They are coming straight along the Southern Ride?" Orlando's face was pale.

"A predictable movement, and not to our disadvantage." Tiresome nodded.

"But-- but it will be a massacre!" The outlaw leader's hand clenched and the pencil he was holding broke with a sharp snapping sound. He gazed blankly at the fragments.

"Just what we need!" Kodswallop looked brisk and cheerful, "haven't had very much action so far."

"You don't understand." Orlando looked anguished, "you see what usually happens is we might get up to fifty mounted Shore Enforcers dropping by to... er... see about things. Well, that's all quite straightforward; my lads get among them with the quarter staves, knock 'em of their horses, and they all go home. But I don't have the men to take on hundreds in hand-to-hand combat. They will simply have to wait in the forest, and shoot them down-- it will be a massacre!" he repeated.

Tiresome looked grave-- he knew very well what a devastating weapon massed archery could be. But Cecil was unmoved.

"Isn't that what you want?" he demanded, "after all, you do want to discourage them from coming here-- I think they'd find being massacred pretty discouraging."

"But most of them are just lads, doing their job!" Orlando protested.

"If they can't take a joke, they shouldn't have joined." The marksman shrugged unsympathetically.

"What we need," Tiresome mused, "is some way of containing them and delaying them until they get fed up and go home. The First Speaker won't want to be away from East Castellian too long."

"Quite true." Montmorency agreed, "Titus Handcarte will wish to record a rapid success and return at the head of his victorious troops as soon as possible. The politics of East Castellian can be... er... volatile."

"Hmm." Tiresome stroked his chin. "Then suppose we allow the enemy to penetrate along the Southern Ride as far as... here." He stabbed at the map with his pointer. "The forest is unusually dense at this point, and this stream forms a natural barrier. Here they can be pinned down. If they venture off the Ride, they can't do so in force, and can be picked off easily. Their only way is back."

Orlando gave an understanding smile. "And then we just sit and wait for them to get bored and go away?"

"Just so."

"Brilliant!" the outlaw leader repeated. Then his face fell momentarily. "Of course it's really going to disrupt business. But that can't be helped."

"We should be able to hurry things along a little." The knight smiled slightly. "Isolated parties will be easy meat, and if enough isolated parties start disappearing, even the most phlegmatic commander in chief is going to develop a low boredom threshold. Now to our organisation..." Tiresome glance at his notes for a moment. "We shall form three task groups: Alpha, Bravo and Charlie."

"We used to have Red, Green and Blue at school," Jacques whispered to Amiens, but not quietly enough, and Tiresome frowned lightly at the interruption.

"Group Alpha," he continued, "under the command of Kodswallop, will proceed to this point," Tiresome's finger stabbed at the map once again, "and erect a barricade across the ride. A good one, Kodswallop, mind you. And extend it a distance into the forest, if you have time. Take two sections of outlaws with you to help-- it will be heavy work..." he paused as if he had just remembered something, "...and perhaps those two young gentlemen should accompany you," he pointed to Jacques and Amiens.

"You know, there's something else you might try," Andrew suggested diffidently. "If you put your roadblock up just after this stream, then you could dam the stream, and that will flood the road. Even if it were only a few inches, it would slow them down a bit."

"Capital idea, Andrew!" Tiresome laughed delightedly, "as always you are the inspired tactician. Do it, Kodswallop. It will be messy work, but I feel sure you will find willing volunteers." He stared pointedly at Jacques and Amiens. "Once you have completed the work, retire a short distance and keep watch. We will warn you when the first column is sighted, but when they arrive do not engage them."

"What! Not even in self-defence?" Kodswallop looked betrayed.

"If small numbers of them should stray off the path, then you may-- er-- defend yourselves. But *do not* show yourselves."

"Ah, I see!" The big fighter smiled happily, "you want people straying into the depths of the forest and not returning?"

"Precisely."

"We can manage that."

"They must stray of their own accord, Kodswallop, remember!"

"Of course!" Kodswallop nodded energetically. There were going to be a goodly number of East Castellian troops straying into the depths of the forest if he had anything to do with it.

"Janus," Tiresome turned to the elf, "you will command Charlie section, with Andrew, Ratbag and Cecil. Take the minimum number of men you think you will need for guides and messengers, and get as close to the main camp as you can. Report each detachment as it leaves and have one man keep them in view. I shall post squads at half-league intervals along the Southern Ride to report on the enemy's progress and take care of their sentry posts. Any questions?"

"I assume, Sir Tiresome, that you will be taking direct command of Group Bravo?" Montmorency asked.

"That is correct, Mage Montmorency. With Clumpface, I shall set up Group Bravo at this point, midway between the enemy camp and Kodswallop's barricade. We shall take the bulk of the unassigned outlaws with us and deploy them as the situation develops."

"Communication will be an onerous task, will it not?"

"It always is."

"I, or rather we, can offer assistance, if you would be willing."

"I should be delighted, Mage Montmorency!" Tiresome exclaimed with relief, for Montmorency had put his finger on the most vulnerable element in their strategy. "It would be invaluable, if it would not violate any...?"

"Not at all. The provisions of the *Unified Code* in that respect principally concern themselves with such activities as evaporation or permanent transformation on frivolous or capricious grounds. There is no mention of communications assistance."

"Then I should be most grateful."

"Very good. I shall accompany you and Bellingham will attend Group Alpha. Group Charlie, of course has--"

"It's own Charlie," grinned Cecil.

"I'm not sure about the communications on my staff," Andrew mumbled, "about the only thing it's ever picked up has been the BBC."

"Just use Tarot 5.1, Cruickshank. Use the five, nine and two of pentacles-- remember the order, Cruickshank, that is five, nine, two-- and place them in the retaining clip on the rear of the spellcaster. It is simple enough."

"Five, nine two," Andrew repeated, writing the numbers down.

"Yes. And one more thing Cruickshank--"

"Yes? What?"

"Please don't shout."

The little group began to file from the room. As he reached the door, Tiresome happened to turn and catch Eric's eye. The young man was still standing dutifully at the side of his chief, but in his face there was an unmistakable yearning. Tiresome paused; it couldn't hurt to take the lad along, indeed with his capacity for silent movement and his knowledge of the hidden forest paths he could be invaluable. The knight coughed. "I wonder whether I might request Eric to be attached to Group Bravo?" he asked casually.

"Eric!" Orlando looked at his assistant, and he too recognised the look on his face. He smiled. "Very well, if Eric can be of use to you he may go."

"Thank you Mr Orlando!" Eric shot through the door like an arrow from a bow. Tiresome caught him up outside and tapped him on the shoulder. "If you are on attachment to Group Bravo, lad, then you had better get properly armed." With a gasp of excitement, Eric raced for the armoury.

"Are you sure that was a good idea, Tiresome?" Clumpface looked dubious, "after all his reputation..."

"Nobody can be that poor an archer without some reason for it," Tiresome responded quietly, "perhaps we shall find out." The dwarf grunted sceptically.

They waited for a few moments while Montmorency whispered last minute instructions to Bellingham, and then the three moved off after Eric. For a few minutes the Headquarters Glade was alive with moving shadows as the three Groups assembled, then was still again as they filtered out into the deeper blackness of the forest.

Captain Lars Porsena, of the Seventh Heavy Dragoons, paraded his men in the ghostly inverse twilight that comes before sunrise. They were a mixed lot-- a hundred of his own troopers, some forty Lancers, two support wagons and their crews and... the Thing. He glanced uneasily at it as he wheeled his horse into position at the head of the column. Massive, and shapeless under its concealing tarpaulin, the Thing was pulled by four pairs of draught horses and came with its own specialist crew from the Technical Branch-- a quiet group of unsoldierly looking men who kept aloof from the other troops. "It is a new device of unprecedented power," Captain Spalding had told him at last night's briefing, "and it may well render all conventional methods of warfare obsolete." Captain Porsena snorted contemptuously at the recollection-- the device might be all that Spalding claimed it to be, but it did nothing for military effectiveness. Why, he could not see an inch of metal on the device with a finish suitable for polishing! And as for the tarpaulin, its shapeless drabness was a disgrace. He checked to see that the colour party was ready and that his two ensigns had taken up their appropriate positions. "Sarn't major!" he shouted. There was a clatter of hooves behind him-- the closest the Sergeant Major could come to snapping to attention while on horseback.

"Sah!"

"The Seventh will advance in column of route."

"Sah!" The bellow fluttered the leaves and, to a blare of bugles, the Seventh Heavy Dragoons, the Fourth Castle Lancers and an unwieldy... Thing under the care of the Technical Branch, started forward.

Andrew lowered the binoculars. "I make that about a hundred and forty horsemen, two big wagons, and something that looks as though it's been pinched from the Roman army."

"Eh?" Cecil stopped scribbling, "what was that again?"

"Something that looks like a catapult," Andrew elaborated with pardonable inaccuracy. The outlines of the wheeled object beneath its tarpaulin had suggested to him some framework with a long pivoted arm designed to chuck large rocks about the place. In fact it would have been more properly called a trebuchet, but catapult was close enough.

"They must be out of their minds," the marksman observed, "dragging something like that about."

"Their's not to reason why, Cecil," Andrew observed and turned to Ratbag. "They were only planning to move half a league at a time, weren't they?"

"That was what they had written down," the nicker agreed, doubtfully.

"Senseless moving that thing half a league," Andrew chewed at a fingernail, "they'd want it as far forward as they could get it."

"Perhaps they've got people like Amiens or Jacques doing their tactical planning for them," Cecil suggested, "anyway, you'd better report it."

"Alright." Reluctantly Andrew assembled the tarot cards and arranged them as Montmorency had instructed. A warning light flashed briefly in the crystal at the top of his staff, and with a crackle the black mage responded.

"Group Bravo. That *is* you Cruickshank?"

"Yes. How did you know?"

"Oh, I have my ways." Montmorency eyed the streak of scorched grass that bisected the clearing.

"Jolly good. The first lot are on their way."

"Interesting." Tiresome stroked his chin, "I think Andrew's right-- they are going to press forward as far as they can. We must warn Kodswallop." He studied the map for a moment, then turned to Montmorency. "Tell Group Alpha they may expect visitors within six hours."

Scarcely had Montmorency finished relaying the message, when Andrew called in again. A broad swath of bracken withered and died before the black mage managed to intercept the signal. "Another hundred cavalry, and twice that number of infantry," he relayed the news to Tiresome, "it seems the First Speaker is in a hurry."

"All the better! I do believe we have them!" Tiresome almost chortled, stabbing at the map with his finger, "they will come to a halt at Kodswallop's barrier and be stuck. They can either all attempt to retreat-- which might be politically unwise-- or they can send messages for assistance-- which we can intercept. Or they can try to make their way through the forest, in which case they will be easily dealt with. The First Speaker will either assume the advance has achieved success, and send more troops to consolidate the gains, or he will assume assistance is needed and send reinforcements. In either case it simply means the chaos at the end of the line will become yet more chaotic!"

Montmorency grinned. "I shall inform Bellingham that more guests will be arriving." He took up his staff once again.

Tiresome had been quite right in his assessment of the enemy's strategy. Captain Porsena had determined to press ahead along the serpentine route of the Southern Ride, halting only if faced with determined opposition. At regular intervals two men from one of the supply wagons would descend and, with some ceremony, hammer a five-foot post into the ground, then attach to it a small blue metal rectangle, with a gold diagonal stripe. This enigmatic task completed, they would return to their vehicle and resume their steady advance.

The second of these signs had just been posted, and the clatter and rumble of the column's passage had barely died away, when the bushes parted and two figures in lincoln green emerged. They eyed the sign curiously.

"What do you reckon then, Section Leader?" asked the first, "should we knock it off?"

Section Leader Pringle considered the matter. "Nah." He shook his head, "we'll wait for something more interesting." The two outlaws returned silently to their hiding place.

Captain Porsena had reckoned on moving the Seventh Heavy at about two leagues an hour, but he'd forgotten about the lumbering device. It soon became clear that his column would be lucky to move at half that speed. Porsena ground his teeth with frustration at the funereal pace and, had he not received very explicit instructions to the contrary, would have abandoned that damned unmilitary device then and there. "See if you can't hurry things up a little!" he called to the sergeant major, "the Shore Enforcers will be catching up with us if we aren't careful."

Barely fifteen minutes after the outlaws had seen the cavalry ride past they heard the tramp of feet and the jangle of equipment heralding the approach of another substantial body of men. From their hiding place, they watched in amazement and consternation as the columns of horsemen and ranks of marching men flowed steadily along the green-vaulted tunnel of the ride.

"There must be hundreds of them!" whispered one of the outlaws, "big lads, too!"

"A hundred horsemen and about two hundred on foot," muttered the Section Leader, who had been keeping count. "Shore Enforcers, by the look of them. Now what's this?"

At the tail of the cavalcade three wagons were creaking along, and as they passed the strange sign left by Captain Porsena's force, one came to a halt. From its back a party of four men jumped down and, working with a speed that denoted long practice, unloaded a dozen or so sections of planking. An order was shouted, and the wagon lumbered off leaving the four men standing round the heap of timber. As the curious outlaws watched, the leader of the quartet walked to the edge of the ride and scrutinised the sign left by the earlier force. He spat contemptuously. "Alright lads! Let's be having you!" he shouted.

The three others sprang into frenzied activity and with a clatter of hammering and a rumble of profanity proceeded to erect a small sentry box on the verge of the track.

"Three minutes!" the leader shouted, lowering a sandglass, as the echoes of the last nail being driven faded away, "not bad!"

"What about the sign, then, corp?"

"Good thing you reminded me, Potter. Put it here." He indicated a spot immediately by the sentry box. While Potter held a six foot post in position, his two colleagues hammered it securely into the ground with their mallets, then the corporal attached a shining metal plate to its top. It was larger than the other and was gold with a diagonal blue stripe. The corporal stepped back and eyed it proudly. "Good! You can take the first guard, Potter. The rest of you men, stand easy!"

Potter came to attention, marched forward, and took up position in the sentry box, while the corporal and the other two men lounged comfortably in the long grass.

Less than twenty paces away, crouched behind a tangle of brushwood, Section Leader Pringle turned to his men. "Alright. This we *do* knock off. Dusty and Nobby, follow me. Dick, you carry on when I give the signal." The four men slid from their hiding place and evaporated into the forest.

Two minutes later on the still air there came a sort of cheeping noise like an optimistic sparrow auditioning for a nightingale's role. It was at once followed by an evil hiss and a nasty *proinng!* as an arrow smacked into the side of the sentry box. The occupant shot forth like a jack-in-the-box and stared open-mouthed at the quivering shaft. "Blimey!" he shouted. As if this had been a signal, three more arrows slashed out from the trees, the first two striking within a hands-breadth of each other, while the third split the first cleanly down its length-- Dick was one of the hazel wand specialists. The sentry gave an inarticulate cry, and joined his companions in the ditch.

"Steady lads!" the corporal shouted, "don't bunch! Prepare to advance under enemy fire."

Two more arrows hissed into the ground inches before the corporal's nose, and a third whined overhead.

"Bugger that!" somebody shouted.

"Alright then," the corporal resigned himself to the inevitable, "prepare to retreat under enemy fire." The four soldiers left the ditch and flung themselves into the underbrush. Half a minute later there was a violent scuffling sound, followed by four solid thumps. Then silence for some minutes.

"Good work!" Section Leader Pringle, uncomfortable in an ill-fitting uniform, surveyed the four trussed figures. "Nobby, you can take guard duty-- just hop into that nice box. Dick, you get back to Group Bravo, report to Sir Tiresome and say please could we have someone along to look after the prisoners. Dusty, you stay in the hide and keep watch."

"Er... one thing, Section Leader..?" Nobby poked his head out of the sentry box like a tentative cuckoo from its clock. "What happens if any more of them come along. I mean aren't I supposed to say something like 'halt! who goes there'?"

"Nah! Don't you know anything about the professional military?" The Section Leader gave him a pitying look. "Just salute and look stupid. You do know how to salute, I suppose?"

Kodswallop and Bellingham, soaking wet, mud-bespattered up to the eyebrows and enormously cheerful, surveyed the sheet of water proudly. "It isn't *impassable*," Kodswallop observed, taking a mighty swig from his bottle, "but it won't make things any easier for them."

"It must be almost thigh-deep in the centre," Bellingham mumbled indistinctly through his ham sandwich.

They had blocked the culvert that carried the little stream underneath the Southern Ride, causing the water to rise and sweep across the road surface, scouring the hard packed ground and making the footing treacherous. Further downstream, Kodswallop, Bellingham, Amiens and Jacques had erected a dam of rocks and stones, creating an ever widening lake which now covered the surface of the Ride for almost fifty paces. It was, as Kodswallop had observed, not impassable, but no mounted man, no matter how imprudent, would ride through it-- he would have to dismount and lead his horse across, feeling his way carefully. And then he would come to the barrier.

A barricade of massive tree trunks, branches and interwoven brushwood rearing almost twenty feet into the air lay across the Southern Ride, and extended into the forest on either side. The only choices open to the East Castellians would be attempting to climb over it, or going around it. To deal with the first possibility, Kodswallop had arranged for a number of outlaws with long poles to station themselves on the far side. Any attempt by an athletic East Castellian soldier to scale the barrier would be met by a firm poke with a long stick through one of the many gaps that had been left for just this purpose. It would be enough to dislodge the climber and send him tumbling into the water below. And as for going around... Kodswallop smiled and licked his lips at the thought. The forest was particularly dense at this point and the only way men could move through it would be in single file and on foot. Men in single file and on foot were, Kodswallop reminded himself happily, easy meat. He rather hoped they would try going around the barricade. He got to his feet. "OI!" he bellowed. Ripples ran across the lake, the trees shook and a number of small birds fell to the ground, stunned. "Right, lads!" Kodswallop beamed happily at the motley crew surrounding him. He knew he was no expert in grand strategy or the formality of complex military tactics, but with this bunch he felt at the moment he could have conquered the world. "Right lads!" he repeated, "we're about as ready as we can get. Will, you and ten of your lads stay behind the barrier with your poles. Have a couple at the top ready to bop anyone who makes it up there." Will nodded his understanding. "The rest of you are in sections of four," Kodswallop continued, "stay well back from the Ride, and keep spread out. Remember you should only bother with those people who actually stray off the path. You are not to go in and grab anybody." The big fighter uttered the last instruction with a certain lack of conviction.

"Kodswallop," a Section Leader raised his hand, "if the East Castellians happened to catch sight of us and try to chase us, would that count as straying off the path?"

"How are they going to catch sight of you if you stay well back?" Kodswallop asked as though he were seeking information.

The man shrugged. "These things happen," he offered.

"Well, in that case it would be self-defence," Kodswallop reassured him, "you grab them."

"Er... Kodswallop," a large, unkempt outlaw pushed to the front, "supposing I sort of tripped up and stumbled onto the Ride?"

Kodswallop beamed at the man. "If your station is forty paces away from the Ride, how would you manage that?" he asked encouragingly.

"It was just a hypothetical question."

"Ah! Well, *hypothetically*, if you stumbled onto the Ride, then you could defend yourself. Hypothetically, of course."

"You mean grab them?" came the hopeful question.

"Only hypothetically." A sigh of satisfaction arose. "Alright then." Kodswallop cast another proud look over his men, "all we can do now is wait."

"All we can do now is wait." Tiresome told Clumpface.

"Aye," the dwarf nodded. "At least two more hours before the first lot get to Kodswallop."

"I need to stretch my legs." The knight got up from the map table and walked to the edge of the clearing where it was bounded by a low cliff-- little more an outcropping of rock, really. Tiresome scrambled to the top and from there surveyed his field headquarters. He fidgeted. There was nothing much he could do now-- everything had been set in motion. He was about to sit down on the brink of this little eminence, when his eye was caught by a familiar figure hastening towards his tent. "Eric!" he shouted, and began to scramble down.

"Sir Tiresome?" The young man met him at the foot, a look of eager expectation on his face. "Is there any news?"

"Nothing new lad. All we can do is wait." Eric's face fell. "But while we're waiting, we might as well get a bit of archery practice."

"Er... yes, Sir Tiresome." Excitement and foreboding struggled for control of Eric's features, and foreboding won by a length.

"Clumpface, come and lend a hand!" the knight called, "this cliff will do for butts." In a matter of moments a few logs were propped up against the cliff-face and Tiresome had marked out fifty paces and pushed a stake into the ground. "Stand here Eric, and let's see what you can do," he instructed. Clumpface looked dubious and, from the verges of the clearing, came rustling sounds suggestive of people getting under cover.

Tiresome took the young man by the shoulders and positioned him facing the target. "There you go!" he said encouragingly, "let's say four rounds, in your own time." He stepped back and to the side so that he was immediately behind the young man-- traditionally the safest position under such circumstances. Eric set an arrow to the string and bent the bow, then gently lowered his left arm a few degrees at a time until he was lined up on the target. Tiresome nodded approvingly-- the lad had certainly been taught well.

There was a twang and a fierce hiss as the arrow flew up at forty-five degrees, grazed the lip of the cliff face, and ricocheted away at a crazy angle. "Oops!" Eric's eyes followed the flight of the unguided missile with a look of betrayal. "Must be a bit of a crosswind," he suggested.

"Never mind! Simple accident, could have happened to anybody, eh Clumpface?" Tiresome strove to keep his voice hearty and encouraging. "Try it again."

This time the arrow sliced obliquely across the clearing and through the top of a tent with an ugly ripping sound. Tiresome blinked. This kind of marksmanship was outside his experience. "Bad luck!" he commiserated. "I think you pulled that time-- remember, just squeeze. Third time lucky, eh Clumpface? Clumpface?" He looked around but could see no sign of the dwarf-- indeed the whole clearing seemed deserted, save for the dark, gaunt silhouette of Montmorency, observing from what he might have thought was a safe distance.

Eric's third shot was the most extraordinary yet. At ankle-height the shaft zipped through the long grass, hit a rock and, with a deep, lethal hum, flew straight towards Montmorency. For a fraction of a second the mage stood motionless. Then, in the nick of time, raised his hand and the arrow disappeared in a puff of smoke. A deadly silence fell.

His face ashen, Eric lowered his bow. "Ah... Mage Montmorency... I-- er--"

"No harm done. It was a simple accident-- could have happened to anybody. Sir Tiresome, might I have a word?" Montmorency drew the knight aside and said something in a low voice that Eric didn't catch.

"Are you sure?" Tiresome's hitherto expressionless face registered a mixture of relief and incredulity, "well we must certainly try it-- or anything." The knight returned to Eric's side. "I wonder," he said carefully, "if you have ever tried holding your bow in the other hand?"

"In my right, you mean?"

Tiresome nodded. "I should like you to try it now."

"I don't know," the young man murmured doubtfully as he changed the weapon to his right hand, "it feels a bit funny, somehow."

"Not half as funny as Mage Montmorency must have felt just now," Clumpface said unkindly, emerging from behind a tree.

"Well..." Eric bent the bow experimentally, pulling at the string with his left hand.

"Target is central tree trunk," Tiresome instructed him crisply, "one round, shoot when you're ready."

Eric hesitated a moment, drew a deep breath, then brought his bow up and fired. The arrow thunked solidly into the central log about five feet from the ground. Eric looked at it, his eyes popping. "But it..."

"Right on target," agreed Tiresome calmly, "now, same target, five rounds, rapid application, shoot!"

It was as if he'd been doing it all his life. Smoothly and effortlessly, Eric sent five more arrows into the log. So rapidly did he shoot that the fifth had left his bow before the fourth had even reached the target and they were grouped so closely that a three inch circle could have accommodated all the shafts.

"But-- but this is magic!" he stammered at last.

"Nonsense!" Montmorency shook his head emphatically, "you have a natural eye. Your problem is that up till now you have been shooting wrong-handed-- wouldn't you agree, Sir Tiresome?"

Tiresome, almost as amazed as Eric, nodded weakly.

"Toxophily is by way of being a small hobby of mine," the mage went on smoothly, "in fact a few years ago I published a trifling little monograph on the subject-- you must remind me to send you a copy."

"That would be most kind, Mage Montmorency." The knight recovered himself with an effort, and turned to Eric. "What are the marksmanship qualifying requirements?"

"Twenty gold in twenty-five shots, Sir Tiresome."

"Very well. Report to the marksmanship instructor immediately. Give him my compliments, and ask him to put you through your qualification shoot at once. And--" Tiresome gave the young man a hard stare, "I shall expect to hear that you got twenty-five gold."

Treading on air, Eric strode off for his qualification shoot.

Captain Porsena was not treading on air, but standing in water-- water which rose halfway up his gleaming boots. He looked at it disdainfully, then at the half-dozen troopers wading slowly deeper. As he watched, one of the men tripped on some underwater obstruction and fell heavily, sending up a sheet of spray.

"Take that man's name sergeant!" the captain shouted, "and be more careful!" He stepped back a few prudent paces, wincing fastidiously with each squelching step. It was criminal to have to use his crack cavalry for such a task! Wading through the water to assault barricades was work for the Shore Enforcers. At least it should not take long. Each trooper carried a coil of rope and, having climbed the barricade, would tie it onto the topmost log. The ropes would be harnessed to the draught horses, and a few good tugs should see the whole structure come tumbling down. The men struggled, cursing, through the water and reached the foot of the rampart of timber and tangled brushwood. They began to climb, but they had hardly got more than six feet up when they simultaneously executed neat reverse somersaults and, amid truncated profanities, descended into the water below. The wavelets lapped at Captain Porsena's boots and he stepped back a few more paces. "Sergeant!" he roared, "what do your men think they're up to?"

"Beg pardon, sir," the sergeant strode through the water and snapped to attention, showering the captain with spray as he did so. "Can't understand it, sir. Lads must be out of practice."

"Well send another squad in!" Porsena told him irritably, rubbing vainly at the mud spots on his uniform.

Another six men waded through the water and began the climb, but they fared no better than the first group. Soaked, they struggled to their feet, and expressed their disapprobation in no uncertain terms.

"We was pushed, sarge!" shouted one aggrievedly.

"Bloody right," agreed a comrade, "blokes was poking at us with long sticks. Not right, that isn't."

"What did that man say sergeant?"

The sergeant saluted and carefully composed his features. "Begging your pardon, sir, but he said there was blokes poking at him with long sticks."

"Blokes poking at him?" Porsena cried incredulously.

"Yes sir." The sergeant remained impassive.

"With long sticks?"

"That's what he said, sir. Mind you I wouldn't set much store by what Dubbins says. He's that thick he wouldn't know a long stick from a short one."

"The Seventh Heavy... *poked with long sticks*!" Captain Porsena roared, his face as black as thunder with the humiliation of it.

"Lieutenant Placebo's compliments, sir," a worried-looking sergeant came up, "the Shore Enforcement contingent should be up with us in half an hour.

Captain Porsena glared at the sergeant. He was on the horns of a particularly unpleasant dilemma. He could either send more men to assault the barricade, and watch them shamefully poked with long sticks, or he could await the arrival of Captain Mortise at the head of his Shore Enforcers and endure the consequent taunts and gibes from that officer when he discovered that the renowned Seventh Heavy Dragoons had been brought to a halt. It was not to be borne, Porsena told himself savagely. He was left with but one recourse. He looked back along the Ride where, looming over the dense throng of dragoons, was the distinctly unmilitary tarpaulin-draped shape of the device. "The man in charge of that... thing," he pointed, "where is he?"

"Senior Technical Officer Robinson reporting, sir," said a voice almost quiet enough to be insolent.

Porsena swung around and stared at the man. The casual demeanour went with the stooped carriage, sallow complexion and general air of seediness that was the hallmark of the Technical Branch. With difficulty Porsena restrained himself from delivering a blistering tirade about slovenliness (abundance of), brasses (unpolished state of), hair (length of) and military qualities (total absence of). He swallowed his anger. "That device of yours," he barked, "will it make any impression on that?" He pointed to the barricade.

"Should be able to take that out in no time, sir," Robinson gave a superior smile, "it's just what the Mark III was designed for."

"Mark III?" Porsena echoed, curious in spite of himself, "what about I and II?"

"A few minor technical problems... improved technology... usual sort of thing," Robinson said casually and, before Porsena could question him further, he turned on his heel and scampered off towards the device, shouting orders as he went. The tarpaulin was removed and Porsena winced as he glimpsed the naked machine-- his instincts had proved correct, for it was the most damned unmilitary piece of equipment he had ever seen in his life. There was not so much as one square inch of brightwork, and the timber structure was devoid of the slightest lick of paint. It was simply a squat wooden tower with a pair of trunnions at its top, supporting a long beam, pivoted at a point about two thirds along its length. The shorter portion was thick and carried a bulbous counterweight at its end. The longer portion was slender and terminated in a sort of basket affair.

As Porsena watched with the repelled fascination of a vicar's wife faced with an unusually explicit pornographic display, the men hauled on tackles, so that the long arm of the beam was pulled down to the horizontal. From a locker on the rear of the machine's carriage a large stone, about the size of a man's head, was taken and placed in the basket.

"Shoot!" shouted Robinson.

CRASH! The machine shuddered as the pivoted beam swung up to the vertical. The rock shot from the basket and cleared the top of the barricade by at least six feet, smashing through the trees on the other side.

"Down two hundred!" Robinson shouted. Two men energetically turned cranks at the rear of the carriage, tilting it further forward. Another rock was taken from the locker and loaded into the basket. "Shoot!" Robinson ordered.

CRASH! went the machine. SMASH! went the rock into the barricade. A small shower of broken branches shot into the air, and Porsena saw the whole structure tremble.

"Down one hundred," Robinson instructed his crew. "Shoot!"

Porsena almost jumped with joy as another shower of fragments erupted from the barricade; it could not hold up for long under that kind of treatment. The sound of a bugle was almost drowned by the machine discharging a fourth missile, and it was not until his sergeant had coughed very loudly that the captain noticed the spruce subaltern in Shore Enforcer uniform.

"Lieutenant Major, sir," he said, saluting briskly, "Shore Enforcement, Second Mounted. Captain Mortise's compliments, and can he be of any assistance?"

CRASH! SMASH! Another rock hammered the barricade. Porsena returned the salute and smiled genially. "My compliments to Captain Mortise, and tell him the Seventh Heavy Dragoons will be through the enemy's principal line of defence directly. After that it will just be a matter of mopping up.

CRASH! agreed the machine.

Act XVIII
ENTER A MESSENGER

You've *WHAT!*" Captain Porsena screamed.

"We have exhausted our ready-use ammunition," Robinson repeated patiently, "our ready-use lockers only carry eight rounds."

"What bloody use is that!" Porsena was almost beside himself. "Even the Technical Branch should know you can't fight a battle with eight rocks!"

"It is the weight, sir," the Technical Officer explained, as to a child, "there's no point in carting tons of rocks about when you can pick them up on the battlefield. According to our figures we can expect to find on average about one hundred rocks of suitable dimensions within a radius of a hundred paces on the typical battlefield."

"A fig for your figures!" the Captain raved, "how bloody many do you see?" Diligent searching had failed to reveal one rock of suitable size. Of stones the size of a man's fist, there were an uncountable number. Of boulders the size of a house, there were quite a few. But rocks about the size of a man's head were totally absent.

"I can only suggest, sir," Robinson replied with freezing politeness, "that we are simply in a low rock probability area."

"Pah!" Porsena turned away in disgust to find himself face-to-face with Lieutenant Major.

"Captain Mortise's compliments, sir, he is sending a patrol to scout a way around the barricade." The Lieutenant accompanied his report with a smug salute.

"Much good may it do him!" snarled Porsena, still smarting from that officer's comments when an earlier patrol of Dragoons, had disappeared without trace. He cast his eye over the chaotic scene. The arrival of the Shore Enforcers meant that now almost five hundred troops and half that many horses were jammed into a *cul de sac*, jostled together and utterly impossible to deploy in any constructive fashion. "Lieutenant Major! You and Lieutenant Placebo get the men to fall back and spread out. We must keep the road clear." The two officers departed, only to return almost at once, dismay written plainly on their faces.

"The road is blocked behind us, sir," Placebo reported, "a couple of trees have been felled. Sergeant Spineways has men working on it but he cannot say when he will have it cleared."

Kodswallop had not been worried by stones crashing through his barricade. The missiles had merely punched through the lighter branches-- inconvenient to the men standing behind, but not endangering the structure itself. The barricade had a slightly moth-eaten look but was still intact, and the outlaws had remained in position, their long sticks at the ready. And the shower of rocks had stopped. The big fighter stooped to pick up one of the missiles and weighed it in his hand. It was a fair old weight to be chucking about the place, he mused. In a fit of irritation he hurled it back over the barricade. There was a festive crash. Encouraged by this, he scouted around until he found a second stone, and sent that after the first. There was another splintering crash. He couldn't find any more of the projectiles, so with a shrug of regret he hastened off in search of straying enemy troops-- they'd already picked up forty-odd, and he didn't want to miss out on the fun.

Captain Porsena and Senior Technical Officer Robinson stared, horror-struck, at the wrecked machine. Kodswallop's first rock had struck the throwing arm squarely, snapping it in two, then gone on to smash the rear axle. The second had struck the left hand trunnion, demolishing it completely and twisting the pivot mechanism beyond recognition.

"At least we've got some ammunition now," someone muttered, seeking opportunities rather than problems.

Robinson turned on him. "You realize what this means!" he snarled.

"We're going to have to go ahead with the Mark IV?"

"Fool! It means there's been a leak-- the Other Side must have the Mark III design."

"Not exactly, sir. Theirs seems to be working."

For a moment Captain Porsena almost forgot his own worries as he watched the rage and frustration on Robinson's face. He tried to console the man. "Cheer up Robinson! While the machine is... er..."

"Down for routine maintenance," Robinson prompted.

"Thank you. Well, while your machine is down for routine maintenance you might want to take the opportunity to clean it up a little-- make it more in keeping with the tradition of the Seventh Heavy. You'll find some paint and cleaning equipment in the supplies wagon-- just tell the Quartermaster Sergeant that I sent you. Get your men to work, and let me see that machine gleaming by tomorrow!" Porsena marched away from the seething Robinson with the warm feeling of having helped out his fellow man in time of crisis.

When he reached the tail of the column he was gratified to see that much progress had been made in clearing the way. One of the huge tree trunks had been dragged aside already and, under the energetic encouragement of a sergeant, a squad of men were hacking away at the second. "Lieutenant Placebo!" he called, "where's that officer from the Shore Enforcers... Major I think it was?"

"Lieutenant, sir," Placebo corrected him, "I believe he has taken a working party to search for more stones."

"Lieutenant Lieutenant?" Porsena spat the words out, "what an absurd name! As soon as this is cleared, have your best despatch rider report to me."

It was getting close to sunset when the last tangle of branches was finally pulled clear and the despatch rider galloped off. The message he bore was short and simple. It reported that the advancing troops had met with an obstacle to further progress and that the device had been rendered unserviceable by "unanticipated technical problems associated with the rigours of the field environment". It requested a platoon of pioneers to remove the obstacle. And it urged that a striking force be deployed against the outlaws from the north west, taking them in the rear at a time when their attention was fully occupied by the Seventh Heavy Dragoons.

The message afforded Tiresome both amusement and satisfaction when he read it some two hours later.

Once again, dawn illuminated the First Speaker's camp with its cold, clear light. Guards changed, bugles blared and the First Speaker's standard crawled jerkily up the makeshift flagpole. Grey-blue smoke from cooking fires drifted up, carrying with it the smell of scorching porridge. Screened from the eyes of the camp guards, just inside the boundary of the forest, a tent flap eased open reluctantly, like one eye of a badly hung-over debauchee. Andrew Cruickshank emerged, rumpled, cold, stiff and bleary-eyed.

"Hallo Andrew!" Ratbag, looking a little grey about the gills, tried to stifle a yawn-- he had been up all night. "Janus is already up. Nothing happened last night."

"This could get dead boring rather fast," Andrew grumbled, half to himself.

"Did you get a chance to look at those papers last night?"

"Bloody hell, I forgot! Sorry, Ratbag. I'll take a look right now." He reached into the tent for the papers, and spread them out before him, weighting them down with stones. Ratbag, his fatigue forgotten, sat down to watch. There was a rustle of branches as Cecil and Janus clambered down from the sycamore tree they'd been using as their watch-tower. "What've you got there?" Cecil asked as he strolled over.

"It's the papers we got from the First Speaker's office!" Ratbag told him, quivering with excitement.

"So what's in them?"

"Haven't quite got round to them," Andrew admitted sheepishly.

"Well bloody get on with it!" Cecil gave him an indignant look, "Miss Prism risked her honour to get them."

"Alright, alright..." Andrew picked up the first, gave it a quick glance, then put it aside. The Articles of Incorporation of Fleet the Time in the Golden World plc didn't look as though they'd be rewarding reading. Neither did the Business Case Study for the same enterprise. But the third document was different. *Application for Usurpation Licence*, it announced at the top of the first page. Andrew read it through very carefully. He read it through again, just to make sure, although he really need not have bothered, for the crabbed handwriting across the bottom of the last page told him all he needed to know: *This usurpation licence is declared null and void, and is hereby revoked*, it began with a commendable effort to leave no possible shadow of doubt as to the writer's opinion, *on the grounds that the Applicant has failed absolutely to provide evidence of any substantive Preparatory Motions within the meaning of the Usurpation Act, Section 2(a).* It was signed *Titus Handcarte*.

"We've got it!" Andrew shouted, leaping to his feet.

"Got what?" Cecil demanded "anything catching?"

"It's an application for a Usurpation Licence, by Roger-- that's the usurping duke."

"Well?" Cecil was unmoved by the intelligence. "He'd need one, wouldn't he?"

"Yes-- but he hasn't got it! Not any more, that is. The First Speaker has revoked it!"

"And that means?"

"It means we've done it! The exiled duke isn't an exiled duke!"

Janus took the document from Andrew's unresisting fingers and glanced over it. "Congratulations!" The elf's eyes were shining with delight, "you said that one of the possible outcomes was the discovery of some secret document, and you were quite right!"

"But I still don't see--" Cecil objected.

"Don't you remember, Andrew told us that there were two possible solutions to the exiled duke problem: either the exile had to be revoked, or it had to be shown that he wasn't a duke. Harold is no longer an *exiled* duke!"

"And that means," Andrew concluded, "Orlando can chase him out of the forest any time he wants to. Of course, we've got to chase a few other people out of the forest first."

There was a pensive silence.

"Just a minute..." Andrew felt an idea start to form, "I think there's a rather elegant way of getting *everybody* out of the forest."

"Does it involve gratuitous violence?" Cecil asked, "'cause if it doesn't, I can't see the others going for it."

"Belt up, Cecil," Janus said automatically, "what have you got in mind, Andrew?"

"We entice the First Speaker into the forest, grab him, then persuade him to withdraw his troops. Kodswallop could do the persuading."

"How do you entice the First Speaker into the forest?"

"We forge a message to the First Speaker that the outlaws have been defeated and that he is invited to come and accept their surrender in person. He'll fall for it-- bloody hell, he's a politician. Show him a sketching opportunity and wild horses won't stop him!"

"I like it..." Janus smiled, "Tiresome can provide us with the horse and uniform-- he must have collected enough of them by now. And I shall play the part of the messenger."

"But--" Andrew started to protest. He didn't like the idea of Janus riding into the enemy camp alone.

"There isn't anyone else, "the elf said matter-of-factly, "after all, your horsemanship wouldn't be very convincing, Ratbag is too small and Cecil..." Janus paused, "with the best will in the world, his appearance is still a little... er... unmilitary."

That was true enough. In any kind of military uniform, Cecil looked like mutiny on legs. "But I still don't like the idea of your riding into that place on your own," Andrew argued, "after all, properly speaking there should be three messengers-- or at least three should start out. You know," he continued, prompted by the elf's look of polite inquiry, "'I sprang to the stirrup; and Joris and he...' and all that sort of thing?"

The elf looked blank. Sometimes he didn't have the faintest idea what Andrew was going on about-- though it was all very interesting. "I am sure the tradition is a sound one," he agreed, "but the circumstances being what they are..." he shrugged.

"It should be a bit of biscuit," Cecil gave a confident grin.

"A piece of cake," Andrew corrected him.

"Get onto Tiresome now," Ratbag urged, "we want the uniform and other stuff as soon as possible."

Andrew picked up his spellcaster and tapped the instrument lightly with his finger. There was a fierce crackle, and Montmorency's voice echoed irritably in his ear. "How many times do I have to tell you, Cruickshank! There is absolutely no need for such a prodigious display."

"Sorry about that," Andrew said automatically, then, "what are you talking about?"

"Never mind, Cruickshank, they are putting the fire out now."

"Jolly good! Now listen, Montmorency: there's something we'd like to try." He hastily outlined the plan. "He's got to go for it!" Andrew concluded, "he's got to!"

"I see. And was this your idea, Cruickshank?"

"Yes."

"You are sure it does not form a vital plot element in one of William Shakespeare's plays?"

"Of course not!"

"I am relieved to hear it. I will relay the proposal to Sir Tiresome. Please stay on net."

Montmorency was back a minute or two later. "Sir Tiresome has approved the plan, although he does wonder whether three messengers aren't traditional in such matters."

"To start with," Andrew agreed, "but only one makes it to the destination."

"Ah, I see. Very good. Sir Tiresome is sending a party with the horse, uniform and message pouch of Captain Porsena's despatch rider. They should be with you in a couple of hours. Signal as soon as you see the First Speaker's party enter the forest, then come immediately to Group Bravo. Do you understand?"

"Perfectly."

"Very well, then. We shall meet at Group Bravo. And, Cruickshank, one more thing--"

"Yes?"

"Don't call me-- I'll call you."

The front flaps of the First Speaker's tent were pulled all the way back to admit the morning sun and give the artist all the light he needed for his work. A few more quick shading strokes with the charcoal stick, and it was done. "It is finished, sir." He held the sketch up.

Titus Handcarte relaxed his pose, and his information officer bustled over to the artist to peer eagerly at the completed work. "Excellent!" he cried enthusiastically, "a most dramatic portrayal!"

"Let me see, Plausible." The First Speaker gazed at length. The sketch depicted a horse, its legs stretched improbably fore and aft, in mid-leap. Upon the creature's back was the First Speaker of East Castellian, a drawn sword in his hand, defying a veritable sleet of arrows. "You are quite right, Plausible," the First Speaker said at last, "most dramatic. And... ah... a speaking likeness, I think."

"Indeed yes, First Speaker!" Plausible nodded sycophantically, "I'm sure we can place this in some of the better broadsheets. Front page material!"

"Front page, eh?" The First Speaker almost sounded gratified.

"No doubt about it," Plausible told him, "Bruce Strident will certainly use it. Especially if we can offer him an interview..." he let the suggestion hang in the air. Before the First Speaker could respond there was the sudden urgent blare of a trumpet, a thudding tattoo of galloping hooves and a chorus of shouted challenges.

"What can all that be about?" Handcarte demanded irritably. The words were scarcely out of his mouth before the figure of his Chief of Staff appeared at the tent entrance holding a message pouch aloft.

"First Speaker!" he panted, "this has just arrived from Captain Porsena of the Seventh Heavy Dragoons." With a flourish he presented the sealed leather pouch to the First Speaker.

Handcarte examined the seals carefully, but they told him nothing except that they were undoubtedly Captain Porsena's. He broke them with a quick gesture, unfolded the wallet and took out a single sheet of parchment. His eyes flickered over it twice, his face expressionless. Then he looked up at the ring of anxious faces gathered around him.

"Gentlemen," he began, with pardonable inaccuracy, "I have here a despatch from Captain Porsena which I should like to read to you." He cleared his throat. "It begins: *To His Excellency Titus Handcarte, First Speaker of East Castellian. May it please Your Excellency to be informed that late last night the Seventh Heavy Dragoons, following an engagement with a strong enemy force, surrounded the headquarters of the notorious outlaws of Stembark Forest. At dawn this morning the Commander in Chief of the outlaws approached under a flag of truce, and requested terms. May I respectfully invite Your Excellency to proceed hither to accept the surrender. I have the honour to remain your humble and obedient servant, Lars Porsena, Captain, Seventh Heavy Dragoons.*" The First Speaker looked up and across his usually impassive features flickered the light of triumph. "Well gentlemen, I shall leave at once to formally accept the surrender. Please request Captain Spalding to summon my personal guard."

The Chief of Staff gestured, and a messenger darted from the tent. The First Speaker began pacing slowly back and forth, then halted suddenly as he thought of something. "The messenger who brought this," he flourished Porsena's despatch, "was he alone?"

"Yes, First Speaker."

"Does not tradition dictate three riders?"

"Three riders who *start out*, First Speaker, but only one who arrives with the news."

"I see. Where is the messenger now? I wish to commend him on his promptitude."

The Chief of Staff thought it highly likely that the man had headed at once for the nearest tavern. "I expect he has rejoined his unit, First Speaker, but I will check." He moved to the tent entrance. "Sergeant!" he called.

"Sah!"

"The messenger who arrived just now from Captain Porsena; has he rejoined his unit?"

The sergeant knew very well that the man had set off for the nearest tavern, but he was not about to give him away to any officer. Besides, the lad had earned his drink. "Rejoined his unit at once, sah!" he explained briskly, "very keen lot they are in the Seventh Heavy."

"Thought so." The Chief of Staff returned to the tent. "As I suspected, First Speaker, the man has rejoined his unit."

"A pity. He shall be rewarded in due course." Handcarte dismissed the man from his mind. "Now, Plausible," he turned to the information officer, "should we invite some of the broadsheet writers to witness this historic event?"

"An excellent idea, First Speaker," Plausible nodded enthusiastically, "especially if you could promise a briefing and a sketching opportunity."

"I have no objection to promising that," Handcarte agreed, with the faintest of emphasis on the word.

"I'll set it up at once. Bruce Strident will certainly wish to come along..." wittering happily, Plausible bustled from the tent.

"Tell them to be ready in thirty minutes," the First Speaker called after him.

"We aren't in any hurry, Spalding," the First Speaker reminded the captain as, for the third time, they were brought to a halt by a sentry. "Indeed this is most praiseworthy! The area has been effectively and efficiently secured-- I am most gratified!"

"Quite so, First Speaker," Captain Spalding agreed. He shouted an order, and the column started forward once more, the sentry rigidly at attention, saluting as they went past.

"Though, Spalding, I was distressed to note that fellow's uniform-- so ill-fitting! Surely the Shore Enforcement Branch estimates are sufficient to ensure that at least the men can be provided with tunics whose sleeves do not stop at the elbow!"

"I shall look into it, First Speaker," Spalding promised, himself a little taken aback by the sentry's appearance-- why, it almost looked as if the man had been wearing somebody else's uniform by mistake!

"Er... First Speaker?" The information officer urged his horse forward.

"What is it, Plausible?"

"Bruce Strident wondered if we might have time for a sketching opportunity."

"We are always ready to accommodate our friends from the broadsheets," Handcarte said graciously. "Spalding! You may order a short halt."

Some hundred paces from the Group Bravo field headquarters the Southern Ride made a graceful curve around a huge jutting thumb of moss-grown rock, that was almost a miniature cliff. Tiresome waved his little assault group to a halt. "Clumpface and Cecil, take the rock. You deal with the rear of the column. Wally," he addressed a grizzled Section Leader, "your lot takes the standard bearers and their outriders, and quickly."

The outlaw gave a confident smile and tapped the coil of rope that hung from his shoulder. "It'll be all be over before they know it's started."

"Good. Janus and Ratbag will neutralize anyone else near the First Speaker. And Kodswallop, you know what to do?"

The big fighter grinned happily, and rubbed his hands. "I'll deal with the First Speaker. I'm looking forward to meeting him after hearing so much about him."

"What will be our signal, Sir Tiresome?" Wally asked.

"The call of an owl."

"Migratory or hibernating?" Cecil asked.

"Ah..." Tiresome hesitated; ornithology wasn't his strong point.

"I don't believe at this stage such subtlety is necessary," Montmorency suggested "a shout of 'hi', or any loud cry, should suffice."

"Thank you, Mage Montmorency." Tiresome shot him a grateful look. "Take up your positions!" The figures melted away into the undergrowth.

"Thank you very much, First Speaker, that will be fine."

Titus Handcarte relaxed from his pose and returned the sword to Captain Spalding, and the two broadsheet writers folded up their sketchpads.

"If that is all, gentlemen, then perhaps we may proceed." The First Speaker nodded to Captain Spalding who shouted an order. A bugle sounded the 'advance' and the column started forward once more. Handcarte felt in a relaxed, expansive mood. The outlaws had been dealt with more swiftly and easily than he had hoped, the coverage in the broadsheets would be extensive and flattering, and it was a lovely day for a ride.

"A picturesque spot, is it not, Spalding!" Handcarte gestured at the looming trees.

"Indeed, First Speaker."

"See how this road that seems to wind so aimlessly, is in fact taking us steadily deeper into the forest. Once the Benbrock-Oldstairs brothers have things properly organized, it will be a delightful recreational facility."

"Quite so, First Speaker," Spalding assented, though he harboured private doubts about that. From what he knew of those two, he would be surprised if they could organise a piss-up in a brewery.

"And this, now," the procession was skirting the ancient outcropping and the crunch of the horses' hooves echoed back from the dark, mossy rock, "see what an ideal position for a scenic look-out."

"Yes, First Speaker, ideal." Spalding urged his horse forward to tell the leaders of the column to hurry things up a bit.

Handcarte was about to ask Spalding what he was up to when he became aware of a sort of scuffling sound from behind him. He turned in his saddle and saw, to his amazement, the disciplined column of horsemen behind him begin to disintegrate as one trooper after another slumped to the ground. Suddenly aware that something was going seriously wrong, Handcarte turned and clapped his heels to his horse's flanks. But even as he did so the colour party before him, and Captain Spalding, simultaneously leaped backward off their horses. The First Speaker was momentarily aware of some huge shape springing towards him, then everything went black.

Act XIX
THE MEETING GROUND

$$\longleftarrow \cdot \diamond \cdot \longrightarrow$$

Right then!" Tiresome looked over his motley crew. "Everyone accounted for?"

"We're all here..." Clumpface stuffed something into his pipe.

"Where's the First Speaker?"

"In here." Kodswallop nudged a large sack with his foot. The sack wriggled agitatedly. Kodswallop gave it a hard stare and the wriggling stopped.

"In there!" Tiresome exclaimed, "get him out right now! And dust him off a bit, make him comfortable. You know the rules!"

Kodswallop grumbled something under his breath. Not being a Knight of Albion, the provisions of the *Unified Code (Combat), Section Three: Victory (Magnanimity In)* weighed lightly upon his conscience-- if indeed they weighed at all. But nevertheless he did untie the sack and, with a brisk shake, decanted the First Speaker onto the grass.

"Well, stand him on his feet, then!"

None too gently, Kodswallop returned the rather tubby figure to an upright position.

"Very good. Now, Janus," Tiresome beckoned to the elf, "I believe we are ready to proceed, if you would care to take charge?"

Janus nodded agreeably. "Kodswallop and Cecil, please set up a table over there. And Clumpface, would you fetch food and drink for the First Speaker?"

"Janus!" Ratbag plucked his leader by the sleeve, "should I get Andrew?"

"Not at this stage," the elf demurred, "Montmorency will observe from a distance. He suggested that the First Speaker might find Andrew's presence unduly... disturbing." Janus turned to Handcarte and gave a slight (very slight) bow. "Now, sir, if you will walk this way, we can provide you some refreshment, and then we can get down to business."

"Lot of bloody nonsense," Kodswallop muttered under his breath to Cecil, "we're supposed to be giving the bloke a good thumping-- a good persuading that is-- not a free lunch."

"Cheer up," the marksman whispered back, "haven't you heard that there's no such thing as a free lunch?"

While Montmorency stood observing the little group from a discreet distance, Andrew was drawn aside by the outlaw chief. "A wonderful success, Wardmaster Cruickshank! And I hear you've worked out how to get rid of...?"

"Yes. As soon as we've got that little lot sorted out--" he jerked his thumb at the table where the First Speaker sat, "I'll show you the papers. It's quite clear: Harold isn't an exiled duke."

"Great news! And we have been fortunate with our prisoners as well. It appears that the First Speaker brought two broadsheet writers with him"

"Broadsheet writers?"

"Yes, Anthony Anguish from the *Thunderclap* and Bruce Strident from the *Daily Lapse*-- two of the most influential writers in East Castellian!"

"You mean newspaper reporters? That is, people who write stories?"

"For the broadsheets, yes." Orlando nodded happily. "It is really is a bit of good luck! I have promised to take them on a tour of the forest, and give them an exclusive interview. This is just the sort of publicity we need!"

"Oh no!" Andrew started back in horror.

"What do you mean, 'oh no'?" The outlaw chief looked puzzled and slightly affronted, "this is going to be our big chance to get Stembark Forest on the front pages!"

"You'll be on the front pages alright," Andrew told him grimly, "what have you told them so far?"

"Well, nothing very much. I was going to give them a few brochures first. Then show them the new Headquarters wing, a quick trip to the island, and finish up at the kiddies' playground."

"Come here and sit down." Andrew pushed the mystified outlaw chief onto a tree stump. "Listen," he squatted down beside Orlando, "you mustn't talk to them. You think they're going to write nice articles all about the wonderful things you're doing in Stembark Forest? About all the opportunities for family entertainment? About the new accommodation?"

"Well... yes."

"Ha!"

"You mean they're not?"

"That's not the kind of article that sells papers-- broadsheets, I mean. No what you'll get is stories *like Inside the Outlaws: Exclusive Interview with Stembark Forest's Crime Boss!!!*"

"What!" Orlando looked stunned.

"Oh yes. You know the kind of thing-- you must read the broadsheets yourself-- *Bruce Strident tears the lid off the seething cesspit of crime and degradation in Stembark Forest.*"

"But-- they wouldn't..."

"Oh yes they would! And they'd probably put a picture of you wearing some kind of awful hat on the front page."

Orlando started as though he had been bitten. "One of them did say something about a sketch," he said, with dawning horror.

"With a hat?"

"With a hat."

"I thought so. Orlando, you mustn't talk to those people."

"But what am I to do? They're waiting for their interview."

"Who is the biggest, toughest, worst-tempered man in your band?"

"Well, there's Oswald." Orlando looked puzzled. "He's certainly big and tough. But I'm afraid he's quite good-natured."

"He'll have to do. Send him to the writers. Have him tell them that he's your Information Officer, and is the official spokesman for the Stembark Forest Outlaws."

"Information officer... official spokesman..." Orlando repeated, writing the words down.

"If they ask to see you, he's to explain that you're tied up in an important meeting all day, but will get back to them as soon as possible."

"Important meeting..." Orlando scribbled busily. Then he looked up. "You know, that isn't really true about the meeting," he pointed out mildly.

"Yes it is." Andrew was firm. "This meeting is important, isn't it?"

"Well, when you put it like that..."

"There you are, then! Now if they ask Oswald any questions-- anything at all-- he's not to say a thing. He can tell them he doesn't know, but he'll get them answers as soon as he can. Or else he can say that he can't answer the question because it would violate an individual's right to privacy."

"... an individual's right to privacy..." Orlando echoed the words, still scribbling busily.

"And if all else fails, then he can just bop them one."

"Ah!" Orlando brightened, "he's very good at that sort of thing. I'll see to it right away." With a preoccupied air, Orlando walked off, muttering "information officer... important meeting... violation of individual's right to privacy... bop them one."

Andrew watched him go, then turned his attention to the table on the other side of the clearing where his friends sat in conference with the First Speaker. He wondered how the negotiations were going.

Negotiations had reached an impasse. From the moment the First Speaker realized that he had been captured by terrorists, his active, supple mind had been busy. He knew enough about the theory of hostage taking to be confident that his captors would be nervous, in an excitable state, and highly suggestible. Or at least, he corrected himself as he observed the calmly authoritative demeanour of their leader, if not nervous and excitable, they would be anxious to negotiate and, with his victorious troops in close proximity, they would be negotiating under pressure. Titus Handcarte smiled to himself; he *always* applied enough pressure to ensure satisfactory negotiations. Then, as he moved towards the table, his eye fell upon the gigantic figure of Kodswallop and for a moment his confidence was shaken. The huge figure did not look particularly vulnerable to pressure and, what was more, looked infinitely non-negotiable. But the First Speaker set his jaw obstinately-- with five hundred troops less than an hour's march away he could afford to be obstinate-- and he pointedly took the seat at the head of the table. "I am a busy man, but I can give you a few minutes," he said brusquely, "what do you want?"

They all gazed, fascinated, at the less than imposing figure, with his round, pale face, watery-blue eyes and sparse hedges of ginger eyebrows. Encouraged by the silence, Handcarte decided to push his advantage. "You have, you realize, made yourself liable for prosecution under half a dozen capital laws including High Treason and Incitement to Rebellion--"

"How about playing a musical instrument without a licence?" Cecil asked, unimpressed.

Handcarte ignored the interruption. "You should also understand that in a very short time you will be in custody," he snapped, "but I can see you are sincere, well-meaning men with some profound concerns. Let us use what little time we have to sit down at this table and try to resolve those concerns, and conclude this matter peacefully. If you surrendered to me before my troops arrive, it would count most favourably at your trial," he concluded with an encouraging smile.

"I'm afraid not," Ratbag chirped, passing the First Speaker his encouraging smile right back with interest. "You see, *we're* not in custody, but *you* are."

"A very temporary situation," Handcarte responded airily, "when I fail to arrive at my destination five hundred Dragoons and Shore Enforcers will be searching for me. And they will not have far to look."

"I don't think so." Ratbag shook his head, "I think they are all rather busy at the moment."

Handcarte gave a mirthless laugh. "Your information is out of date, boy! The Outlaws of Stembark Forest have been defeated, and I am on my way to formally accept their surrender."

Ratbag shook his head once more and, still smiling, took a sheet of paper from his pouch. "Do you mean this?" he asked, and began reading aloud. *"May it please your excellency to be informed that late last night the Seventh Heavy Dragoons, following an engagement with a strong enemy force, surrounded the headquarters of the notorious Outlaws of Stembark Forest..."* Ratbag looked up. "I think it was a bit dishonest not to mention the Shore Enforcers, don't you?" he asked gently.

The First Speaker almost leaped from his seat. Involuntarily his hand flew to his wallet where Captain Porsena's despatch lay, then he regained control of himself. "Since you have already read the despatch from Captain Porsena, then you must know your position is hopeless," he responded calmly.

"I didn't read the despatch," Ratbag's smile held a slight razor edge-- he hadn't liked being called 'boy'-- "I wrote it."

"You--"

"The First Speaker should realize that he has been labouring under something of a misapprehension." Janus spoke with careful formality. "The document purporting to come from Captain Porsena was in fact prepared by Ratbag, a stratagem we adopted so that we might have the opportunity to exchange a few words with the First Speaker."

"And persuade him!" Kodswallop added, an anticipatory gleam in his eye.

"Your words, then!" Now Handcarte was feeling considerably less sanguine-- the slender elf-like figure was not bluffing, he was certain.

"It is very simple," Janus said quietly, "we wish you to withdraw your men from Stembark Forest and leave the outlaws to themselves. It is a sensible and a humane solution."

"Ha ha!" Handcarte was genuinely amused by the naivete of the proposal, then he choked the laughter off as he realized that the naivete was neither here nor there: this was the proposal. "You are surely jesting!"

"We are not jesting," Janus told him, "we are simply making every attempt to save lives, and arrive at a peaceful solution."

"The peaceful solution would be the submission of these outlaws to the forces of justice!" Handcarte snapped, "and that goes for you people too. Now I don't want to be unreasonable about this, but unless you release me immediately, and escort me back to my troops, I am going to become extremely concerned about your health."

For the first time in his experience, Titus Handcarte found that this awful threat had no observable effect whatsoever. He began to wonder whether these brigands had actually been telling the truth about Captain Porsena.

"Enough of this idle chatter!" growled Clumpface, "just prepare orders for your troops to withdraw from the forest and to return to East Castellian."

"And if I do not choose to do so?"

"Then we will inform your troops we hold you hostage, and that if they hold your life at any worth, they should withdraw!" The dwarf was getting impatient.

"Might not be a good idea," warned Kodswallop, "they could be glad to see the back of him."

"We could cut off his finger and send it to them," suggested Ratbag, "that's often done with hostages."

"An ear is more traditional" Clumpface objected.

"Sod the ear! I know what we can cut off." Cecil looked very pointedly at the First Speaker and played idly with a long, slender dagger.

"I don't know if we can do that," Kodswallop grumbled, "what with the *Unified Code* an' all." He gestured at Tiresome.

Titus Handcarte followed the gesture and breathed a silent sigh of relief when he saw the Red Dragon insignia on Tiresome's chest. He knew no knight of Albion would permit the kind of unspeakable mutilations these dacoits had been discussing so casually.

"Tiresome could always go for a walk," Cecil suggested, cleaning his nails with the point of his dagger.

"Nah... wouldn't do any good." Kodswallop shook his head sadly. Much as he would have enjoyed bouncing the First Speaker up and down for an hour or so, the big fighter was simply incapable of maltreating a defenceless prisoner-- even one so demonstrably deserving of maltreatment as Titus Handcarte. The others shook their heads in mute acknowledgement of Kodswallop's point-- with the exception of Cecil.[16]

"I want to make myself perfectly clear on one point." Handcarte's voice was steady. "I have no intention of issuing any orders for my troops to withdraw. On general principles, the government of East Castellian does not negotiate with terrorists."

"We're not asking you to negotiate," Kodswallop explained, as to a child, "we're just telling you to sign a withdrawal order. There's no question of negotiations," he added with the triumphant smile of a salesman who has just made a telling point.

"And I am just telling you I have no intention of doing so." The First Speaker's voice did not quaver.

Whatever else you could say about the man, Janus reflected, he did not lack courage. "Very well" the elf shrugged, "then we will simply have to draft the order ourselves and have Ratbag provide the signature. It will be indistinguishable from your own."

"And what do you expect that to achieve?" Handcarte gave a contemptuous laugh. "Temporary confusion, at best."

---

16   To Cecil, a defenceless prisoner was an opportunity, not a problem.

Andrew joined Montmorency about ten paces from the table and, tactfully, behind the First Speaker. "Negotiations seem to have reached an impasse, Cruickshank," the black mage murmured, "the First Speaker is no poltroon and is resistant to physical threats-- especially when he recognises they are empty threats."

"I can't see much empty about Cecil's threat," Andrew observed, "he's looking bloody murderous."

"All he can do is look," Montmorency pointed out, "Sir Tiresome will tolerate no violation of the *Unified Code*, and alas, the First Speaker is fully aware of that fact. Physical intimidation will not avail us, I fear. A more subtle approach is called for."

"Yes." Andrew agreed, and started to think.

Montmorency looked momentarily disconcerted as he saw Andrew's eyes narrow. "I fear I did not express myself clearly just now, Cruickshank. I should have said I must develop a more subtle approach-- there is absolutely no need for you to trouble yourself."

"It's no trouble, Montmorency," Andrew replied absently, his mind on other matters.

The black mage muttered something that Andrew didn't catch. "What?"

"I was saying Cruickshank, that you have already been abundantly subtle enough for today, and there is no need for you to over-exert yourself. I can be subtle too, and after all it is my turn. Besides, it would look a little extravagant having two mages being subtle at the same time. Overdoing it a bit, don't you think?"

"Listen Montmorency, I've just thought of something!"

"Indeed! Congratulations, Cruickshank-- you are having a busy day." Montmorency's eyes glinted violet and green and, to his very great surprise, Andrew realised that Montmorency was actually having fun! So taken aback was he at the incipient grin threatening to disfigure that usually austere countenance that he was speechless for a few seconds.

"Well..?" Montmorency prompted, "what was the something you had just thought of?"

"The First Speaker. I've never been quite clear what he is, or how he got his job, but would it be fair to say that he is some kind of politician?"

Montmorency drew in his breath in shocked disapproval. "The First Speaker is the principal citizen of East Castellian," he said severely, "a position he assumed following the untimely demise of his predecessor who succumbed to a severe cold following a meeting up a dark alley with three representatives of the electorate. The First Speaker has been accused, justly I believe, of raising peculation to an art form and, equally justly, of being an assassin, a thief on a grand scale, a corrupter of youth and a betrayer of public trust. But he has never, so far as I know, sunk to the level you describe."

"Oh."

"Was there some reason for the question, Cruickshank?"

"Well there are these two reporters-- that is broadsheet writers-- we captured with the First Speaker."

"Indeed?" Montmorency's nose wrinkled fastidiously, "it must have been a most unpleasant experience."

"Yes. You see they were supposed to be covering the First Speaker's campaign."

"You mean writing about it? For their broadsheets?"

"Exactly."

"I rather doubt *that*," the mage observed, "but writing something, at anyrate. And now they find themselves without occupation?"

"Not necessarily," Andrew said slowly, and began to smile. When he had explained what he meant, Montmorency began to smile too.

Montmorency beckoned Janus away from the group at the table, now seething with silent defiance on the part of the First Speaker and barely restrained grievous bodily harm on the part of Cecil. "Janus," he whispered, "if you would allow us a few minutes with your client we may be able to arrive at some resolution of the matter."

The elf frowned uncertainly, but when he saw Andrew's expression, his own worried features relaxed into a smile. To his friends, Andrew's face was as transparent as plate glass and the look of triumph it now bore was unambiguous. "You are in control Andrew, Montmorency," he said with a slight bow, "we shall take our lead from you."

Montmorency swept up to the table with a style and flourish that Andrew could only envy. If he tried anything like that he knew he would trip over something. There was a clatter as the black mage tripped over a chair, followed by a viciously hissed imprecation and a livid flash of lightning. But he quickly recovered his poise and beckoned Andrew forward. "Gentlemen, pray give us place a while," he requested the others.

They rose from their seats and grouped themselves at the far end of the table watching, fascinated. Cecil muttered, "bloody negotiations. Bloody waste of time!"

Andrew silently agreed with the frustrated marksman. Negotiations were the sort of thing that were entered into once a course of action had been determined. Negotiations were what took place when verbose hypocrites and sanctimonious poltroons sat down to share a free lunch. Negotiations might affect the selection of tunes played by the ship's orchestra on the Titanic, but they'd do nothing to keep the vessel out of the ice-pack. Andrew and Montmorency were not going to negotiate. They were going to threaten... to blackmail... to coerce or, as Montmorency would have said, to advise.

Montmorency assumed his seat with the smooth precision of some lethal machine. His staff hovered obediently at his elbow, eagerly awaiting the summons to go forth and wreak destruction. Andrew just sat down-- anything he might do would be an anti-climax. He tossed his staff to one side and it clattered ignominiously to the ground-- once again he had neglected to set it to the "safe" or "park" mode. Blushing furiously, he grabbed at the recalcitrant instrument and a stream of crimson light blasted a deep smoking furrow in the grass.

The echoes of the detonation died away as Andrew belatedly set the staff to "safe", reflecting that perhaps he hadn't been as anti-climactic as all that.

The First Speaker lowered himself back into his chair, from which he had involuntarily risen. "What manner of men are you?" he asked, his voice only the slightest bit unsteady, "I warn you I am not to be diverted by magician's parlour tricks!"

"I am glad you asked that." Montmorency smiled very thinly indeed. 'Magician' was not a word to use lightly in his presence, nor indeed was he best pleased by the expression 'parlour tricks'. "Before I make the introductions, let us have some refreshment." With a wave of the hand he materialized a decanter of brandy and three glasses, and poured out three healthy measures.

"You-- you are mages?" Handcarte's voice for the first time betrayed some slight concern.

"That is correct." Montmorency slid a glass across the table to the First Speaker, and another to Andrew. "I am Montmorency, Senior Level Black Mage, and my colleague is Wardmaster Mage Cruickshank, of the Crimson. Cheers." He raised the glass to his lips.

The First Speaker spluttered and choked. *Cruickshank!* He shot upright. "The mage who is not the usual kind of mage. *You?*" His voice rose as he pointed a trembling finger at Andrew. Thanks to Montmorency's meticulous attention to detail, the glass he had released stayed floating upright in mid-air.

"You see, Cruickshank, he *has* heard of you!" Montmorency said, with the delight of a hostess who has managed to find common ground between two strangers at a cocktail party.

"*Heard* of him?" Handcarte was almost screaming with rage, "the one who turned my Shore Enforcers into stone? The one who destroyed Hamerslake Castle? The one who--" He stopped abruptly. There was no point in bringing up the humiliating episode of the white mouse.

"I never!" Andrew said hotly, "I never turned anybody into stone... did I, Montmorency?"

"I do not believe so," Montmorency agreed, with an indulgent smile, "but we did not come here to bother the First Speaker with old arguments about who turned who into stone, did we?"

Handcarte was recovering his equilibrium. Undoubtedly the two men he faced were potent mages and one of them was, on the evidence of his past behaviour, a dangerous nutcase to boot. But as he registered those facts, something else popped into his mind, and he gave a bark of relieved laughter. "As mages you are bound not to interfere in the affairs of ordinary mortals!"

"In the absence of a formal contract, or if it cannot be shown that our intervention is required under the conditions of the Inter-Universal Stability Regulations, that is quite true." Montmorency nodded. "And to clear up any possible misunderstanding, First Speaker, let me make it very plain that we have no intention of interfering in the matter between you and these gentlemen." He gestured toward the silent group clustered around the far end of the table.

"No intention?"

"None at all, First Speaker, isn't that right Cruickshank?"

"Oh yes! Absolutely no intention." Andrew nodded enthusiastically

"We are quite neutral in the matter, are we not, Cruickshank?"

"But of course!"

"It would be wrong of us to attempt to influence the outcome of this... ah... disagreement, would it not Cruickshank?"

"Inexcusable," Andrew agreed.

"That is most gratifying." The First Speaker was only half-relieved-- his sensitive antennae told him there was something extremely fishy and extremely threatening about these two. "Then what, if I might ask, do you wish to talk to me about?"

"It is something of an ethical dilemma..." Montmorency began, then hesitated, affecting some slight discomfiture. "Cruickshank, perhaps you will explain."

"Of course." Now they had started, Andrew felt calm, in control, and was thoroughly enjoying the situation. He took a sip of brandy, leaned back and placed his fingertips together. "Mage Montmorency was recently approached by two members of the-- er-- that is two broadsheet writers, in his capacity as a source of unimpeachable integrity--"

"Unimpeachable integrity," the black mage echoed, demonstrating a marked tendency to over-act.

Andrew shot him a warning look. "These two writers-- Strident and Anguish, I believe their names are-- were on assignment to cover some trivial military activity in Stembark Forest, however since that particular affair appears to be no longer newsworthy, they are now working on another story, and such was the nature of the material they had gathered that they asked Mage Montmorency, as a man--"

"Of unimpeachable integrity," the black mage prompted

Andrew glared at him. "As a man who had some knowledge of the matter and of the persons involved, whether he could confirm the essential features of the story. Because the story touches you intimately, First Speaker, Mage Montmorency thought it only right to acquaint you with the essentials of the matter so that you might be the better prepared to provide your own perspective. Undoubtedly it is some trivial affair at bottom, but possibly open to misinterpretation and, in the hands of a sensational or scurrilous broadsheet, might possibly cause a gentleman in your position unnecessary distress or embarrassment." With some satisfaction, Andrew waved for Montmorency to continue.

"Thank you, Cruickshank. You have outlined the matter with your usual lucidity and elegance. First Speaker, the fact of the matter is that these writers have uncovered what they claim is a shocking story of corruption, degeneracy and abuse of office."

"Pah!" Titus Handcarte gave a contemptuous snort. "Stories like that appear all the time-- nobody gives them any credence."

"I am delighted to hear you are so confident, First Speaker," Montmorency replied smoothly, "though it did seem to me that the sixty thousand readers of *The Daily Lapse*, to say nothing of the twenty thousand undoubtedly better educated readers of *The Thunderclap*, might find Miss Prism's story not totally unbelievable in all respects."

"*Miss Prism!*" The First Speaker's face went ashen, then turned to an unpleasing mottled red. Once again his brandy glass went flying, only to be saved from certain destruction by a deft gesture from the Black Mage.

"Come, First Speaker," Montmorency gave a soothing smile, "we are all reasonable men." He saw Handcarte's bulging eyes turn on Andrew and added hastily, "well, two of us are reasonable men. I am sure that Miss Prism's account of sexual harassment and seduction--"

"*Seduction*!" The First Speaker croaked the word.

"--will just be put down to an understandable momentary lapse by an overworked, tired and emotional public servant. However the accompanying breaches of security and the disappearance of secret government documents, to say nothing of the unfortunate incident last year when the government of East Castellian was in the paws of a white mouse... well..." Montmorency shrugged.

"You-- you--"

"I am sure that the appropriate inquiry will determine that the allegations of any breaches of security are without foundation, or at least highly exaggerated. But alas, the headlines! *Sex Romps in Secret Castle Downing Love Nest,*" Montmorency intoned sadly.

"Come on Montmorency!" Andrew interjected, "the serious broadsheets won't do that."

"No?" The Black Mage raised his eyebrows in polite enquiry.

"Of course not! It'll be something like *Sex Romps in Secret Castle Downing Love Nest Raise Security Questions.*"

With an effort the First Speaker regained control of himself. "Security breaches? Impossible!" he retorted, glad to feel on safe ground.

"With the greatest of respect, First Speaker, it seems all too possible." Andrew slid a thick packet of papers onto the table, "unless, of course, these are elaborate forgeries."

"As indeed they may be," Montmorency encouraged him, "but there is a risk that in the course of the searching public inquiry you will doubtless institute, certain unhappy, deluded people will come forward with fantastic tales of assignations in Castle Downing. All without foundation, of course. But in the hands of the more sensational broadsheets..."

"*Government Love Slaves Reveal All,*" Andrew suggested

Montmorency gave him a pained look. "Really Cruickshank! This is hardly the time or place for such predictions, however accurate they might be. You are upsetting the First Speaker."

"Sorry!" Andrew was instantly contrite. "The serious broadsheets won't treat it like that at all-- and after all, they are the only ones that matter. They'll probably say something like *Secret Service Fears Government Love Slaves Revealed All.*"

"I don't think you're helping, Cruickshank," Montmorency told him severely. "I-- What was that, First Speaker?"

Titus Handcarte was an intelligent man and could recognise defeat when he saw it. The titillating revelations (or fabrications) from Miss Prism on their own he could weather. The disappearance of a set of confidential government documents could be covered up by a full public inquiry. But combined, the stories could destroy him. It was true that he had no electorate or public opinion polls to bother about. However it was also true that there were a number of colleagues (the Deputy Third Speaker, for one), not to mention senior officials in the Revenue Branch, for whom these revelations would signify the loss of the First Speaker's Moral Authority to govern. And once he lost his Moral Authority, Handcarte knew it was just a matter of time (a few weeks at most) before he would find himself having full and frank discussions with a few hooded figures up a dark alley. He decided to enter one last protest. "You have no right to interfere," he croaked, without very much conviction.

"Interference could not be further from Montmorency's mind," Andrew told him, "indeed, he was hoping to be able to avoid involvement in this whole sordid affair. But if he's asked direct questions, as a man of unimpeachable integrity he has no choice in the matter."

The First Speaker's antennae were quivering now. There was something about Cruickshank's tone of voice, and choice of words, that alerted him to the fact that a deal was being offered. He cleared his throat with a dry rustling sound. "Is there no way in which Mage Montmorency can avoid direct involvement?" he asked.

"Alas!" Montmorency shrugged elaborately. "Under normal circumstances I would be unavailable since I would be supervising the field work my graduate student is undertaking in support of his dissertation. As you may know, work of this nature must be carried out in a relatively unpopulated area. But with all these troops around..."

"I understand. And that-- the--" Handcarte's voice failed him, and he merely pointed at Andrew.

"Wardmaster Mage Cruickshank would likewise be fully involved since he has graciously consented to act as Bellingham's external examiner."

"Eh?" Andrew snapped upright in his chair.

"In addition to his other commitments," Montmorency added.

There was a long silence while Titus Handcarte ran the whole thing over in his mind once more, searching for a way out. He did not find one. He reached for his glass, thoughtfully refilled by Montmorency, and drained it. "Should the troops be withdrawn, would you be able to return to your work?" The question seemed to be slowly and painfully dragged from him.

"At once," Montmorency reassured him, "I fear we are seriously behind schedule already."

"And the writers?"

"We should send them our regrets that we were unable at the present moment in time to be of assistance to them."

"They would pursue the matter no further?"

"Oh no," Andrew reassured him, "in fact I rather think they'd be more interested in a sort of human interest story; how in the course of observing the annual field manoeuvres of his troops, the First Speaker managed to reconcile two estranged brothers. Quite a moving tale, I believe."

"Benbrock-Oldstairs?" The First Speaker showed his teeth.

"Harold and Roger," Andrew confirmed, "they will be returning to East Castellian shortly after your departure."

"Indeed." Handcarte began to see how something could be saved from the ruin. The elder brother, he knew, had taken with him to

Stembark Forest the bulk of the family fortune-- something over four hundred thousand. It would be a matter of some satisfaction to relieve him of this burden. And of the dukedom too, Handcarte told himself viciously. "In that case I believe I can arrange the speedy withdrawal of my troops from Stembark forest."

"Then there is nothing that need detain us here longer!" Montmorency exclaimed jovially, "if the First Speaker would care to issue the orders withdrawing his troops..?"

"I believe Ratbag has drawn up a form of general order," Andrew pointed out, "the First Speaker merely has to attach his signature."

"Capital!" Montmorency beamed. "Ratbag!"

Silently the nicker wafted up to the table, laid two sheets of parchment before the First Speaker, then wafted away once more. He did not feel comfortable in the presence of a man like Handcarte.

"It does not appear that I even need attach my signature!" Handcarte held up the parchment where, plain to see at the bottom, the name *Titus Handcarte* was slashed in spiky handwriting.

"Then just your initials, First Speaker," Montmorency told him, "on both copies".

The pen scratched bitterly at the parchment as Handcarte complied. Montmorency gave the ink a quick stare to dry it, then handed the documents to Tiresome.

"Thanks Mage Montmorency. And you too, First Speaker," the knight bowed slightly. "I will arrange for your escort to take you back to your encampment, and for delivery of this to Captain Porsena." The knight marched off to issue his orders.

Another long and rather uncomfortable silence followed, broken at last by the arrival of Captain Spalding. At Montmorency's suggestion, Andrew discreetly withdrew-- he and Captain Spalding had met once or twice in the past.

Feeling tired, and a little desolate, Andrew led the rest of the band to the edge of the clearing, where they paused to watch.

The First Speaker was on his feet, Captain Spalding at his side, and half a dozen troopers in attendance. With the gaunt figure of the black mage standing a little apart, Captain Spalding assisted the First Speaker into the saddle, then mounted his own horse and, with commendable smartness under the circumstances, the little party moved off.

Montmorency remained motionless, a lonely dark obelisk in the setting sun. Then, with a violet flare of Heron-Gough discharge, he dematerialized.

"Where's *he* off to, I wonder?" Andrew asked of nobody in particular.

"I expect he's gone to collect Bellingham," Kodswallop suggested, "good lad, he is, too. He was staying to keep an eye on Captain Porsena and his troops."

"He could have said goodbye," Andrew complained.

"He'll be back tomorrow, never fear," Clumpface assured him, "told me he wouldn't miss the final scene on any account. He wanted to know if you were going to use *As You Like It*."

"No," Andrew said quite firmly, "this time it's going to be as I like it."

Act XX
EXUENT OMNES

Cecil ran his eyes over the Headquarters Glade with the disillusioned stare of a man who has been up too late the previous night, and consumed rather too much beer. He frowned at the gay bunting strung between the trees. He sneered at the brightly coloured banners. He raised his eyes to the outlaw flag hanging limply from its pole, and nodded slowly. He knew how that flag felt. "Ugh!" he said.

"Could be worse," Kodswallop grunted sympathetically. He himself felt perfectly fine, and he was sorry Cecil seemed a little off-colour. "Looks as though some of the lads were busy last night." He pointed to the far side of the clearing where a number of hand-lettered banners had been strung between the Administration Office and the Staff Canteen. *NO DUKES*, announced one, *OUTLAW RULES OK* added a second, while a third tactfully suggested that *WE DON'T WANT TO LOSE YOU BUT WE THINK YOU'D BETTER GO*. Cecil didn't exactly brighten, but his countenance did become a fraction less gloomy.

"That's more like it!" he said, with a slow and careful nod of approval, "it gets on my wick, all this 'please be so kind as to' and 'with the greatest respect' stuff. We should just call a duke a bloody nuisance and tell him to sod off."

"The gentry don't do things that way," Kodswallop replied with the air of a missionary explaining the social significance of lunch to a cannibal, "they have to be indirect."

"Why?"

"Well... er..." Kodswallop wrinkled his brow in thought, "it's a matter of the social compact," he concluded decisively.

"The social compact?" Cecil echoed, "what's that mean?"

"The gentry go about in small groups so they're socially compact," the big fighter told him, "an' they're supposed to be better educated than us, too," he added.

"Who's better educated than us?" the marksman asked belligerently.

"Well, Andrew is, for a start."

"Well *he* said the dukes were a couple of suppurating piles of wombat droppings!"

"And who are we to argue with that?" Kodswallop challenged, as though Cecil had just proved his thesis.

"But you just said the gentry--"

"Andrew's got nothing to do with the gentry." Kodswallop's brow darkened with anger at the perceived insult to his friend, "but he knows a pile of suppurating wombat droppings when he sees one." The big fighter stamped his foot, and struck an attitude.

Cecil recoiled as a shower of dislodged debris and a few unconscious birds drifted down from the trees above. When Kodswallop struck an attitude it stayed struck. "It just goes against the grain to let them walk out of here when they've caused so much trouble," he ventured in a very soft voice;

"I know," the big fighter agreed, "people like that are always more trouble than they're worth, just like the MBAs-- you remember?"

"I mean he could *transform* them into something. Something really nasty."

"Cecil," Kodswallop shook his head sadly, "would you really want Andrew to try transforming somebody into something?"

"Ah... now you come to mention it..." Cecil paled at the prospect.

"Well, there you are then! What we'd like to have done to them, we can't. But there's always the fact they *know* what we'd like to do to them. And they *think* Andrew can do it any time..."

"That's something..." a happy smile spread over Cecil's features.

"And there's another thing," Kodswallop added, "when they take a look in that treasure wagon of theirs, they'll be in for a nasty shock."

"You mean Ratbag?"

Kodswallop nodded. "More or less cleaned it out before the two of you went off to East Castellian."

"Got a few bob, then?"

"A few hundred thousand. And a coronet."

"*What!*"

"But the coronet doesn't fit anyone."

"Bugger the coronet! *How* much did you say Ratbag got?"

"About four hundred thousand, I think." The big fighter shrugged. "It's always difficult to keep track with Ratbag."

"Four hundred thousand..." Cecil contemplated the sum.

"Of course most of that he'll leave with Mr Orlando--"

"How much is most?"

"About three-quarters."

"Ah well..." Cecil contemplated a hundred thousand, and found it eminently satisfying.

"Hallo! Where is everybody else?" Andrew, with Janus, Clumpface and Tiresome in attendance, followed by a handful of outlaws, sauntered into the glade. Andrew carried a bundle of papers under one arm and every now and then he fingered them anxiously to make sure they were still there. "Aren't the others here yet?" he asked.

Kodswallop stared. "I thought everybody was supposed to here for the final..." he searched for the word, failed to find it and concluded, "er... thing."

"I thought Orlando would be here by now." Andrew was puzzled. "He was very interested--"

"Wardmaster!" Eric, resplendent in lincoln green, with a brand new marksman's insignia gleaming proudly on his left sleeve, ran into the glade. "Mr Orlando will be here directly. He is with the escort party."

"He went down to meet them?" Tiresome asked, eyebrows raised.

"Yes, Sir Tiresome, he was very anxious about the party on the island and wished to meet them as soon as they returned."

"Anxious? They could surely come to no harm there?"

"No, indeed," Eric agreed, "but you know what Mr Orlando is like."

"That is true." The knight gave a knowing look which, to Andrew's eyes was rather un-knightly. In fact if it hadn't been Tiresome he'd have sworn that he'd actually winked.

"What about Ratbag?" Andrew looked about vainly for the little figure, "I thought he was with you."

"He went down to the lake with the escort too," Eric told them eagerly, "he said he was very anxious to see the two dukes and the others as well."

Cecil chuckled. "Bit pointless that, seeing they've probably got nothing much left by now."

"And Montmorency?" Janus asked, "I had thought he would be here before now."

"Not him!" Andrew snorted, "he won't make his grand entrance till everybody else is here to watch."

"That is a most ungenerous remark, Cruickshank," came a familiar voice. There was a subdued violet flash, and Montmorency materialized before them. "I may have some sense of the theatre, but I never let it over-ride my professional principles."

"What never?" Andrew asked, openly sceptical.

"Well-- hardly ever." The mage sank slowly to the ground. "Now where is Bellingham?"

The branches of a nearby beech tree began shaking agitatedly. Montmorency gave a resigned sigh, raised his hand, and the figure of his research assistant tumbled into view. Arms flailing, he hit the soft turf with a solid thump.

"Bellingham, Bellingham!" Montmorency wagged his finger, "you really must do something about your transport routines. Remind me to ask your instructor to schedule a few more hours dual." He turned to Andrew. "Cruickshank, allow me to present Bellingham, one of the Guild's most promising graduate students."

Bellingham, rather dishevelled but otherwise undamaged, scrambled to his feet and, blushing furiously, shook hands. "An honour to meet you, Wardmaster," he mumbled, "I do apologise for the disturbance."

"Think nothing of it," Andrew waved the apology away, "I've always said that a good landing is one you walk away from."

The black mage looked as though he were about to take issue with this distressingly liberal view (for he was no enthusiast for modern educational theory) when there was a short burst of cheering and into the glade strode Don Orlando, Ratbag skipping eagerly in his wake.

As if this had been a signal, the glade began to fill with outlaws. They did not walk in, or lower themselves from the trees by ropes, nor even debouch from any of the headquarters buildings, but rather seemed to materialize. It was, Andrew and his friends agreed afterwards, one of the most amazing displays they had ever witnessed, as better than two hundred figures in lincoln green filtered into existence before their eyes. With the exception of the occasional shout of "who d'yer think yer shoving?" they stood in watchful silence.

The outlaw chief was looking extremely spruce. His tunic was immaculate, his boots gleamed like black mirrors, and he wore a trim feather at the regulation angle in his bonnet. Only the cloak rather spoiled the effect, with its ragged hem and tarnished clasp-- he *still* could not seem to find his best cloak.

While Ratbag disappeared from view, prompting a suspicious growl from Clumpface, Orlando walked briskly over to where Andrew and his comrades stood. "A beautiful morning, Wardmaster!" he exclaimed with what seemed to Andrew to be excessive enthusiasm. "You have the papers?"

"Here they are." Andrew handed him the cancelled Usurpation Licence.

Orlando ran his eyes over the document. "Excellent! No doubt about it, eh! The man's certainly not exiled. And the notes for my speech?"

"I really don't think you should use them after all," Andrew told him uncomfortably, holding them back, "they just don't seem appropriate somehow." Despite his confident assertion of the night before, and despite the fact that he had laboured long and hard putting together what had seemed at the time to be a pretty good final speech for the outlaw chief, now he came to look over what he had written he realized it just wasn't right.

"Not appropriate? Let me look." With a swift movement, Orlando relieved Andrew of the notes. "Ah... now let me see... *I am not furnished like a beggar, therefore to beg will not become me...* that's true enough in all conscience!" Orlando flashed a bright confident smile. "And what's this... *the duke hath put on a religious life, and thrown into neglect the pompous court...*" Orlando shook his head, "that doesn't sound very plausible to me..."

"With respect, Mr Orlando," Montmorency raised a hand, "it does not have to sound plausible-- it just has to work."

"Ah... I see." Orlando returned to the notes. "Now I do like this: *Yet with my nobler reason 'gainst my fury do I take part: the rarer action is in virtue than in vengeance.*" He raised his eyes from the paper. "That is very good, you know. And this: *As I foretold you, all were spirits, and are melted into air, into thin air.* Are you sure you don't want me to use this?"

"Quite sure," Andrew said firmly.

"Well what *should* I say?"

"Just tell the brothers to go. Leave... depart... exit... retire... withdraw... agitate the pavement... hop it... bugger off."

"I see. Just that?"

"And immediately, if not sooner."

Orlando fluttered the notes indecisively. "It does seem awfully brusque."

"Come on Orlando! It's your forest, it's your outlaw band-- you can be as brusque as you like. You're the boss."

"That's right." Orlando folded the notes and put them away. He straightened his shoulders. "I *am* the boss. Come on!" He marched off.

As the others followed, Montmorency caught Andrew by the arm. "You could have suggested *Stand not upon the order of your going, but go at once.*"

Orlando led the way to a broad avenue of elms where the two brothers, the toadies, a huntsman with two hounds, and the two cousins stood under the grim eyes of a section of outlaws (grim because they'd been doing guard duty on the island instead of participating in a perfectly good punch-up). Like a lincoln green tide, the outlaws from the glade flowed down the avenue, taking up position on each side, two deep and ready for action.

"Sorry to keep you all waiting," Orlando breezed forward, "but this won't take a minute. Is everybody here?"

"I think they're one short," Cecil observed. He had been counting.

"It's Pebblestroke!" Anne held out a large jam-jar in which a frog squatted. "Something happened to him."

"You mean *that's* Pebblestroke? The jester?" Orlando peered at the frog, "are you sure?"

"Yes. He was in the front room of that little house, and there was some machine there. He just touched it, and--" helplessly she pointed to the jar.

"Perhaps I can help," Montmorency offered, "it is possible he encountered a small technical problem of some description. Tip him out onto the ground." Decanted onto the grass, the frog rolled its eyes pathetically and gave a rasping croak. Montmorency levelled his staff and murmured a brief incantation. With an understated *pop*, the repellent figure of Pebblestroke materialized. He gave a terrified squawk, then collapsed to the ground, curling himself into a foetal position.

"He should suffer no permanent ill-effects," the Black Mage observed calmly, "and the habit of trying to catch flies with his tongue is likely to disappear within a week or so."

"Perhaps you could return him to his earlier state. He was infinitely more acceptable as an amphibian," Buckingham suggested. Alone among the toadies, he looked fairly smart and alert.

"That will do, Buckingham!" Duke Roger (ex-usurping) gave his chief toady a censorious look, then addressed himself to Montmorency. "We thank you for that service, mage, and you shall not find us ungenerous."

"You are too kind." Montmorency's eyes glittered and, had he not been a scrupulously fair-minded man, recognising and honouring Orlando's primary claim on the repulsive fellow, it would have gone very ill indeed with ex-usurping duke Roger.

"Not at all." Sublimely ignorant of the mortal danger he had just courted, Roger turned to Orlando. "You, sir, I take it are chief of the outlaw band that frequents these parts?"

"Indeed I am," Orlando responded automatically, with his habitual courtesy.

"I am pleased to know ye," Roger said carelessly, "you have informed this fellow of our plans?" he asked his brother.

"I-- er--" Harold hesitated, more alive than Roger to the slightly menacing atmosphere.

With a hiss and a thump an arrow buried itself in the ground a full twentieth of an inch from Roger's foot. "Less of the fellow, fellow!" Eric shouted, nocking a second arrow.

Roger jumped back a pace and one of the hounds gave a mournful yodel.

"Thank you Eric, but that was quite unnecessary." The outlaw chief tried to conceal his smile of satisfaction. Then his eyes fell on the two hounds. "Put those dogs on a lead, at once," he ordered sharply.

"But these are hounds--" the huntsman protested.

"I don't care if they're very well-disguised poodles," Orlando snapped, "put 'em on a lead. Now."

Protesting under his breath, Peel tethered the two animals while Orlando watched him stonily. When the task was completed to his satisfaction, the outlaw chief turned his gaze upon the two brothers. His face had changed from its normal open, good humoured expression to become harder and harsher. The wide, generous features had turned rigid and the jaw jutted out like a piece of granite. Don Orlando was mentally reviewing the destruction and disturbance these people had brought with them and it was making him very angry indeed-- in a quiet sort of way. "I won't keep you very long," he told the two brothers, "you are obviously very busy men. Or are about to become very busy men."

"Good of you," Roger interrupted, "we simply wanted to establish--"

"That you will depart this forest now." Orlando finished for him. "The First Speaker kindly agreed to provide your baggage trains escort-- by now they are out of the forest and on their way to East Castellian. It only remains for you to follow them."

"But--"

"I want to make one thing quite clear," Orlando ignored the interruption, "we have nothing against the aristocracy as such. But we do not want dukes in the forest. We do not want hunting in the forest. We do not want Clarence Snout and his Arboreal Arcadians in the forest. And if there's any roistering under the greenwood tree to be done, then *we'll* do it! ***DO I MAKE MYSELF CLEAR?***" As Orlando paused for breath, the nasal twanging lamentation of a zither floated faintly through the air. "And we don't want any of *that* either!" he shouted. The music stopped.

"That's better." Orlando drew a deep breath and added in a quieter, but no less deadly tone. "You may leave now. Stand not upon the order of your going, but go at once."

"Good sir," Harold found his voice first, "but season your displeasure for a while. You know I am no duke, but a poor exile, thrust forth from the pomp and splendour of the court and thus constrained to hold acquaintance with rude nature--"

"Knock it off!" Orlando interrupted.

"Eh?" Derailed from his eloquence, Harold looked about helplessly.

"I said knock it off," Orlando repeated, "you are no exile." He held up the Usurpation Licence. "I have here in my hand a piece of paper signed by the First Speaker. It revokes your usurpation-- read it for yourself."

Reluctantly, Harold took the document and read it. When he reached the First Speaker's scrawled instruction at the end his jaw dropped. "If the matter in this paper be certain--"

"It is," Orlando told him confidently, retrieving it, "and let me tell you how happy I am to be able to bring you the news that you can return to your proper sphere-- out of the forest. It's a long way to East Castellian, gentlemen. And it's that way." He pointed.

"I-- I do not believe you--"

"Do I have a speech impediment?" Orlando demanded, "is there something wrong with my articulation? Which part of the word 'go' do you not understand?"

The two brothers stood in stunned silence. Orlando turned away from them. "Will!" he shouted, "take your section and escort these two gentlemen to the end of the Southern Ride." His eye fell upon the group of toadies and the huntsman. "And you can take those with you as well!"

The deathly silence was broken by the bustling, rattling and bad language attendant upon the preparation and mounting of horses. It was a subdued little group. The two brothers still looked stunned, and moved like automata. Bushy, Bagot and Greene were sullen and defeated. And Buckingham had the look of a man who was mentally updating his *curriculum vitae* with all possible speed. It was just as Herbert, miserable and confused, was climbing into the saddle to follow the others that a voice shouted; "I say! Spotty Herbert!"

Herbert jerked around, swayed dangerously and half-jumped, half-fell to the ground. From the silent ranks of the outlaws, Jacques strode forth, a beaming smile on his face. "It is 'Spotty' Herbert! Fancy seeing you here! Don't you remember me?"

"It-- it isn't 'Joker' Jacques, is it? From the Upper Fifth?" Herbert stared incredulously.

"None other, Spotty!" Jacques yapped happily, "you were just a little tick in the Lower Third then. How are you doing?"

"Not very well, I'm afraid, Joker," he lowered his voice, "apprentice toady to him," he jerked his head in the direction of Roger, "but I'm not sure that sort of work is really my cup of tea."

"I should say not!" Jacques agreed, "come over here. I want you to meet someone." Tugging Herbert by the arm, he approached Orlando who, his foot tapping impatiently, was awaiting the departure of his uninvited guests. "I say, sir!" He gave the outlaw chief an encouraging smile.

"What do you say, Jacques?" asked Orlando absently.

"Fren' of mine from school, sir. Just now looking for a job. Make a fine outlaw, sir. Very sound chap."

Standing a little apart, but still within earshot, Cecil dug an elbow into Ratbag's ribs. "*Another* one of 'em," he whispered, "what's the betting he says he did archery at school, and was head of house?"

The nicker giggled. "I wonder if he had somebody hold the bow for him?"

Orlando looked Herbert up and down. He seemed a reasonable enough lad, despite his disadvantaged background. "Any sort of... um... qualifications or experience?" he asked.

"Head of house in archery, sir."

"Jolly good. Alright, Jacques; see Walter about a qualification shoot."

"Thank you very much, sir!" Jacques gripped Herbert's arm. "Come on, Spotty."

As they walked off, Herbert's voice could be heard faintly, "... of course at school we *did* have a man around to help out with the technical stuff..."

Ratbag and Cecil exchanged glances.

Orlando watched the two disappear with a benign smile, which changed to a scowl as he beheld the group of horsemen. "Will! Get this lot out of the way. Now."

"Right chief!" The Section Leader wheeled his horse about to face his charges. "We shall be taking the Southern Ride," he told them. "perhaps the most picturesque of the routes through Stembark Forest, it offers unique--"

"Will!" Orlando interrupted, "get on with it!"

"Of course chief." The Section Leader cleared his throat. "Please do not stray from the path, gentlemen: you will be shot if you do. Walk-march!"

Flanked by half a dozen mounted outlaws, Will bringing up the rear, the little cavalcade moved off down the avenue. Everybody watched in silence until they reached the end, and turned onto the Southern Ride.

"Well *that's* all sorted out at last!" Orlando clapped his hands together. "Stand easy, everyone!" he ordered, "resume scheduled activities. Duty Section Leaders meeting will be at fourteen hundred." The ranks of lincoln green evaporated silently into the forest, and Orlando strode over to join Andrew and the others.

"A most satisfactory outcome!" he beamed amiably at them, "and I have you to thank for it, Wardmaster."

"Not really," Andrew mumbled, acutely conscious of the extent to which his plans had gone awry, "it was Ratbag and Cecil who got those documents."

"But it was your strategy!" Orlando reminded him.

"And if it hadn't been for Montmorency..."

"Come along, Cruickshank! There is no need to be over-modest."

"But it just didn't work out the way it was supposed to," Andrew complained.

"How can you say that!" Kodswallop exclaimed indignantly, "You said there'd be a usurping duke, and there was one. You said there'd be secret papers discovered which would sort everything out, and there were. What more do you want?"

"Kodswallop is quite right," Montmorency agreed, "after all, the process followed the classic pattern of conflict, confusion, resolution and reconciliation."

"But there's all these loose ends!" Andrew gestured towards Julia and Anne who, with Charles, were standing somewhat apart, engaged in quiet conversation. "And that!" He pointed to Pebblestroke who was squatting comfortably, putting out his tongue at passing flies.

"Well, as to him..." Orlando gazed at Pebblestroke thoughtfully. "Court jester, are you?" he asked.

Pebblestroke croaked loudly, then bounced to an upright position. "Just a poor fool, nuncle, yet not so witless as some wise men that count themselves as wits," he cackled, then looked vainly about for his bladder.

"Less of the 'nuncle', if you don't mind," Orlando told him with a slight frown. "Tell me, what sort of things can you do? Song and dance? Monologue? A spot of Punch and Judy for the kiddies?"

The jester coughed. "No kids stuff! Vicious little tykes, kids are. Sooner take up lion taming. But I done the clubs, stand-up routine mostly. The odd song... sort of adult stuff, if you get my meaning." He leered suggestively.

"I see..." Orlando stroked his chin. "Perhaps we might be able to offer you an engagement here-- I need an Entertainment Director. Would you be interested?"

"I wouldn't say no, guv." The scrunched figure seemed to straighten a little. "Do me good to get back into something a bit more professional-- something wif a bit o' intellectual challenge. Anyfink's better than soddin' about wif that bleedin' bladder."

"Excellent!" Orlando slapped him on the back, raising a cloud of dust, "you get along to the main office, and ask for Section Leader Taylor. He'll issue you some new clothes."

"Ay thankee, nuncle! They say the clothes oft make the man-- but then some man must make the clothes. Hee hee!"

"I *did* say about the 'nuncle' bit..."

"Right guv, so you did. Sorry, force of habit. Won't happen again." Pebblestroke scuttled off.

"One loose end tidied up, you see, Cruickshank," Montmorency pointed out, with a smile.

"Yes, but..." Andrew's gaze returned to the two women and Charles. "You see, properly speaking we should have finished up with a couple of marriages."

"Ah yes, well..." Orlando looked rather sheepish. In the background Tiresome whispered something to Janus, and they both laughed. "Yes, well..." Orlando repeated, then beckoned the three over. "The fact of the matter is that while I was on the island, Anne and I got talking and... er... what with one thing and another..."

"You mean that you and Anne--"

"We will have a trial arrangement, Wardmaster," Anne said with a smile as she took the outlaw chief's arm, "and if that works out, we shall make it permanent. We do seem to have a lot in common. And I can help Don out on the business strategy and planning side of things."

"Well-- that is marvellous! Congratulations!" Andrew shook them both by the hand.

"Two down, two to go," said Montmorency in a voice so quiet that only Andrew heard.

"And Julia, I believe *you* have some announcement to make," her cousin suggested with a smile that tried to be arch but succeeded in only looking mischievous.

"Yes. Wardmaster, I do apologise for misinterpreting your questions on the island."

Andrew turned to look at the taller woman and noticed for the first time that she was wearing the copper coloured satin cloak, the leather waistcoat and the knee-length supple boots of a duellist. "What--"

"Charles and I are travelling together to Nova Castria."

"Together? You mean...?"

"Yes. We have come to a tentative arrangement." Julia's dark, sharp features flashed forth a happy smile. "In Nova Castria I shall enrol at the Duellists' College. Charles believes I show promise."

"Julia has the eye and hand of a fine fighter, Wardmaster," Charles said, enthusiastically, "and since a duellist travelling with a female companion can give rise to unseemly comment, Julia has adopted the disguise you suggested."

"Ah... yes... Congratulations. My best wishes to you both." Andrew stammered, then recovered his composure. He had just thought of something. "I do not know whether there is anything about the air in this part of Stembark Forest," he pronounced, "but it seems to me that the number of engagements is significantly higher than that which statistics have laid down for our guidance."

"A masterly recovery," Montmorency whispered to Bellingham, "when I have worked out precisely what it means, I shall explain it to you."

"Not 'engagements', sir," Julia smiled, "but 'arrangements'."

"Yes, yes, quite."

"'Arrangement' is the better word, Wardmaster," Anne agreed, "for 'engagement' carries the overtones of combat or battle, and that is not what we intend."

"Of course not," Andrew nodded, "and I'm sure you'll all be very happy."

"If we are, we shall know who to thank for it." Orlando folded the papers he had been carrying, made to offer them to Andrew, then, at the last moment, withdrew his hand. "The Usurpation Licence I shall give you to return to the First Speaker as you promised. But the notes you gave me, I should like to keep, if I may."

"But of course." Andrew accepted the Usurpation Licence and tucked it away.

"Yes... some fine language there," the Outlaw chief murmured, re-reading the lines, "but there is one serious error."

"What's that?"

"Where you say *Our revels now are ended.*" Orlando looked up and shook his head. "Nothing could be further from the truth."

A tide of lincoln green had flooded the parlour of Three Pigeons, spilled down the passageway through the back door and was even now lapping at the boundaries of the tavern's back garden. The night air shook to the rumble of conversation, rang to the shouts of laughter and shuddered briefly to the occasional crash of the resolution of argument. It was not a solid green tide. Flecks of other colours moved to and fro in the eddies and occasionally drew together like leaves borne on the surface of a swirling stream.

"You return to Nova Castria immediately?" Orlando was asking.

"Soon," confirmed Janus, "Andrew is going to direct us in a play for the Summer Festival."

"Yes. We're doing *Blood on The Rooftops, Blood on the Tiles*," Kodswallop announced proudly.

"A grand play!" Orlando nodded with vigorous approval, "perhaps we might travel up to see it?" He turned to Anne.

"I should like that of all things!" she agreed enthusiastically, "and I bet I can guess *your* role, Kodswallop!"

The big fighter blushed. "Aye. Don Pedro d'y Angina."

"Not 'Immaterial' this time?"

"The Immaterial is immaterial," Kodswallop said, with dignity.

Herbert and Jacques were exchanging school reminiscences while Amiens and Bellingham listened.

"And there was 'Mad-dog' Marriott," Jacques chuckled, "the one who set fire to the clock tower."

"I don't think Mad-dog did that," Herbert objected, "wasn't he the chap who kept goldfish?"

"No, no, no. You're thinking of 'Truro' Albany."

"Where were you at school, old boy?" Amiens asked Bellingham suddenly. The two others stopped in mid-reminiscence and cocked their ears for his response.

Bellingham told them.

"Oh!" The sneers were unmistakeable.

Bellingham shrugged, and transformed their beer to cold porridge.

From the far side of the crowded room, Montmorency watched the transaction with an approving smile-- Bellingham was learning fast. He beckoned the graduate student over, then turned to the crimson robed figure at his side. "Come Cruickshank! You are not drinking!"

"Put my glass down somewhere, and can't find it," Andrew mumbled.

"Allow me!" Montmorency materialized a full tankard and passed it over. He had been doing this all evening, much to the relief of Rowley who, sweating at his pumps, was having difficulty in keeping up with demand.

Andrew drained half the tankard at a gulp and was only mildly surprised to see it refill itself.

"Capital work Bellingham!" Montmorency clapped him on the back. "Did I not tell you this was our most promising graduate, Cruickshank?"

"First class!" Andrew agreed, and took another long drink. "I suppose you'll be going back?"

"To Blytham-by-the-Water, yes, tomorrow morning. Bellingham and I have much work to complete." Montmorency materialized himself a refill. "So Cruickshank, this time we could not see it through to the finish. A pity in a way, for we had just reached the crucial juncture, and I flatter myself that I was just ahead on points."

"Why, Montmorency?"

"Why?" Montmorency looked puzzled. "I believe I had you on the run. By interfering with your activities, whatever they were-- and I must frankly admit that I could not begin to fathom their rationale-- I managed to regain the ground I lost through your extremely clever piece of misdirection. One which, I should say, was brought to my attention by Bellingham. The usual scoring system under those circumstances would give me an edge by--"

"I didn't mean that, Montmorency!" Andrew's strangled shout caused more than one head to turn in their direction. Then turn back hurriedly as soon as it was realized that two mages were involved.

Andrew breathed deeply, then began again. "What I meant was why did you come here in the first place?"

Montmorency sighed. "How many times must I explain to you, Cruickshank, that we are Designated Opposites? How would it look to my colleagues, not to mention my students, if I allowed you to go ahead in any enterprise without trying in some manner to thwart it? 'He's losing his grip' they'd say, and they'd be right! And for you, Cruickshank, where would be the achievement in completing a mission without serious opposition? Professional ethics demand some kind of competition, surely!"

"But I thought-- I mean, we *have* worked together--"

"Of course. And shall do so again from time to time, I trust." Montmorency drank deeply. And you will doubtless be visiting us at Blytham-by-the-Water later on in the year to review Bellingham's work."

"Well-- I--"

"Splendid! Then it's all arranged. Now Bellingham, of the three of us you have the most objective view: what were our relative positions when the contest had to be broken off?"

"I'll-- I'll need a minute to work it out, Mage," Bellingham answered pallidly. The shock effect of Montmorency's request was quite sufficient to drive the effects of four or five pints clear from his system. But what should he do? On the one hand, an answer that favoured the Wardmaster would be favouring the more powerful of the two. On the other hand, an answer favouring Mage Montmorency would be favouring the mage who would be assessing his dissertation. Bellingham's mind raced back and forth-- it was an intolerable dilemma! At last he came to the only possible conclusion-- he'd have to review the figures properly and give an accurate answer. The truth was not a pleasant thing for an apprentice mage to be forced to tell, but there were times when it was unavoidable. Watched closely by Montmorency and with polite incomprehension by Andrew, Bellingham went swiftly through his log, adding the scores, calculating the loading factors and applying the one hundred and one different corrections and adjustments that are necessary in reckoning up the results of such a complex engagement. At last he finished-- and then nearly dropped the instrument in dismay. He blinked, hoping that the numbers would go away, but when he opened his eyes they were still there, blinking in the heart of the crystal. A perfect tie! He groaned under his breath-- there was no doubt that this was the worst possible result and would make both mages equally irate.

"Well Bellingham?" Montmorency raised his eyebrows.

"It's-- um-- like this--"

"Like what, Bellingham?" Montmorency was showing signs of impatience.

Wordlessly, Bellingham handed him the log.

Montmorency stared at it for a full minute. "You are sure of these figures?" he asked eventually.

Bellingham nodded.

"Excellent!" Montmorency gave one of his very rare bursts of laughter. "Cruickshank, it turns out we tied exactly! Couldn't have asked for a better result."

"No?"

"Certainly not! It is always a problem when a contest is decided on points. If you lose by a large margin people assume you are past it. If you win by that margin they assume you had no serious competition. If you lose by a small margin they assume you made stupid mistakes, and if you win by that margin they assume you were just lucky. But if you tie, then they assume a hard-fought campaign between mighty opposites where both emerge undefeated and ready to do battle again. And who knows, they might be right."

"I still think you were leading when we stopped," Andrew admitted.

"So do I," agreed the Black Mage, "but the record tells us otherwise. Come Bellingham, we must pay our respects to Don Orlando." With a wave to Andrew, Montmorency disappeared into the swirling crowds.

"Andrew! We're looking for Bellingham-- have you seen him?" Kodswallop loomed over him, two mugs gripped in one fist while Ratbag, looking even more diminutive against his huge comrade, dodged about his heels.

"He went over there with Montmorency," Andrew pointed, "what did you want him for?"

"Oh-- er-- just to show him something..." Kodswallop looked evasive. "Aha! I see him. Oi! Bellingham!" He began to cleave his way through the crowd.

"See you later Andrew," squeaked Ratbag as he followed the big fighter.

Somewhat puzzled, and not a little suspicious, Andrew watched as the apprentice mage greeted Kodswallop with a delighted grin. The big fighter whispered something, then the three of them began to make their way through the crowd to the back door.

"You are rapt, Wardmaster."

Andrew jumped. Julia and Charles had worked their way through the crowd and were standing at his elbow. The duellist gave him a quizzical look. "You are surely not pondering some new assignment tonight?" he asked.

"No, just worrying about those three."

"What three?"

Andrew looked again. The trio had disappeared from view, undoubtedly bent on some nefarious errand. "Kodswallop and Ratbag. And Bellingham." He jerked his thumb at the back door. "I wish I knew what they were up to."

Probably just going over old times about the hermitting business," Julia suggested, with a half-suppressed chuckle. "Come, sir! You have not drunk our health." She produced a full tankard which Andrew accepted gratefully. Already he had lost track of the one Montmorency had materialized for him.

"The very best to you both!" he toasted them.

"You will travel with us?" Charles asked.

Andrew shook his head. "You leave first thing tomorrow. I expect we'll have one or two things to sort out before we can get going."

"Well, we shall meet in Nova Castria, then." Charles did not look bitterly disappointed. "But we have to thank you, and all your friends for-- everything. Even if," the duellist added with a smile, "it did not all work out exactly as you had originally envisaged."

"I'm sure it all worked out for the best," Andrew replied firmly. "With a good cast it usually does," he added.

The duellist's deep lustrous eyes sparkled with understanding. "I have always found that myself," he agreed, "even a good script should be shaped to a good company-- and you have a good company. Until Nova Castria, then." Charles raised a hand in farewell and followed Julia through the crowd.

"I cannot seem to find Bellingham." Montmorency appeared at his side. "I saw him leave with Kodswallop, and I cannot help wondering what they are up to."

The words were no sooner spoken when the tavern was shaken by a series of thundering detonations, and blue, green and scarlet light bloomed through the windows.

"It sounds as though whatever it was, they have just finished," Andrew winced. The tavern remained still as death for a few seconds then, as the last blaze of scarlet light died, a great cheer arose outside.

"We did it! Well done Bellingham! Now *that's* what I call good hermitting!" Kodswallop boomed joyfully as he and Ratbag burst into the room dragging Bellingham with them. They were all soot-blackened and their clothes were torn and scorched. With a casual wave to the stunned company, they went to the bar to replenish their glasses.

"What the--" Andrew began.

"Cruickshank..." Montmorency laid a hand on his arm, "sometimes it is better not to ask. Come, let us sit down over there." He pointed to the far corner of the room where two empty seats were tucked in close to the dartboard.

Dixon and Orlando sat in companionable silence and watched the party swirl about them. At last Dixon knocked out his pipe, drained his glass and sighed with satisfaction. "You must feel happy it's all sorted out now."

"More than sorted out, Dixon," Orlando said, with a proud glance at Anne who was deep in an animated conversation with Janus and Tiresome.

"And the Wardmaster Mage and his friends came up to expectations?" the constable asked with the faintest of smiles.

"Exceeded them!"

"Even the nicker?" Dixon asked.

"Most assuredly! Do you realise Dixon, that he left almost all the treasure he took--"

"Found, Don," the constable corrected him gently, "found."

"Almost all the treasure that was formerly in the possession of that exiled duke," Orlando continued, choosing his words carefully, "it must be three hundred thousand! He said to look on it as a long-term investment, but I do feel rather guilty about keeping it."

"You could always send it back to Duke Harold."

"I don't feel *that* guilty."

"Nor should you." Dixon nodded sagely. "Dukes, books in running brooks, sermons in stones--"

"Tongues in trees," Orlando reminded him.

"Was just coming to that," the constable agreed equably, "that sort of thing may be all very well in its place. But not in Stembark Forest. Or in Lecter."

"Right! And all that bloody horn blowing and hounds baying first thing in the morning. To say nothing of the music!"

The two fell silent again, then Dixon caught a brief glimpse of Ratbag flitting through the crowd. He looked at his friend. "Something happen to your cloak, Don?" he asked with elaborate casualness, "looks to me like you're wearing your old one."

"Um... yes... can't seem to find it..." Orlando shifted uncomfortably. Then something struck him about his friend. "Dixon! What's happened to your helmet?"

The constable looked once again for the fleeting form of Ratbag, then shrugged. "Can't seem to lay hands on it. But I've no doubt it'll turn up one of these days."

The two old friends gazed at each other with perfect mutual understanding.

From behind the bar there was a slight scuffling sound, as Rowley strained on tiptoe to reach some glasses from a high shelf. As he did so his shoulder brushed the edge of the dishcloth that hung tactfully over the clock. With a slither, the towel fell to the floor. The roar of conversation died away, and everybody waited transfixed as the Lecter Constable stared expressionlessly at the clock. This was unprecedented! The Three Pigeons prided itself upon its spotless reputation for scrupulous observance of the licensing laws. Was that reputation now to be sullied?

In the corner by the dartboard a black cloaked figure arose. "Perhaps, ladies and gentlemen, you would permit me..." Montmorency gave the clock a direct but not unfriendly look. For a moment the clock face was limned by a violet glow. The figures wrinkled and twisted. The pendulum twitched convulsively. It went *tock-tick* once, quite loudly. Then the figures resumed their normal shape, and a gasp of relief and admiration arose. The hands of the clock unambiguously indicated a time that was at least two hours before even the most rigorous enforcer of the licensing laws would demand "last orders" be called.

"Now *that's* good maging," Dixon observed, with the hearty approval of the connoisseur.

"Yes. Although I'm sure the Wardmaster would have been just as effective," Orlando maintained loyally.

"True. But Rowley would not have had a clock left after he'd finished," Dixon pointed out, "nor a back wall either, if I'm any judge of the matter. I've seen Wardmaster Cruickshank in action before, remember. Gets a little over-enthusiastic sometimes, he does."

The outlaw chief looked over to where the black cloak and the crimson were sitting together. "I wonder what they're talking about," he pondered.

"Technical stuff probably," Dixon sighed, "way beyond the likes of us."

"Interesting," Montmorency was saying, "so you cannot start until you get one of these inside that outer ring. And then you start counting *downwards*?" He examined one of Andrew's darts with the curiosity of an archaeologist who has just unearthed an incomprehensibly shaped bone.

"That's about it," Andrew agreed, "and you just have to finish on a double as well." He was not sanguine about getting a good game-- Montmorency had claimed that darts were a mystery to him.

"I see." Montmorency weighed the arrow-like missile in his hand. "And how is it determined who goes first? It would seem to me that the first man to throw has an advantage."

"We throw one dart each," Andrew explained, "the one who gets closest to the centre starts."

"It is very good of you to explain all this to me, Cruickshank," the Black Mage said politely, "may I try?"

"Go ahead."

Montmorency took the dart, gazed at the board with narrowed eyes, and threw. There was a thud as it buried itself in the woodwork. "Dear me!" he recoiled in shocked surprise. "I'm sure you can do better than that, Cruickshank."

"I'll try." With a sinking heart, Andrew addressed the board-- the black mage was even worse than he'd suspected, and he'd have to try not beat him too badly. He casually launched his dart at the board, landing midway between the treble ring and the bull.

"Well done, Cruickshank! It looks to me as though you start first."

"That's right." Andrew retrieved the two darts, and returned to the line.

"Would you care to have a small wager on the match?" Montmorency suggested, "loser buys the drinks, perhaps?"

"Oh... alright," Andrew agreed uncomfortably. He took aim at the double six-- his best double. He might as well start, he told himself, then he could throw wild while Montmorency caught up. The three darts in rapid succession arched towards the board. Andrew clicked his tongue-- all outside, though one was actually nestling the wire.

"You started?" Montmorency asked innocently.

"No." Andrew shook his head and handed over the darts. "Your shot."

"Very well." Montmorency took a dart delicately between thumb and index finger, aimed and threw. Like a homing missile, the dart landed slap in the middle of the double nineteen.